LIKE ANYBODY WOULD KNOW A CROW

Like Anybody
Would Know a Crow

by
NEAL CLAYTON

RESOURCE *Publications* · Eugene, Oregon

Like Anybody Would Know a Crow

Resource Publications
An Imprint of Wipf and Stock Publishers
199 W. 8th Ave., Suite 3
Eugene, OR 97401

www.wipfandstock.com

PAPERBACK ISBN: 978-1-6667-4836-9
HARDCOVER ISBN: 978-1-6667-4837-6
EBOOK ISBN: 978-1-6667-4838-3

VERSION NUMBER 090222

To all teachers, among whom are my parents,
and to the place that locates me.

BY THE WORD OF THE LORD WERE THE HEAVENS MADE; AND ALL
THE HOST OF THEM BY THE BREATH OF HIS MOUTH.

—Psalm 33: 6

MASTER, CAREST THOU NOT THAT WE PERISH? . . . AND HE SAID
UNTO THEM, WHY ARE YE SO FEARFUL?

— Mark 4:38, 40

Contents

Prologue

Round
Reflective
Shining face of the waters, yards down in the dark,
A tilting circle of light in the round of earth.
We see the sky, but the surface breaks, cold, like the hard stone glass, obsidian.
"This is no way to go," I had yelled.

In the Yucatan, the shining face of the waters waits. Natural caverns, open to the underworld, open to the sky, formed over ages by rain washing away soft limestone. The Maya called them *tsonot* and the Spanish made the word *cenote*. Sparkling water, the blue-green color we loved, carries sunlight far into the passage.

Obsidian is fire long dead, given out and resting in the ground. Veins and arms of earth glow red hot, molten, burning and melting. Then dead, cold, a stone-hard glass. Found and dug, shivered by a craftsman's skill, treasured and shining, fiery, bloodletting and frightening like the wet electric of a living eel, like a newly reborn serpent shining and alive from paper skin, a deadly slippery blade.

Many yards down, the Mouth of the Waters waits. The layered walls pass quickly, blurring beyond seeing, many lengths a person's weight to fall into.

"This is the way," the jaguar said.

It is not the whole journey. It is an opening. Sometimes you go to a wilderness. It's like a test. What are you? Who awaits?

"The Devouring Mouth is always near," he said to me.

What is it? A place of heat and breathlessness? Freezing cold? Chambers of fright? Words sink into you and wait for sleep so they can rise up in dreams. The Lords of Death salivate to have you.

"It is the mirror," he said.

It is darkness and he goes among shadows. He is able. In darkness like fever, like inflammation, like a sickness. The blue form of the jaguar, the dark form, the indigo tiger, where the earth goes into shadow, and stars burn in the indigo blue, and the jaguar burdens them on his back, the depth of night.

I did not see him now, the jaguar called Inha. The golden sun of his coat was gone. But I knew he was there. He had not left me. I knew he was with me.

The limestone walls sang as I passed. The circular face of the waters broke open. Green light from the world of plants, the world of life, tried to reach me. But I shot through the surface into the depths. Away from sky and away from light. Blue-green waters swirled around me, deeper and darker as I sank. Lower and lower, further and further. The body of water held me, buried me, and I went deep, deep.

I

Mountain Lions?

A thunderstorm hit us the same morning Brandon first showed up. People's papers were flying across the parking lot, the white pines twisted and roared, and dark clouds rolled in every car's windshield. Kids were running, yelling about tornado warnings.

All he ever talked about then was surfing. Like he knew so much. I thought it was just nervous gibberish, him being new. Way before he got the puma tattoo that I drew.

I had just come running in, length of the parking lot. And people were still heckling me, even then. "This your hurricane, Fuller? Finally happening for you?"

Ha ha.

And now we had a whole new project to figure out, and I had no ideas.

The rain began a walloping hoofbeat just as I got to the covered walk at L Wing.

I curved into my seat and Mr. Collins was already up there, fanning out the exam papers, and right next to me was this new kid. Right where I usually put my stuff. He looked grim. Dismal. Like he might be in a gang. Later I thought he probably had a bunch of skull tattoos and clown faces, ugly stuff you'd have to live your whole life covering up. He looked pallid and angry. All in black. The late bell was bleating as I held out my hand.

"I'm Chris. How's it going, man?"

I was used to people thinking I was weird. Muriel said I was "one of the originals." Which at first I didn't know what she meant, and before I knew

3

her better I even thought she was laughing at me, but later she told me it was because "you don't follow the fashionable crowd. You're just yourself." Maybe that was right. Or maybe, I wondered later, it was a remark about my clothes.

I figured I was half-cool, half-loser.

But I wasn't expecting this grimy new kid to act like something was wrong with me. He didn't smile. He wasn't friendly. He had on a dark fleece jacket and it wasn't even cold. He kept shooting his eyes over without turning his head. Like I was something to watch out for. At least an animal growls before it bites. Finally he decided to unfold his arms and shake my hand.

"Brandon," he muttered.

"Where're you from?" I managed to ask before Mr. Collins started.

For a second I thought he was going to laugh, but it was just a gruff breath. A smirk.

"Colorado."

"Wow," I said. "Mountain lions?"

"Yeah?" he said in a weird voice, turning his eyes wide on me like I was crazy to ask.

We were in the middle of a mythology section, world creation stories, ancient beginnings and order from chaos, and this exam was about the ancient Maya and their stories, the god Huracan, the Hero Twins Hunahpu and Xbalanque and how they defeated the Lords of Death even though they died. And the four men made from corn, and someone called Dark Jaguar, who did not have a son, and some unexplained thing about a jaguar who carries the sun through the Underworld.

Martin said it was all "false trash." It was the first thing that had made him and all his people at lunch so glowing red with fury. "We're going to get our parents up here," he had said. "We're going to get our preacher up here. We're going to get Mr. Collins fired for this pagan trash."

I liked it.

"OK, my people. This is your exam!"

"My people." Mr. Collins thought we loved taking his exams.

Now the new kid was staring straight ahead. Some kind of stain on the cuff of his jeans, blacker than the black of the jeans. Running shoes gray and dingy. No books, no paper, nothing to write with.

Great. I'm about to get stuck beside some jerk who hates everything. I could see it in his eyes. And in the way his dark brow clouded up his whole face. I could see his jaw muscle clenching, biting.

I liked it better when that desk was free and I could put my stuff there.

Right after the exam started, Mr. Collins came down my row toward the back.

"Brandon, while they're taking their exam would you come up front with me and tell me what books you all read at your old school? I'd love to hear what you thought about them."

Brandon. He got into this class by mistake, Mr. Collins. He's probably in this school by mistake. You need to get him moved to another class, like one of those trailers between the gym and the science building with all the kids who'd rather leave school early and go work in a fast food restaurant.

There he was loping up to Mr. Collins' desk. Mr. Collins turned to get a chair for him, smiling with all his love of books and poetry and his pictures on the wall, Vincent van Gogh with his ear bandage, the Flowers of Shakespeare, his map of the English Speaking World. And this kid was spitting on all of it. A kid like this wasn't going to care what we were reading in here.

Some people think van Gogh was just plain crazy, like some of the girls in my class. They said the business with his ear was all just gross and sick. And that he did it for the sake of a prostitute too, how immoral and disappointing, and they would never look at his pictures the same way again. Not to mention what they thought about his supposed suicide. It was one of our class's many controversial moments. But that's where most people just don't get it. If he did cut off his own ear, what else could you expect? Anybody who had his kind of intensity might respond in all kinds of ways. They might just number their days. It's the wretched rawness of reality and when people like him, and people like Brandon, see it, they cannot always be contained.

Our English classroom did not have a window, but as I took the exam, I could hear the wind and the storm outside anyway. It was furious on the roof like the sound of fire trucks and emergencies and a great spirit of rushing wind that had come from a long way off.

2

A Thin Line of Words, and a Bird

When I got to the locker room that afternoon the first thing I saw was Brandon sitting on the bench by the door trying to get his shoelaces out of a knot.

"So it's Brandon, right?"

He shot me an upward look and kept messing with his shoe strings.

"You running with us?"

That smirking breath-laugh again. "Looks like it."

Was that his real voice or was he mocking me?

He looked kind of pale and wiry in running shorts, maybe like a runner, but I knew looks might not mean anything. I wanted to see him go against Coal Train.

This ought to be good.

Coal Train has power-speed that comes out of nowhere. It hits and he's gone. And he's tough. It was before my time, but everybody still remembers how one of his shoes came off a few minutes into a race. He just kicked off the other shoe and ran in socks and missed first place by a few seconds. Hardly any fans were there but the team carried him on their shoulders. Coach spray-painted his socks gold, didn't even wash them, and put them in the trophy case.

"Got it," Brandon said.

He had his head held high as we walked out the door and down the steps to the field. The rainstorms of the morning were gone but the wind kept gusting. Clouds stacked the distance like stage sets, white mountains to surround us, like it was us and the school buildings drifting past so small.

Running is great. Running might be the opium of my reality. I'm not the fastest or the best, but I'm distance. It makes me feel the breath going into me. And I can feel my body getting stronger. It's good for you all over.

Brandon turned out to be a real runner. Real good. Close enough to challenge Coal Train. He didn't say a word the whole practice. He didn't joke with anybody. Lots of us were joking around in the wind, jumping up to fly, leaning against it to let it hold us up. Brandon just kept his face stern and far away. Olympic god material. On the way back the girls were saying he was a show off. Stuck up. In the locker room the guys were already on Coal Train, teasing him, the other top runners. They were like, ooh, he's quick. Brandon could have been talking junk. Other guys would have.

"Colorado," I said. "Mountain lions are out there, right? Don't they kill people? Because I saw somewhere, I read it in the newspaper . . ."

"Puma!" He turned on me, eyes real wide, his breath right on me.

Coach called him over to his office door. Explaining something, showing him something on his clipboard, writing with a pencil. He looked up and smiled and they shook hands. Brandon went back to his locker and got his stuff and walked out. The other guys were caught up in their penny throwing game, but I was ready to get home. Ready to eat supper. This huge sunset was happening right when I went out, right where you step out the door. Brandon was at the edge of the practice field, his hair flaming up in gusts against the sunset. I turned toward the student parking lot across campus and I could have just gone on home. But I stopped. I had never moved to a new place in my whole life, and I just thought, Well . . .

"Yo, Brandon. You waiting on a ride?"

He didn't even turn around.

"You sleeping here tonight?" I said it sharper than I meant.

He jerked around, like he was about to come at me, and I just kept staring right into his eyes. Puma? I'm not scared of you. We can fight right here if we have to. I'm going to end up fighting this kid. And I'm not a fighting kind of guy. And he must have seen something in me then. His expression changed.

"Nah. I forgot to tell my mom. She probably figured I'd ride the bus."

"I might be going your way. But not all the way to Colorado. Not tonight, anyway."

He looked down and kind of laughed.

"OK." He stood up.

"Car's over there," I motioned with my head toward the student parking lot.

"I live somewhere in town. Pine Grove or something like that? We just moved in."

That's what put a lightning bolt through my stomach. "Pine Grove or something like that." Like it was just some ordinary thing. My head swam for a few seconds. Piney Groves Estates. That lie of a name. So this is who they destroyed the pine forest for. Find your own way home, jerk.

"Come on," I said. "That's on my way. I know exactly where that is. That's right by my house."

I just started walking. Toward the library. I wasn't thinking straight. I was staggered.

The pine forest.

How could I not have figured out that the newest kid at school would be moving into the newest neighborhood in town? And now I was about to take him there. And I had made my vow never to go in there.

Along the back wall of the science building we stepped through a muddy circle of cigarette butts and footprints. Rough kids tried to smoke back here between classes.

"This the way to the parking lot?"

"There used to be woods up there," I started. "A pine forest. There used to really be pine groves."

But what was the use of telling somebody like him something like that? You're just throwing words away.

"I used to go up there."

I'd tried to tell Muriel about it, back when the destruction started, but I couldn't get all the words out. I turned away. But I know she saw tears come to my eyes. At night, even a long time afterwards, even now, I would hear the machines again. The hum-hum-hum. The ringing harp in the saw blades.

The fury of it pounded in me round and round and round. Waves against a rocky shore. When they did it, when they started the destruction, I imagined myself coming to the point of violence: breaking their windshields at night, peeing on the seats and the control panels in the open cabs of the bulldozers, spray painting, throwing dirt, pouring oil all inside them. I had been on the threshold several times in my mind, on the edge, and then one evening I set out to really do it.

The student parking lot was a deserted plaza, long black shadows, red-orange sun streaks burning up the white pines where I parked. The breeze was still gusting the light in them.

"What was your other school like?"

That smirking laugh again. "Stupid. Full of posers."

"What?"

"Posers. Kids who put surf stickers all over their cars and wear surfer clothes, and they've never even been on a surfboard. They couldn't even get up on an ironing board flat on the ground."

I was surprised by how much he laughed about that.

"Well," I said, "I don't know the first thing about surfing."

I unlocked the doors and we got into my little Honda. I'd had my license only a few weeks.

Let Brandon start talking and suddenly he was the expert.

"Best surfing in this state is out on the Banks, at Hatteras. That's where you find the real thing. Of course, it's nothing like out on the North Shore, or anything like the West Coast."

You're saying a lot, to be from Colorado.

"The North Shore?"

"Hawaii. Big Island. And of course, that's not to mention the whole of Australia."

His voice was zinging with enthusiasm, and with an accent that made me think maybe he was from Colorado. Or was he trying on purpose to have a surfer accent, like I had heard of with people in California?

Poser. That was his word. Let him keep talking.

A thin line of words is all that kept me from doing that violence.

I had been already on the way there. Already walking. Already had it all planned out. Nobody would have seen me. I was halfway through the back way, under cover of the Out Back after dark, when the words started up inside my mind. Just a thin line of words, fragments, that I didn't even know I would remember.

"He deviseth mischief upon his bed. He sets himself in a way that is not good."

That was from the Bible. And I didn't want to be one of those people. That simple. It wasn't because I was virtuous or all about doing good. It was all about me. I didn't want to be one of those people, to "set myself in a way that is not good." I was too good, and that was enough to stop me and turn me around.

Brandon had killed me out on the track. He was so much faster than me. He would be one of the best runners on our team. No point in letting that aggravate me. But I wanted him to know I knew my way around here.

I'm from here. Maybe that's why I gave him a ride. I wanted him to know. He was the outsider, not me. But why did I care?

Later, another little line of words had come to me. Unexpectedly. I was outside raking up mowed grass, like a medieval peasant raking up all his livelihood in the back yard, wheelbarrow loaded full of this green hay Dad wanted for compost.

Another little line of words.

"Do unto others as you would have them do unto you." And I was so glad at that moment that I hadn't done anything, none of that violence I'd planned and dreamed up laying on my bed. I was just so glad I could say I hadn't done it. I was still free. I could just put it out of my mind and not have to wish I hadn't done it. Because I hadn't done it.

But that didn't help me. The pine forest was destroyed, and nothing I could do about it. It was gone. I was burning up, making my heart pound, disturbing my sleep, hearing the saws.

"Even Florida has better surfing than here. Except for Hatteras. That's the Holy Mecca, man, for North Carolina. But New Zealand is the coolest place. That's where it's real. That's where I'm going, because everything is environmentally friendly, everybody's surfing and everybody's vegetarian. Well, except for a few rednecks." His voice sharpened to scornfulness and he turned to look out of his window. I had never heard of rednecks being anywhere but here.

I could feel the wind pushing my little car. I gripped the wheel and imagined the tires gripping the blacktop, humming us forward.

We were in town now, bumper to bumper, brake and creep, waiting for our chance to turn at the light. It wasn't dark yet.

All that sounded great, Hatteras, New Zealand, Hawaii. Whether I cared about surfing or not, and right here were those crazy seagulls flapping over the dumpsters at one of the fast food restaurants. Seagulls, way up here. I could see the person in the drive-through handing food to a reaching hand. But I was ready to get home. My supper would be ready. The intersection came into view.

North, South, East and West, all eyes facing this little square of road, like this was the holy crossing place of all people. People were waiting to go. The people who had the green light zapped past in front of us, lines of cars, and all of us little particles, round and round and round.

In French they call it circulation.

Our turn. We curved in our lane with the other cars in their lanes and fanned out westward onto Gilead Road. We were about to cross the

Interstate. We had a couple more stoplights to get through because of the on and off ramps, but I could see them up ahead, turning green for us. Open country. The clouds were gone and the whole sky was clear crystal blue, the color just before twilight darkens over the earth. The thinnest crescent of moon was cutting in, and the first stars, little map points connected to each other by the straightest lines that made the shapes and animals, the Zodiac. Sea islands dotting a glowing blue sea as the sun sank away.

Or, rather, as the earth turned to the point that we could no longer see the face of the sun. Muriel was trying to get me to think that way. Trying to get me to see that Earth was a body "in relationship," she said, with the sun and other heavenly bodies. It's not all Outer Space, it's the space we're in, she kept saying. She had the cool science teacher.

And then just like that Brandon was shouting. "Pull over! Pull over!"

It scared me. He was so far out the window I thought he might jump.

Cars were right behind us. I pulled over, tall grass whipping the underparts of the car and Brandon burst out even before we stopped. He went running back, thirty, forty, fifty yards. Left the door wide open.

"What are you doing?" I yelled, squeezing out of my door, but my voice was nothing in the evening rush of cars and wind. Other drivers gawked. There was Brandon, way back up the road, crouched down, on the bridge. "Stupid kid," someone yelled.

Cars rushed, lights wrapping us, flowing over us. My supper, I thought. It was Friday. Mom and Dad would be waiting on me. Brandon was huddled over a small dark shape.

"Brandon," I started, jogging toward him, "I need to be getting home," and then I thought, what if it's his dog? I wouldn't care if I missed supper. I would help him get it home. I came around and knelt down with him. But it wasn't a dog, or anything like that. It was the biggest crow I'd ever seen. Its eye was still open, a little dome of twilight, but it was dead.

I stood up. The whole road was trembling, with a pulse in my feet and knees, all that traffic ramping across the bridge, and the bolts of wind. Both sides of the Interstate beneath us were a mesmerizing, glowing river in two directions. I had never been out on the bridge before.

"That's not a regular crow, is it?"

No answer. He lifted the dead bird. I drew back.

"Hey, take it easy, isn't there a virus or something from dead birds?"

Brandon looked at me and then without saying anything put the bird back on the pavement and began taking off his jacket.

"What are you doing?"

He knelt down and scooped up the crow and began to wrap it up in his jacket. Beside the dull fuzz of the jacket, the black of the crow was shining jet gloss blue black.

"You're leaving your jacket out here?"

"The least we can do is get it off this road. Get it to a quiet place."

We?

"You said something about woods? A place where we could bury it?"

After a moment, I said, "Yeah, but those woods are gone."

Your stupid neighborhood destroyed them.

"I guess we could probably bury it at the back of our yard," I said. I just wanted to get out of the road, off the bridge. That's the only reason I said it.

"But why?"

"Only not tonight. It'll have to be tomorrow. At your house, OK?"

"Yeah, OK." I just wanted to get back in the car and get home. People were having to swerve around us. Horns bled a weird smear on the air. Here he was holding this dead crow in his arms like a baby. The bridge rumbling and thumping. Could it come apart while we were on it? Cars were bigger and faster when they were zooming by, and we were right against the metal guardrails.

"Well," I said, back in the car, "I would like to know what kind of bird it is, anyway. It seems too big to be a crow. Do ravens live around here?"

But he just looked out of the window. From where we had pulled off I could see the pines up at my house, black shapes against the twilight. My headlights cut us a place into the flow of traffic.

"Piney Groves Estates" said the entrance sign. I turned right. The golden letters flared up as my headlights braised over them. The entrance had fancy brickwork, iron lampposts and flaming oil lamps. Like it was some ancient estate. Now here I was. The vow I had made was about to go up in flames.

"Piney Groves Estates," I snarled. "Just look at all the pines." Bitterness gripped me, and instantly I thought it would have better not to have spoken.

He seemed about to say something but then didn't. And if I had heard that smirking breath-laugh at that moment I might have reached for his throat.

The whole place was one big circle of the same house over and over again.

"You said you live in this neighborhood?" he asked.

"No." I felt the blood drumming in my neck. Now it was my turn to make a breath sound. "I did not say that. Near it. Just take a right out of this entrance. We're the second house on the right. First house you'll come to is

Corin's, then ours. And we do still have pine trees. You'll see them as you come up the road."

If you even know what one looks like.

Then we had nothing else to say. We rounded a slow curve and the stars were coming out all over the sky. I saw the crescent moon sailing through a couple of left over scraggly sweet-gums. Somehow they had escaped the tree-chopping machines. The houses were all jammed in close together.

"That's it."

I pulled up the driveway.

Brandon's house wasn't much to look at. Just sitting there, a few bushes jammed into the ground around it, bare cement walk up to the front door. The grass in the yard broke up before it got to the house. Red mud splattered on the foundation. It was all brand new and already looked worn out.

"Thanks." He got out and leaned back in through his window. "It's Chris, right? Thanks, man. I appreciate it." He was holding the wrapped bird close, cradled with one arm, and I noticed when he talked one of his front teeth was chipped.

"No problem. If you still want to bury that, I'll see you tomorrow. Your mom doesn't care if you bring that thing home?"

The smirking breath again.

"She won't know." Then with an upward nod of his head he ran in front of the car and up the walk. The door glass caught the crescent moon, flung it back. Thin blue light from a television filled the house. A figure was standing against it in the dark.

As I pulled out onto the road I remembered the signboard the developers had put up when they first started building Piney Groves Estates.

"Why are so many people flocking to our area? It's the green open spaces, naturally! And the friendly atmosphere out here in the country. Come and be part of something special!"

3

Hating Piney Groves Estates

Stark fear jolts me. The machines are back! They're in our yard. They're cutting down our trees.

Even months later I would hear them.

It always started like that, me half awake, half asleep. Trying to see the woods again, trying to get back to the pathway among the trees. Still as possible I lay, not to disturb the powers, the spirit, to take me back. Don't try to grab it. Let it come to you, like remembering a dream.

But then I would hear it: the hum, hum, hum. And the dull thud of tree trunks hitting the ground.

To anyone on the outside, a ghost is someone dead who walks unbidden and unknown in a place. But being a ghost isn't about being dead or alive. It's nothing to do with that. It's about one thing only.

Love.

I had to believe it. If a person loves a place, they can return to that place. They are not kept out by space or time. They are free to return. I had to believe it. I kept trying to make it happen.

Evening was coming. The moon was a blur in clouds, yellow gold in rings of blue grey, like a blemish on pottery where somebody else's glaze dripped onto yours.

'Relinquished to the fires of the kiln,' the art teacher had said. 'Not ugliness.'

Relinquished.

The hill crested ahead of me, a little high place at the edge where the trail ran up to overlook the Interstate.

I knew it was coming. A day of destruction is coming and I cannot stop it. I looked and I stood, silent, trying to see the forest as much as I could before it was gone forever. Trying to take hold of it with my eyes and with my feelings. And there she was, a doe, silent. She looked at me, I looked at here. Her eyes were round and dark as the globe of an unseen world. The treetops shifted and a flight of birds, scattered, shed the last beams of day-light from their wings and moved on. The doe reared back. I saw her small black hooves gleaming as she turned to leap away.

"I have seen you now," I rushed to tell her.

Dry leaves and pine needles sounded, crashing in the distance and soft away through the nightfall.

"I didn't want this," I called after her. "I would not have chosen this."

Everything was destroyed. And like some kind of distorted leech, I began to feed on the sick sweetness of the hatred I had for Piney Groves Estates. I wanted its destruction. I made my heart pound wishing for it. Cars passing on the road sent fans of light through my open blinds, shadows running like water on my wall, and I was laying there grinding my teeth.

"Don't let it bother you so much, son," Mom told me when the bull-dozers first came. "This is the way the world works. The people who owned that property did what they wanted with it. I don't like it either. But you are resilient. You'll be OK. You'll see."

But these were ancient pines. Why weren't they protected? Years, cen-turies, circled in their trunks. The wind moved them way up at the tops, among the needle greens, and the whispering sea-song came down hoarse into the shadows. The only thing to say: This is a cathedral. A church. Even if you've never been to a cathedral. This is a sacred place. Your face turns up-ward, rises up. Can nobody else feel this? Why isn't this protected? It made me stand and walk and run and think and talk, even into the air by myself, to whatever, whomever, was listening. I was in an ancient place. The scent of pine breathed into me. It was clean. It was good. And it was unexplainable.

She never went up there. She didn't know. I made my vow, my private declaration, never to go into that neighborhood.

Every time I went by there, every day, I steeled my face. But in the end I couldn't keep from looking. It was so close to where I had to go every day. I couldn't keep my eyes from walking over the strangeness of the sight, the trees gone, the land turned over, ripped open. The land came up red after red, layer after layer, day after day. Seven reds, eight reds, each darker than the one before. The last layer came from the very blood of the core. The face of the land I had known had been cut away.

And now my vow was broken.

I kept going to the window the day the machines came. It sounded so close. I kept looking. The earth shook every few minutes. Our windows shook. A smell filled the air. Green leaves and living tree sap mixed with the raw wet clay. All of that mixed with diesel. It was a rotting throat-stench you couldn't wash down, because the red in the clay is the same as the red in your blood and they join together to make you know sorrow for the torn up ground. I kept my eyes straight in front of me every day. But we still had to drive through the red mud that the trucks and vehicles tracked onto the road. When I finally did look, finally went and stood looking, it had become an unknown place. It might have been any place. All the rings upon rings of tree growth rippling in circles for all those years had all gone in a few days. And I knew then that even the Earth wears out, the mighty Earth. Even if it's rock and ground, it does not last forever. Not as we know it. Nothing remained that anyone could know and remember. It ripped me open and I suffered.

But it was only my own blood I heard on those nights, half awake, half asleep. I finally realized that. My own pulse, hum, hum, hum, round and round and round. Blood churning against my ear drum like waves on a rocky shore. Probably not even normal. Probably some kind of congestion clogging my ear. The machines were long gone, the pine forest was gone, and nothing I could do about it.

So call me ghost, call me dark and melancholy, call me ridiculous. I don't care. If a person loves, they can return. I have to believe it. In some way, even if it's all in your head, it is real. As real as you are.

And now you know what's under the surface of somebody who's one of the old originals. You might think he's just an ordinary half-cool half-loser teenager. He's a person who cries about trees. All I had left to me now all my own was the darkness of night in the wide open places.

4

Ghosts

But Muriel said I was wrong about ghosts.

"It's not about love. It's about trying to hold onto the past. Some people can't let go. They can't move on. That's what makes somebody a ghost. They can't rest in peace. But nobody can turn back the clock. Nobody can make everything like it used to be."

She was looking at me with her eyes like a green ocean not turning away and I didn't know what else to say. I thought I had figured something out, but now I didn't know.

"But I'm not talking about dead people," I started to say.

But I didn't say anything.

What was she anyway, some kind of authority on spiritual things?

5

Jaguar Steps Hurricane

Saturday morning, Dad yelled up that Corin had called for me on the phone. Something about somebody being over there that I would know about. Brad, was it?

Brad?

"So could you get on up and get over there? And your mom and I are on our way to get carpet samples. And maybe paint samples. And we left a few pancakes for you and they're getting cold. So get on up."

Brad?

So Mom was serious about new carpet. That was because I had left my mythology textbook on the kitchen table, Mom had seen it, and that was it. We needed new carpet. Because the cover of the book had this circular picture divided into quarters, with an ancient Mesoamerican man wearing a jaguar skin, next to Heracles wearing the Nemean Lion skin, next to Gilgamesh wearing a lion skin next to some Greek guy wearing a leopard skin. From then on it was "this old carpet is jaguarish."

"Just like having a wild animal skin," she said.

I tried to tell her jaguars were magnificent and mystical and anybody would want to have jaguarish carpet on their stairs.

Jaguarish carpet's just not what I have in mind, dear, she replied.

"But you should hear what the ancient people thought about jaguars, Mom! They . . . "

"It's just not what I want on our stairway, Chris."

That wouldn't be Brandon over there? At Corin's?

Up the wall by my bed was a National Geographic map, "The World," and the newspaper's annual "Hurricane Tracking Map." It was Corin I had interviewed for the point of view of a hurricane survivor. My hurricane project had been so easy. It all just came together. And then it all went wrong.

The news back then had been all about a hurricane coming this way. Maybe. The path of the storm would change every few hours. I got the people in the school office to let me go on the morning announcements, on the school TV. I was tracking the hurricane. Each new report might be the word of doom. If it was coming our way, how bad would it be? Total destruction? Would we be left without a house or a school, all our stuff in a pile of mold and mud? Dad at breakfast would be saying things like "almost a Category 5 now, winds at 155 miles per hour." It was out there. I could feel it. Clouds start to show up, and everybody says, Is it here? Is this it? The sky gets a weird green light at the edge like a dying lamp mantle and before you know it you've passed into a shadow under heavy grey, blue-grey, purple-grey, dark grey, row on row, layers and layers of upper darkness. The wind blows from strange directions and people rush around trying to be ready. By that time, summer has been so hot for so long that people say the hurricane, even though it's tropical, feels cold. But it isn't the cold of winter or autumn. It's a sick cold, like a fever, like a chill. You get under a blanket. It's the humid chill of the sun jelled over with thick water. But really the only extra clothes you need is a long-sleeve t-shirt.

That was my project. Daily updates on the storm. People I didn't even know starting thinking I was a hurricane expert. And the hurricane really was moving toward us. I wasn't wrong about that. And it did grow into a full force hurricane.

Hurricanes are part of the lore of North Carolina. You grow up hearing about them. They're simple storms in West Africa and from thin air they take their deadly spin. They writhe counterclockwise. The power comes from hot air meeting cold air, and the rotation of the earth, and the storm churns all the way across the Atlantic. How could the meeting of two different temperatures start a movement so destructive? How could something that has been so far away be able to damage us? The very dust of the Sahara can be carried to North Carolina. With hurricanes, you can talk about the updrafts and the down drafts, low pressure, high pressure, all that stuff.

But I didn't care about that. There was something else, impossible to explain: the feeling the hurricane gave me. Even if I had never been around during a hurricane. It was the feeling of danger, knowing that in a few days you might lose everything just because of the weather, and nothing you could do would stop it. You were waiting, hoping, watching, praying. Standing on the porch, looking out. Outside, but inside. And that was it, the feeling: the familiar porch, the wooden house, windows and the open sky. I felt it deep down, deep in me. Like I really lived it. Somehow like I had been standing on a porch on a Caribbean island. A curtain drapes over the land. The shadow. You go out to the porch to look. Does it take the danger to make you feel the safety? And if you enjoy that kind of feeling, is that the same as wishing for destruction? Corin said you need the closeness of the sea to make you feel the land.

You might even need a jacket, even if it was still summer.

But it was more than that too.

It meant we were part of the tropical world. The hurricane tracking map includes us, every year. The danger goes from the Caribbean coast of South America all the way beyond New England to the Atlantic Provinces of Canada. It's the Atlantic. Tropical places like Jamaica and Barbados, the Virgin Islands and the Yucatan are different from Cape Cod or Cape Hatteras or Nova Scotia. But during hurricane season all of those places are on the hurricane map. I felt the closeness. I felt it. I was living in a wooden beach cottage, even if I really wasn't. The map ripples with concentric circles, and North Carolina is right in the center. Out of the whole Atlantic: North Carolina. We have had our legendary moments with hurricanes.

And after a hurricane, people have to make do for days without power. That's part of it. People share things, like chainsaws, whoever has them, and work together to clear fallen trees from roads and cars and yards. They light candles together and share food from their freezers, because without power food is thawing and has to be eaten anyway. That's what I learned from Corin. I could feel it just from him talking about it.

But trying to explain feelings on school TV just ends up turning in circles. That was one of my big mistakes. We are not in the Florida Keys, Martin said afterward. We're not in the Caribbean. You're wishing for destruction, he said. Like I had committed a violation. He was the only one on me then, before my prediction didn't happen. What kind of death wish do you have, he said, his eyes squinting like he couldn't quite see me, like he might not recognize me anymore. Jabbing at me with his finger. You seem like you're wishing for a hurricane. Despair is a sin, he said.

Good grief.

And Muriel. Like she can see into me somehow, with her eyes like a gleam of light in green glass. She didn't say anything harsh. She didn't jab at me like Martin did. She saw deeper, and left me where I couldn't say anything.

"When I saw you come on the school TV and start talking about a hurricane, I almost thought you were about to say maybe that hurricane was coming to destroy that neighborhood," she said, her eyes clear and bright,

right at me. "But I know you wouldn't want anything like that, to destroy people's homes?"

It was like she saw me better than I saw my own self.

But waiting for a hurricane is like waiting for a wild animal to come out of hiding. Like waiting for the world to get pregnant with a monster. You don't know what you'll get. I got caught up in my own thoughts. I called on Mr. Givens to shut down the school. By this time next week, I said, everything we have could be destroyed. Mr. Collins cautioned me, something about being careful not to incite inflammatory feelings. But in the end the hurricane went over a hundred miles out to sea. All its raging and we didn't even get rain. The project was turned in and graded and school kept going, and the only thing anybody remembered was that I wanted a hurricane.

I rinsed away traces of syrup from my plate and went out. But instead of going up to the gate like any normal person, I ducked behind our basketball goal on the driveway into the bushes under the high pines. I used to always do that, but this time I got my shoe tangled in a holly bush and ripped up my favorite shirt. On Corin's side I fell out onto the prickly bed of pine needles and dry cedar fronds. His crazy trees hung low in shaggy curtains.

Cedar, cypress . . . I couldn't remember. Some of them were the ones that shed their leaves. His wife had wanted it like she remembered from California, "a house tucked into fragrant woods" or something like that. Photographers used to come, dad had told me. Plant people, magazine people, from out of town and out of state, just to walk around on Corin's brick pathways looking at trees and plants. Camellias, azaleas, rhododendron, all that stuff. But even though his garden and trees were famous around the state, Corin was famous in our town for just one thing: Being crazy. Crazy partly because of his yard and his house. The house was wooden, just like the shed, but not painted, except for the mossy green door and trim. Everybody else painted their house, if it wasn't brick, usually white. And it was built weird, people said, foreign looking, with upper porches on the sides. Was it Asian style or Black Forest style? I had heard both. Or California Bungalow style. The roof was dark green tin. Tuck that house up under all the cedars, like a Christmas tree forest, and that was the other thing people faulted him for: he had no real yard to cut grass in. And no easy way to visit without feeling like you were having to find your way into all that.

"Snaky," people said. Like one step in there and right away snakes would be wrapping around your legs.

But when his wife died and they had the funeral, so many people came that the church overflowed. The stories went on and on of good things she had done for people.

Now here I was at the old shingle shed. A fallen cedar lay nearby, dead whale bones white and smooth. The little brick walkways turned off into high shrubbery.

What was the point in having pathways winding you all around?

I heard voices.

Around the half-circles, through the little meeting places and then, framed in the hedges, human beings. Corin with his snowy hair, out here in a wooly sweater on this humid day, and the thought hit me, had I really never seen how old he was? And Brandon, both of them at the outdoor table, and the branches of the Himalayan cedar draping down over them like a pavilion at the center of all this.

"Oh, and Chris, one more thing," Dad had said to me before they left. He came all the way up to my door. "Your mom and I have been meaning to say something about this but we just haven't yet. But if you're going over there I might as well say, be careful around Corin. He's . . . well, he's not as sharp as he used to be."

"Huh?"

"Well, he's getting older, and I've noticed lately, I think he might be showing signs possibly of the beginning of dementia or something like that."

"What?"

"I'm just saying, if he says anything that seems unusual, or if he seems to be lost for a few minutes, just realize he may be . . . well, I don't know how to put it exactly."

"Losing his mind? Dad, I'm sure he's not crazy."

"Well, no. I don't mean he's losing it, exactly. But son, people do begin to lose some of their faculties, with age. I'm just saying, keep your eyes open and if he says anything weird, just realize he may not be totally himself."

There they sat like they had known each other all along. Eating something. And a little black cat was weaving around under the table, pushing against Corin's hand. And right there on the table lay Brandon's black fleece jacket with the dead crow right on top. Corin sitting there looking unshocked. Like it was one hundred percent normal to have a dead crow laid out on your table while you ate breakfast and drank tea.

I came stumping up shoe in hand, trying to get the knot out as I walked. Brandon with his dark brow, eyes on me, my torn shirt, like I was the one out of place. He was sitting there in the same crumpled clothes from yesterday.

"Hello there Chris," said Corin. "I was wanting to ask you, is this your little cat? She's been visiting me all night and I don't know whose she is."

I took a seat.

"No, not ours. But it looks like a nice cat." She came over, let me rub her head.

"Blueberry muffin?" He poured another cup of tea. "She's a she, and she is a nice cat. I suppose she has found herself a home then. Unless she belongs over in the neighborhood?" He looked over at Brandon, like this delinquent would know anything, and then at me and then he turned back to Brandon.

"The pine grove, you were saying. Now you might not know this, but Chris here is mighty sad about his pine forest."

He looked at me, and I mumbled "yeah," trying to sound like it was nothing, but I couldn't keep my face from blazing red.

"It's true," I said.

"And we did hate to lose that forest. But I'll tell you what, Chris. Much of this whole country is a forest waiting to grow. Not all of it, but much of it. And not just the pines, though much of this area was once rich with those virgin pines. Not just the pines. All of our native trees. Right here where we live is the place of an ancient forest. I don't mean ancient like something dead long ago and gone forever, the way an ancient sea used to cover part of our state, and left its traces in fossils and seabed limestone. I mean a vast and living forest, all the way up and down the eastern United States, from the coast to the mountains and beyond. That forest is here right now. We're holding it back all the time. It would grow back if we let the land be. I've seen it every day, out in my plantings and my beds. I have to pull them up, because they act like weeds—little willow oak sprouts, little sweet gums, little maples and cedar trees popping up among my shrubs. Pine seedlings. I wouldn't be able to have my garden if I didn't pull them up. In the gutters of my house even. Look up there. Little trees growing. I've got to find somebody who can get up there on a ladder and clean those gutters out. The seeds don't know where they fall. They're just in the air. And that's the ancient forest, remembered in the air, you might say. Just as soon as we leave it be, that forest will return."

Yeah, I thought, looking over at Brandon. You and your stupid neighborhood. Looking at me like I'm wrong. Sitting there in some freaky "Ghost Rider" t-shirt. Broken tooth. A surf expert, from Colorado. You've never even been in the woods. Sometimes your shirt gets torn. This is North Carolina and we're at the heart of this continental shore. We were the first colony. The Lost Colony, anyway. We have our tragic mystery, and the first English person born in the New World. You've never even heard of that. We're at the heart of a mighty and ancient forest, living and indestructible. You heard him. Vast isn't the word for it. It's Continental. The whole East. No roads, no buildings, no interstate. Nobody's house. Nobody's neighborhood. I felt my face burning hot. I felt my heart pounding in me.

Corin's words were ringing around me. He called the pine forest "virgin pines." Back to the unspoiled beginning. And then our ancestors got here. Sir Walter Raleigh and all them, stepping off boats in puffed-up velvet clothes, swords out, and conqueror's flags to plant. It wasn't like some long ago sea with dead fossils crying in the ground. This forest was still here. Still waiting. Remembered in the air. Then why don't we just leave it alone? Why don't we let it grow? Nothing in my lifetime could replace the pine trees I had known up there. But a new grove could take root any time we let it. I felt blood pounding in me.

"We found that yesterday out on the bridge over the interstate," I said, pointing to the dead crow on the table. Breaking myself out of the spell.

But why am I saying 'we?' Why do I need to say anything about it?

"Yeah," Brandon was saying. "Do you know this one?"

Does he know this one? Like anybody would know a crow?

A cloudy look came over Corin. For a second I thought he might cry.

"Where'd you say you found him?"

"Out on the bridge. Over the interstate."

"Yes, I know this one. He's been nesting in an old tree back there at the bottom of the garden now for a good while. Maybe a year or two. Him and his crowd."

The blue sheen on the feathers rolled up ahead of Corin's hand. The bird lay there perfect and clean, the eye shining like it wasn't dead, like a little mirror-dome if you looked close, the beak as smooth as stone. The wing feathers fanned out, each one pristine. The feet curled down to claws perfect like the beak.

"Oh, I have seen this one. Bright light coming off him, and how he came down . . . Will you young fellows know that a time comes for each one of us here on this earth, when the angel will come down. 'It's your time,' his voice will say."

"So . . ." I began after a few seconds of not knowing what to say, "he's an ordinary crow, then?"

"Because I thought he might be a raven, the size of him. I don't know. Don't you think ravens might live around here?"

"Hold on a minute. I'll be right back." Corin slowly got himself up and headed toward the house. When I saw the doorway shadow drape over his snowy hair, I turned to Brandon.

"What're you doing here?"

"You said come over."

"I said two houses down." One, two. I held up fingers.

Idiot.

"Old guy made me drink this stuff," Brandon continued, holding up the tea cup like I hadn't said anything. Corin usually had weird stuff like green tea.

"Old guy?" I started. You're lucky he didn't call the police, the look of you. I was about to grab him by the neck. "This is my neighbor, and you don't know anything about him," and there was Corin already back, at my elbow without my having heard him. He wore a colored strap around his neck with a camera attached. Yes, he really was going to take pictures of this dead crow as it lay on his outdoor table. When you live alone, I thought, and only have plants and now a little cat to talk to, I guess it comes to this.

The camera snapped with a soft click. When he had taken a few pictures, he said, "Now come and take a look."

The old tree gnarled up at the back of the garden, down beyond the shed, past all the winding pathways, past where I had scrambled through. It was an old cedar in a livid state like one of those coast-blown trees you see in sunset photographs of California. It still had green branches, but chunks of it had been shattered off by some long ago blast of lightning.

Up in a clutch of broken out space was what Corin wanted us to see. It looked like a rabble of sticks. With a ladder we climbed up to peer into the crow's nest. White droppings and feathers were all over the place. And the crows' secret collection.

"Don't you think it might be a raven?"

"Well, I've never known if ravens live around here. But ravens have a ruff of feathers around their necks. This is a big crow, but I think ravens are bigger."

Bits of broken glass, plastic, shiny metal, little things gleamed among the nest twigs. Even a small twisted chrome piece that might have come from a car. A few things had fallen to the ground at the tree's roots.

"He was a glory to see, up in his tree with his people all around, crowing and cawing and flapping their wings. I wonder how this happened to him. You didn't see anything? Just fell out of the sky?"

"He was just there on the side of the road," I shrugged, "but if he was flying... I don't know." We stood there a minute, looking up, wondering. Things that fly, wing tips brushing the cedar branches, at home aloft among twigs, up off the ground. It was such a different life.

"Here we are." Corin wanted us to look at his greenhouse. His eyes were bright. "Right now there's not much in here more than weeds. Spider webs. The summer fills it up with grass and all these maypops and things and now I've got canes of blackberry trying to get in here. Cold is coming, not that far away. We could have first frost in a few weeks."

I saw old clay pots, plastic pots, a couple of wooden benches. Spiders' egg sacks. On the far end the greenhouse plastic had ripped open along the pipes that made ribs.

Corin said thanks for coming over, we were good lads. And would we consider helping him get the greenhouse in shape for freezing weather?

"Sure," I said, "that would be fine." The thought hit me again, Corin, over here all alone. I noticed the bird feeders at the back of his house. Think of him inside all winter watching birds eat seeds. How alone do you have to be that you follow the ways of the birds?

And, I told him, I can easily get up on a ladder and get those gutters cleaned out. I've done that at our house.

Brandon just stood there, said nothing. He took the bird with him, wrapped in the black fleece, and what he did with it I had no idea. But before he went, when just me and him were walking up Corin's driveway, he stopped at his bicycle and turned to me.

"There's this." He opened his hand and held out a little seashell. It was small but it was one of those whelk shells people are always trying to find.

"What's that?"

"It was in his beak, out there on the bridge."

"What, like he was bringing it here?"

He just raised his eyebrows at me, upward nod, like that was a way to say anything, and pushed off one-armed on his bike.

"But I thought you wanted to bury . . ," I called to the distant shape of him as he turned out of the driveway.

"Yeah. Later," I muttered after him.

6

Something Unholy

Somebody on your porch roof making idiotic crow sounds at midnight is not normal. I knew right away it was Brandon.

Why had I been so foolish as to tell him where we lived? I was already in bed, reading by lamplight.

The face in the glass mingled eye to eye with mine, eyes shining white, teeth snarling and some kind of weird swooped up hair do. What was this, practicing for a Halloween costume?

"What are you doing?" I demanded through the screen. You're crazy.

"Buried the dead crow myself."

"Where?" Rummaging around in our yard? I wasn't used to people showing up at our house in the middle of the night. It was an invasion.

"And what have you done to yourself? And why are you here?"

"Where, what, why! Come take a look."

I couldn't have him come inside, and I wanted to know what he was up to.

Into shorts and old running shoes I slid, raised the screen and crawled out onto the roof. The night air was alive and fantastic, still buzzing with night songs, crickets and tree frogs. Leaves and dampness and earth smelled good, spicy with sweet gum.

It was only later that I thought how like a burglar he was.

"What in the world." Was that blue paint on him? No shirt, face and body painted with spirals and weird animals and unknown symbols, and in his hair, some kind of crown or headdress of . . .

"No way. You did not get those feathers from…"

"No?" he said, smiling. The broken tooth caught a chip of light. Absolute maniac.

"Where'd you bury it? And what are you doing on my roof?"

"What, where, why!" And then he leapt. Wildcat. I wasn't that agile. Fumbling, scraping, nearly falling, I hit the ground beside him and he was off.

"Wait," I shouted and whispered at him, galloping to catch up. I already knew he was faster than me. "That's not our yard." He had already vaulted the gate.

"You wanna see or not?" And he vanished under Corin's shadowy trees.

"But wait," I began. I had never gone into Corin's yard like this, never just on my own without it being to see him, and certainly not at night. We didn't make his yard our own to roam around in. I lingered for a second, but I thought, I might as well, because if Corin hears him out there and thinks a prowler is there, I would be able to let him know it wasn't. Or that it wasn't a robber. Because it was a prowler. A sort of prowler. An uninvited person roaming around in the dead of midnight. And with him dressed like that, half man half crow idiot. He was someone in a dream. He really is insane, I told myself. I'm out here in the night, in the living hour of this wild man.

I almost caught him in the back of Corin's lot, down at the bottom near the slat fence, by the blueberry bushes. I used to help pick blueberries, I suddenly remembered. How had Corin managed this summer? I had offered no help. Why hadn't he asked me? He always gave us as many blueberries as we could use.

We ran through the cedars, the cypresses, the shaggy green groves. I could see Corin's lights in the windows through branches. Or was that just the glint of street lights from Piney Groves? And then I heard the shout. Corin's voice.

"Let no unholy thing come into this garden!" He was the main reader at our church, so he knew how to make his voice loud. But he sounded weak and straining, and I felt embarrassed for him. And for me, half naked and ridiculous, caught in a circle-round with this kid Brandon. How would I explain my being over here? But Corin sounded so old and small. And a little crazy.

"Brandon, come on," I whispered as loudly I dared. "I don't care for this. Let's get out of here. We don't need to be messing around in here."

"Scared?"

"No. I'm out here aren't I? I don't like doing this to Corin."

And then the blast, powerful, chock-full. A shot gun. Birds flew up, squawking out of sleep. The crow family went crazy. Surely he was just trying to scare whoever was out here? Not actually shoot them? Not actually shoot us? That was it: enough of this.

"I'm out of here, Brandon. Now I've been shot at! By my own neighbor!" His face looked different, like the game was on now, and he was running. I was running and I saw the golden blur of Corin's lights as I ran back through the trees.

But we couldn't go back the way we'd come without being seen, so I yelled now as loud as I dared, through clenched teeth, "Brandon, this way." I motioned in the dark: down through the Out Back, the wild area under the power lines, and then back up into my yard.

I caught a glimpse of Corin. Old Corin. Wearing a plaid robe, shotgun in his hands, on the back terrace, he called it, of his house. This was his worst fear coming true, that when they built the new neighborhood, kids would be all over his garden and he wouldn't be able to stop them. He had said it would be the end of his way of life. The pine forest used to cover him on that side. And maybe it was like Dad had said? He really was starting to lose it? To be out there with a gun, shooting into the dark? At kids?

His big trees were so dark they made the night sky seem light, dusky, grainy. Open door-light rayed around him. He stood there not knowing who might be out there, how many there might be, when they would be coming back. We could have been anybody. And I wanted to tell him, don't worry, it's only us, we're stupid and it won't happen again, if I can help it. I almost did yell that. But now was not the moment to go running toward him, not with a gun in his hand and me on the dark side of the night this time. And this freak in feathers running in front of me.

The crescent moon was long gone by that time. It was on the other side of the world. Or was it still where it had been and the earth had moved? I wasn't sure.

Even without moonlight the running trail in the Out Back showed up fine in the night. It was smooth, lighter than the rough places where plants were growing. It's hard packed North Carolina clay, I thought. Was it by starlight that we could see? Starlight is what people in books, out at midnight, see by when the moon isn't there. The stars didn't seem particularly brilliant. They looked rather weak and spotty above the fog of light from the shopping center and the exit ramps at the Interstate. But there was the clay path, loping off across the little hills into the distance, under the dragon-neck power lines that snaked and glistened in the dark.

We were running fast and my thoughts were jostled. I felt elation. The darkness, and just being a human person running wildly underneath the lines unleashed something I had not felt in day time. We leapt. I knew the path. I knew all the leaps, the low places, the steps to avoid. I wasn't back in my room until after 1:00 AM. Do people realize the power in those lines is so strong you can hear it? It crackles and sizzles and mutters in the dark. It speaks a word that would blast you to oblivion. Leave nothing of you but a charred wreck of human framework.

But the most infuriating thing of all that night, the thing that drove me across a line, was that Brandon had already been out there. He'd just moved in and he'd already been messing around in my places. And he found something out there that I had never seen. In the madness of our running, I had followed him and he had followed me, me trying to show him, and him trying to show me, me trying to lead, and then he was refusing to follow me. On my own paths. He circled back toward the back side of Piney Groves, where the Piney Groves people had stuck a white plastic fence on the high ground, the way the land crested up. A skull-grin in the dark, a gaunt jaw jawing up defiant. Why put a fence anyway? To fence out anything true and wild? That was all they cared about: cheap fence. And then I saw why Brandon was going that way.

For all my trail-making and exploring, all my running, for all the years I had lived there, I had not known that just a little way down from where my trail used to come out of the pine forest a group of boulders was nestled down low in a gully.

I had been by here one million times, but the lay of the land and the strangling bushes concealed this fold. It must have been impossible to see from where you came out on my trail, up in the pine grove. I know I would have seen it. But you had to come right up to it. It opened up when you made a way through and behold, mighty boulders rising up from a little ravine, a gully. They were massive stones. Boulders. But no, I thought, no, it could not have been like that when the pine forest was still here. The bulldozers must have uncovered these stones. So I couldn't have known. Because once the bulldozers came, I didn't go into the Out Back for such a long time. It put me in such a dark place. I let go of all that was mine. And now Brandon was acting like he owned this place.

It made me furious that this outsider should be able to show me something. Didn't he know how to respect other people's property? I just stood there, stopped in my tracks by the sheer mass of the rocks. Trying to understand. How could boulders this big stay hidden from me? They had to have been underground.

Brandon ran tearing forward through weedy grass, leaping up the first boulder and over, swallowed out of sight. Into the rocks, like it was the home he had come from. And I just kept standing there under that gaunt jaw. And then he was back, on top of the next rock. And there he stood, Lord of the Stones, silent, glistening with sweat under star-light. And the boulders looked silver, hunched, ancient bodies lain here like whales and dinosaurs. Monsters greater than all our experience. The dinosaurs themselves might have grazed on tree ferns right here beside these very stones. Or had this been ancient sea floor, that whales and the mega-sharks swam above?

Feathers against the sky: ancient man stood right before my eyes. And when he came down is when I made to tackle him. Half joking, but really halfway fighting him. More than halfway. I wanted to push him down. Halfway wanted to hurt him. Angry, and ashamed of my anger all at the same time. I wanted to say, Just stop for a minute. Why did you come here? Why did you have to come to my class, to my window? Just stop and realize this is my ground, my place. I'm from here. I'm the one who lost the pine forest. I'm the one who had to put up with your stupid neighborhood. You don't even know how big a loss it is. But we forgot words, forgot language. We grappled and spilled, jumped up and dodged and circled. We grunted, growled. Anger rushed out through my arms and hands, gripping, grabbing. I felt the strength in him pushing me back. I felt anger from him too. We grabbed headlocks, pushed, hit the ground. Red clay smeared our sweat. We were out in the dark; we were grappling. And then we were running again.

I owned all of this. Not by legal means or with signed deeds, but in a more real way. I was the one person, I was the only one, who had ever cared to come out here, who knew what was out here. I made these trails. I was the one who loved the pine forest, and here was this outside newcomer with his idiotic Colorado accent living in the neighborhood that destroyed it. But already it was gnawing at me: Had I just started something, and settled nothing?

By the time I got back in my room it was way after midnight. I rushed through another shower just to knock off the sweat and the wrestling dirt. The water swirled pale red into the drain. North Carolina clay. And flecks of his crazy blue paint. Mom and Dad probably thought I was crazy. Probably thought I had woken in the night again thinking it was time for school. And before I slept, chambered in the dark of my room, the words of Corin came rushing back to me, embarrassing me all over again. Is that what I am now, something unholy, something to be shot at?

7

As When Someone Blows Breath

"You have crossed a line. Come, you will go with me."

Dark of night swirled around me, murmuring, chiming, the world turning, the moon turning. Solar System turning. I saw stars and the grainy indigo sky. I saw the painted face in night's glass, the dead crow's eye, feather tips, finger tips.

Who are you, I started to say. His voice had a quietness that made me feel trust.

"You have crossed a line. You can no longer belong to yourself."

The air shivered.

I was turning away from the world of light.

Drums sounded, deep and low, rumbling in waves, the sky and the drumming rolling toward me. I felt the tremor and the rumbling inside me.

And I heard the sound of the people of that place.

"Come, Guardian. Call down thunder."

"Call down your voice." they said. "Shake down the sky."

"Keep our fields from devouring mouths."

"You have crossed a line now," he said again.

Who are you? Maybe I already knew.

"I know I crossed a line."

I said it out loud, out to the deep indigo darkness.

I could feel it eating at me already. I had crossed a line. Brandon would be at school now all the time, and he lived in those stupid houses. Right up the road. He would be running with us now all the time. But the drums boomed and my words seemed to go lost, seemed to spread thin into the deep indigo.

"What are you going to do about it?"

"I can't take it back."

"He's faster than you. Does that bother you?"

"I hate it. Maybe. Maybe I don't really care. That's not what made me fight him."

"What made you fight him?"

"Everything else." The pine forest. No, not the pine forest, but the way I felt about losing the pine forest. And the way he was running around out there like he owned everything.

Nothing could be the same anymore.

"I don't want to have to keep on being in a fight with somebody."

"You have chosen a path Come."

"My eyes are bright," he said. "I am as an ember flaring: As When Someone Blows Breath they call me, for as a moon bearing sunlight passes through broken clouds I bear a likeness to the shadows. When I go along the forest borders or when I rise on silent foot up from the dark depths I rise with eyes shining. But I pass by unseen. From shadow and from light."

"I didn't mean to disturb spirits," I said. "All I wanted was the pine forest . . . "

I thought again my words went lost in the dark, in the wealth of star-washed indigo, letters and words arching, expanding. But they were not lost.

"We are not disturbed. We are always watching."

We?

"You have come here," said a voice soft and small but sure and strong.

A shimmer, a blue-green iridescence, passed in front of me. She hovered, fluttered. She glided softly in gentle circles.

"You are among us. Do you know that you are free to walk among your trees? The love you held for the forest is not gone. You will walk there again. It will come to you as a gift. I will give it to you, and it will come to you."

I would walk there again?

And the same voices, singing, the same people, but it was soft now. It was calm and sweet. It was as the sound of children clapping.

"Come, Guardian,
Call the Child Rain to come and dance in our fields.
Come and dance, come and dance in our fields."

I did not see him then but I heard his voice calling down thunder, calling down rain. It was like the roaring of a great cat and I woke shivering in my room of darkness. Wild sleep had torn the covers off me. Grimy light lined the edges of my window curtains. Thunder tolled. Sunday morning was rising in a rainstorm. No sleeping late today. Breakfast, and a wet raincoat for church.

8

At Church

Sunday mornings we sit in our usual place. This building is old. Colonial. Ancient. Brick outside, plain wood inside. The floorboards run dark and smooth, the years coming and going with church folk. Dark and high up, Gothic beams branch and arch like trees. Light fixtures hang on chains, like the medieval lamps night watchmen lift at gateways. I wandered among the ceiling beams during the long service. The organ pipes gleam up there, vertical, dark-mouthed slashes of sunlight.

Arched windows are water green, as old as the building. Over the years the glass has wavered, withered, slinking down by gravity, the slowest flow of liquid on Earth. Everything through it made wavy and bubbly. Not invisible, but blurry, lost to detail. To keep us in from the outside while we are here, Dad said. But it did not separate us completely from the outside. Sunlight came green in summer, the fullness of the oaks in the churchyard. But this was a rainy, sleepy, dimly glass green day.

And what I dreaded was there: Corin. Over in his usual place, the reader, front row, with the people who weren't able to go forward, who had the Bread of Heaven and the Cup brought to them. And at the end of the service we would be standing outside on the walk speaking to him, as usual. Mom and Dad might even invite him for lunch. And what if he had seen us out there last night? What if he knew that it was me? Something to be shot at? And I didn't want to be dreading talking to him. My own neighbor. And even more, it was eating me that I should go ahead and tell him it was us, get it over with, me and some idiot kid, rather than let him think that some gang was attacking him or something. Put him at rest a little. He doesn't need to be worried. I didn't want him to be troubled. So I decided I had to tell him. I had to say I was sorry.

I was about to die from the service, the long, sleepy duration of it. My leg rested against the wooden support under the pew in front of me. I couldn't go anywhere, not out of either end of the pew. I was deep in the middle and surrounded on both sides. Mom would frown on my scraping across everybody to go out. And on my going out in general. And the pews were as old as everything else in the church. They magnified movement with squawks of condemnation. That made Mom frown too. And the floor: Just shifting your feet was enough to make it groan, and more movement brought snapping pops, as if the building mocked your need to get up and move and stop being still. So I tried to sit without moving. I shifted my back, trying to get some comfort.

I was in a coffin. I just stared straight ahead at the Gothic beams. The pulpit had its green banner, the Chi Rho, and my eyes wandered over that, the Greek letters. The X to take in the four directions, the Rho like a shepherd's staff. This little place would be my last. This little coffin. It was OK. I was not in luxury, not in a comfy bed but I was OK. I was in a place made of stable wood. I would rest against this wooden bench. It all became so simple. I was perishing here so nothing else mattered. My leg rested easily against the wooden support in front of me.

A reader stood, and it was Corin. White hair burnished under one of the hanging lamps as he leaned toward his reading. Psalm something or other. His voice quivery but not weak, sounding like the old dark wood all around me, like a bow on a cello.

And I drifted away. I floated. Words coming, words going
He bowed the heavens also and came down . . .
Brightness and clouds removed . . . Darkness his secret place . . .
Hailstones and coals of fire . . .
Hailstones and coals of fire

Music. Piano. And it was something I had heard before but I wasn't sure what. These are the last things on Earth for me. And I am comfortable. I can't recall the name of the music, but I never really listened before. But I am listening now. It is soft and nice. Gentle. Every note like a sheet of paper floating.

I am gentle. I am music. I am dwelling in this place and I need never worry about anything else again. All of it is gone and I am floating away. I did not think it would be comfortable like this to stop and to be still. The glass in the windows bending with light. I have never been quiet before now. This is quietness. Nothing can harm me now.

Then all around me everyone was moving, standing, the organ rushing with a wind storm, the wood of the floor screaming and I was sinking, engulfed, feet were scuffling, and Mom was nudging me and whispering sharply.

"Get up and act like you know how to behave in public!"

Later that afternoon true horror was breaking out all over me: a rash of poison ivy. My arms were already welting red and itching. It was on my hands and fingers. My chest, my back. I knew it would start red, whiplashes, and then blister in clusters, a gross boil of skin on me. I knew from bitter experience that it meant days of misery, oozing crust, itching.

Mom kept saying, How could it possibly be so much, and so all over me? How could you have gotten this? She couldn't figure it out. But I knew. It could only be from the wrestling in the Out Back. I knew how to stay out of poison ivy. I knew what it looked like. I had a mental map of all the places where it grew. I ran out there all the time without getting into it. I had never let it get me out there before, not once, after I learned how to see it. But last night had been different. I had crossed a line. And now I would have to suffer. The late night shower hadn't been enough.

It was a torment. I must go and see Corin as soon as possible, and I would have to face Brandon and figure out how not to be living with strife between us. But for now nothing was possible but misery. I was incapacitated. Decapitated. Despicably disfigured. Because it would spread to my face, it always did, and swell over my eyes and I would be blinded for days. For a few days. Then it would heal up. I would return to normal. A glimmer of hopeful perspective remained. I lay in bed. Mom said No School Tomorrow. It was as bad as that. So I could call Muriel. Maybe she would gather up my schoolwork for me, at least for the classes we had together. History and our wretched Geometry. Mr. Collins would see that I got on with English.

Corin didn't eat lunch with us this Sunday. But he did stand outside after church talking to Mom and Dad for a long time. What he told them made me stand there secretly sweating, secretly desperate to get away. He had heard noises in the night and he had seen movement and he had gone out with his gun. You just don't know what is going to happen these days, kids running wild over there in the development. He had actually shot his gun! His hands had been trembling, and his shoulder was still hurting from the blast.

"I told you I heard something!" Mom said to Dad. They talked of nothing else the whole way home.

Of course I already knew the story. And I just stood there the whole time we talked, saying nothing. Too scared to own up to my own foolery. Too embarrassed that I had had any part in upsetting an elderly man. Neighbor and friend. I told myself I would do everything I could to try and help him out.

9

Sick Stillness My Putrid Face

We walked out from the city on the sacred way. It is a way of reckoning. Do not set foot on those white stones without knowing what waits: The Shining Face, the One Singing in the Darkness. The One Without Fear in the Darkness. You step up to the edge and you will throw something. It might be gold or a precious stone, it might be some kind of work you've done and loved and sweated over. It will be something valuable. You're throwing to the blue-green, breaking the surface beneath sky. The water rocks and pivots and rolls outward. Long minutes pass before the circle falls still again.

All I did all day was lay there trying to figure out the new project. I scribbled down stuff but every time, after a few sentences, I marked it all out. It was just a bunch of dream fragments. Use this time away from school, I thought, don't waste it. Get an idea. Then everything will be OK. Was an idea hovering in front of me but I just couldn't see it? I couldn't get to it. I couldn't see anything that would actually "meet the requirements," as the instruction sheet put it.

"Don't scratch," Mom implored.

I'm trying not to scratch. Trying not to itch. Might as well try not to breath.

I spent the whole day staring at the maps on my wall.

"Hurricane Tracking Map."

"The World."

I absorbed the shapes into my mind. If the world ever wanted to make itself a flag, we already had it: our homelands and continents all on a field of ocean blue.

I found Norfolk Island. It's a dot way out in the Pacific. Their flag had a tree, I knew, because of the little tree I had in a pot in my room. On the map all the distance out to there is flat blue, but if you're floating in the air it's easy to see the ocean full of salt water, rolling and tilting and moving, pulling and moving with the moon and the earth's rotation and the power of gravity. It's easy to see how its a real place, not just a tiny dot.

Do people in other countries have to worry about poison oak when they go into woods and fields?

Sea water is what I needed now. The mystical salt had power over the blisters. I threw myself into the glassy waves curling up to the dark tree shore of Norfolk Island.

I tried to enjoy not being at school, tried to enjoy looking at the windows, the way the sunlight runs through the trees during the day. But I was getting behind.

All I did all day was lay there like a corpse listening to the radio. Half asleep half awake. Wrapped in the sheets of the white tomb. Trying to be still. Trying to not even breathe. Hating the crust of sandy calamine painted on me. Sick stillness, my putrid face. Boiled over and swollen red. Not running with the guys but laying here painted and wrapped.

And Brandon would be running with them. One of the fastest. Jerk.

Green light from ferns and hanging plants rays down to strike the waters. It's yards down to the surface. Something sails over the edge; the splash shouts in the forest. Birds start up, squawking, animals spring up running. Then the forest falls back in, flattens back to a regular hum and conversation. But in the pool rings of sky roll across the face of the water, silver rings to the darkest edges of the cavern, the limestone walls flickering blue from above, and back and forth, light and shadow rolling until waters are flat again, an eye on the Earth gazing up.

I didn't do anything all day but listen to Muriel's station, the classical music. She knows every composer and every orchestra. All the foreign names and words, the different music, the conductors, the instruments. All the foreign cities and orchestras. Concertgebauw, Leipzig, Philharmonic. Tempesta di Mare. All those words.

But I did know about jaguars and leopards. I was drawing jaguars in my notebook in math class and that was how we met, when she turned around and said she liked my leopards.

"Leopards!" I had said.

"Yes? Not cheetahs I don't think. If they are, you should make them thinner, lankier."

"Not cheetahs and not leopards. Have you ever heard of South America?"

"No! What is that, another country? Like the Confederate States?"

That, I thought, was the beginning of another "southern boy" mockery by yet another transplanted person.

"Ha. If you know what South America is then you should know jaguars live there. The differences between leopards and jaguars, and cheetahs, are not at all difficult to grasp. First, and I guess most obviously, are the spots. All the same? A golden-yellow cat sprinkled with dark spots? Not the same at all. The leopard's spots are smaller, more numerous, and more evenly placed. They are called 'rosettes' because they are rings of dark. The jaguar also has rosettes but they are larger, more wide-spread, and they may have spots or dots inside them, and the jaguar can have other spots too and dashes and marks which..."

"You sound just like a textbook," she had said, turning away to face the beginning of math class.

She always writes with a peacock ink pen, the kind you have to put cartridges in. I saw the turquoise-green on her fingers that first day, and the writing in her notebook.

And the cheetah, well he just has pepper spots, I went on, whispering right behind her. Nothing like the mighty jaguar. And then you have bone structure. The leopard is agile and wily and strong, strong enough to haul a dead gazelle straight up a tree trunk, but also slim, lithe. The cheetah is thinner, lankier, and famously fast. The jaguar is much more stocky and more muscular than either. He's stout. And what sets him apart is the massive jaw: able to crush a human skull easily. The muscles of his jaw are so pronounced that his head can sometimes look square. Some of the native peoples used the same word for jaguar and for dog, because the jaw looked so much alike. And that's not even to begin talking about the melanistic forms of the jaguar and the leopard . . .

"Just like a textbook," she turned and mouthed at me again.

"Let's have your full attention in the back," came the command from up front.

That was the first time I talked to Muriel.

But I wouldn't be laying here with poison ivy all over me if Brandon hadn't moved here. I'd be running with the guys right now. And none of this would have happened if they hadn't torn down the pine forest anyway.

And how does throwing something valuable into a cave of water solve anything? Tourists swim in the cenotes now, like in any swimming hole, but to the ancient people the cenotes were openings to the Underworld. Sometimes they even threw people in as an offering.

At least one person survived being thrown in. I had read that somewhere. Maybe others survived? Would it just mean you had to swim and float all night until the ones who threw you in went away? Did you have to die for the power to work, or maybe just going in could be enough?

10

The Rich Get Richer

"So have you done anything?"

"For what?"

"For the project!"

"It's too early to be worrying about that."

"It's never too early! It'll be due before you know it. You can get it done now while you're at home and then you won't have to worry about it."

"There's plenty of time. I'll get it done."

"But you do have ideas?"

"Uh, yeah, maybe, one or two. What do you know about God K?"

"Who? Are you talking about cereal?"

No. Maya storm gods. Like Huracan, who clouded human eyes so people would not be able to match the gods. And there was Chaac, and God K, and God L. Maybe they were all the same. It was kind of blurry to me. What I liked was the idea of storm gods. In our book Chaac's face was stern. Mocking. Sticking out his tongue like a fat and deadly knife. But the more you looked at him, the more you saw: he doesn't care. He doesn't have any emotion. His eyes are locked in the terrible spiral, the hurricane, staring blankly. Hypnotized by his own whirling power.

"Chris. Hurricanes, again? You're already . . ."

"Already what?"

But I knew what.

"Already . . . known for projects about hurricanes. So I guess you won't be doing that again. But don't let it get to you. It's only something for school. Are you going to be OK?"

"I don't know. I might get blown away. Might get wiped out. Yeah, I'm going to be OK. And you can go ahead and say it. I'm already known for being an idiot about hurricanes."

"I wasn't going to say that."

"Well, you could have. Everybody thinks that. But the real reason I'm crazy is I never know what to do and my projects always get bogged down and then at the last minute everything rushes together. Like I can't get an idea until I'm running out of time."

Why was I telling her all this, like some pathetic person on a talk show? She had this way of getting me to say things.

"That's because you wait so long to get started. Maybe if you made yourself a schedule, some kind of plan?"

"Yeah. Maybe. I guess I already know what you're doing?"

"You'll never guess! My teacher's helping me transcribe the *Tempesta di Mare* . . . "

"The what?"

"I could just play the one for violin, but I wanted to try transcribing the one for flute. It just makes for a better project, like, doing something unusual . . . "

"What did you call it?"

"*Tempesta di mare*! It's Italian. It means "the storm at sea." I noticed it back when you were talking about the hurricane . . . "

"Oh now you're just making fun of me. I see how it is. Doing your project about a hurricane. But that's OK Muriel. Go ahead."

"No, really, I'm not making fun. I just thought it would make for a good project. It's a good concerto for me to learn about transcription, rather than my just playing something."

"Well, I wish I was a musician. It all just falls into place for you. The rich get richer!"

"It's not easy. I practice 6 . . . "

" . . . hours a day! I know! I'll be OK. Eventually. I might survive this what did you call it, tempesty? This hurricane. I'll just be maimed and half-drowned but I'll be OK."

"Chris, don't make fun of that! Hurricanes are serious. My aunt's whole house got devastated a couple years ago and they lost all their stuff. They had to stay in a shelter."

"I know, I know. I remember. You told me. I know hurricanes are serious. I'm not making fun of anybody. I'm just using it for an idea. A metaphor! Don't you have those in music? I'll get an idea for my project. I just can't give you a definite idea yet."

And how did some guy write a thing of music about a sea storm but he's not getting ridiculed?

"So what went on at school, anyway? What have I missed out on?"

"Oh! I meant to tell you. You did miss something. Some weird kid that nobody knows was out at the cafeteria courtyard and he almost started a riot or something."

"A riot? What? Are you talking about Brandon? Did he have crow feathers?"

"What? I don't know who it was, but he was doing some kind of tricks out there. I couldn't see because of all the people."

"Tricks? Like what? Like a dog catching a frisbee?"

"A dog? No, I wouldn't think so. Not at school. I don't know what it was. Everybody said he was doing tricks. I think magic tricks maybe? Anyway, I never saw it, like I said, because of all the people. I didn't know anything was going on until it was almost over. The security officer came over to break it up."

"When was it?"

"During lunch of course. All these people were out there."

Were there any new kids besides Brandon?

"So anyway, I have an idea. What you should do is, find someone from history that you admire, and get into a conversation with them. Start talking to them. Any runners you admire? Like maybe someone from the Olympics a long time ago? Talk to them."

"Muriel, now you really are making fun. And I'm more than a runner, anyway."

"I'm not making fun. My violin teacher talks about it all the time. She can talk to people in her mind. It's something she taught us to help us get better."

"What are you talking about?" I had never heard Muriel say anything like this before. "You mean just thinking about somebody and then pretending you're telling them something?"

"No. I mean connecting with somebody and telling them something."

"How do you do that? And who is your teacher anyway, somebody with a traveling circus?"

"Chris! You're mean. I am not talking about anything like that. I'm talking about connecting with people, you know, through caring about them. Through caring about the same thing as them. Through our common human connection, and love, and stuff like that."

"What? Valentine's Day?"

"No. Don't be ridiculous. I'm talking about through the fact that you care about the same subject, music or whatever, you can communicate with someone from another time."

"How? Like prayer somehow? And talk about being ridiculous??!"

"No, not like prayer. I don't guess. He isn't God. I'm talking about... I don't know. But my teacher is not some goofy . . . stop laughing! She isn't. She was talking about having a dream about someone and feeling like she had actually talked to them. And she told me about how when she is having trouble learning a certain part in a piece of music, she will have conversations with Tartini and Paganini and other people like that. Other violinists. I don't know. I don't remember everything she said. But don't you believe in powers that we can't see?"

"Well . . . sure. There's gravity. That's one."

"Chris! You're just being difficult. You know what I mean. Powers outside of ourselves."

"But I thought you meant me talking to someone in my mind. That's not outside of ourselves."

"Oh you know what I mean. Talking to each other . . . no, not 'talking to each other' but connecting. That's the word: connecting. Making contact. Across time. Maybe it is like prayer. Or like a dream. I don't know, but the way my teacher talked about it, I really did like it. I think it's good. When I was working on some music by Tartini she suggested I talk to him."

"Well who the heck is Tartini anyway, and that other guy you said?"

"They're violinists. Tartini was also a composer, from Italy. In the 18th Century. And that's another thing, he wrote this fabulous piece, the one I had been working on, all because of a dream. He dreamed one night that the devil came to him and showed him how to play this music, and when he woke up he wrote down the part he could remember, and it's called the Devil's Trill. It's fantastic and famous and I've played it."

"OK. That's fine. I see now. You want me to talk to the devil. Nice one Muriel!"

"No. I didn't say that. I just think the world is bigger than just what we see when we're awake with our eyes open."

"So what happened when you talked with Tartoni?"

"Tartini! Stop laughing! I did talk to him. Well, at first I didn't know what to say or what she was really talking about, but then while I was working on this one really hard passage in a piece of music he wrote, a place I kept having problems with, I just slowed down and worked note by note by note, and at the same time I was trying to think about Tartini and talk to him. And I started thinking about how he had written those very notes that I was trying to learn. The same exact notes! They're such small things, just a few seconds of music, but I was looking at them just as he had looked at them. It gave me chills! Because it felt like I was there when he was writing them. Or he was here when I was practicing them. He was telling me how to play them. He was encouraging me. I really felt it!"

"Wow. That is really cool."

"Now you're making fun."

"No, really. I don't not like it. I'm just trying to understand. It would be awesome to do that."

There was a pause then, and I was trying to figure out what to say, and I wondered several things all at once: if she really was more strange than I had realized; if what she was talking about might be possible; if she thought I didn't really care about what she was talking about when I really did think it was interesting; and whether or not girls were always like this, able to talk so unexpectedly about such crazy things.

"So," she said, "any ideas yet? Someone you could talk to?"

"Uh, no, I don't know."

"See you later then. You'll be back to school soon?"

"Yeah, soon. Uh, yeah, I hope …"

"Oh yeah, I never even asked, how's the poison ivy? And I still don't get how you got it so bad. And did you say someone had been climbing on your roof?"

"It's getting better. Still terrible, but going away. And yeah, the roof. It was this new kid, Brandon, he had this dead crow and . . ."

"Chris! Off the phone, now!"

"OK, Muriel, I have to go! See you when I get back to school."

11

Going Back to Look

I went back later to see in daylight what Brandon had discovered. Even if looking at the rocks forced me to admit that Brandon had done something awesome by finding them.

I saw how with his coming and going he'd already made a path. Already made foot trails. Already made his place. And I saw how our wrestling had knocked down stalks and stems and flattened grassy weeds. I saw the poison oak leaves.

And a few days after our wrestling the thought came to me: this is where Brandon buried the crow. Corin's angel. Somewhere out here.

Even this waste land wasn't mine anymore. Nothing would be the same.

In among the rocks the space was almost like a cave but open to the sky. It made an inner room. Deep in the middle you could not see out. No one could see in. How would such boulders get here? Dragged by Ice Age glaciers, ripping furrows across the ground? Or had they always been right here, an original part of this place?

But were any of the original places left? Hadn't it all been churned up and split up and dashed back together all through the ages? Hadn't the Earth been through change upon change, rearrangement, tectonic movements and shifting of the plates?

I tried to go leaping up one of the rocks but I had to jump back. Almost fell back. I had to admit it. Brandon had done something awesome by finding this.

So when I saw Brandon again I didn't know what would happen. I had thrown him down. I had let raw anger take hold of me.

Up above the Rocks, the white plastic fence of Piney Groves Estates was already dingy with common green scum, grinning down over this monument like somebody's ill kept teeth.

12

The Violin

I thought playing Muriel's violin looked easy.

But when I ran the bow across the strings, nothing close to music came out. It squawked and bleated. It was an ugly voice. Rosin fumed up white and dusty.

"Not like that. It isn't a dead fish," she said. "Here."

"It smells like a pine tree."

"Well, of course. The rosin is made from pine sap. Resin."

She shaped my hand with her hand to the neck part. She curved my fingers in her fingers, to press against each string, to make the notes. She put her right hand around my right hand and moved my fingers into the right way to hold the bow. Thumb in the little notch and fingers spread. Balance and control the bow. It was a lot to keep going all at once, the bow, the balance, the violin crammed up against your neck and chin, holding your left wrist straight with your arm, your fingers against the strings. I felt her breath on my neck and my ear and I fumbled it all quite a bit.

I hadn't even noticed before: four strings. Each string higher than the one before it. A little staircase, taking you into that world.

Music.

She just rolled the fingers of her left hand as easily as anything, and struck the bow to the strings, and the music rang out. A real voice. A real song. The rosin smelled warm, almost like wood-fire, like the old pine rooms in Corin's house. It was dusty over the strings. The sound came out like the wood was willing to give up its secret. Out of that wood and smoky rosin I saw forests in Germany and the ancient domes of snowy Russia.

What is the secret of the power of music, I whispered to her.

This, she said. And she played a simple scale, note upon note upon note, clearly, simply, resoundingly. Each finger had power, each movement of the bow had a voice. She was giving herself away to each note as she played it.

I already knew enough to know that I was not capable of playing that simple scale. She was with the power of every note.

This violin is old, she said. It had been her Great Aunt's. As she played, light played, the stage lights in the auditorium and the tracery of mother of pearl inlaid in the dark ebony of the fingerboard. A light went up from the violin with each move, responding to the music she was making.

"And you, mister, considering the violin? You have a hall pass? Muriel? You need to be in place now. We're ready."

The orchestra teacher. First teacher ever to investigate a hall pass.

"Just on my way to the library," I stammered. "Just stopping by for a second."

"Be on your way then. You've taken the shortest route possible, I see." Her eye and that sarcasm when she looked up from reading the pass said, Think twice before you hold up my class again.

13

Water Under the Earth

But when I went to English, expecting me and Brandon would still be on fighting terms, the seat beside mine was empty. Mr. Collins called the roll and Brandon's name wasn't on it, and I realized I didn't even know his last name. So he did belong in a different class, after all? Or maybe he had poison ivy too. Could a person die from it?

Mr. Collins surprised everyone by announcing that our next world origin story would be from the Bible. The Creation and Flood stories from Genesis. Some people objected. What is this, church? Martin and his people rejoiced. Finally, they said, the word of God instead of pagan stuff.

This is not church, Mr. Collins said. This is your English class. We are going to read this extraordinary work, this masterpiece. You will participate and you will benefit from reading it and you will learn from it assuming you apply yourself and do not become foolish. And later we will put this alongside stories from Mesopotamia, stories of Gilgamesh and his friend Enkidu and how they venture together into the Cedar Forest to cut down trees, and how Gilgamesh goes on a quest to find the life-giving plant.

Right from the start, this Genesis was all new. It had two creation stories, not just one. I'd never heard it like this. And I've been to church. I would have said I had read this.

But it made good sense this way. Chapter One first: Waters of disorder and chaos are already there when the story begins, and God divides them and puts up barriers to hold them back. Waters above, and waters below, and in between go the dry land and the sky and the regular sea, the places where God will put the living things.

Water under the earth, Mr. Collins said. His eye was sparkling when he spoke, but dark, and you could not tell what he might say. Water so deep and so frightening we call it the Abyss, and we've made the word 'abysmal' for awful things. Water above the sky, he said. He turned his face upward and we did too, following his gaze beyond the ceiling tiles to a place no one could see, beyond the clouds, beyond the blue, to where he said immeasurable tons of watery chaos weighed down upon the firmament.

Don't be afraid to admit that we today don't think about the earth and the sky and the physical universe in this way, Mr. Collins said. Imagine the roiling, endless sea in the eyes of ancient people. It was unfathomable. It still is. It makes a good symbol for instability and disorder. The ancient culture behind Genesis pictured it as a sea monster, perhaps like an uncontrollable giant crocodile, or a water dragon.

The Flood Story will help us understand. We will see God open the barriers that hold back the waters of chaos. Barriers above, and barriers below. Chaos will flood down from above and gush up from below. It will engulf Creation. It's not ordinary rain we're talking about. All the carefully ordered places God established will almost be lost in a swirl of disorder, and Creation will almost be wiped out.

And in Genesis, that's because of human violence.

Martin was against this. No matter what. He was complaining in the lunch line, looking right at me. Like I was the one who needed to answer for it. Everybody knows that water is in the sky, he said. Rain? He looked around at his friends, brows raised, hands turned up for agreement. He looked right at me. Everybody knows water is underground. People dig wells?

Mr. Collins was trying to undermine the scriptures, he said.

I wanted to say something then but I didn't. And what was the other stuff Mr. Collins was talking about, people in another story going into a cedar forest to cut down trees? I wanted to know about that.

The lunchroom was a regular mash of talking, laughing, clatter and chatter, table drumming and screeching.

Back at the beginning of the year everybody else seemed to have lunch organized with friends all around them. I just went to a seat near Martin because I knew him. And then a couple days later Muriel was there. Like a heavenly miracle. She had to get her schedule changed and that made her be in my lunch.

So on my left was Martin and his church people. Still griping. If you're saying Genesis doesn't talk about the world as it is, a Solar System, earth as a globe, then you're saying it can't be true. Because we know that earth is a globe and part of the Solar System. And if you aren't talking about 24 hour literal days, then they can't be real days you're talking about. And if Genesis isn't true about these things, how can any of the Holy Scriptures be true in what they talk about? Mr. Collins was trying to undermine the scriptures. Martin got redder and redder, louder and louder.

They were always like that, troubled and severe. One of them had reached out to an atheist student and proven he was so wrong on so many things, how empty his life was and how their lives were full because they had God. Most of them weren't in my grade. They were unhappy with me when I started sitting there because Martin had been on me to come to their Bible study and I did go one time but I hadn't been back. Now what they wanted was to completely leave this school behind. They were hoping their church would build a school of its own.

On my right was Muriel and the music people, kids who were in the school orchestra but even more important, in the city's youth symphony. She was wrapped up talking and laughing with them.

I spent every lunch lodged in this little space. Usually doing homework while I ate.

I was drawn toward the music people. Not just because of Muriel. They were serious about music and that made them crazy about everything else. When their youth symphony gave a concert at school, they metamorphosized. Their whole face was different. Their hair looked tangled and wild and you could see where a couple of them had walked onstage with their shoestrings undone but they wore tuxedoes and Muriel was like a movie star in a black dress, and on their faces you could see they were carried away by the music, the intensity. It was an invisible shining cloud that had risen up around them, the experience of music, and they were so involved in it that they went into another world. That was what made them be able to laugh so much at everything else. They had their other world to escape to. Even if they did bad in some classes, like Muriel in math, they could just turn their back on that. Because they had music.

I poked my Jell-o, green, which I regretted getting. I had seen the dessert lady coming from the back with a tray of other choices but I didn't want to wait. The Jell-o had pallid grey grapes molded into it. Staring at me. It seemed best to dissect, extracting these small bodily organs, and eat only the green congelation.

"I got you an appointment with the guidance counselor," Muriel announced, leaning across to me at the lunch table.

"The guidance counselor?! I don't need guidance!"

"Well what are you going to do about the project? Aren't you worried? You do need guidance. Remember what I said? Someone from the past, someone who can help you? Like a spiritual guide."

Does a Maya rain god count, I wanted to ask her. A voice in a dream?

But how can you talk about important things in a room full of noise?

"Gwoing to wibwawy," I globbed with my mouth full of Jell-o.

I got my tray to the dish window right before a big mob lined up. I could salvage some time in the library. The cafeteria door closed slowly behind me and all that noise sank away, a whole world filtering back into its bottle.

But outside, from the covered walkway, I thought I saw Brandon. All the way on the other side of the practice field. So he wasn't dead. It was the same dark fleece jacket, same gusting hair.

He was walking away from the field house straight for the woods. Straight for where a pipeline ran, where the running trail started. I almost called out. But then another guy was walking in the other direction from behind the field house. Something about him made me stop.

He was older than us. That was easy to see. He looked old enough maybe to be out of college. He had on dress clothes, a slick shirt, with long hair that feathered back as he walked. He kept jerking his head back, jostling his hair. I watched him stride past the tennis courts and along the row of pines at the edge of the parking lot. Right beside my car. Then he was out of view down the side driveway.

Brandon was already at the pipeline. It was perfectly normal for people to be outside during lunch, but only kids who skipped, kids who smoked and worse went into the woods. We saw their bottles and food wrappers and cigarette packs when we ran the woods trails.

Wow. You really are one of those kind of people.

I forgot the library and went dodging through the group of mobile units at the side of the gym. The openness of the practice field was between us, but I kept myself hidden at the gym corner. Was it Brandon? He was going straight into the woods.

Toward the skippers little hideout? Or just on the running trail? That trail circled all the way across the woods, a good little way. The highway was on the other side. You could easily get down the bank there. All a delinquent kid had to do was arrange with someone and get picked up at the side of the road. Once you got into the woods, what teacher or principal was going to come searching for you? I darted across the practice field. What was I going to do, crunch along behind him through the leaves in the woods?

Then the bell was ringing. I had to run back pretty hard. And even then I walked into class just after the late bell. Sweat on my face. I had never done that before for any class. I earned a glare of dark surprise from Mrs. Burton. Like I had insulted her and her own children or something.

And the library. I had a sudden feeling of "I've got to get this together or I'll go crazy." But I wouldn't have had much time there anyway. And Mom was right, what she had said when I told her about the crow. Brandon was disturbed. I would be better off not to be around him.

Or maybe he was just going through the hardship of being new at school. But to go into the woods? Shouldn't I turn him in? But why would I do something like that? It wasn't my business what he was doing.

He was already in the locker room when I got there. Bent over with his head in one of the sinks. I heard snorkeling, sniffling, and then he rose up and burst into sneezing and snot blowing.

"You alright?"

I couldn't keep an edge out of my voice. It all came back, the wrestling, the fighting.

"Course," he snuffled between sneezes. Blowing and wiping his nose with a big wad of toilet paper. Something toppled from the sink and shattered against the floor.

"You missed English." I looked down. A salt shaker. Like the ones in the lunchroom. The chrome shaker top was still screwed on but the glass was everywhere.

"How'd this get in here anyway?"

"English? Oh, yeah. I wasn't there. Anywhere. I mean, I just got to school about an hour ago. Just in time for my last class." He mumbled something I couldn't hear and disappeared into another seizure of sneezing and nose-blowing.

"You got sick over the weekend?" I felt bowed up, looking down at him. Like it was up to me to push him around or something.

"Uh, yeah, maybe a little bit. Mostly just a lot of sneezing."

"Is that salt?"

"Yeah, it's salt. What else would it be?" He shot his eyes at me and then was glancing behind me. The other guys were coming in. "What are you anyway, an investigator?"

He was trying to kick the glass into a little pile. A broom and dustpan were over in the corner. You can't just leave broken glass on the floor of a locker room.

Coach poked his head in: Down to the track to begin with. Then we would run over in the business park across the road.

"Salt?"

"Salt? Huh? What about it, it's salt, it's salty. What do you care?"

"OK." I went over to my place, started getting changed.

"Never heard of sinus?" he demanded. Like I was a complete dope.

"OK," I said. Then he flung open the door and we all headed across the field. I felt like I was about to punch him.

But you can't argue with his running. I wanted to beat him so bad. I pushed myself at the track. Sometimes you give it all you can and all you do is show your limit. I made it plain for anybody to see. Wow, coach actually said, about his sprinting. The girls didn't say anything else about him being a show-off. He just doesn't bother with all the guys' joking and chatter when we're running. He was serious. He didn't have to say anything.

And then, when we were going back, he was like "PUMA!" right in my face. Like it was the most mystical word.

"I'm not from around here," he said.

"I know. You already said."

"I'm from a place where lions roam the mountains."

"OK. Good."

"You don't see the lion until he's ready to be seen. I'm different from everybody in this place."

"Yeah, that's right."

Coach said, "Good running Chris, good timing. You're getting better."

Yeah, Coach, we both know you're just saying that.

Eddie started telling me about his project. He was going to fire off some model rockets and predict where they would land by measuring the wind direction and wind speed and use trigonometry. He would send up messages with them so if they got lost somebody might respond. I thought, wow, that sounds intelligent and interesting. Even Eddie already has a project idea. I have nothing.

I ended up giving Brandon a ride home again. It made sense. We lived so close. I didn't have to like him to do that. I didn't care anymore. I would just go into the stupid neighborhood. I didn't have to hang around in there. He didn't seem to have any other way home.

On the way he wanted to know what Eddie was talking about, the project.

"They haven't told you? Maybe you don't have to do it."

"But what is it?"

"Everybody has to do something or make something and write a paper about it and what it means. It has to incorporate stuff you've learned in school into whatever "life interest" you happen to have."

"Everybody has a life interest," the teachers kept saying when they introduced the project.

"Everybody has been assigned to a grading committee of teachers, but usually its your homeroom teacher you work with. You can have mentors too, volunteers from the community. If they didn't tell you about it maybe you don't have to do it, since you just got here. They didn't assign you to a grading teacher or anything?"

The look on his face told me he'd never heard of any of it.

"But what's it got to be about?"

"Anything. That's the problem. Anything you like to do or know how to do. Something you want to learn about. You just have to show how it's important or connected to something you learned about. Most people hate it."

"What's yours about?"

"I don't know. We've been reading about mythology. You should ask your homeroom teacher if you really want to know, but really, dude, you ought to lay low and not mention it. It's not fair anyway to make you do it, since you got a late start. We've had all this time to be working on it. I know some kids who are already finished with it. Who'd you get for homeroom, anyway?"

"The art teacher. Round glasses, kind of bald. Blake? So this project can be about anything you want, anything at all, just as long as you tell why it matters?"

"Yeah, pretty much. You have to work with your project teacher, tell them what you're up to. They're supposed to approve the idea but I think they're so busy with regular stuff that you really just do what you want. One girl, Muriel, she plays the violin and it's like she's got a free ride. She plays music all the time anyway so for people like her, they don't really have to put anything extra into it."

Why was I telling this jerk about Muriel?

We turned into Brandon's driveway. He looked right at me. Face lit up like sunlight.

"This is going to be the best project ever done in a public school. I can't believe they're letting us do this!"

"What?"

He got out of the car then crouched down to look back in.

"I know exactly what I'm doing. No problem. It's as good as done."

He clapped his hand so hard on the roof of my car I thought he might have dented it, and then dashed up the walk to the door.

He had an idea that quick?

And I'd forgotten to ask him about the poison ivy. Some people never get it, never have to suffer like I did.

But he was lying, anyway. He was a liar. Because I was sure that was him going into the woods at lunch time. He had been at school way before an hour before practice. Out there smoking? Catching a ride with that disco guy? Anybody going into the woods during school is up to no good.

14

Starting the Carpet

"So," Muriel asked me, "did you go to the library?"

"No," I growled.

Don't remind me. "Never made it. Don't worry about it. I'll get it done."

"I'm not worried about it. But you seemed worried."

"I'm not worried. You're the one asking about it."

That sounded mean.

"Well you aren't going to see me or hear from me without me asking you about it from now on until you do have a project idea."

"Don't worry about it! It'll all work out. I'll stay up all night at the last minute if I have to."

I'm not worried.

This is not what worried feels like.

"I'm just letting my mind have time to figure things out," I told her. "Don't you do that?"

"Not really. You've got to do something to get an idea. Don't you think so? Go to the library."

Framed in the window, the dusky evening bodies of oaks and hickories trundled up into the shining foil of turquoise sky. I could see car lights beaming on Gilead Road.

"The earth has turned to the point that we are moving into its shadow," I ventured. "You see, I have been listening to all your science talk. Your obsession."

"I'm not obsessed! Just interested. And that reminds me, you'll love this, did you know that Galileo was part of secret society? The Academy of Lynx! They were scientists at a time when they felt it was dangerous to be known..."

"Lynx? Are you talking about the wildcat? Is this true?"

"And I'm not sure about my project now. I may have fallen in love with the brain."

"What!"

"Did you know that your brain is growing and branching out from a stem, just like a beautiful green broccoli?"

"Nobody's brain is like a beautiful green broccoli. Mine's not. And you're not really doing the brain for your project. You've already got your project."

"Well, I am thinking about the brain. So what are you doing?"

"We're about to rip up our carpet! See you tomorrow."

"Here," Dad directed, "take this scraper, get under the edge, all along this side. Like this. Then we can get hold and pry it up."

We gripped the loosened edge of carpet between thumb and forefinger, on our knees at first and then rising, pulling, the length of the hall. The jaguarish carpet came up howling and screeching, like the opening of a stoney vault, the door to some ancient tomb. Long strips unraveled, ripped ragged, clinging up close to the floor moldings.

As it gave way, we discovered that the people who laid the carpet had used black foam padding underneath. All the years of us walking around had crumbled the foam to dust. We had to put on air masks.

The twilight and the early stars filled the hall window, the evening heavens in a frame. The inside light and the pale yellow walls made the outside blue deeper, stronger, more real than the inside colors.

Without the bookshelves and the lamps and the chair the hallway seemed smaller, even though there was more space. The overhead light threw odd shadows and sharpened the corners. But it sounded bigger. Cave noises echoed.

Now I had a more tedious job. Down on the floor. Some of the black padding had turned to a stiff crust that had to be scraped away. Dad began clawing at the carpet on the stairs. That was a one-man job because of the tight space. He was disappointed to discover that the carpet on the stairs was in separate pieces, each step individually. Getting it up would take longer because it wouldn't come up sheer in big sheets.

I put Irish fiddling on the CD player. After a while of scraping I got out the vacuum to suck up loose bits of black dust and foam. Then I had to scrape some more, until behind my kneecaps I felt the ache of crouching down. Every time I looked Dad was moving a little further down the staircase. We were taking this project a little at a time, after school and after Dad got home from work. We would not get finished tonight. It meant we'd be living for a while with the stairs and the hall roughed up. But it was OK.

"OK, Chris, let's take a break."

I fell back. Dad was already downstairs in the kitchen. I could hear him through the floor. He was under the stairs, rambling around the pantry.

"We have Fig Newtons and brownies," he yelled.

If I could cut a hole through the floor I could just reach down through the ceiling into the pantry. Floor and ceiling. Or I could run down the stairs, take a right into the kitchen, take a right across the room, take a right and go into the pantry under the stairs.

Dad came out into the hallway eating off a paper napkin.

"I'm thinking this might take longer than I expected," he mumbled through crumbs, "getting all this carpet off the stairs."

After I ate fig newtons I was back with super-strength. The sky framed in the window deepened, ink, indigo, stars pulsing among oak limbs. I leaned down and channeled myself to the perfect angle for scraping but not jabbing the plywood of the floor.

Our work exposed black swoops on the bare plywood where remnants of foam clung to the glue. They were marks of the carpet layer's motion as he swept the glue back and forth when the carpet was new and being placed. He'd left the arm of his work right there on our floor, hidden under our carpet. As I scraped and sweated and worked over the black marks, they began to move and rise up around me, swirling with the whistling and drumming, Irish music, a cloud of Corin's shining crows, wings tracing me, flapping my face and my arms with soft feathered wingtips, and the floor fell away beneath me.

15

Tree of Knowledge, Tree of Life

"But of the tree of the knowledge of good and evil," the LORD God tells them, "thou shalt not eat of it."

But Adam and Eve did eat of it.

Mr. Collins would let people argue, but it had to be orderly, and we could not attack people.

But these were new ideas: 'Adam,' the word for human being or humankind? A metaphorical representative of all human beings, rather than one historical man? Eve, her name being a play on the verb 'to live,' a symbol of the power of life-giving birth?

I watched Martin and his crowd grind their teeth. They were chewing rocks. They contorted at every new idea. They were on guard, like they couldn't smile or be at ease.

"What do you think, Chris?" Martin said to me later, jabbing at me in the hall. "You gotta be with us on this. You know this isn't right, Chris. Why don't you ever say anything?"

But all Mr. Collins was doing was letting us hear a new idea. They couldn't stand it. While they lashed themselves into another strangling argument, I didn't know what to say.

It was confusing. Is only the tree of life in the middle of the garden, or both the tree of life and the tree of knowledge? Every time I read it I felt blurry. God tells the human not to eat of the tree of knowledge, then the woman tells the serpent they are not to eat of the tree in the middle of the garden, but we've already read that the tree in the middle of the garden is the tree of life. The serpent keeps talking to the woman as if the tree of knowl-edge is the tree in the middle of the garden. Are we supposed to think both trees are in the middle of the garden? But they don't say anything else about the tree of life, but you would think its being in the middle was important, central to everything? But it's not the one they eat from. Then at the end, when God sends them out of the garden, it's not because they ate from the tree he told them not to eat from. It's so they won't get to the tree of life and eat from it.

To go along with this Mr. Collins put up a poster of an absolutely naked Adam and Eve. They were being forced out of the Garden, out of Paradise, right there in front of us. People around me laughed.

"They're naked," they whispered.

"Why, Mr. Collins, would you put this in front of us," Martin objected.

But it was Renaissance art by Masaccio. Adam and Eve's anguish was real. It was bitter sorrow. They were weeping and crying. A stern angel bore down on them with a sword and pointed the way out. No other way. Then later some of the guys in the locker room pointed out that I looked "exactly like that skinny legged Adam."

Ha ha. Y'all are so funny.

"Then why did God make the trees in the Garden in the first place?" Josh was asking. "If he knew all along Adam and Eve would disobey and eat them. Why put them there at all? Why make the possibility?"

Mr. Collins' sparkling eye made it impossible to know what he was thinking. He wanted us to think about things.

"If this story is going to be about human reality, these two trees have to be there. They have to have somewhere to grow."

"Yeah Josh, stop trying to deny their growth," Russell said.

"I'm not denying them, I'm trying to figure out why they exist, if they're going to create so much disaster. Just don't put them there in the first place, and none of this would have happened. The humans and the animals would have kept on living in the perfect garden, with all this good food, and rivers of water."

"Think of this story as a description of the way things are," Mr. Collins said. "Maybe even more so than as a story of how things began. So the trees are there. This is the human situation. We eat the fruit of one of the trees, and not of the other. We do not live forever."

"Don't underestimate the power of the serpent's words to Eve. To be like God? Is it true that having your eyes opened, gaining knowledge, good and evil, is what it takes? All the varieties of knowledge, good and evil, hang there before us, good-looking fruits alluring to our eyes. Is all knowledge attained as easily as the picking of an apple? We might ask Sir Isaac? And when we do come into knowledge, into a state of experience, are we really like God? When we go from a state of innocence to a state of experience, we gain something, but something slips away from us, too."

"God wanted to make me," Russell chimed in. "That's why God put those trees there. So Adam would eat them, and know about sex, and then God could make me."

"This story can be seen as about each individual person as well as about humankind," Mr. Collins went on. "Each one of us grows from childhood to adulthood, from a state of innocence to some level of experience. From a helpless baby needing parental care to a state of responsibility for ourselves and for others. Each of us reaches a point where we must eat the fruit of knowledge. We won't be able not to. It's part of growing up. And in both of these journeys, of humankind to civilization, and of each individual from innocence to experience, we gain some things and we lose some things. Dreadful ruptures and problems and disconnections can occur. We come into a state of knowledge, powerful knowledge. Knowledge about ourselves and about the ones we love. The ability to produce children, Russell. The terrifying ability to create life. Soon this story will take us face to face with the human ability to destroy life, to kill. Each of us has to make how many choices in a lifetime? Thousands? We have the ability collectively, as a civilization, to wreak havoc on the world, or to be good caretakers of the world. Will we honestly face who we are? What are our limitations? Are there boundaries we cannot help crossing? Are there boundaries we should never cross? Is there something in us that tends toward havoc?"

"But if the trees had never been there," Josh kept on, "then no problems would have happened."

"And humans would never have reproduced, don't you see, would never have known anything" said Chantal. "Eating the fruit is a way of saying they got knowledge. Adam and Eve would just be friends together in the garden, in the woods. It's like they were blind, in a way. Like they were walking around asleep. How could you be going around naked with each other and not know it? Like it didn't mean anything. They can't have been really aware."

"No," Martin said. "God commanded and Adam and Eve did not obey. That's what this is about. The trees are there to give the opportunity for Adam and Eve to sin. Like a test. They had a choice. They chose wrong. They sinned against God and against God's commandment. And therefore they must face judgement. And it's not just 'they would be friends running around in the woods'. It is much more important than that. If the trees had never been there, Adam and Eve would have continued in perfect relationship with God, for all eternity."

"Well then none of us would exist, Martin, if the trees had never been there. Isn't that right? Adam and Eve would go on being naked and not knowing anything about it. Two human beings only, ever. But what would be the point of having the name 'Eve' if you aren't going to have children?" Chantal's face got red as her voice got louder.

"Well, she only got that name after they found out they were naked," someone said. "And because it said 'she was the mother of all living.'"

"Of all living what?" someone said.

"There would never be problems with overpopulation," someone else said.

"And besides, Martin, if they were going to live for all eternity like you just said, what would be the point of God keeping them away from the tree of life?"

"God would have fed them daily from the tree of life if they had not disobeyed."

"How do you know? And what are you saying, it takes a dose of fruit daily in order to keep you alive? Like vampires having to keep finding blood? Wouldn't one bite from the Tree of Life be enough for all time?"

"No. Nothing to do with vampires."

"So what would have happened if they had gotten to the tree of life before God stopped them?"

"They would have lived forever. It says that."

"So God meant for them to get old and die all along? And not live forever?"

"Don't let yourselves get caught up in questions the story is not going to answer," Mr. Collins said. "Maybe the biggest one would be about the nature of the LORD God. This is not really about God's personality, or about God's intentions, that God was mean and didn't want people to know anything. God's ban on them eating from the tree of knowledge, and the humans' eventual breaking out of that boundary, is a way the story talks about the way human beings have broken some of the bonds of animal life. It's not without problems, so it makes sense it would be portrayed as a trespass against an original situation. The gaining of knowledge can or usually does change the status quo for people. Our gaining knowledge disrupts, plows up, rearranges things. It's happening right here and now. People are growing over the course of life and of history, learning new things always, and it's a momentum of growth, change, pain and resettlement, adjustment, return to calm. Stories like this have mythic power to tell us the truth about ourselves. In fact, people do have god-like knowledge that other creatures in creation don't seem to have. We know from science that human beings evolved from a state of being much like other animals to the kind of creatures we now are, with brains capable of culture and thought and powers that other animals do not manifest. With those powers come the responsibility of caring for this world. So the commandment provides a friction that will make the story work. And such an outcome as you are imagining, the humans eating from the tree of life, is not here because it would not represent us. It wouldn't be our story. Let the word 'represent' help you. This story, and others like it, re-present us to ourselves."

A guy named Kenneth said, "Maybe this is a positive, that they ate this fruit. I mean I know they end up being cursed, but anyway, maybe it's like saying 'you can get on with your life now, because you're starting to know stuff.'"

"What, so you'd like to be cursed?" said Martin.

"That's an interesting idea, Kenneth.," Mr. Collins continued. "So let's focus on what does happen. Martin has a point. This story has some concerns about humans and their place in the scheme of things. Knowledge was there for the taking. Just like a ripe fruit—probably a pomegranate in the mind of this writer—glossy, suggestive, red and beautiful, hanging from a branch right in front of you. All it took was the suggestion of an idea by the 'subtil' serpent. Don't underestimate the power of the words the serpent speaks to Eve. Eat this fruit and you will be like God. That was the temptation that did them in: wanting to be like God."

"Serpent? The Devil, you mean," snarled Martin. "It's Satan you're talking about." And at the same time Josh said, "So you are saying God didn't want people to have knowledge or to have children?"

"The serpent, actually, is what I mean. One of the creatures. A creature 'more subtil' than all the creatures the LORD God made, and what's more, one of the story elements you won't be surprised to find here if you know the story of Gilgamesh. All of you, refer to our handout about the role of a trickster figure. Though he is not God or human, the serpent here has the ability to speak. This image of the serpent may be a descendent of a more ancient image of the sea monster of primordial chaos. Imagine giving Chaos a form, making it into a character, and have it slip into a story to try and disrupt what God is up to. Chaos has a way of being present in our everyday lives. And do people have a way of wanting to be gods? Wanting power? And a good question would be, are these characters, the man and the woman, caused to surpass their boundary by the serpent, or is their trespass a result of who they were all along? And what about that word, subtil? It's an older spelling of 'subtile,' which is like 'subtle,' but it has its own entry in some dictionaries. Don't expect me to look it up for you. Other translations of this story have used the word shrewd, or cunning, or crafty. Other texts in the Hebrew Bible, such as the Proverbs, use this very word to name a contrast to foolishness, usually translated into English as 'clever' or 'prudent.' The word play is important. Don't overlook it. Is punning a way that the Hebrew writers highlight, or emphasize, a point they want to make?"

"Chantal, keep thinking in the direction you're going. This story has been interpreted in more than one way. When we get to the Gilgamesh story the character called Enkidu might help us. Going from being naked to wearing clothing is important in this story.

"Wait. Are you saying God didn't want people to know anything?" someone said.

"Wait," Martin was pointing at Jeannie. "What was she talking about, 'humans would never have reproduced.' God had already told them to be fruitful and multiply. You keep on putting God's word against itself."

"Yes, Martin, in the First Account, in Chapter One, God blesses them and says be fruitful and multiply. It is a depiction of the ordered world. We can find a similar thought in Psalm 104. In that telling, things work like clockwork, everything in its place. Creatures live, and creatures die. You might think of it as an overview on a grand scale. But it is the Second Account we are talking about here. That's where we get a different picture of humanity and the world, with different concerns. Concerns about morality, yes. The contradiction you're feeling is the result of the two different accounts being set together, side by side, but not merged or harmonized, by the ancient writers."

Martin's face was getting harder and harder. He was shaking his head. I already knew: the word contradiction was going to devour him. He would be sitting there at lunch unable to get over it.

The bell started ringing just then.

"And remember, all of you. Pay attention to the puns. List them in your notebooks. The word play. You'll find them in the footnotes. And you'll probably find them on an exam. And take note of the handout I have given you about various things people in the ancient world thought about snakes. It might surprise you."

So did God not want people to get knowledge? That question didn't get answered. And maybe the confusion I felt about the trees was just a way of saying how crazy the real world is. And like Mr. Collins said, if they had eaten from the tree of life, it wouldn't be our story. Because people do die. And people do get knowledge, and they do get into problems, so they had to eat of that tree for it to be our story.

And had the humans really become 'as one of us?' Like God? Was that possible? That's what God said. Because the humans had knowledge.

But the way to the Tree of Life is kept, I thought. At least that wasn't lost. It was kept by the cherubim, and the flaming sword which turned every way.

We already knew from Mr. Collins what the cherubim are. Not the fat little flying babies of Renaissance art. He showed us those. Even then some people kept getting it mixed up. Check out the book of the prophet Ezekiel, Mr. Collins said, if you want more of the cherubim. They are conglomerated creatures, like griffins or hippogriffs, part something and part something else. The Sphinx of Egypt is one such thing, and the winged bulls of the Assyrians. He showed us pictures of those. They stand guard at thresholds to palaces or temples, at sacred places. In the book of Ezekiel the cherub guarded the humans in the garden. And cherubim can be what storm gods ride, like a king on a horse or in a chariot, as they storm over the waters of chaos.

16

Round and Round

The library had nothing that I could find about Maya weather gods and nothing about any weather gods. It had a few dusty old books about Maya pyramids and artifacts. A lot of the ancient Maya writings got destroyed. Archaeologists were still learning about it.

But I did find a book about hurricanes I had not seen before.

"You reading about hurricanes? But aren't you the guy who did that project? Predicting a hurricane?" It was Mr. Thomas, Muriel's science teacher. My face burned red no matter how much I didn't want it to. But he wasn't interested in giving me scorn.

"You're really into this, aren't you? Ever been through one? Hugo came right over us some years ago."

"I've heard about it."

"That was something else. The very eye came right over this school. Right over this room right here."

"The eye is pretty big, right?"

"Yeah it's big. About 40 or 50 miles wide, something like that. We were just about right smack in the center. Not quite."

"What's it like to be there, under the eye?"

"It's calm. Quiet. You've already been through one half of the storm. The wind's been blowing all from one direction. Everything is bent that way, trees, everything. Birds are clinging to tree branches. Then comes the eye. Everything gets calm. Wind stops. People who have been holed up in the house come outside. Everybody wants to see what's happened. What all the damage looks like. You can't believe how still it is. You look at all the damage, tree branches down, all kinds of leaves and trash and debris everywhere. Hopefully you don't see anything awful like a dead animal or injured maybe. But you know it isn't over yet. The other half is on its way. Then it hits. The wind starts blowing from the other direction. Everybody goes back inside. You know, you wouldn't believe how much trouble some of my students had understanding that. They kept saying, once we got back to school, we were out almost two full weeks, they kept saying the storm changed directions. I had the hardest time trying to get them to see that it didn't change direction. I even had other teachers in here talking about 'the storm changed directions.' But it's not hard to understand. It's just a circle. The wind is blowing in a gigantic circle. If the eye goes over you, you are in the absolute middle of all that. You're only halfway through. You got the whole other half to go. With a hurricane, well, the wind is blowing in one direction, all the time, it's a circle, but when you're on the ground and its coming over you, it seems like the wind changed direction. The storm itself is moving in a direction, usually north or northeast, by the time any hurricane gets to us, while the circle of it is blowing round and round. Draw a picture of it if that helps you.

"I think I understand it. It's a circle spinning around and moving across the map too, at the same time it's spinning around."

"Right! It's not hard to understand. It's just those students were down under all that. Once you've been down in it, it's hard to see the big picture sometimes. Hey, I'm glad you're interested in hurricanes. Maybe I'll see you in my class next year?"

"Did you know that hurricanes start out in West Africa?" I said to Muriel when she asked me again about the project. "They come all the way over here from Africa."

"I thought you said no more projects about hurricanes?"

"The sky lowers down, sick and weird. Green light fills the yard, the street, the town."

I had loved writing about it, the heaving tropical seas, the surge and race of waters, the upheaval. Mr. Collins had said my description was vivid, and some girls in my class said it was "so scary to think about."

Muriel said, "Haven't I heard this before?"

"Rain crashes down. Roadway lights smear into liquid in the distance. Power poles blow up. Roads and ditches rush away like torrents. People need shelter. Birds blow away, helpless. Shells and things long forgotten wash up from the seabed. Anything that can float gets carried along, anything that can be lifted on the air, cars and boats, even germs and dust from Africa and from the Indies. It's the world turning upside down, the world turning counterclockwise, and people see the power of the heavens. It's easy to see why people thought of the god Huracan and other weather gods. People feel the threat. People feel their own smallness. It's real helplessness and real danger."

"Just like a textbook! You're really doing this? Hurricanes? Again?"

Such a huge thing, a whole system all its own towering into the sky and it had no mercy for us. We were desperate in its path.

"And it's counterclockwise! See? It's like I was telling you. Counterclockwise! Just like water going down a drain. Just like how I see the year going around."

"You!" she said. "You can't be doing this again."

No. I can't do another hurricane project. I would be crazy to.

It was weird though, two directions at the same time. Because it was a circle.

And counterclockwise. Counter. Turning back time. Not everything works the way they say. Some things do go counter.

17

The Metallic Robotic Voice

Then, at lunch, when I came through with my tray, Brandon was in the line. Little groups of people chattered together behind him and in front of him but it was obvious he was all alone. Maybe I was the only person who ever spoke to him. I went up to him.

Even if he was a liar. And a kid who goes into the woods. And how could someone like that be such a good runner? It didn't seem right.

"You in this lunch now?"

He just nodded upward. Like that was a way to say something. I pointed out where I was sitting.

It was weird to see him in the lunch room at all. But every person has to eat.

The whole cafeteria was clamor, clatter, chatter. No room for any extra person. People had their tables. If a chair was missing, or if someone got the idea of changing tables, it would mess up a whole table, and that would mess up a whole row of tables, and that would mess up the whole room. Something somewhere would have to give way. Someone would get pushed to the extremities. The domino effect was dominant. In some mysterious way, everybody knew not to mess with the balance.

But I swiped a chair anyway, from a table behind my seat, across the big aisle, before anybody got to that table. I squeezed it in at our table and put my books on it. The people at the other table would just have to work it out. The people at our table would have to adjust. What was a new kid supposed to do?

The music people were soaring. But that was music. If you had that ability, you were set apart. You lived in a glowing aura of unspoken esteem.

After a few minutes Brandon walked up with his tray. One of the church people said "Is that all you eat?" Like it was a violation. So, I thought, he's going to be weird about what he eats. He just stared at them for a few seconds and sat down. What he had was a whole plate of salad, two bowls of green beans, bread, and some oatmeal-chocolate chip cookies. That's not much to run on, I was thinking. Protein?

Introduce him to everybody: that would be the normal thing. But I wasn't really part of either group, and in the loudness, and with the church people already sealed over into their severity, and Muriel laughing over something with the people beside her, only Oliver met Brandon. He was a keyboard player. One of the best, according to Muriel. It was exactly the auspicious moment for Brandon to join us, he said, because they had been working on the Brandenburg Concerto Number One, and "my man Robbie here threw down on the hunting horn in the opening movement." He threw his arm around Robbie's head. Brandon said "That's cool."

"In fact, we have tapes." He handed me a cassette tape from his book bag. It had a photocopy picture of round trumpets on the front.

Maybe Brandon knew what the Brandenburg Concerto was. I didn't. I was getting out my math stuff, trying to get homework done while I ate. And now, Muriel was saying, they were working on some of the Planets.

"What do you mean?" I asked. I had my head down in my notebook, papers in my lap.

"It's music! Holst. He wrote one for each planet, and I'm thrilled. I love it. I mean, talk about a life conjunction. I couldn't believe it when our conductor announced it. We've been doing planets in science!"

"What do they sound like?"

"They sound like...they're symphonic music. They sound like flying through Outer Space. He's trying to describe each planet with music. We're doing Venus and Jupiter and I think Mars too."

"And what about good old Earth? Leaving him out of it?"

"Well, he didn't write one for Earth."

"What?"

"Well, it's not one of the ones you watch in the sky and all that. 'Planet' is a Greek word for 'wanderer'. We know where Earth is. It doesn't wander. We wouldn't be sending a robot or anything out into space to go to Earth."

"We don't need to! We're already here. And you could still write a symphony for it. It is a planet, Greek word or no. So that's what you're doing for your project is it, writing music about Earth?"

"Well, actually, Muriel," Oliver said, "Holst was describing the Greek mythological gods more than the astronomical planets. That's why Mars sounds ominous, with trumpet blasts of war, and . . ."

"Where's my seat?" I heard behind me. "No way, this is not happening! I will not be separated from my table!" Then from Martin's direction I heard the words "primate" and "anthropology" and I knew it was about Social Studies. I had already heard him say he would memorize a list of reasons and arguments why he could not agree with evolution and believe in it. Why evolution could not square with God's words about sin and death and if evolution was true, that meant God's word would be unreliable. Adam and Eve have to be a fact of history, Martin was saying.

I ate the cookies and the green beans, and the chicken wasn't bad. And the bread. The bread at our school was the one constant, the one rock of culinary stability you could count on in a school lunch.

The music people started going crazy about something. Muriel honestly could be the loudest among them. I was drawing in my math notebook. Forget trying to do the math. I saw myself from above: bent over the table, face peering straight into the page, pencil in hand, rain jacket on. All around me everybody talking and talking. A few people glanced at my intent self bent like a scribe and thought, That's the exact definition of what a loser looks like. Doing schoolwork in the lunch room. The voices melded together into indistinguishable clatter. How can people talk so loud? I just let my pencil draw. Tried to close out all the noise. I kept my eyes watching the lines as they drew out of my pencil. I blurred my eyes down to one little narrow aspect, squinting to see it from far away, squinting to keep my close focus on just the move of the lines. Jaguars and lions came growling up, an elephant, puma and snow leopards, wildly contorted or straight-legged, half drawn, emerging from solid rock or wildly given the tail of a sea mammal. I could quickly fill a page with them. Brandon interrupted me. His voice, his sharp accent, cut through the noise like steel.

"Chris, I'm gonna need help with my project. I don't have a car. I'm not allowed to drive anyways."

I had trouble drawing jaguar mouths and noses. But this one was OK. And then the man wearing a jaguar skin. No, it was part man, part jaguar. I didn't know.

What's all this, I wondered. You're not borrowing my car. No way.

"What is your project, anyway?" I asked. I kept my face down near my paper, squinting my eyes. The jaguar man was emerging, jaguar head with burning eyes. I was penciling shadows and caverns of darkness in the earth around him. Clouds of smoke.

"Can't say. Not in here. It's secret."

"Then how can anybody help you?"

"I need somebody to drive me around. Probably more than once. Lots of times maybe."

"Drive you where?" I didn't want to be this freeloader's chauffeur. I was already taking him home from school.

"All over. Out in the country. And you know these roads. I can't ask my parents. They won't understand. I'm hunting for something."

Hunting?

"Why is it secret?"

"Just for now. You'd know what it was once we got started. What d'you say?"

"Well, I might be able to help you. Or I might have to spend all my time working on my own project."

"What is your project?"

"I don't know yet."

"Do you really not know or is it a secret too?"

"I really don't know. It's not a secret." I wished it was a secret. It was all too obvious. I had no idea what to do.

"There's all this stuff with the Maya," I said.

I showed him a picture of the god Chaac. I showed him the eyes with their whirling spiral, like the weather man's symbol for a hurricane. A rain god, a storm god. Some said he had scales like a reptile, a crocodilian, a kind of dragon. Archaeologists found images on pottery and on incense burners and other stuff. He had associations with water. And with the letting of blood. He strikes water-snakes for rain with the axe of lightning. And he struggled with a jaguar carrying sunlight through the waters of the underworld.

Just like a textbook. Brandon just sat there.

A storm god is frightening, I said. Like Huracan. Nothing can be normal when a hurricane comes over you. You realize you're at the mercy of something way beyond you. But not having rain would ruin your way of life. When you live in a place with almost no sources of fresh water, like the Maya living in Yucatan, you have to depend on rainfall. So you might be willing to ask for a hurricane. You might have to.

The thought hit me as I was saying the words: You might be willing to risk the hurricane, the hundred mile an hour wind, the drowning sea floods, the fiery lightning, just so you could get some rain.

"You die one way or another, anyways," Brandon said, his eyes dark and clouded.

While I talked I had drawn a spiraling storm. I lined out a little map, the long loping line of the Outer Banks, the shapely sounds behind them.

That was the famous profile of North Carolina. The astronauts had taken pictures of it from Outer Space. The storm I drew spiraled across the Atlantic towards the coast of North Carolina. I put little arrows, drew the winds blowing counterclockwise, the classic hurricane direction. Hands of destruction, hands that overwhelm mankind and all animals, hands that turn back time. Taking whole cities back to the days before electricity, the days of candle and fire, days of darkness at sundown. Days when people have to eat together or not eat at all. In the middle would be an open eye. The plainest, most immoveable Eye, unchangeable and unfeeling, where not a breath breathed.

Brandon sat there the whole time watching me draw. Nervous energy jittering through him, drumming out some secret rhythm with his fingers on the table, his pallid face, his dark eyes.

"Make a bigger version of that hurricane right there. There's your project," he said. "That's a sweet design, man. You don't even know that. You don't even know. That could be on tee shirts. That could be on surfboards. You're done."

"Maybe. I don't know."

Could it?

Or is that something you say when you want to get somebody to drive you all over the place?

"No, I'm not going to do that, because I'm already associated with hurricanes and I'm being mocked because of it."

"Mocked? Who cares. Own it, dude. And it would be about the Maya, whatever, all that stuff you just said. But I hope you won't be looking for sacrificial victims. Didn't they do that, ripping out hearts? Yeah, we could act it out. You could rip a fake heart out of me or something like that."

The victim of sacrifice held down by four over a stone altar atop a pyramid as a priest comes forward with the obsidian knife . . .

"You want to go up on a stage and do something like that?"

"Not really."

"Me neither. And I don't want to make them out to be savages, whether they really did do human sacrifices or not. I don't know enough about it."

I don't really know much about Chaac either. Or hurricanes. Not really. I needed something to hit me. I need some kind of idea.

The robotic, electronic voice of the school bell rang and we all got up, robots responding, and marched our separate ways.

18

Mountain Lions, School Forest

"Colorado," I ask. "Mountain lions are really out there? Running loose on the mountains?"

But he didn't say anything.

This is the "School Forest," Coach calls it. Like it was so vast. Like it was such a deep hold of ancient growth.

It's just the woods behind the school. Not a paradise. The road is never so far away that you can't hear the cars or catch glimpses of chrome flashing past. These woods aren't deep and big and sacred like the Pine Forest I lost. None of the trees they call virgin pines are here, the mighty lodge poles of the sky. But it is enough of the woods that you are among trees. Some big tulip poplars grow here, where quietness comes down. We hear ourselves running, crunching on leaf fall. We hear birds, maybe an airplane with that rumble in the sky. It and its passengers sit up there in another world. The sky over the branches is perfect sapphire, where it bowls up to the deepest blue straight overhead. Usually I don't care if I'm last, don't care if I'm first. Because I just want to be out here. These are the only woods I have now.

The trail was coming around to the part where the woods narrow down to a strip between a playing field and the new elementary school. You have to jump the high banks of the creek to get there, or tromp the muddy place below. Then up, into a little place of open trees between the elementary school and the field. And beside that field, low in a ditch under cover of Virginia scrub pine, is where the delinquent school-skippers have their little hideout. Ragged plywood, a few two-by-fours, a busted up ping-pong table with no legs, a muddy tarp, and other throw away stuff. A couple of dead tree branches. Their sad little hideout. It was a hovel in a ditch where they could crouch. You can't even stand up in it. They had a little fireplace black with ash there. Sat out here poking a little fire while the rest of us were in school. How did the school people not know about this? They had to know. Why didn't they do something about it? Is this the place Brandon comes to? Out here smoking with them? Didn't he know what kind of people come out here? Had he been put in such low classes that these were the people he was with? But we run by here every day at practice, and he says nothing. But today, I'm keeping up with him. Or is he running just a little slack?

"Mountain lions. Yeah," he says. "Right up into the edge of the city where I lived. In the neighborhoods. In people's yards. In our yard. People wake up and see a lion standing near their door. Out there you just call them 'lions'. They're really out there, and they eat runners like us."

We half sprint the playing field up and back and then back into the woods, back around, where one part of the trail meets another circle of itself before it goes back around to our practice fields. Piles of old cut field grass decay at the edge there. We stand breathing and Brandon just stares at me with his wet hair all spiked up.

"What do you think? A kid just like us," he jabs at me with his finger, "high school runner, just like me and you. Killed in broad daylight in the woods behind his school. On his school's running trail. Doing nothing but his normal run. Right in the middle of a sunny afternoon. Lion dragged him off, way up high to a hidden place. Took the searchers days to find him. What was left of him. But out there the woods are different. Here, it's all closed in. I feel like I'm in a tunnel out here, trees all tight and dark around you. Out there in Colorado, the woods are open. It's ponderosa pine, trees and boulders out in open land, and it's bright. You can see. Lots of times they catch a lion up a ponderosa pine."

Ponderosa pine? Was it different from our pines?

"What was that like, this kid who got killed?"

"Unbelievable, dude. Can you imagine? This lion stalked him for days before it ever made its move. Weeks, maybe, before it made its move. This kid had no idea. He got jumped from behind. That's how they do it. That's why people hate them so much. That's why they call them sneaky and dis-honorable. But really people are in awe. People are terrified. Because lions own the woods. They're the perfect hunter. Wolves depend on a pack, but lions take down prey all alone. What they always say is, by the time you've seen the lion, the lion already knows you. Knows your every move. It's been watching you a long time. If you see the lion, it's only because it lets you, and it lets you because it already knows you're nothing to be afraid of. And that's the moment when it's too late. They found this guy's eyeglasses, somewhere, a few yards away from his body. But the guy's face was fully ripped away. His body was just a shell, a ribcage, with the insides all eaten out."

I tried to imagine it. The attack from behind: like being struck by lightning. The ground hits your face; you know you need to fight back but you can't turn around. And if he had lost his glasses, maybe he couldn't see good enough to fight back. Maybe his neck was already broken before he hit the ground. Maybe he was instantly paralyzed, the wild fangs piercing nerves? Or maybe, for about one minute, he felt the deadly mouth, the gripping teeth, felt himself being dragged.

"Man," I challenged, "what do you know about woods? Not being from the East?" Forget Brandon's ridiculous idea that these woods are so dark and deep. I jabbed at him with my finger and was off. I would match him stride for stride! I thought I was going to. We passed the people's garden who live near the school. I was making the woods my own, looking out in secret, making the turns of the circle, lost in the wildness, the lion, running on the sunny afternoon.

And in the afternoon sunlight, bright sapphire orb of October, light came down in arcs and in the circle we were running. I thought I was going to match him. At my side I saw flashes, sunlight, golden gleaming that I could not catch when I turned to look. And I was trying to match him.

And in the circling of the circle as I came around, I saw him standing in the path. Not the lion, not the puma.

The jaguar.

The fiery head, the body, splendid in the light, gleaming like silks, darkening with his shadows like the crush of velvet, mossy, golden, ochre. He wore the somber shadow-fleck, the shadow spirit, of forest cats.

Watching me. His eyes and his stillness told me nothing but that he was immoveable. Unapproachable. One move from me and he was an engulfing flame. One flicker from those amber eyes would be blood and violence and fatality. I kept still. He wore rings of leaping gold, the sun's corona at the dark edge of eclipse.

What had Brandon just said? If you see him it's because he's already seen you. Already seen what you are. People are in awe.

Nothing from him. No movement. No knowing what he might do. I stood unsure. Then he spoke.

"You fear I will destroy you?" he said. "How may we look at one other? Human and wild animal? We have been enemies. You are in awe. For you, my kind is a threshold of death. Some words must be said, words from all the way back at the beginning. You humans made yourselves great, and the animals answered the call of God. I have tasted earth's metal in your blood. I know what you are made of."

"I didn't mean to disturb animals. Is that the final word between us?" I asked. "Is that all I am?"

The jaguar opened his mouth and the air trembled. Energy spilled out in visible waves, set the world in motion. Waves of heat and waves of water. All colors rippled over my vision. Everything reeled, upended, and the tremor went through me. On my knees and not even knowing I had fallen. I heard something like voices shouting.

"Your kind followed your eye," he said. "You opened hunger in the world, and we hungered. I could destroy you. My mouth blazes with flames of lightning. My paws are Knife and Slash, Sharp and Deadly. I could paint my face in the streams from your heart. Drag the organ-cords from your body, leave your empty rib-shell for birds who pull and twist. As readily as we tore any monkey from the forest, I could devour you."

Was it a true judgment? Wasn't it just natural that living things would be hungry? Was that our fault? And was I nothing more than a taste of metal? And I had thought he was some kind of spirit, anyway. I tried to steel myself but I was bolted to live electricity, trembling, unable to move. Don't run, Brandon had said. Try to look big.

"I taste the fear in you. I taste it coming from you. You are wise if you truly fear me. Wise again if you see and fear yourself.

"The sun burns high and runs its course, day follows day, and time runs away from every life. But I who speak to you am a fire in the deep of the mountain. A fire that will pass through waters. I am not here to destroy you. And now, how may we look on one other? You take away my eyes but you are blind. But I will be a father to you. You will run with me and go in my line. I shall lead and you shall follow. We go to the Waters. I pass by unseen, untouched by devouring mouths. Come, place your hand upon me and do not be afraid."

Several minutes, it seemed, passed. His face changed, softened. Just like a cat. The blazing brightness became autumn forest sunlight.

My hand seemed small against him, resting on the bristles of fur. What sort of fool's world was I in, to put my hand on the shoulder of a wild jaguar? Run with him? I'm dead anyway, I was thinking.

"As When Someone Blows Breath? Is that what they called you?" I asked.

The fur was ember velvet, with dark constellations apportioned over him to suit each part of him: smaller dots on the head and face, larger dots on the thickness of the legs and from his neck across his mighty shoulders, his back and sides; flaring rings, coronas, dashes; marks of black ash, circular and oblong, carrying smaller marks and dashes.

"You may call me Inha, if you want a name to call me that only you will know," he said.

The other voice came, as before. The shimmering blue-green.

"What happens is this: We pass through waters. It is dangerous, where are angels and wild animals. Who is helping you and who would harm you? Come with us. We will not lose our way."

It was the butterfly, small as she was, moving lightly and speaking as boldly as the jaguar. I could not catch her fullness with my sight. Were these two always together?

"My body is small," she said, "but my full stature is in my words and in the corridors of my heart. Hummingbird they have called me. Everything tends to devour. There is water under the Earth. We make our way through narrow portals, water mirrors and black stone glass. Flames of Fire, Water, Lights in the Sky! Light Dancing on the Waters, and Flowers! These are the ways we fly. These are the ways we go. I draw spirit in the nectar."

"What we are going..." I began, trying to say something but fumbling for thought. My mind seemed as flittering as she was. Was he saying I was blind?

Inha raised his head, his throat moved as he roared, and the ivory knives worked their power in the air.

"Tongue In Your Blood they have called me!" The golden coat shimmered and threw wide arcs of light. "Earth's Metal in Your Blood I will call you."

And we ran, pure sunlight, shaping the earth and all its inhabitants out of stone cold darkness. Shadows fled back and we ran. Colors blurred, flared, brightened, and the ground gulped away in my strides.

Run with me and you will see.

But the path was a trail that led back to the school, back to the locker room, back to the laughing guys and back to my homework. Math and French and history. Back to the project and confusion.

Brandon was scorching me, fast on the trail. Coming out of nowhere, back around again. Like the hands of a clock, head back, always speeding up. I couldn't pretend now. I had to admit it: I could never catch him. He cut past me in strides. I could not run as fast. He would always beat me. How was he so good? We were the same, size and build.

So I made to tackle him. Leaping out, a lion! Drag him to the ground.

"Show me how to run like that!" I could demand.

But what good would that do, grappling in the fallen leaves? I hadn't won it off him the first time, and all I got for it was days in white, in a shroud, painted with calamine. Even if I wrestled him till morning I wouldn't win it off him.

But this time he leapt. And this time we found words.

"Puma!," he shouted. The most mystical word. I just had to laugh. Laugh at myself, laugh at it all.

"Man, where are you," he said. "Come on! Everybody's gone in."

Inha the Jaguar opened his mouth, roaring, and the air trembled.

"You gonna run another hour? You're distance, man. Distance. You don't even know that."

But I did know.

Run with me, Inha said. Run with me and you will see me. Put your hand on my shoulder and run with me.

19

Scarlet in Seconds

"Chthonic?" I said to Martin. "Was that the word?"

"What?"

"Where a serpent climbs a tree that connects the sky to the underworld?"

"Ah! Who cares. Mr. Collins is a serpent. Contradictions is what he said. You heard him, Chris. Contradictions. In God's Word."

"You're tearing up the scripture," Martin had said, staring straight into Mr. Collins' face. He stayed behind after the bell just to say that to Mr. Collins.

I stayed too. I wanted to say, It isn't like that, Martin. Mr. Collins isn't trying to do something bad.

"I warned you Martin," Mr. Collins said. "We might be reading these texts differently from how you grew up reading or hearing them in a church. This is a different setting and a different context for understanding. Our concern is literary. We are reading with the same sensibilities we would use when we read any other work. I do not intend to violate this text, although I believe I may have violated your prejudices about it."

"Prejudice!? And you're saying this is all made up by some author. Or authors. But it is God's Word. What this is about is sin and Satan. First and foremost. The first sin. The reason for all the sin in the world right now, and the reason for death. Eve led Adam into sin, and that has been reproduced right down to the present day. So stop deluding all this, stop tangling it all up."

"All I mean by 'prejudices' is 'the ideas you brought in with you.' But Martin, you have to notice that the word sin is not used in this story. When we get to the Flood story, we will see that the Flood happens because "every inclination of the thoughts of their hearts was only evil continually," as the King James has it. Rather than because of human overpopulation and noise, as we will see in some other ancient flood stories. So yes, evil or sin, if you want to use that word, is part of these stories' theme of humans reaching beyond the boundary set for them. What is it about these humans? Is evil in them? Is it just human appetite? Are sin and appetite the same thing? Is the serpent responsible for what the humans do? Isn't it that the serpent is exposing the humans for who they are? I understand the connections people have drawn between the serpent and Satan and the devil, but I insist we recognize that those connections were made later.

"Satan is not in this story," Mr. Collins calmly insisted. He wasn't going to stand there and be lectured to by Martin. He went back over things he had said in class.

I ran my eyes back over the lines. The word Satan wasn't anywhere. Only serpent.

"The Hebrew writers are perfectly capable of writing about The Satan when The Satan is the one they want to write about," Mr. Collins continued. "We know that by reading the book of Job, where the Satan appears. And that would be well worth our reading. And I am aware that later on, both Jewish and Christian thinkers would link this serpent to ideas about the devil. But what we see here is one of the creatures. A creature called 'serpent.' One of the created beings. A fellow, if you will, to the other creatures, the other animals and the Man and the Woman. And that, and the ambiguity, is more interesting than just turning it into 'the devil.' If evil is here, if disobeying God is sin, where does it come from? Who brings it into this scene?

"You do see that God sends the humans out of the garden, saying that they have become "as one of us." They have become like God, because they have knowledge. Does that sound crazy? They have breached a boundary in this story. They're reaching. 'Trespass' might a good word for their actions. Is it that they're out of control? And now God sends them out of the Garden so that they won't eat of the Tree of Life and live forever. God isn't going to take away their ability to reach and take. God will establish a boundary they cannot cross. It reflects our reality. We can reach, we can take, but our reaching can result in disaster. We need help knowing how much is too far sometimes. Similar to the boundary he establishes to hold back the waters of chaos.

"I want to take your comments seriously, Martin, and I hope you will see that I'm not trying to damage you. The learning process can be disruptive and challenging. I want you to be able to be flexible and understand ideas. That is not the same as demanding that you accept them as your personal beliefs."

"And that's why," Martin kept going, as if Mr. Collins had said nothing, "none of the evolution ideas can be true, because that would mean that millions of living things would have died before the existence of any human beings, and how could that be true, since human sin is the cause of death?" He went through all that again while we were standing there. Like if he kept saying it, Mr. Collins would finally agree. But Mr. Collins didn't agree. He stood there calmly, looking like he was trying to figure out the best thing to say. He said he didn't think that these stories in Genesis were to be taken as historical events. That we need to be careful not to take away the myth-logic in this story to tell the truth about human beings. Martin was gripping his hand to the lectern like he would crumple it, crumple the whole room, like he would force an agreement out of Mr. Collins. His whole face went scarlet in seconds. His neck had a pulsing vein I could see above his collar, moving inside.

"This isn't right." Martin said in a low voice as we left the room. He turned to look straight at me. "You heard all of that. Why don't you ever stand up with us and turn against this? Why don't you ever say anything?"

I could see why Martin disagreed with the ideas. But he acted like he needed Mr. Collins to agree with him. Like it was eating at him.

"What do you say, Chris?" Martin was demanding, jabbing at me in the hall. "You gotta be with us on this. You are with us, aren't you? You know this isn't right, Chris. Why don't you ever say anything? What do you think?"

"Well . . . "

"Don't just say 'well.' Come on, tell me right now you're with us."

"But . . . "

"Don't just say 'but.' Come on, Chris."

He stared at me and then turned away and I wanted to grab him and say, Why can't you just listen to a different idea?

And he was still furious at lunch. Still going on about the Anthropology reading.

"I can't believe we have to endure this," he said. "I can't believe any person has wasted their life writing this stuff. I am not an ape. I will never believe that. I am not in any way related to these gross, ugly things. I don't care if I fail this class. I'm not reading this. If that's the kind of stuff they want us to learn about, it's not a real class."

So he slammed his Social Studies book down on the lunch table. He pretended to pour iced tea onto it. I thought he really was going to. He acted like he was about to squirt ketchup all over a picture of a group of Homo habilis. All of them laughed. I don't think Martin knew, but I was watching him.

Or maybe he didn't care.

20

Guiding Spirit, Fall Break Comin'

At practice Coach had a schedule for each of us, with individual things for us to work on during break. He put pictures of famous runners on it, triumphant runners, to remind us.

Brandon asked me again, would I help him with his project.

He still wouldn't say exactly what he wanted. He sat there at lunch drumming the table, this secret rhythm.

"You look like you're about to jump out of a plane," I told him.

"Open the door. I'll fly."

He already had most of the paper for the project finished, he said, before he even started the other part.

Could that even be true?

"OK," I said. "I'll help you." Break was going to be dull anyway. Everybody else was going to the beach. Most everybody. Dad said maybe next year. I knew they wouldn't let me go. And who would I have gone with, anyway?

We were going to use some of the break to put down the new carpet. Dad had some days off work. And I was going to help Corin.

I had to get my project going. My face was suddenly blazing. Sweat broke out on my scalp. How are other people so calm and cool? Ideas nestle down on their shoulders like friendly birds. No bird was descending to me. Who was my guiding spirit that Muriel had told me about, someone I could talk to? It was only me and the destroyed pine forest, us two ghosts, together, a floating dream world, my slaughtered pine trees.

Only me and this jaguar now, harrying me with talk about judgment and devouring, or either stone-stillness, half-sphinx, saying words about blindness and taking his eyes away.

My face was burning hot. I had to get some kind of idea.

21

School Work

Standing in the woods behind the school, in these trees in wet late afternoon before evening, I breathe out long plumes of foggy breath. Autumn chill has come down on us. I am the dragon, sending trails of mist high into tree branches. I could fill up these woods with mountain sea fog, obliterate the school and all the roads and all homework with the silver grey fog of my breath. Turn the woods into the Middle Ages under layers of silver, into a time and place where we could be free to defend castles and fight with swords against real monsters right before our eyes. Instead of homework. If I could just stay here till dark. But the prospect of late afternoon schoolwork is raw on me. I'll be going in, sitting there for the rest of the afternoon, and then again after supper, on into the night, staring at algebra problems.

Now the cold shows up, now that I've stood for a moment. The sweat, the wet, making the chill race over me. I breathe it in deep to replace the grey streamers of smoky breath. I am the Great Smoky Mountains. I hear leaves drop in the rainy wet woods. This drizzling rain will bring some of them down, pink leaves of sourwood, red and orange and yellow of maples and of sweet gums purple, hand-prints and stars. My shoes are soaked. The ground is a rainy leaf carpet. Wet if you sit on the ground. But I'm too wet to care anyway. This is the season when mist is rising. You see it white in the distance, but not up close. It's not bitter freezing cold. The ground is covered, carpeted, soft and thick in fresh flexible wet fallen leaves. I am trying not to go in yet. Trying to see all of this. Yellow glows in this misty light.

The purest yellow, hanging in the air all the way to the top of the forest. I just stand there looking at it. The other fellows consider me crazy or don't even notice. They just go on. I don't care if I get left out here.

This is the day when trees have no shadows except shadows of yellow and gold. It is a day that comes maybe one time all season, just exactly like this. The poplars, two or three of them, are round towers along this part of the trail. Maybe the other guys feel it. They stop talking. Quiet falls over us as we go among them. You hear the leaves touching down.

Clouds shift. They're in no hurry. Lights lower and rise. Clouds cover the sunlight. Diffuse it.

What will emerge from this bringing down of the leaves, from this dragon mist, is the skeletal body of earth in Winter. Silver arms up to the sky. The sky will clear, and each night Orion will rise, the silent, to guard the walk of sky till morning.

And then I hear music. Elven music. Like voices, like birdsong of unusual birds. As if I've never heard the sound. A little squawky, a little rough edged. Then sweeter, softer. Notes of music coming through the tree branches. I hear people breathing in for making the notes. The marching band out here in the woods? They practice on the football field. Would flute notes come out foggy like ordinary breath?

"Chris!"

Running along we were ambushed. I see them now. Other people in the woods always look strange, unexpected, the colors of human clothes and faces suddenly among trees. It's some of the music people, the orchestra people. Oliver and Robbie, Mark and Justin and Jessica, a bunch of them, organized by Muriel. Some of the marching band. Marching through the woods. Oboes and bassoon and clarinets, flutes and pipes.

To startle us? To provide music for our running? And where is your violin anyway?

We have to step back, out of the way. They march up the trail, a scene from a dream, and march on past us trying to keep playing while they smile at themselves and meld with the foggy air in the pillars of tree trunks, curves in the path, gold and yellow shadows.

"You runners aren't the only ones who get to use this forest," Muriel told me. "I'm learning conducting too, not just playing."

They were playing old style woodwinds. Replicas. Practicing for their trip during Break, to a Renaissance music festival in Washington DC. Some of the fellows stood there, sweat fuming off us in the chilly air. Some ran on.

"But how are you not freezing out here in barely anything?" she asked me.

"Pure steel," I said, knocking on my thigh.

And all these leaves out here. A sudden thought rushes on me sometimes, a picture that I don't know to expect: all of these golden leaves are wealth, the pure riches of the Earth, lying freely all over the ground. Hundreds, millions, all we could ever need.

I pick up a leaf. One of our sweet gum leaves. Star-shaped. Such a deep crimson it's nearly black, glistening wet. I hand it to Muriel with a bow as the formality of the marchers falls into the casualness of the runners and everybody starts laughing and talking. "I bet they've got security cameras to see us out here with these instruments." "Run madly then!" A game of chase breaks out, people gather in groups, a pretend football run in the woods. She holds the leaf up between us. Somehow she knows about the people's farm, their garden near here. The trail goes right up there, if you take one of the little trails off the main circle. A pear tree is there, growing in their garden. And she wants to show me how to drink water out of a cabbage leaf. Where she comes up with this stuff, I don't know. Something about her Dutch grandparents maybe?

Isn't that where babies come from, I ask. I see her blush before she turns her face away.

Leaves are such thin tissues, miraculous with the ability to produce life for the plant. And the ground is covered with them, layer upon layer.

"Chris. Out of all the leaves out here, out of all this beautiful gold, orange, yellow. Out of all that you choose the darkest leaf of all." She was shaking her head, with that look in her eyes. 'I just don't know about you.'

"You hand me the darkest leaf of all."

22

Hominid Mama

"Here come some of my people. Some of my family." I held up our Social Studies book, the picture of a group of *Homo habilis*. I was pushing it. Pushing myself. I had never addressed the whole table like this. These *Homo habilis* were facing *Dinofelis*, a saber-toothed cat on the prehistoric savannas of East Africa. I was facing the whole table of Martin and his church people. They looked disgusted that I had ever been near them.

"See how the mothers run for safety? The babies cling to them, and the males turn and gather against the monstrous cat. They live in fear of these predatory cats. *Smilodon* and other saber-toothed cats. And this is some of my family."

I caught a glimpse of Muriel.

What's this, her eyes were saying. Just like a textbook, I was thinking.

Martin was right up at me.

"Your family?" he said. "What are you doing, showing us a picture book like we're a bunch of second graders? These ugly things. That's a sacrilege against God and against humanity, against God's dominant creation, to say that those things are your family. You ought to be ashamed. You ought to be shocked at where you are right now, Chris. You're in a crisis."

"My people," I continued, "are not a sacrilege to speak of. They are people of the Earth and must live as they are able. They stick together. If they do not appear beautiful to you, they are not ashamed of it," I said. "Here. Hold out your hand. Put it up to mine. We are the same. We are primates. My people had hands just like us. Almost."

"Don't ask me to touch your hand. You're going downhill fast. You need to turn around, Chris. You're heading for damnation."

"Martin, chill. Take it easy."

"No. This is deadly serious. This has implications for eternity. We're losing you, Chris. We have been for a while now. We've talked about it at Bible study. You're slipping away. We've been praying about it. You're quickly becoming a loser, Chris. Becoming Lost. Calling this your family? Look at these things. What are they? Nasty looking ape-dogs? You want that for a family? Look at this naked ape woman loping around like a baboon, or I shouldn't even say 'woman' because she's not a woman. She's a baboon-animal, covered in dog hair. These things never existed. Archaeologists just have the bones mixed up right now. They find bits and pieces but they haven't got them put together the right way. They've let themselves be influenced by their preconceived ideas. They started with the idea that these things existed, and then they say these are the bones of those things, and they put together a bunch of total nothing out of a few pieces of ape-dog bones. Come on, man."

"Don't you talk about my people that way, Martin. That's our ancestor you're calling an ape-dog. That's our Homonid Mama. She's not..."

But the next thing I felt was Martin's knuckled fist slamming against the side of my mouth. I'd never been in a fight of any kind at school, but now here I was on the cafeteria floor, tasting my own blood. Realizing how fragile and suddenly thick lips are, wondering if my jaw had been dislodged and if it would go back into place and feel right again.

Martin had knocked me down with one punch. Pathetic.

One of the school janitors got there first, put his hand on Martin's chest, his other hand down at me where I was on the floor.

Here I was with my mouth bleeding, suddenly surrounded, central to everything. Punched in the mouth. But I wasn't going to be ashamed to be from those hominids. What if we really were from these hominids? Imagine what they went through. Imagine the mothers screaming when their babies got taken, eaten by predator cats like Dinofelis. Look at their hands and feet. Look into their faces. Imagine that we came down a long, long line all the way to us. What if that line had been broken?

The principal's office was all new to me. Never been there. Neither had Martin. Mr. Givens and his desk, a block of immoveable oak, sat filling the entire room. His high diplomas and certificates declared him from the walls. You hear of delinquents being whipped and caned and sent straight to some kind of wretchedness. But it didn't happen like that. Our fight was not one the school's more spectacular ones, and the principal was confused by it all.

Maybe he was glad that some of his students had been fighting over an idea rather than the usual kind of thing.

"I must say I am rather puzzled by this, both of you. Neither of you has anything like this on your record. What I want to know is, is this kind of thing going to continue, or can we get back to a more appropriate level of behavior such as I would expect of two decent young men who come from good families? It's a good thing the break is coming, because both of you appear to need some time off. Martin, you know I am astonished about this. You struck the blow. What should I say when I contact your parents?

That was the dreadful part. I saw right away that the principal knew he didn't need to bother whipping us or anything like that. My parents would know about this as soon as they saw my busted lip. I would just have to trust them to be able to understand. But the response I got from Muriel was the most infuriating.

"But you didn't even fight back. I mean, are you a pacifist? I hadn't thought of you as a wimp."

"Well there I was on the floor. And Martin was kind of surprised too, I think, and our fight just kind of fell apart. Mr. Lewis was right there, and I was tangled up in chair legs, and by the time I got back up it seemed more funny than anything else. I mean, it was Martin. We used to joke around all the time. And I kind of liked it, anyway, that for a sheer idea, I made him so angry that he punched me. I kind of like that. He's so easy to get inflamed about something. I just pushed it too far. So, no, I wasn't really being a peace lover. I was pushing him on purpose. I knew I was going too far, and then after he hit me I was really just trying to get out of the center of attention."

"Well, it did sound like you said his mother was a cave woman or whatever all that was. And you are now thought of by some people as a wimp."

"Well then they're just a bunch of stupid people. Maybe you should tell them I said so, if they're so into me and my ways."

"Well, I don't know. What are you saying, you want more people to come and fight you, so you can show them? Where did all this violence come from? Should I be worried?"

"But I didn't hit anybody. So do you think I'm bad now?"

"I think you're a little more crazy than I used to think."

"Good crazy or bad crazy?"

"Well, it's good crazy that you are apparently not a wimp. I mean, that you had a reason for what you did. Nobody understands a person who didn't fight back, but now I know that you were really fighting beforehand, by bringing it on. You had already been antagonizing him, so getting punched was really just coming to you, and you recognized that. So, yeah, that's kind of cool I think, that you were fighting for something you believe in. And I don't care what other people think either. Not that I'm against the idea of you being a pacifist. But I just didn't know you would be the one to get in a fight."

"Wow. You have all this analyzing power now. Because you've been studying the brain?"

And Brandon. He saw the whole thing. Standing right there. I figured he would see it like I did. I thought he would. And that he would agree Martin was being a jerk. But he just stood there shaking his head. Like he disapproved or something. Like he was some kind of man of ancient wisdom up on a mountain top. Like I was being foolish. So I was wondering, if it came down to it, maybe you're not someone I could count on to jump in and give me a hand? And right as they took me and Martin to the office I heard him ask me, when I passed by, if I thought it was possible I might have a violence problem. I just let out a long breath and kept on walking.

Martin couldn't let it rest. Even after he had belted me. Even on the way to the principal's office.

"They are not your family, Chris. Not your people. Not almost or not by a 1000 miles, they are not."

"Enough," snapped Mrs. Stiles, before I could begin to reply. She was pointing her finger with its long painted fingernail back and forth at each of us as she led us to the office. She handed me a tissue to hold against my swelling lip.

23

October Running

That afternoon the clouds were the thing. They bellied across open sky, grey bottomed but glowing gold-white on top and all around. Like they were ships seen from below in evening sunlight. They were towering, emulating, moveable and changeable. They were the continents of another world, bodies of another existence that we ran underneath and could not get up to no matter how we wanted to. They were lumbering deities lounging back in all their glory, too content in their sailing to notice our strivings up the hill roads, our silliness and the improprieties of outdoor running school boys.

I felt a weird throb in my lip with each stride. But these are some of the best days for running, this October air. The elation and the sheer energy comes forth and you fly.

The church people had called me "unbeliever" at the lunch table. But it isn't true. I believe in the total universe under one almighty power of love. I believe in the celestial winds that blow and I believe in what they represent. I do believe in God. I believe in the sheer and safe abandon I felt running on the road, October, when I tore off up the last hill with a gust and the guys all laughed and said I was just a wind runner.

24

Hominids

Martin confronted me the next day. Like he had been waiting for me. It was the last day before break.

"So you do believe all this," he said.

Martin and I weren't blood enemies. We went way back. Sometimes people take a different turn and friendship changes. But you still know the person. You still go to the same school as them. You still share all the old connections. We always had almost all the same classes. We had been standing in Mr. Given's office together, both looking at the floor like two shamed men in chains, and I knew he was no more a school fighter than I was. I used to go over to his house. You can't ignore someone you've known that long. But now Martin was drawing back from me as I spoke to him. Shaking his head.

"Sure," I said. "Of course. All those things are real."

"What things?"

"All those creatures. Those beings. What else would you say? Tell them they aren't real, when their bones are right there in the ground?"

"Chris, I don't know you anymore. I don't want to fight, and I know I shouldn't have hit you, but you're getting mixed up with stuff that's bad for you. This is not the path to life. It's taking you away from God. You actually believe that this is where people come from? Don't people mean more to you than that? Doesn't God mean anything to you? You're going to end up away from God. You're turning away from what's right. You are entering into Error. You've got to turn back before it's too late."

Sometimes I just don't know what to say. Where to begin. Muriel had called me a flat sky person. But did flat earth people not care what was in the ground?

"Because God is not going to accept this from you," Martin went on. "God is going to deal you a blow to set you straight." The bell was ringing. He was looking at me, like, Why don't you say something, and then he walked away, shaking his head.

Imagine: What if we went back in time, what if the ground opened up and what used to be came back, and we spoke to them? We would seem like angels to them. We would be unbelievable. Because we do such things that they did not do. We talk. We have complicated thoughts. We wear clothing. We make clothing. And all our different kinds of technology. We drink tea!

"Tea! Ha!" Muriel said later when I was telling her. "They drank stuff too, even if they didn't drink tea. They ate fruit."

"Ate fruit? What made you say that? Anyway, what would they drink except drinking out of a creek or something? They didn't have cups and silverware."

"I just thought of them drinking, and I thought of fruits having juice, and I thought, they ate fruit. So they would know what fruit juice was like."

And we barely know anything about them. We barely know where we came from. And we came from them. We were them. Without them, we wouldn't be who we are. We wouldn't be. Finding them is like finding angels to us, treasures, golden treasures kept safe in the soil of the earth, and now in museums and universities. Golden figures standing silent, from a world far away from us. All we can do is piece together a story from little fragments, and wonder. Out of all of them who ever lived, this one little person's bones would be found, out of all of them. And these bones have become golden fragments, kept safe. This skull is a golden mask like King Tut's, and each of our own heads holds a skull.

And imagine their skulls being crushed in the jaws of their great enemy, the Saber Toothed Cat. We had learned about the caves full of primate bones, where hominids were the favorite food of the prehistoric cats. We primates grew up with it printed in our minds, deep down: a roaring, monstrous cat. Jaws open in the moonlight. The last sight some poor fellow saw was the deadly swords of ivory falling down upon him.

Mist of the ages settles over everything.

25

An Idea

Fall Break was better than school, even if me and dad were working on the carpet while other kids were at the beach. Even if Muriel was gone to Washington DC with the music people. Even if black gritty dust peppered my sweaty arms.

The people who built our staircase had taken plain pine boards, not plywood, and measured them and marked them and cut them. They had carefully held each 8-penny finish nail upright in their fingers. A burst of hammer hits rang out against the raw wood and sheet rock of our unfinished house.

Our feet, up and down the staircase all these years, had worked a few of the nails loose. How many times had we walked these steps?

In a matter of seconds I hammered all those years back down through the nail heads. The scraping blade would stump against them if I didn't. And it would snag in the soft places of the swirl of pine wood grain.

When we stopped for lunch I sank my teeth into soft chocolate brownies and pulled up a chair in front of the staircase.

What are stairs? How did we get them? We have them. We, I kept saying. People. Where did the idea come from? Someone thought of it, living on a mountainside?

In the Bible, Jacob had a dream of stairs going up from earth and down from heaven, with angels coming and going. That was weird. Up, down, but in the same place. Where does it start? Which way is it going? Who invented this?

Suddenly I was laughing and I couldn't stop.

"Chris?"

"Chris?" Mom was laughing too, but her look said "Stop?" She grabbed me by the head. I was going out of my mind right before her eyes.

It was something to be amazed about: Stairs. The floor.

The stairs were part of the upper floor that spilled down through an opening. And the stairs were part of the downstairs floor, taking you up.

If you start at the bottom you're downstairs but when you get to the top you're upstairs. On different floors. We walked up the stairs all the time without thinking about it. How could I explain this?

When the floor got above us, it was the ceiling. We were in rooms. In a house. I could see it all like in a cut-away picture.

I'd been living with this staircase all this time. It was a sacred mountainside right here in the house. It was a solid object. I had spent all this time scraping it. I could put my hand on it. The parts I had scraped looked old and weathered, but clean. I could see the swirling grain of the pine boards and the pine resin deep in them.

Ingenious!

A masterpiece, a work of art, right here in the middle of the house. Like the house existed to surround it.

Everything was OK now. I was about to bust through the door and fly all the way up the road. I felt my face moving into an uncontrollable smile. I could eat supper and enjoy this break and not be worried. I was getting an idea! I would start drawing in the morning.

26

Idea: Some Kind of Deer

There's Brandon, standing at our door. Holding a camera. A nice camera, expensive.

"Ever been hunting?" he asks.

"Hunting? What, like with a gun?"

He holds up the camera and nods upward. Like that was a way to say something.

"That's the name of this project. The Wild Hunt."

"You already got a name for your project?"

"So you ready now?"

"Uh, yeah, I guess."

"Hold on. What's all this stuff? You've been drawing? This is your project? This little baby monkey?"

"Yeah, drawing. But not a monkey."

"And all these deer, or what are they, gnu?"

"Gnu?"

"I thought you were doing something about the hurricane, and all those leopards you always draw? And the hurricane, all that stuff you said? All that stuff you draw at lunch?"

"Those aren't leopards. They're jaguars. They're different." Everybody knows that.

How did I end up with this?

I had just followed the drawing graphite. The lines rounded out together and made a shape. It seemed to be waiting for eyes, a pair of little round eyes, staring.

It looked real. Not photograph-real, but real as a face. The eyes were the right size for it and it was looking at me. But it needed a body, legs. It was so easy to draw that it just jumped out of the graphite.

Before I knew it, without meaning to, I'd drawn about a dozen others.

I stood back to look. They weren't all identical. They were individuals, each one, but they were also alike, of the same kind. They were standing at the upper middle of the staircase. A herd.

They were great. They were really good. But what were they, and why had I put them there? I'd meant to draw a person.

Try again. Wouldn't it make sense to draw myself as a baby this time? Wasn't this supposed to be about my beginning?

The graphite rumbled again. It felt as soft to the pine wood as chocolate brownies had been to my teeth. It was like I could feel my mouth biting into the graphite, a mineral from inside the earth, the pine grains biting into it while my hand carried it and made lines. A head. Round eyes. A little too big maybe? Oh well. I was still getting used to this stuff. A small body, arms, legs. Ears? Hands? Feet? These things are complicated to draw.

And then there it was, drawn, looking at me just as intently as the little herd of animals. Waiting for something. They were all waiting, staring at me.

It was the traces of black carpet padding and the old carpet glue that had given me the idea. They were made by the carpet layers' arms sweeping, flying across our floor, swimming in an ancient sea. Traces of human work, human existence, had fossilized onto our staircase.

Archaeologists have uncovered Maya staircases where each step was carved with writing to tell the history of a king or of some event. Somewhere at the top, lost in the bright rays of sunlight over the pyramid, was the other end of the story.

So that was the idea. A story of pictures on a staircase, my own life from a baby to now.

But where do you put the beginning? If you start at the bottom, a stair-walker could start at the beginning of the story and travel with the story up the staircase.

Or would it be better to begin the story at the top? That way, to walk up the stairs would be to walk back to the beginning. Back to the beginning of time, even.

You would be stealing up for a look into the Garden of Eden.

But there could be no going into such a place, could there? It was too exalted, too holy. It was Paradise, and it was guarded. Even if Adam and Eve had stolen back to try looking in, the Flaming Sword was there, turning and flashing, and the immoveable Cherubim.

I looked back at pictures of Maya pyramids. At the top stood a little building. It had an open door, but it was all dark inside. Only the priests or kings, whoever was supposed to be up there in that high place, would know what was in that darkness. The sacrifice victim was the only one who goes beyond the darkened door. Only they would see what was beyond, but they weren't coming back down.

So it was grim and perilous to climb back up the passages that lead to the sacred places of the beginning. Maybe it was best to stay away from there.

But it seemed right that the beginning be at the top. If the story needed more room at the bottom, it could just keep going down the hall and into the living room, and on out the door and down the sidewalk and the driveway and Gilead Road, across town, out of the county, into the eastern reaches of North Carolina, the Coastal Plain, and down to the Atlantic shore. Just like the white lines people had painted on the road, and like the power lines that stretched all the way to California.

"So you ripped out the carpet and everything," Brandon was saying. "This is your project."

"I don't know. I don't know."

And it's not a monkey. But I didn't say that again. Because the more I looked at it, the more it did look like a monkey.

"You've got some sweet designs, man. I keep telling you. You don't even know. This stuff could be on t-shirts, surfboards. Whole companies of surf shirts and boardshorts could have this. Logos, designs. You don't even know."

"Want a drink before we go?" If this was my project, I didn't know what a herd of gnu or a little monkey had to do with it. "I'll just write Dad a note and then we'll be off. The Wild Hunt, you say?"

The upward nod. Like that was a way to say anything.

The gnu and the baby monkey flickered underfoot as I took the stairs two at a time up to my room to get my keys.

"And bring that tape, the one Oliver gave you," he yelled up after me.

27

A Red Fox

"We'll be stopping a few times. I won't know where until I see what we're looking for."

We, again. Like how he said did I know of a place where we could bury the dead crow. And the sight of him cradling that dead crow in his arms, out there on the bridge…

No. He wouldn't be thinking of something like that.

He can't be thinking that finding a dead animal would make a good project. Nobody would think that. Even if it crossed their mind as an idea, they wouldn't follow through with it. They would just let it pass on out of their minds. They would say 'wouldn't that be a crazy project?' But no one would ever do that.

"You got that tape?"

"Is that why you don't have a car?"

"What?"

"Like, being a vegetarian of driving. So you won't hit one?"

Somehow he knew what I meant. His voice was quiet.

"No. I would have a car if I could."

Then I thought, I shouldn't ask him. I remembered how his house looked. It was new, but it wasn't like the huge places going up in some of the new neighborhoods around town. I'd never heard him say anything about his family, like where his dad worked. Maybe they didn't have a car at all. No, that couldn't be right. How could anybody live without a car? You couldn't walk everywhere all the time. I shouldn't have asked. At practice he never talked about anything, and if he did say anything it was about surfing or running shoes or basketball.

"Which way, then, captain?"

"Straight ahead."

"Straight ahead."

"And turn up the music. I want them to hear it."

Them?

The Brandenburg music soared around us. Muriel was the leading violin. Oliver's friend Robbie was playing the hunting horn. The whole thing sounded like horse riders running through open country, the call of the horns, but it also made me think of sunlight shining above a high city, striking towers and arches and windows and steeples.

Across the bridge, up Gilead Road. The town square, the old stores, old houses went past and we thudded over the train tracks. I saw a few people out on the sidewalks but not many. People at the stoplights did turn and look when we blasted the Brandenburg, windows open. The old rusty water tower clambered up on the left and then we were falling away in a sharp curve, rushing under tree branches and flashes of sky. Porch rails and mill houses spindled past, the road flickering through a shadowy depth of vines hanging. A tumbled down house trailer teetered on creek-edge. Junk lay thrown down the shadows of the bank. Then we curved back up and into open sunlight where new neighborhoods stood on both sides of the road. New houses filled what used to be open fields. A famous old oak tree used to spread over the fields there, the haunt of crows in autumn, the perfect Halloween picture. With all the houses I couldn't tell if the tree was still there or not.

"Did you see the old water tower . . ." I started. But that was just more grandfather tales. Out here the houses were exactly like the ones in Piney Groves Estates. Beige, gray, no other colors. Maybe people didn't care about house colors. I would paint my house bright moss green, like Corin's door.

"OK, now. Now!" he shouted.

"Man! You're giving me a heart attack."

Nowhere to pull off except a steep ditch. My tires left lines in the tall grass.

But he was already out, straddling and jumping the ditch, jogging down the white line on the edge of the road. I got out watching for traffic, wondering if the car would be stuck.

It was just like last time. Brandon was crouching over some little shape at the edge of the road. This time it was bright orange: a fox.

"No way. You're not bringing that into my car . . ."

Then he was kneeling, sprawling, lying full out in the road. Face obscured by the camera, like the dark lens was all he had for eyes. "Watch for me," he called. "Watch for me." Like it was a blindness he went into, his hand circling the lens, focusing. The camera worked with a clutching sound, catching the pictures in the air.

How could this animal be real, a fox, such a bright color? Marks of silver and white and black made the face vivid and alive, like an actor caught offstage.

But the fox was dead. It lay there with its mouth open. The little pink tongue draped out over the teeth. The front legs were raised up away from the ground at impossible angles. What would it be like to be hit by something so much larger than you are? It would be bright lights paralyzing you, the ringing sound of the tires filling your head, then a rush of forces in a vacuum of darkness. You might lose your senses. You would be caught up and then it would all be over.

The little paws were clean and delicate and shimmering. How could something that lived outside, that lived in a den in the ground, have its feet and claws so clean?

"OK."

Brandon was standing by my shoulder. Camera in both hands, like he was holding a small box filled with gold.

"You got what you want?"

That was it? Brandon's big secret? The Wild Hunt? What can you do with pictures except show them to people?

"Oh yeah!"

28

Idea: Monkey Baby

Back on our side of the Interstate, Corin was outside, white hair bobbing in and out of shadows, trying to wrestle a ladder up to his upper porch. Was he lifting the ladder or the ladder lifting him? We jumped out and grabbed the ladder.

I didn't mind helping Corin, and I didn't even ask Brandon if he wanted to or what. But he did help, even if he didn't know how to do anything. Like not even how to set up a ladder the right way.

"Corin, let us do this."

"Careful--the woodwork on the railings. I cut those by hand, you know." Cut-out heart shapes, Black Forest style, like people said. Bungalow style.

"Nearly broke one yesterday."

"OK," I said. "Let us do this."

"Thank you, young lads."

We cut tree branches that slapped against the house and windows. Corin had instructions. He knew each different tree. Some of them we cut along the branch. Some of them he wanted cut at the trunk. We went all around, moving the ladder with us. In the tree tops it was either deep forest shadow or blinding Alpine sky. The whole upper part of the house was like a tree house, dewy branches, the cinnamon smell of conifers all around you, the scent like oranges, like Christmas.

The crows, finding land people up in the trees, scolded with rough voices and then crossed the sky in a casual drift. Trying to make us think they weren't keeping an eye on us.

Then Corin was talking below, maybe offering us a drink? No, he was in the flower beds talking to butterflies.

Monarchs. They came sailing in, two or three together, landing on the flowers, then lifting off and away. Corin standing there like the butterfly wizard among them.

You could watch their tongues drinking the nectar from flowers. Corin showed us. They would soar in circles around the garden and glide back to drink more. Stopping off here for food on their migration, Corin told us. They're on their way to the religious forests in the mountains of Mexico, he said, where they cling through the winter to tree branches. It's the groves of Oyamel, he said. Corin spoke to the butterflies, "Is this the Oyamel? You've farther to go, little friend. You've a long way. But stop here and take your rest."

They sense something we don't know how to sense, Corin told us. They feel the earth's magnetic field. That's how they find their way. And now my little house is part of the map they carry with them. When they are following the right way, they know it in themselves.

That's how we spent the whole break. Working on our projects and working for Corin. Splitting firewood for his fireplace; getting old brush chopped up and away from his shed; working in his Fall garden of greens; but one of the main things would be getting the greenhouse ready for the night of first frost. That night was coming soon.

Then he went inside and came back holding two bags of turnips. Earth still clinging to them.

He handed us the bags and then suddenly clasped Brandon by the head, like he was being ordained or something.

"Yes, this lad will make a fine gardener. Some day he's going to put in a garden of his own."

Brandon turned bright red and just shook his head a little and didn't say anything. But he liked it. Right before he left he started talking about me and him meeting up tomorrow.

"More?"

"Yeah I want more. Lots more. How about 6:30 in the morning?"

"Are you crazy?"

"I want to get on with it. Come on."

"You're for real about that? 6:30 AM?"

"I'm for real."

At home a roll of foam padding, ocean blue, was waiting in the hallway. A rolled up sea ready to spill out and flood down the staircase.

The herd of gnu I had drawn looked at me. Asking me, Why did you call us into existence? Give us the space of earth to run in and we will eat grass, run under the sky, and keep to ourselves.

"It was for my project," I told Mom and Dad. "It was supposed to be like a Maya pyramid, with pictures going up the steps. Would it be OK if I just finished up my idea, real quick, just a few days, not a whole lot of trouble, just to get a few pictures drawn? And then I could take some pictures of it with the camera? Before it gets all covered over by carpet, and that would be it. It would just take a couple more days."

Photos. Brandon's project had made it obvious. I couldn't take the actual staircase to school.

"Well," Mom said, "we can manage like this for a few days longer. A few days. If you're not talking about something dragging on and on and on . . ?"

I had a way of running after dark where I went up the driveway, back down it, through the backyard, down through my Out Back trail, and then repeat all that if you want.

Running is that great thing that jostles the human mind. Because of the increased oxygen, Coach had told us. I thought he was joking, but I also thought it was because of putting your whole body into motion. Not sitting. Being upright and moving. And that was how I saw myself then, looking down from above: a human being, taking long strides across the silver land of starlight. Air went into my lungs and out again, and I was in the air and air was in me, and air was also the sky, the deep indigo. Electromagnetic power was ranging invisible all around me, all through the atmosphere, filled with knowledge that even butterflies can understand. I opened my hands, held them up, tried to feel it, tried to sense it, tried to receive it. The soaring power lines, dragon neck, buzzing and crackling, beams and buttresses, made a night cathedral of the whole sky. Powers are in the air without us seeing, moving in secret because we don't notice, flights of butterflies across continents, and flocks of birds, starlight on silver wings.

And that was when my real idea was born into my mind, what I should do. I saw it all plainly, as if a staircase went up into the sky right in front of me. It was just like what Brandon said: it's as good as done. Confidence surged through me. Running builds you up. That's how I felt. I saw everything in front of me and it was perfect. All that remained was for me to put the drawings in.

That little monkey baby I had drawn wasn't a monkey. Not at all. It was a hominid, an ancient creature from another time, almost like from another world, and just as I was a runner, I saw that line of hominid ancestors up-right, running. Standing on their legs under the vast and beautiful heavens. What did they understand? Did they know how to read the electromagnetic waves? Did they look at the stars? What would they think if they could know the controversies their bones had caused?

The church people at lunch said "I know I didn't come from any mon-key." But I was going to draw the whole line of human ancestors. All the hominids I could find. But that wasn't all of it.

I would divide the stairway in two. Roughly in two. Because things had already gotten blurry. The gnu were crossing over, in the middle. They would be part of both sides. The hominid baby and all its line would be on one side, with stars and indigo sky. And on the other side, there would be The Creation, Adam and Eve, Cain and Abel, however much of that story I could get on the steps before the steps ran out. Both stories, side by side, going up the same staircase. Going back to the beginning. And I would go right up through the middle.

That night I stayed up. I kept drawing. While this idea was alive and burning in me, I kept on going.

I had the Days from the Genesis First Account paired up like Mr. Collins had put them on the board. Chapter One. That was one more thing that had made Martin so crazy. Mr. Collins would not agree that these had to be 24 hour days. Martin kept saying none of the scriptures would be true if this wasn't true.

But no one could argue with this layout. It made sense.

Day One, Day and Night, paired with Day Four, Sun, Moon and Stars, the bodies that go with Day and Night.

Why would anyone argue that they had to be 24 hour days, when the sun didn't exist until Day 4? It's a pointless argument, Martin! Everybody knows that. You're just letting something pointless hold you down.

Day Two, A Dome or "Firmament" to separate the Waters Above and the Waters Below, paired with Day Five, Water Creatures and Sky Creatures.

Day Three, Dry Land separated from Waters, with plants, paired with Day Six, all the Animals of the dry land, and Human Beings.

Simple drawings, coming down the staircase. No one could argue with that. And Day Seven, the holy day. The Sabbath. The day God rested. A day for humans to rest, to restore, and to remember: we are not God. We have to let it all go someday.

And if I could get some of the things from the Second Account. Adam and Eve, the Trees, the Fruit, the Serpent. I could have the Cherubim, the Sword Turning. I might have room for Cain out in the field slaughtering

Abel. Draw a close-up, Cain's hand with a knife, Abel's neck ripped open. Real violence, real human blood pouring to the ground.

I drew, I moved the graphite, scraping into the early hours past midnight.

But I barely knew any of the hominids, the early human creatures. I would have to go back to the library. My own ancestors, and I didn't even know them!

29

Up Early

Early next morning I was tired but I got myself awake. Outside my window, over the line of dark trees and the pylons, Orion the Hunter stood shining. He would be rising earlier every night, soaring over us while we slept. Some cultures called him Shepherd. The Pleiades clustered near him.

The world opens its doors early.

Mom stuck her head in the kitchen door while I was crunching cereal. She asked what Brandon's project was and when I said "Secret," I knew instantly: the wrong word. Her look of concern could not be hidden.

"I'll let him tell you about it. I'm sure he will."

But she won't want to know.

I pulled in at Brandon's at exactly 6:30. I was admiring my ability to be there at the exact moment we had said. To the dot. I was expecting him to be outside, ready and waiting. But he wasn't. Only then did I pay attention to the fact that we hadn't said anything about meeting outside.

I thought I could see light in their windows. Maybe. Or was it a reflection from the streetlights outside?

Did I really want to knock on somebody's door at 6:30 in the morning? If I had known which window was Brandon's I could pay him back with some of his own crow calls. But to knock on someone's door at this early hour? I couldn't see any light in any of the side windows. Why wouldn't he be waiting outside? That was the sensible thing. Anybody would know that.

With the knuckle of the middle finger of my right hand I tapped gently on the middle of front door.

No one. I thought I could hear the TV going. Maybe they hadn't heard me? Just leave, I thought. But I raised my hand to knock again and before I could knock, the door opened a little. A woman's face appeared, blond hair tied back. Hand over her throat like she dare only just risk opening the door. I saw a tattoo.

She smiled slightly. "Yes?"

A complete stranger, 6:30 in the morning. I must have looked confused or lost. I must have been crazy.

"Uh, hello. I'm Chris, from down the road. I was supposed to meet Brandon this morning. I know it's early. Sorry about that. I hope I didn't wake you up."

She opened the door wider. The chunky sound of television chopped around her. She wore a robe colored bright with Hawaiian flowers.

"Oh no, hon, you didn't wake me up. Brandon's not up. If he said he'd meet you, I'll get him. Come on in."

Deep shadows moved with her, above her, darkening the walls and ceiling in a cone of blue television light. The smell of someone else's breakfast was heavy in the room.

"Had breakfast? Hungry?"

"Oh, no, thank you. I had breakfast. Thank you."

"Sure? It's no trouble. We've got sausage and eggs and bacon and . . ."

"No, thank you. I appreciate it. Thank you."

"Well just make yourself at home, hon. Bran? Expecting someone? Have a seat and make yourself comfy. Like a drink?"

"I'm OK, really. Thank you."

It was all one big room, living room and dining room, and around a corner must be the kitchen. Another TV was blaring there.

I sat down and fell back, sinking into a fuzzy white sofa that was deeper than I thought. I was squirming to get back upright.

How could anybody watch two televisions at the same time?

"Here," I started saying, "I can just see Brandon later." But she was gone.

"Bran honey, somebody's here to see you." I heard the sound of inch long finger nails drumming on a door. "Get up."

It was too late to leave so I just bolted my eyes to the televisions, back and forth, engulfed in the fuzzy couch. The TV nearby showed one of those big TV church services. The one in the kitchen was showing a pair of women modeling jewelry. Prices were scrolling across the screen.

The TV preacher could have been a football player, the size of him. He stood at a pulpit in suit and tie. At his feet dark red carpet flowed down the steps and into the congregation. A choir surrounded by ferns pyramided up behind him.

His face was bulging and he gripped his pulpit with mammoth hands. His voice gonged out, robust.

"Friends, this evening I want you to just join with me as we come together in this ministry. And I'm talking to our friends out there across the airwaves of this great nation too, this beautiful nation of God's blessing, from sea to shining sea, where even you might be at this very moment. Thanks to our brothers and sisters that have sacrificed that we might be able to continue this televised ministry of the Word. God's Own Holy Word! He said it wouldn't come back empty and folks, I'm here to tell you, it doesn't. It just doesn't. It overflows. It continues, thanks to your gifts. And friends out there, I want you to know, that this evening, at this very moment in time, we are coming to you from the very throne of God . . ."

Across the room, a man had joined the jewelry ladies. While he talked they showed the sparkling rings on their hands. Aquamarines, exotic sapphires. Tourmalines. Call now! What a deal! A bonus for shoppers who act in the next fifteen minutes! Gems of the highest quality, rings of 24 karats, the kind of ring you never see on television, except for this special offer.

The church service went to an ad for one the preacher's books. I heard muffled talking. Brandon's mom was back. I half-waggled half-rolled myself up to the edge of the sofa, planning to leave, when a saw-blade voice cut in from somewhere in the dark of the kitchen.

"Tell that boy to get up now, Marva, or I'll be in there. Boy, get up."

I heard a door open, and Brandon's voice. "I'm up. I'm coming. I don't want breakfast. You know I don't eat that stuff. And I didn't forget anything."

Standing there in the ice blue television light was the shadow-cut face of a ghost. A specter.

"Ready," he said. "Come on, Chris." He was already at the door.

"You're not going to eat anything? You need to keep your strength up. You look so . . ."

"I'm fine. Come on, Chris. We're going."

I thought I should say something to Brandon's parents, but I couldn't see his father, so I just smiled and mumbled "nice to meet you" to his mom as I followed Brandon. I pulled the door shut behind me and felt the living rush of clean fresh air.

In the light outside, the contours of Brandon's skull showed in a fine dust of glistening bristle.

"You got your hair buzzed? Man, where were you? You did say 6:30 in the morning?"

"Sorry about that. I meant to meet you outside. I accidentally set my clock for 6:30 PM. So yeah, I am sorry about all that. Nobody should have to go through all that."

"I hope your mom doesn't think I'm rude, so early and all."

"She's not my mom. Not my real mom."

The sky was lightening as we curled our way out of Piney Groves Estates. Jagged wings broke loose from the pylons: the crows, winging outward. Late stars shining at their wingtips. We had the music on again, same thing. Brandon said, let them hear it, it would bring the animals to us. We drove around for a while but didn't see anything. About 8:00 we were starving. Even though I had had breakfast. Brandon refused to eat any kind of fast food or even go into a fast food place, so we stopped at a grocery store at one of the new shopping centers. We bought muffins and golden raisins. He wanted soy milk. I thought maybe soy milk was something like liquid yogurt. We went across the parking lot to a coffee shop.

Inside, the line snaked around. Two girls from school were at a table across the room. I had known them back in elementary school. They would start asking me about the fight in the cafeteria, I figured, Martin punching me. Muriel had said people now thought of me as a wimp or worse. I would have to explain and defend myself. These girls were the kind who liked to tease, and I had been tongue-tied in sixth grade when they turned their arrows at me.

But when they saw us, it was "Brandon's here." "Look at his hair." "Oh my God, like an ax murderer!" "No, I like it." While I was still at the counter waiting, he was already over there with them. I heard them say "the project." When would the pictures be ready, when could they see them, how did they turn out, how did they look?

So, this project, this big secret. Like he needed me to drive him around, like I needed to meet him at 6:30 AM, but here were these girls knowing about it?

And these girls. They weren't what you would call nice girls. I knew that much. They were the girls who stood smoking with guys behind the science building, and if you went into the woods, they were the ones you would find in the little hut made of old plywood and junk and dead tree branches. What they would be doing up this early I could not think. Hadn't even been home from last night probably. And Brandon. Had he really been put into such low classes that these were his classmates?

Then when I got my coffee he was standing at the door ready to go.

"Brandon, really, son, who are you talking to," I began with him outside. "How do you know these girls?" But then I started thinking, maybe I don't even want to know.

"What? These are some girls I've been taking photos of. What about it?"

He said it so strongly, such a grown up sounding way, that I said nothing else about it. But I thought of the ladies modeling jewelry on the television. Did he mean photos like that?

Then, at the car, a girl older than us, maybe a college student, noticed Brandon's camera and asked if we were reporters. Wow, I thought, this guy attracts attention at every turn. Because she couldn't possibly think we were reporters. Me standing here in an faded Outer Banks hoodie and shorts. Hurricane wear. Brandon with his ax-murder haircut.

He said we were, but then he said it would be more accurate if she referred to us as photographic artists, because we were involved in one of the year's most important stories.

We, again.

"It's for every generation," he added.

"What is it," she asked.

"You'll have to wait for the show. Once it's all together and presented, you won't be able to miss it."

30

Outsiders Both of You

Out of the parking lot and into standstill traffic. Here they were, the people of the working world, staring straight ahead, gritting their teeth, waiting for green lights. Business clothes, work clothes. Automobiles sitting congealed in their own invisible jelly of exhaust.

These people did this every day, while we were sitting in our classrooms.

But the sun was shining, the whole sky triumphant in bright blue. We crept along through more stoplights at more shopping centers until we broke free into open country.

We hadn't gone far before we saw what Brandon was hunting for. He ran back and was down, crouching, sprawling, flat in the road. Blind, obscured, hidden behind the camera. "Watch for me," he called. Watch for me. The filthy smell of rot was strong and Brandon had the neck of his T-shirt up over nose and mouth.

The animal's body was flattened. It was hard to understand, this little raccoon, how a living body would go through this. I couldn't keep from thinking about it. You would try to escape but you wouldn't be able to. You would be pulled down. Death would come over you sometime during the crush of the tires over you.

We found another raccoon a few miles on. It looked like it was asleep at the side of road. But it was dead. The breeze ruffling its fur made it alive again, made it catch my eye.

Then we kept going, windows open, on beyond the river and the dam, across the county line way over to high fields beyond. Hay fields and green pastures lay before dark woods with gravel roads going up into the trees. Not everything was destroyed by shopping centers and developments.

Where we turned around was an orchard with an apple stand. We got a few apples and they were making fresh cider. Then right beside it was a little store, a gas station, one of those old stores where people sit around out front. A group of young guys was out there in hunting clothes and camouflage. A sign said "Hunting Gear on Sale Today." A couple of neon orange shirts on hangers floated up on the breeze.

"That's it!" Brandon was saying. "Come on."

Right away those guys were looking at us. They heard Brandon's sharp voice, Rocky Mountain accent. Saw his skull bone buzzed head. I saw them looking at our running shoes. I looked at theirs, like a reflex. Cowboy boots, brogan work boots. Running shoes? What about it? Is that so weird? Anyway, it's Brandon who's the outsider, not me.

Outsiders both of you, their faces said.

"That's exactly what I want," Brandon was saying, striding past them, grabbing the shirts. "Here." He threw one to me. "It's exactly right."

"What do you want this for," I said down low to him. "They're for people like them, hunting deer and coons and stuff like that."

"Exactly. We're hunters."

"Mornin', boys," he nodded upward as he pushed his way to the screen door and into the store.

"What you boys hunting up this way?" one of them said as we came out. Like, are you planning on tromping around in our fields and woods?

"Uh, yeah, animals, that kind of thing," I said, turning as we were getting into the car.

Back at home, the house was choking with a chemical sweat. Paint scent. Brandon came in and the whole time I kept being scared Mom would ask him about his project. And he did look different from most people. Not just the buzzed hair and the chipped tooth. It was in his eyes. He didn't smile quickly like most people do when they want to get along with everybody. It was good she didn't ask about the project, because what would anybody think? What normal person goes out to take pictures of dead animals on the road? In the car Brandon had put on his new hunting shirt, saying this is unbelievable, this shirt, this project.

He got onto telling Mom Corin was letting him plant his own little garden for kale, his holy plant, and I didn't know if that was even true, and then he was off, talking about vegetarians and Mom was saying Oh, you don't look like a vegetarian. And I was like, Mom.

"Well, there's just some young folks at work, you know, who are doing that now, and they just started looking sort of pale all of sudden. That's all. But you don't look pale. You look healthy."

"Mom, I'm sure he's fine. He runs like he's not quite dead."

"Chris, really. No one mentioned death."

My trail in the Out Back crisscrossed the landscape, pylon to pylon. I hated people knowing where it was, but I couldn't keep them off it. Sometimes now we saw kids on dirt bikes, heard their mosquito-buzzing from the house, saw their dusty orange clouds. After people started moving in so much, sometimes we'd meet them out walking their dogs or even with babies, in that dire place. It's a wild place. The power company people come out there checking on their towers and chopping back the weeds. All manner of weedy things grow there: Brambles of blackberry and foot-tangles of honeysuckle. Milkweeds, loco jimson weed, thorn-apples, Johnson grass, poison oak, hidden hands of beggar lice, orange trumpet vine. And wild roses that smell like raspberry, honeysuckle buzzed by hummingbirds, all kinds of star-shaped yellow flowers all summer long and white in autumn in many types.

The space out there is not a normal place. It's like the Interstate: a long place that keeps you facing forward. I am sure you could go all the way to California by going pylon to pylon. You are in a place not connected to the places you pass unless you pull off and get out of it. If you try to picture it from above you have to think like a map. But you're on foot.

But we weren't going to California. Not now anyway. We were running and again we came around to the Rocks, the Gaunt Jaw smiling down, and we leapt up the rock faces and stood breathing on top.

Muriel always said, "How do you do it, all this running?"

And I said, "I don't know. I love it."

"I hate it," she said.

And I saw the faint trail Brandon had made from the Rocks, from the Gaunt Jaw, up to Corin's back fence, going up there to plant kale.

On the way back Brandon said I needed to come surfing sometime. We needed to go to Cape Hatteras.

"Yeah, that's fine, but I don't have a surfboard."

"No problem. I have two."

"And I don't know how. But yeah, going to the beach, sure."

"You'll learn how. And we can camp out. I know some campgrounds where I've been before. Right at the beach, at the national seashore, practically at the door of the lighthouse."

"Sounds awesome. Yeah, sure."

"When you catch the first wave, that's something you'll never forget. The thrill of it, like your whole life stops going round and round and just kind of hangs there with you in it, like you just came alive. You're in a floating world, you feel gigantic and you feel better than you ever have, but you also know you're small but it's in a good way, like you're OK being small in the great open sea. Like you finally found out where you fit with everything, and the moon and gravity and the motion make the waves, and you're feeling that cause you're on the water. And once you've been there, you'll be living for more."

Yeah, I wanted to go. It sounded awesome. It would depend on what Mom and Dad said. If they would let me go somewhere like that. If they would let me go with the disturbed young man.

He kept on going. "It's perfect. You're on top of the water, you're in the curl of a wave . . . "

The expert. But when we were working at Corin's, he knew nothing at all about splitting wood with a maul and wedges. Never heard of it. I had to show him how.

31

Helping in the Greenhouse

We stepped into the ribcage of a whale. Sky and sunlight broke in. Shredded plastic flapped in the breeze. Fallen sweet gum leaves crunched underfoot. But the wooden framing at the bottom and at the ends and in the doors was still good. Still sound. And, Corin said, it was natural for things to decay and wear out. Natural for things to be replaced. It was the opportunity for renewal. It was the way of the world.

We weren't out there freezing ourselves to death. It was perfect autumn weather. Football weather. Sweater weather. Hayride and pumpkin weather. Leaf raking weather. Greenhouse rebuilding weather. First frost is coming, Corin said, and he had to get his plants under cover.

Corin called the plastic sheets clear, but they aren't clear like glass. They're cloudy, milky. Vague shapes and shadows show through. The greenhouse has electricity because a wire runs to it underground from the house. So you have to be careful never to dig in that area of the yard. He's got a lamp out there and a little heater. On deep winter nights when cold bites down, we see the greenhouse lit up and Mom always says a spaceship is out there. There's a brick floor and a couple of wooden benches. But sitting is for later when we get it put back together. This time we just helped get all the old plastic off.

Corin is pretty old. He had already been out there by himself trying to get the old plastic off. He has a hard time reaching up. His arms and shoulders have problems. He said several times, he kept telling us, freezing weather could come any day. He's worried about it.

Corin let me take the ladder and get up into one of his shaggy old cypress trees. Just climbing up higher in the branches you hear the sound of the breeze. It's like hearing the ocean. You don't even know the wind is blowing until you get up there. It must be every needle-leaf responds to any slight brush of air. I looked over to the rooftops of Piney Groves Estates. Late afternoon sun made them golden, glowing. Anything that's left of the pine forest is what's inside me. I try to see it. My eyes see the houses of the neighborhood. I strain memory. I try to force it. The forest stays hidden. I can't make it happen. The destruction, the trees like stacked corpses, the land dug and re-dug, the neighborhood, the streets, the houses: Those things fill my eyes.

The forest is lost. We're both wandering ghosts now, each trying to find the wandering other. I'm afraid of losing my memory of it. Sometimes I remember it just before I go to sleep. Sometimes I can't remember it when I want to. What happens to all the good things of Earth that have been destroyed?

What are you doing, Brandon asks. So I come down. Start telling him. Some of it. The parts that don't sound too crazy.

Right past Corin's, right here, I show him, from the side of the road, a little path went back into the woods. Hidden from the road. Corin would see me going up there lots of times. It was not all pine trees. Dogwoods and sourwoods grew there, black gums, sweet gums, maples, under the higher heights of the ancient pines. It was the pines that made the whole forest dark. They were not small pine trees. It was a place of cool air. The ground was sanctified and hushed under layers of pine needles.

On the other side you came out on a high crest that overlooked the Interstate and the exit for Gilead Road. I could be there without anybody seeing me, watching cars go on the Interstate, watching the stoplights change colors in their cycle. People on the Interstate rushed by in their little vein of motion, without a thought about what was up there.

What's up there, Mom would say.

The Pillars of the Sky, the heights of green sunlight, the cleanest air. The scent of pine. The soft cushion of pine needles. It went up hill, a crest. And there was, I remembered, a little crest of rock just sticking up. Maybe that was the top of one of the rocks Brandon found.

You would have liked it up there, I tell him. Anybody would have liked it up there. Nobody cared about going up there but me.

After the bulldozers, the smell of crushed pine hung in the air for days. Especially at night. It mingled with the dankness and dampness where they had torn open the deep beds of clay. It was a foulness like spilled blood that stained everything.

The bulldozers pushed all the green branches into piles. Dad said they would bury them or grind them up. They hauled away the trunks on truck beds. By then just a few small trees were left, along the edges. That was the day I quit looking.

Until the day I drove Brandon home.

32

Chase

Somewhere out on Concord Road we found a dead possum, the most killed animal in the world. You could always see one dead on the road. This one died with a grimace of saw-blade teeth.

It was like before, Brandon running back and then crouching, bending, laying in the road for the sake of a few pictures.

"Watch for me," he called.

We were glowing in the shadows in the neon shirts.

But no cars came. The music of birdsong was all around us and I was startled when a gruff voice spoke up behind me.

"What y'all doing?"

I jerked round to a stern face staring at me from the other side of the roadside fence.

"Oh, uh, nothing. He's just taking a few pictures. Don't mean any harm," I stammered.

"Well get on out of here. You belong in school, anyway."

"School's out," I started, but Brandon was saying, Come on man, let's just go.

"We're just taking pictures," I said again.

"Well I don't want you up here in my fields."

"We're not..."

"Come on, man," Brandon was saying. "Let's go. I've got what I want."

Back in the car, I was angry.

"We're not up there in his fields. We're on the roadside. It's public, it's the right of way."

"Forget it," Brandon was saying. "Just forget it."

When I pulled in at the school, Brandon clamped his hand down on my skull. "You're crazy."

I took an extravagant loop through the empty student parking lot and then pulled up in a spot near H Hall and C Hall, at the front, where I never got to park.

"I just miss school so much. Don't you? I just want to walk around a little."

Brandon really was astonished. "You are crazy."

"No, I just need to go into the library. I thought maybe they would let me in. I'm looking for a couple books on hominids. Human evolution. Stuff like that."

At the library door I saw people through the glass, so I walked on in.

A sharp voice met me straightaway. "Stop right there, young man. Students are not permitted on school property during break. We are doing inventory work..."

"Uh, yes ma'am, but I really need some books for my project. Just a couple? I'm not joking."

She rolled her eyes and let me in.

I got back to the parking lot with three books and found Brandon outside the car crouched down like he was hiding. Neon shirt glowing in the car's blurry gloss.

A dark sports car was idling at the far side of the parking lot, racing its engine. Right where I usually parked, right by my roaring white pines.

I jogged back to my car and ducked down beside Brandon.

"What's going on?"

"Let's just get out of here." He raised up just enough to look at the dark sports car. He pulled open the car door. "No, don't stand up." He grabbed me by the arm. "Get in, let's go." He was trying to hurry me through the passenger side.

"Hold on, OK, we'll go. What the heck is going on? I can't get in this way, climbing across."

I curved around the front of the car and into the driver's seat.

"Go," his voice pushed at me. He had himself lowered down in the seat.

"Who is that? Do you know them?"

As I cranked my car, I heard a sudden scream of rubber. I turned in time to see the black car tearing out by the side driveway, by the baseball field. Then the trees blocked my view, and I couldn't see whether it was still there or had driven away into the road.

I pulled around and headed out the main entrance drive.

"Go left," he said. "Just get out of here! Don't let him catch us."

"Sure. OK. But what's going on?"

We had the green light at the intersection, so I just hit the gas and tried to go as fast as I could and stay on the road. I was afraid to look if any police might be around.

"Don't let him catch us."

I didn't want a ticket, not this early in my driving career. Mom and Dad would take the car away. But I also didn't want to be known as a person who didn't take action. And I didn't want to get caught by some kind of bad guy. It was all split second and I just gripped the wheel and put down the gas and met the curves that were coming on fast.

"Is anybody really chasing us?" I asked.

We scooped around a curve and emerged from the overhanging trees onto a straight stretch that paralleled the train track. I looked back. The rear view mirror framed empty road. I looked ahead. Another sharp curve. I looked back into the rear view mirror and jumped as all at once the mirror filled with dark racing shapes and gleaming lines. My ears filled with the sound of clattering tracks and the sudden blast of a train's whistle. Right beside me. Moving rail cars raked my peripheral vision. We were being pulled backwards, my car failing and losing power, even with my foot pressing the gas, and then just as quickly we broke free and burst ahead as the road curved. I saw the front of the train's engine as we raced away.

We leaned into a curve to the left and then back to the right and there was a stop sign.

"Go right, just don't stop. Don't let him catch up." Brandon said, looking back.

"No, I'm going left. We can make it."

As I turned left, toward the tracks, the black car appeared, edging into my rear view mirror, squealing in the last curve. The railroad signal was already gonging and flashing. Hazard. Stop. Train is coming. The guard arm was about to fall as our car thumped over the tracks. The black car blacked out of my rear-view in a rush of train cars, train whistle wailing, like a devil spirit angry that I had breached the space. I knew I had done something foolish. Something serious and dangerous. A tremor run through me, all over me, but I didn't let on.

"Yeah! Whoo!" I shouted out the window. "Just like Bigwig's escape," I grinned.

Brandon was still looking back. He came up in his seat, and he did look pale.

"So what was all that? Somebody's after you?"

Brandon let out a long breath and sat back. Said nothing. Finally he spoke.

"Somebody from before. Somebody I knew from my old school. Somebody I never want to see again in my life."

"I guess not. But they couldn't have known you were in my car. How would they? I mean, they couldn't have been chasing us. They were just going the same way we were. But that was fun."

"Not if they saw me. Back at the parking lot."

"Did you actually see who was driving? I didn't. Maybe it was just a car like the one you thought it was?"

"No. It was him. That's how he always drives, hiding down in the seat. He thinks its cool. That was his car. No question. I know it. They're . . . I've already seen them around here." He hesitated and then said, "Look, it's OK. Forget it. It's not something for you to worry about. It's just . . . I don't want to see them again. He probably thought I would be at school today, and then he left when he saw school was out."

"I'm not worried about it," I said. "Just wondering. You make it sound strange and that makes me curious, but that's all OK, man. Leave it in the past if that's what you want."

"I do want to. Just . . . Don't be so fired up about what just happened. He wasn't really trying to catch you. Or he would have. He just wanted to let you see him."

Let me see him? I didn't believe that.

Brandon didn't say more about it. I glanced over and he was looking out his window. Then, for a second I thought he was about to open up and say something. But he didn't.

Later I wondered if all our driving around was really him looking for that black car. But that didn't seem likely.

We came to the stop sign at Concord Road and turned left off Asbury Chapel. He started talking.

"I wish I could just get out of here. Yeah, I wish we could go to Hatteras right now." He turned to me with this look on his face like, Maybe we could do that right now?

"Yeah, sure," I said. "I reckon they won't need us at school for a couple of months. And we have lots of money in our pockets right now to pay for food and gas and a place to stay."

In Brandon's room the blinds were half open, striping everything with tropical palm leaves, sun and shade. He had the flags of New Zealand and Hawaii over the bed. Surfing posters filled the other walls. The ocean water was unbelievably blue, turquoise, green, sparkling. Clear as glass. I had never seen the ocean be that color in real life. You'd have to go to the Caribbean or Tahiti. Some distant place. Surfers surfed the towering curl of a wave. Brandon knew all the top surfers' names, like they were regular basketball stars on TV. I pictured that rush of water curving over my head from behind, a cape of liquid glass, my legs alive with the wavering board under me. I saw the coastline blur and the golden sun a fire through the veil, then the water roared and powering motion swept me forward. Surfing wouldn't be bad.

He had a real surfboard leaning in the corner by the foot of the bed. Another one under the bed. Clothes and shoes were scattered around. Next to the door he had a small desk with his books all in a stack, and a chair. Pencils and paper. Normal teenage bedroom.

On the wall opposite, black and white photographs were pinned to a cork board. I went over to look, but then something else caught my eye.

"Hey, is this the crow's shell, the one he had in his beak?"

"Huh? What?" he called in a muffled voice. He was fitting a new spool of film into his camera.

The shell was light grey, almost blue. It was the classic spiral, perfect and true, ever widening. The little sea creature lived a curled, spiraling life. I guess it didn't mind. Darker lines rippling along the outside in both directions, tiny blurry lines, following the contours. Sea waves, written on the shell. Just like the ocean waves that sounded inside it, if it weren't broken, if it were bigger, if you held it up to your ear. What was broken was part of where it wound around into such smallness, the crown of it. The break let you see inside. I couldn't keep from running the tip of my pinkie finger around the inside smoothness. It was glossy with tiny highlights of the window in its curves. You could look into it and it was a spiraling room you follow your way into. And that was the Maya observatory in the Yucatan: they had designed it after a conch shell. Now it came back to me. Now there's an idea. That would be a project. Ushered up to the heavens, to look at the stars through an opening seashell.

How did a little sea creature, some kind of snail, come up with something like this?

"Chris? Ready?" Brandon was standing in the doorway.

His mom was asleep on the couch. Blasted away by television volume. The preacher's gonging voice blanked the whole room.

"No. Listen to me, people of God, the signs are in, they're registering before our eyes, just as we have them written for us in holy scripture. The Last Days are coming! People will fall before delusion, and sway under the weight of their own troubled minds. Don't let yourself be caught in it."

A telephone number and the words "P. Radley 'Bull' Brown Ministries" floated across the bottom of the screen.

"The world is worse today than it was yesterday, and tomorrow it will break open with the sores of disaster. Storms, earthquakes. The signs we find in Scripture are coming true. The nation is failing. God is taking his glory away. We have turned our backs on God. God is lifting his protecting hedge from around us. We've shaken our fists at God. The forces of the Evil One are waiting on the borders."

"Amen," cried voices of the crowd.

"Glory," a woman's voice said above the others, and the voices faded into applause and the cameras drew back and then suddenly there was P. Radley 'Bull' Brown in a sweater sitting by a fireplace.

"This is Bull Brown and I've got something I'd love to share with you. Under no circumstances will you want to miss this! You won't be under any obligation, but these end time days are too important . . ."

"Come on," Brandon said, "unless you want to stay for more. I've seen that about a thousand times."

What if, I thought as I cranked the car, we really could go straight to Cape Hatteras right now, go stand at the foot of the lighthouse, and go surfing into that curling glass struck with fiery sunlight?

More driving trips, more hunting, more dead animals. He wanted more.

33

Helping in the Greenhouse 2

We got the new sheets of plastic wrapped over the framework. We secured them with thin strips of wood and staples. Chilly wind was already blowing. Leaves swirling around. We worked on into evening by the outside lamps at the corners of the house, the lamps by the door. The shed light threw a widening angle of green-gold onto dark ground.

The greenhouse is a protected place. Under cover. It was time for closing off against the cold. The door would have to be kept shut. The heater would have to be working.

Nights will freeze. Earth is moving, tilting away from the sun. Bowing toward darker days. There will be beautiful winter nights, Corin said. Clear and shining with stars and moonlight and the December meteorites. But these nights will be cold and frosty.

Day will bring sunlight to warm the greenhouse. It will be a capsule of the tropics, where the plants will be safe.

The greenhouse is a great idea. People ought to live out there during the winter.

We hauled the plants to the greenhouse in his old wheelbarrow, one by one, two by two. Some of them were heavy enough. Lift with your legs. That was a rule. Big clay pots, old with mossy green on the outside. Lime tree, lemon tree. Lots of other things. They had spent the summer outside. We helped him get them arranged inside. We got them all in, room for everything, and situated. And with room to get around in there. The two wooden benches fit snug in the corner.

34

Road Running

We run up Gilead Road from my house, against the crazy traffic, through high grass at the roadside. Because when cars are flying past, they don't want to move over and allow human footsteps to touch the road. And then we turn off to a smaller road.

These used to be country roads.

Brandon and I were of few words running in the evenings. This is how we spent our break. We were like the running gods of ancient Greece. It was power, a force between us running together. And your lungs are breathing full of air. It was the way your legs, your feet, your full body moved you forward into the distance of the next step.

As the year turned toward late autumn it was getting darker when we turned around than Mom would have wanted me out in if I was running alone. Not quite twilight. The place where we turn around is a curvy place in the road, up the crest at a field with a lonely mailbox. The field is for sale. We've run on the dirt road that winds through that property. The sign says Keep Out, No Trespassing, and we saw it, but we both knew without saying: we just ran on in and around. We meant no harm and did none.

Just looking. Just running through.

Other people did harm. They left beer cans and bottles and junk and ruts from spinning tires in the mud.

From up there I could picture the house back home. Lights were on in the windows, and I might pretend I was just returning from a walk across the United States or across North Carolina, some huge distance and I was just now making the final steps back home. What would it be like, that final distance of road measured the whole way by nothing but human footsteps?

We see deer grazing in the field edge. What they said to us: this field is still wild. This is the only thing left to us. Go back to your houses, human beings. We are wary of you.

This was the turning around place because it was time to be getting back. Houses up there had lights on. If someone else, from the other direction, had been out running, and turning around there, we would have met them just as we turned around. But no one else was ever there.

Back along the curvy crest, back into the wooded part, back down to the bridge and the creek, back down to the indigo blue and the evening shadows. White tee-shirts, white socks, running shoes aglow.

Back uphill, back at Gilead Road. The cars never stop. The wheels keep turning. But humans go on two feet, walking or running. Not like the animals who go on four. Or more. So take notice, Automobiles. Human Beings are coming among you. Crossing this road. Two Human Beings approaching on foot. Upright. Standing tall like they were made to. Hand shape and leg shadow stride the road as we cross in car light.

Back home, we'd see the windows lit orange and gold and I knew Mom was there making supper. I would still have time to help set the table and stuff like that. Brandon would take the cut through Corin's and through the brush, the secret way, to the Rocks and the Gaunt Jaw, to the place that destroyed everything, the Piney Groves Estates.

35

Streetlight Candles

We came to the glowing spaceship. Golden eyes flickered inside. Fallen sweet gum leaves stuck damp to the outside.

We yelled.

"Course I'm in here," he yelled back. "Come in, come in, and don't stand with the door open."

We hustled in and the door clicked shut.

It was already Thursday night. The greenhouse was different than during the day. Darkness filled all the spaces around us, hid the corners, jelled over the plastic dome. Corin was sitting there with candles burning on the brick floor in front of him. The snugness of the space felt warm enough.

"Come on in. This here's my little home for camping out like."

It was about maybe 10 foot by 10, or 12 by 12. The two wooden benches had room enough to sit on.

And it was a jungle, packed with the plants. Tall plants and small plants, all organized, with a passage down the middle.

"Come and have a seat, lads. This here's just an old man's occupation."

A drip of water hit the back of my neck. This place was membranous and clammy. Like we were tiny things inside a microscopic cell. But when we'd been working in here it made us cough and spit, so dry and dusty in the afternoon sun, getting all the weeds and grass out of it and sweeping up and hauling the big potted plants in.

Corin with a pocketknife was carving one of the candles. Some of them were half melted. He was cutting in to get to the wick so he could light them now.

"You'll think it's a waste, bothering like this with old candles. Just throw them out and get new ones, you'd say."

We hadn't said anything. I wasn't thinking that. We were just watching him. The other candles were burning, flickering on the brick floor. The place felt like a cave, a little grotto. A little chapel. He picked and jabbed and cut at the wax for a few minutes. He didn't say anything, just kept trimming and whittling. The candlelight created his face from the shadowy darkness, shaped lines at the eyes and mouth.

"I thought you had lights in here, Corin. Electricity."

"Oh I do, sure enough, right there behind you. But this is nicer. It won't disturb the plants, you see. They're sleeping. I sleep out here some nights, just once and a while, now and then. Well I used to. Well, one time I did. Just to see what it was like. Just think of all the good air in here. This is the air of the tropics, lads. Breath it in!"

He took a deep breath.

I breathed in. I felt my lungs rising. I breathed the air back out slowly. Now it was carbon dioxide. Now the plants could breath it in.

"Here," Corin motioned, hovering his hand round and round over the lit candle flames, a wizard working magic. "Put your hand just so, right above the flame, just right about here."

I stretched out my hand flat there, above the candles. Not too close. Warm air was rising straight up into my hand. Like a force flowing upward.

"Another little bit of warmth on a chilly night. No, it's not much. But do you know, year before last, when we had snow and we lost power for a couple of nights, you'll remember it Chris, I think, only thing I had to keep this greenhouse warm those nights was three old candles. Just three. Just like these here. They burned all those nights through. Never went out. I'd look out the window in the middle of the night, out in the lonely dark hours, and they'd still be burning. And that little heat you feel rising was what filled this little room with enough warmth to keep my plants alive.

"But tonight I'm just getting them ready. This little heater works just fine. And it's not that cold anyway, tonight. OK, now. Let's see."

He took a little dry straw, old grass, broke it and stuck it to one of the flames. It lit, a new flame, and he touched it to the wick of the candle he was working on. We were facing around the candles like people at a campfire, our faces huge and bright. I held my breath without even thinking about it, not to blow out the little flame. The tiniest flame in the world sat glimmering on the candle wick. I didn't know a fire could be so small. It was too small.

He cut away some more wax.

"Yes, this is a crazy thing to do. Anybody would say I'm wasting my time."

"No, you're not."

"No," we said.

He lit the piece of straw again, relit the candle wick.

The little flame sat on the wick, again. And went out again after a few seconds.

"This is what people do when they've no idea what else to do," he winked.

"No, it's OK to do this," I said.

"You see, I'm trying to not cut away too much wax. My Dear One used to call me a slave to this greenhouse. All the trouble I put myself to. Out here watering plants, summer and winter, moving them in, moving them out, keeping them warm all winter long. I've left my warm bed many a night and come out here, middle of the night, seeing to them, making sure the heater's running, those deep cold nights in January and February."

This time the candle took a flame that grew tall.

"Yes," he said. "Breath of the tropics. That's heliotrope. Have you seen it before? From the mountains of Peru. Are they green hills? I don't know. Never been there. They're the hills where the Inca ran on pathways for a thousand years."

"Those are different sages. Some from Brazil, some from Mexico. Central America. Hummingbirds love them."

"How'd you get them? How did you know about them? You haven't been to all those places?"

"No, I haven't. But people have gone around the world just for the sake of looking for plants. And they bring back seeds or cuttings, and grow the plants, maybe in a little glasshouse or in a garden."

Now I saw what this room was: a little island of live plants from parts of the world far away, precarious and stranded in a cold winter country.

The night sky as I went home, the known stars of our hemisphere, made a familiar flag over me. The streetlights way up Gilead Road at the Interstate danced like piano music, circles of blue hovering in the dark. I did remember the power being off a couple winters ago. We had all eaten together, at Corin's house and ours, and that was before Mrs. Sarah had been so sick and died.

36

The Hayfield

Mom said one of the Davis boys called. They're hauling hay. They would pay me and probably feed me and they were good to work for, nice folks, and we had known their family from before I knew of. So of course I would. And it would be kind of bad manners to say no, since I was able, and they had asked. And, he had said, if I knew any buddies who could come along too, maybe one or two, they had enough to do and could use the help and of course pay them too.

So of course. Let's see what the Colorado boy makes of this. Nothing is really like a fine hay field, in chilly weather, when the sky is bright and a breeze is blowing. The work is good for you, not too hard, just hard enough. The mowers have already gone around, cutting the high grass. The sunny weather dries it out, and they come on a tractor pulling a rake to flip the hay, finish its drying. Then they come again and rake it, shape it up into a neat row, mounded up to the right height for the baler, round and round snaking all over the field. All that takes a few days, depending on how fast it dries out, and how big the field is and all that. Then they come with the balers, running along that little path of mounded hay. The hay gets swept up into the baler, baled inside the machine and tied with twine, and falls out the back baled up and ready. That's what would be our job, to follow around after a tractor pulling a hay wagon, throwing each and every bale up onto the trailer, all over the whole field. One of them would be up there to catch it and place it neatly in the trailer. So all it amounts to is walking around a mowed field, lifting and swinging up a slightly heavy bale, and enjoying the perfectness of the whole place.

What is perfect about it: the smell of cut grass and hay, for one thing. Why does it smell so good? It is a kind of sweetness. Is that why animals eat it? Grass is related to corn and to sugar cane. And the smell of the tractor fuel. Something is sweet about it too, and it mixes slightly but not too much with the smell of the grass. Something is perfect too about being out in a broad field of grass on purpose, for a purpose. You enjoy it and you also enjoy it more because you know you have to because you know your being out there will end. It is for a limited time. And the field feels clean, all the grass. It isn't dirt or briers or anything objectionable. You feel you could just lay down, under the open sky, and it's always pleasant weather or you wouldn't be out there.

So we are out there working. Brandon is fine. He works just as hard as you would want him to. He's really helping. No problems. Nothing weird. They were teasing him and joking, so I knew I had brought a good worker with me. If he wasn't, they would have just kept quiet the whole time and been glad when it came time to be rid of him. And we worked hard. It was perfect weather, cool, not cold. It feels good to do work like that.

Then, it was past normal supper time, which was fine. Mom and Dad knew where I was and they knew how you just had to keep on until you finished something like that, so they weren't expecting me until whenever I got home anyway. And the Davis's, several of the brothers and some of their cousins or somebody was up there, and they brought out a grill into the yard right where we were coming off the field toward the barns. They had a table set up and drinks under the trees and everything. And they were going to grill hamburgers right there, and they were already started when we got there, and it smelled so good. You could see the flames in the grill just glowing up even from out in the field, it was starting to get twilight, and I was so hungry and the smoky smell of grilling burgers was just making me so much hungrier. I could eat five of those right now, I said out loud, realizing my rudeness as the words spilled from my mouth. And of course they invited us to stay. They probably would have anyway. It was like the banquet of the lost sheep of Israel, tired and hungry men rejoicing from the fields and nobody had to worry about how clean your hands were or anything, we just devoured these burgers, and corn on the cob and potatoes grilled on the grill. I didn't even think about Brandon at all. I was caught up in the joking of the Davis brothers, who always teased people and had all their farm jokes that were designed to rib you and prove you were a 'city boy,' no matter who you were, if you didn't live on a farm like them. Sam took up one of my gloves and said if that was his, he'd throw it as far away from himself as he could throw. Because it didn't fit me right, and kept folding over my fingers whenever I picked up a bale. I hadn't even cared about it, but he had noticed it. You could have done a whole lot more work with gloves that fit, he joked. I knew it was just their way of joking. I just had to laugh along with them, because I never knew what to say.

And I looked over at Brandon. Sitting there with slaw and bread, potatoes and corn. OK. That's not a bad meal. I guess I was used to that from him by now. How anybody could resist the overpowering smoky smell of the burgers, I don't know, but he did it. It was what he believed in and it was OK. But what they would think, I thought I knew. Sam came up with a burger for him.

"You sure you don't want one of these, buddy? I know you got to be hungry by now. I would eat that thing down in a second."

"No, I don't. I'm OK. I'm fine with all this. It's great. Thank you."

He won't even eat a burger. I could feel them thinking that.

"OK," Jim said. "I see how it is. You don't like our food. I see." All he really wanted was to understand.

And Brandon never turned down the opportunity to explain to an audience about being a vegetarian. I felt my face burn red hot when he started on about the way meat is bad for you. You are talking to people who raise cows, I was thinking. You are sitting here at their table telling them this. But he went on. Like it was his God given audience. His Colorado accent was like a metal scrape blade cutting the air.

And in the end, it was his hard work in the field that made it OK. They were OK with his weird eating. They said so. They said, well, you are a strange one like I've never seen before, but you did do a fine afternoon of work out there and we'd be glad to have you back sometime.

37

Vagabonds of the Blood

While I had been gallivanting around with Brandon, Mom and Dad had finished all the painting. I hadn't helped them, and now it was time to put the new carpet down.

Mom said I had one more night to finish to my drawing, no matter how tired I might be. So now it was the prehistoric hominids. The other side of the human lineage.

But there were more of them than would fit on the staircase. I had to choose a few.

And I had to depend on the library books to know how they looked. So it occurred to me as I was drawing that I was copying someone else. But that was just one more criminal act I could add to the cafeteria fighting, and the fact that I was associating with these unholy hominids at all. And I had got shot at by Corin.

I drew the first facing right, the next left, and so on. I put the names with them, these powerful words. Names we have given to unseen bodies yielding from the earth.

Australopithecus afarensis
Australopithecus africanus
Homo habilis
Homo erectus.

Could there have been a time without human beings to give names to things? The world of animals and birds and plants with no human being anywhere to know about it and think about it and say a name and write it down?

The boards rumbled as the graphite ran over the grains of wood. Drawing is powerful. It can mesmerize you. Put your face down close as you work. You see the line being made. I knew I was doing the same thing some of the most ancient people did. Some of them drew animals. They crawled deep into caverns. They took a burning torch into the rock, into dark twisting passages. They took charcoal from the fire and drew animals on stone cavern walls. They took ochre from the ground. I heard them breathing with me, at my shoulder as I drew. Why did they draw? They had seen animals and they were able to draw them. So I held my graphite. It was a mineral too, brought up from inside the Earth. I heard it rumble on the pine boards as the lines came grumbling out.

Here I was, calling these forbidden Hominids. Drawing them down to this house, down to our stairway. Bringing them near from all their distance, where they lived beyond memory, forgotten in a twilight. I made my pictures look like that: faces looking out of the dark eons. Faces from so far back we wouldn't know how to recognize our own. Here they were, breathing beside me. I heard their sounds. They had voices. I wanted to know their rugged faces. What kind of life did they live? Did they scream like chimps? Did they cry and love and have good will toward each other? Did they give glory to God as they understood things? I felt rebel blood surging through me. These are your people, Martin. Like it or not. They existed. They are our blood relatives. Don't turn your back on them. They belong to us and we belong to them.

Drawing all this, I had to look carefully. Each Hominid was different. Each one represented how many years?

I looked back up the length of the staircase. My drawing wasn't perfect, but it wasn't bad. Now here were these ancestors alongside the scenes from the Garden. Adam and Eve. The Trees. The Serpent. A human hand reaching for the apple. And they were exposed, naked, for what they are. Not God. But not animals either. And then Cain standing over dead Abel, at the place where human blood spoke from the ground. Human violence happened.

Two lines, two stories. Both going up the staircase. The herd of gnu I had drawn first ran between them. Creatures of land running, migrating, chomping grass, alongside us all the time that this human story has gone on.

Let Brandon impress girls with the Wild Hunt. My project was a landmark. The Human Staircase. When Muriel got back from Washington she would be astonished.

But the drawings were just one part of this. I got Dad's camera and clicked pictures. I got the whole staircase, and I got each individual drawing. These photos would be what I turned in. I couldn't turn in the staircase. It never occurred to me then to see about inviting Mr. Collins to come see it. He might have come. The roll of film had 24 exposures and I used all of them. That would be just about it. I was finished. I couldn't stop looking at it. Over and over, top to bottom, bottom to top. It all went together. I couldn't believe I had drawn all of that. I wouldn't have if they hadn't made me do it. But now that I had done it, I loved it.

I still had to write something about it, but that would all come together. No problem.

Brandon said one more hunting trip. At the gas station he went in to pay while I put gas into the tank.

When we crossed the Gilead bridge, the Interstate below us was at a crawl, an artery circulating its blood in slow motion. Me and Brandon, soaring overhead, were wandering particles. Vagabonds of the blood. We had just passed over the heads and bodies and beating hearts of people without them even knowing. Maybe one of them looked up and said "there goes a little blue car over the bridge. I wonder where they're going. I wonder who that is."

Then we were on country roads, curvy roads, gravel roads only a local person knows. We were like a TV commercial for cars. We crested over open hills. We shadowed the roadways where trees canopy over. Out here was just the same as everywhere else: farmland and woodland, relics of our local storybook America, being devoured by new houses, shopping centers, new neighborhoods. How much more before all of the land is gone? Corin said the forest is always ready to come back. Always waiting. But couldn't we push it too far? We came to a place where the machines were ripping down trees, right then. No point getting so upset about it, Dad had told me. But I couldn't help it. Hatred rushed through me. My face got hot with anger. The rapid motion of driving made me feel free and untouchable, and I screamed fury at them from the window as we passed.

The road ran down hill, a dark curve. A little bridge double thudded under the car wheels and then everything opened up into wide pasture on either side and barbed wire, honeysuckle and cedar trees.

"Up there," Brandon was pointing. "Something big."

We flashed past it as I slowed down and pulled off. The roadside banked up to a fence. Brandon the Hunter was quick as ever. He had his eye to the camera before I even got away from the car.

I'm watching for you, I said.

A deer. The most magical animal of all for a hunter.

The closest I ever came to a herd of deer, I felt like I was seeing angels. I wanted to run and tell Mom and Dad but I knew if I stood up the deer would all run away, so I stayed crouched down. I didn't have any idea of killing them. It was a whole herd, maybe ten or fifteen or more, in the dark, coming from the Out Back. I didn't even see them at first. I heard them, and I waited. I could feel my whole upper body swaying with my heart beats. The deer were coming closer, not stopping. They didn't know I was there. They didn't hear me, didn't smell me. I could hear their teeth tearing mouthfuls of grass from the ground. Will they walk right up to me? Will I be crouched here while they surround me? Closer and closer, and I could see that they were shaped half out of moonlight and half out of shadow.

But I had to move because my knees were breaking. I changed my position as slowly as I could but within seconds the deer knew, and burst away, repelled from me. Gone like somebody blowing out candles. A couple of shimmering leaps and they had all passed together through a veil of darkness.

But now here in broad daylight I could look at a deer all I wanted, see how it was made. Look it in the eye or look in its ear. This deer looked like she couldn't even be hurt. Her eyes were open, like she would jump up at any moment.

Her eye was not the eye of fear. It was looking straight ahead, like she was going on forever. I waited for tender words to come out of her mouth that could match the look of her eye. "I know what I am about," she said. "It is the way of things that I will die. I belong to the natural world. Let me be uncomplicated. Let me return." Her eyes were lit with that tenderness even if tenderness seemed like the opposite word for strength. It was the only word I had for it. It was nobility.

"Hey Chris."

Brandon was standing on the bank above me. He pointed across the field, through the fence.

I grappled up the rough grass and saw a group of deer, six, standing across the pasture at the edge of some trees. Not far from us. Staring in our direction.

"They know," Brandon whispered.

I looked back at the doe, and a car roared past, radio blaring out of open windows. I saw a face blurred with open mouth yelling words at us that sang into the windy rush of motion. The horn's blare flattened away into the motion of the road.

"Idiot!" I yelled. I turned just in time to see the white tails of the herd flicker in the shadows.

Back in the car Brandon said, "They can always tell people who eat meat, you know."

"What? How?"

"Smell. A bad smell comes through your skin."

I sniffed my arm and frowned at him.

"I don't smell."

No different from anyone else. They ran away because of that car, anyway.

Back at home Mom invited Brandon for supper but he said he couldn't stay. We were in the driveway and started trying to dunk, trying to grab the rim on our loose basketball goal and just messing around. He said something about going to his mom's over the weekend. He said it was going to be a nightmare. Then right before he left he turned back and said I was lucky and I ought to be happy. I thought that seemed weird but I said yeah, I guess so.

On Monday break would be over. I still had homework I hadn't even thought about. It wasn't till I got back in the kitchen that I realized Mom had invited Brandon to eat chicken for supper with us.

"Mom?"

"Oh, I didn't even think about it. He didn't say anything, did he? It's OK, honey, I'm sure it's fine. He probably deals with that all the time."

"Yeah, he does, I've seen him."

"Well, I didn't mean to forget. I'll invite him another time and make sure it's something he'll want to eat. It does seem a lot to have to think about though, all the things you couldn't eat, if you were doing that. Sure does seem like a complicated life."

After supper Dad said it was time to start getting the carpet padding down. Time to get on with this.

The good thing was that we were using staples, not glue. So my drawings would still be there, not messed up with glue, and at some distant day there might be a time when we would take up this carpet, when it got old, and then I could see my pictures again. So now it was time for the blue green waters to roll down and flood everything. Adam and Eve, Cain and Abel, the Trees in the Garden, the Serpent. *Homo erectus, Australopithecus, Homo habilis.* And the little herd of gnu who ran between this double helix of human timelines.

On my way upstairs after supper I just had the light coming up behind me from below, and at about halfway up the steps, a brilliant star or maybe a planet was lined up perfect in the hall window above me, in the crystal blue that comes before the darker dark. A planet was being born from among the hickory branches outside, to wander upward into wider sky as the night drew on. And if someone famous could write a bunch of symphonies to the planets, then my project was going to be fine.

38

Why

That night Muriel's violin sang out in the woods behind the school. Half-birds I'd drawn tried to burst out from the treetops but clung, half-made, not yet fully formed. A crow called, his raw language just beginning to take shape.

The deer was there.

"We found your body," I told her.

"I followed the way of all life," she said. Her mouth looked small as she spoke. "I fell and the earth met me and the breath rose out and did not return. The earth received my body. Do not say that my blood did not speak from the ground. My blood runs now in my people."

I woke, burning hot with too many blankets. I stood looking out my window. Why are we in this scheme where somebody has to die? I had already tumbled my mind about the dead animals and the cars and being a vegetarian and chopping kale plants to death and the deer hunters who just wanted antlers. Something was going to die no matter what. And then all of us would die too, lying in the earth one day being walked over by the next generations of people. Layers of earth would eventually cover all memory of us. How many people remember their own relatives, say, seven or eight generations back? The remains of ancient people might be under us right now and we would not know it.

Trees outside moved in the wind, like so many hands reaching up into the heavens. I got back into bed and let the quiet darkness come up all around me.

The hunters would say they would eat the meat they shot. The car drivers would say they have to get to work to make a living. The kale would say you're eating my leaves, my body, and killing me instead of killing an animal. Maybe the deer would say the grass it ate would grow back. The vegetarians would say the kale doesn't suffer. It feels no pain. And the deer hunters would say if we don't kill some of the deer, all of them will die from diseases and over-population. Some people would say that edible animals are here to supply us with food, and it is a gift to us.

Part of me agreed with Brandon. I didn't like the idea of killing animals. If it was up to me to run a knife across an animal's throat or to shoot a bullet into its head, I don't know if I would do it. Would it be hard to be content with just eating beans and corn while others were roasting pork over the fire? I had not starved before. Real hunger might make me do things I didn't know I would do. It might overthrow my mind and my ideas and my beliefs. Brandon was taking a stand to do something he believed in. He had been standing there with us in the hayfield smelling great food just like I was. He must have been getting hungry from it. I couldn't see how anyone wouldn't want to eat that. He was just depriving himself on purpose. Maybe that was a way to live with it in your face all the time: the fact that something's wrong. Something has to die. Because I couldn't keep from thinking that: Something is wrong. Even eating corn or peas means killing seeds, killing potential plants, taking life. And how could Brandon go through life being so different? Like Mom said, making everything so complicated? You could never be at ease and just join in with people when they said 'come and eat with us, celebrate, let's enjoy good food.' You'd always be having to wonder if what they would offer you was going to mess you up, mess up your beliefs.

But other people would say nothing's wrong, it's just the way life is, enjoy the good food of life on earth and don't be so troubled. Don't trouble yourself. You're thinking too much.

I smelled the skin of my arm again. I had eaten meat, but I couldn't smell anything unusual. Faint traces of the soap I'd used in the shower. Nothing offensive.

Rain poured down all weekend. At night, in between the rain showers, fogs rose up and separated everything from the ground. All the houses, buildings, woods and trees, everything was dark and grey. Dad and I drove across the Interstate to the shopping center to get milk and other stuff for the weekend. People were staying in. The streetlights and parking lot lights were caught in their own globes of mist under a low orange sky. At the drugstore I filled out a film envelope, slipped my film cartridge in, sealed it, let it drop into the bin of things to be developed, and that was it: as good as done.

Along the road tree branches and power lines marked out black arms, black lines. From the dark edges at our backdoor light came the trickling sound of dripping water.

I worked on French, English, history, math and the paper for the project. Mom did a lot of reading and some sewing, sitting on the couch in the golden dome of lamplight. Dad was working on some of his stuff. By Saturday night we had all the carpet padding down.

On Sunday afternoon I drove back to where we had found the deer. I wanted to look at it again, for some reason, like that would tell me something. But the deer was gone. Where it had been was the perfect shape of its body embedded in the grass, like it had sunk away whole into the ground and left a shadow-impression of itself.

39

Devastating Photos

Deep plunges of cold air in the dark of Sunday night pushed away the soft blur of weekend mist and rain. Break was over and we were back to stark reality, in jackets and sweaters and toboggans, just a few days after running in shorts and no shirts. But it felt good somehow, the deeper cold. Frost sparked on the grass.

I saw Muriel before first period. Just for a minute. She was all in a hurry, telling me everything. The Renaissance music festival in Washington . . . Oliver and the others . . . second place for group performance . . . first place for historic interpretation including their costumes which Muriel helped design. Oliver got top prize for solo performance. Muriel got third. And their group had gone to about a hundred music performances. It was awesome and they all went insane and stayed up all night and she couldn't believe they had met some well-known musicians at a reception, and they had real champagne and they had been invited to visit Philadelphia by a professional group.

And what about my project?

"Wouldn't you rather hear all the stuff I did during break? Me and Brandon went . . ."

"I just want to know whether you got yourself together, got your project settled. So you won't be so troubled about it."

"Troubled? I'm fine."

I went over the whole thing, how it was kind of an idea I got from the ancient Maya, a staircase that tells a story. It's about all of us, I said. It's the human story, where we came from, and how we are right now. What we are like. Human origins on one side, and the human place in the scheme of things on the other side. Both on the same staircase.

Like what we had said in English. But Muriel wasn't in my English class.

"Well what are we?"

"Vulnerable to the suggestion that we can be like God. And we have taken on some ways of God. Like Eve. Giving birth. And people can kill. So my project shows both these things, both of these realities about people."

All of that made perfect sense, but she said, "Giving birth? Maybe if I could see it."

"Well," I said, "you could have seen it about three days ago. Now it's all covered up by carpet padding."

"What?"

I explained all of that, and she said, "You mean you did all that work on something that was just going to get covered up?"

"Sure. But I've got pictures of it. I will have soon, at least. It's OK. But don't you like the idea that it's all under there, waiting to be discovered some day by an archaeologist?"

She just rolled her eyes.

I wanted to tell her about the deer and how weird it was, how I could hear it speaking even though it was dead, and then again in the dream. But I didn't.

"It's just like your music," I told her. "You play it and then it disappears forever. All those sound waves spread out across the air and go into people's ears and mix with all the other sounds in the world and nobody can ever hear them again."

"But I can play it again. And besides, people remember it. Music lives in our hearts."

"Well, my staircase is living in my heart, along with all the hominids and Adam and Eve and the trees in the garden. So what about your project?"

"I can't wait. That's my favorite part, when I get to perform. And are you coming to our concert, our symphony concert? You said you would. You better start making plans now to come hear the Planets. It's not far away."

Mr. Blake was letting Brandon work in the dark room during lunch. Developing his pictures would take all week. On the way home he was talking about how he never stopped thinking about them. At night going to sleep he was thinking about them, how they would float in the developing fluid, how the picture would start out faint on the paper, and then grow stronger, and how he would lift them out with tongs, let the fluids drip away, and wash them. They would have a devastating effect. He could remember every single one of them. All these dead animals.

We stopped at the pharmacy to get my pictures. I ripped open the packet right in the parking lot. Those weird seagulls were back. Their baby crying sound was ringing all around us and Brandon was all the way half out of the car window calling back to them, a high gargling throat sound trying to sound like them. Anybody who saw us would instantly know he was out of his mind.

The first photo in the stack had one of those little stickers on it, 'adjust lighting' it said, something about it not being the developer's fault.

The next one did too, and the next and the next. All the same, every single one. They were too dark or too blurry. They might as well have been pictures of a large coffee stain on a black sofa, or of a caramel ghost in the middle of the night. Just a blurry blob of brown surrounded by dark grey and black.

I had grabbed Dad's camera and gone crazy.

I stuffed them back in the packet and cranked the car. Brandon pulled himself back in the window and I began to drive off.

"Where are they? How'd they look?"

"Oh, I don't know. They'll work out somehow."

"Let me see."

"Nah, that's OK. I'll show you later."

I acted normal, just sat there, didn't yell out the window. Didn't say bad words. Just sat there staring. But then I knew. This was my prediction. I had misread it. Not the school, but me, wiped out. Hurricane. Chaac with his knife blade tongue. Huracan, heartless, with his spiral eyes. I felt myself getting hot with embarrassment and anger. It was a disaster, and I couldn't blame anyone but myself. I was supposed to have my school work under control. How could I not be able to do something as simple as take a few pictures?

"Let me see them. What're you trying to hide?"

"OK, take a look at them." I tossed the pack at him without even looking at him.

He looked through them without saying anything, then said, "You've still got time."

"Yeah." My face was hot and red.

"It's just a stupid project for school."

It was my turn to laugh the smirking laugh. "Yeah."

By the time I got home the grip of fear was gnawing in my stomach. I had burned up all this time and now it was all for nothing. I was stuck. Why in the world had I thought that this would work? I loved the drawings, but now they were covered up.

As I got out of the car it occurred to me that I could ask Dad if we could take up the padding and make more photos. The final carpeting wasn't down. It was just the under-padding. I felt like I was sinking. I came up to the door and went in. Dad probably wouldn't mind. I knew he wouldn't. He was easy-going about stuff like that, and the padding hadn't been that much trouble. It would come up easily. And I would offer to do it all myself.

I stepped inside and there was Dad, smiling. Sweat dripping down his face. His shirt was sweaty. The new carpet was making its way down the staircase. It looked really good, really tight, nicely cut and everything. Beautiful. He had taken a day off just for this, to start the carpet. And nobody had been here to help him. He had done over half of it today.

"Hey Chris, nice day at school?"

"Yeah, just fine." I dropped my book bag. The devastating photos were inside. I pulled off my sweatshirt and went out into the kitchen to get something to eat. I would just have to get on with it. Get on with something. I couldn't ask him.

"Wow, Dad. You got a lot done. It looks great."

40

Man Lost at Sea

Dreams come from inside you. That's what health class taught us. Dreams are the way your inner mind, your subconscious, works on its problems.

But some dreams come from somewhere else. They have to. Because you hear words and passages you cannot believe were already inside you. You hear things you would not think of yourself. Things from holy, secret places can come to you.

And that scared me. Because maybe Martin was right.

Maybe God was dealing me a blow. Because I had taken graphite and drawn those hominids down into our house.

In the depth of my sleep a dream came back, same as one I'd had during the hurricane project. I appeared to a man lost at sea. Except this time when I woke I was thinking, that's me I'm looking at, lost and halfway dead.

I hovered over him from banks of fog and he could see me and talk to me and I didn't touch the water. His voice was rusted and croaking, and he held his throat with one hand.

"I died a month ago."

He looked up out of the hold of his broken boat with his eyes big and bright like dark jewels. He was crusted and salt-white, rag-bearded. His hair spiked up from his head in breezing clumps. His clothes were grim and frayed.

"I died a month ago and that yellow fire up yonder burnt clean through me. Burnt me wide open. Skinned the meat right off the bones and I was a little tiny scrap of breath."

He gripped my arm and breathed right up into my face.

"And this little boat give me birth, right here. It give birth to me into a little envelope. Happy are they," he huffed out the words onto me, "happy are them who go down to the sea in ships, and let it be unto me," and then he fell back. His eyes rolled and he whispered to someone else in a rush of breath, "from all the perils we beseech thee." And he opened his mouth wide, gaping.

He pulled back close to me, rolling with the gentle sea surface, "I saw white all around me. I saw white fire leaping off in bright rings."

I see the bright rings. I see the fire. I rise away. And I wake. Heart pounding.

But no. I couldn't blame God. No matter what Martin said. I'm the one who took the pictures. I was holding the camera. I'm the one who didn't know what I was doing.

41

Into the Woods

When you feel desperate weird things happen. You're on the edge. Maybe I fell off. Maybe I got too close to being something I never thought I would be. Not having my schoolwork ready, facing a disaster, I was in a new place.

But going into the woods wasn't anything bad. I mean, we did not do anything bad. I'm not the kind of person who does stuff like that. It was during lunch, and we are allowed to go outside during lunch. I wouldn't have gone if it meant skipping class. I didn't miss any part of any class. It was just during lunch.

I don't know if any teacher ever looks around the cafeteria taking roll for lunch.

Brandon said we could go on the running trail during lunch. It would be OK. He kept saying it like that. It's OK, man. Stop worrying. It's fine. It's no problem. It's OK. It really is. It's nothing to worry about. There are real things to worry about but this is not one of them. He kept saying that stuff. Later on I wondered, What exactly was he trying to do to me?

You just need to shake yourself up so you can get back to normal. Stop worrying about this project. Make a T-shirt design. I've been telling you. You don't even know. You've got it. You don't even know.

So I said OK. I would go. But I was worried we would get caught. He was so calm. So casual. Walking along the side of the practice field. Like it was 100% normal to walk that direction during school. It was allowed for us to be outside. People threw frisbee out there sometimes.

Just walk like you're doing exactly what you're supposed to be doing and anybody who's looking will automatically think you can't be doing anything wrong, Brandon said. Don't skulk around like you know you're doing something wrong. And then when we get near the trail opening, we just make for the shadows in a burst of speed.

We did it just like that. I went out of my head a little bit. My body just automatically did it. I could feel it. My feet just kept walking and there we were and there was the opening, the woods, the shadows and the tree branches and we were bursting into the crunching sound of leaves on the woodland floor. I felt a lash of freedom and fear. It made me dizzy, kept me looking in all directions, hoping not to be caught, suddenly knowing we had crossed through into shadows. It was nothing like being in the woods after school when we were running, when we were supposed to be there. I never stopped worrying, never stopped looking all around. I couldn't get comfortable. My eyesight couldn't rest and be at peace. I could only think about how much trouble I would be in. I could only think about not getting caught. And this was only lunch time. If I let the time slip and I missed class or was late, I wouldn't be able to explain myself.

But it was fun too. Everything was electric and vivid. Time started running in a way it never does during a normal day. I couldn't stop thinking what would I do if something went wrong?

The woods out there are not thick and closed in, except down at the creek sides. You can see ahead for a little ways, see who's coming and stuff like that.

But what did Brandon really want out there? I was magnetically resistant to letting any of the regular school skippers see me. I knew they would be out there. I didn't want to go near them. Because them seeing me would make me one of them. And I'm not one of them. I'm not like them.

At first we stayed on the running trail. The big circle. Brandon started talking about running and the lay out of our school trails, talking about how he plans his running in his mind. It made me realize all over again: I'm not a racer. There's a real difference between how we think about running. I just like being out there. I like the running and I like the woods. I don't care about the blood-thirsty winning. I'm just being alive in the outdoor world. So that made me see, me and Brandon think different.

Only later, I thought maybe he was trying to tell me that I was letting the team down, by me not caring so much. Because that was true, and he had seen it in me. And I did feel bad for a little while but in the end, I had to admit, that's just who I am.

But once we got in there, once the big circle took us toward the highway, Brandon got cautious. He had been so cool when we were in the open, going across the practice field, where any teacher, anybody, could have seen us. Now he kept looking everywhere, watching out, even getting off the trail, going behind heavy drapes of green brier vines down in a low place that was usually wet. He was holding his hand up, like, Be careful. And then he made straight for where the side trail curves down to the creek, where the new elementary school backs up to the woods. Where the school skippers' hideout is. Straight to it. Like he planned it all along. So I didn't go. I stayed back far enough but I kept watching him. What are you doing, I said to him, as he went on ahead. Nothing, he said, looking back at me. Just want to speak to some people. I stayed back, where a trio of oaks are, a place to stay covered. But I could still see. Those girls, I was thinking. I was looking at my watch. There they were. The ones from the coffee shop. Nobody would call them nice girls. Not the way they are. They used to laugh at me back in 6th grade. Now I was nobody to them. He was talking to them. Dude, I was thinking. What are you getting mixed up with? And I thought, you said you needed all your lunch time to work on the pictures?

I could see them but I couldn't hear them. I checked my watch. We needed to get going. If it came down to it, came time to go and he was still over there, I would just have to take off on my own. This was pushing it too far. I could not risk being late.

One of them had on a t-shirt, black with a red "Wild West Nights" right across the front, and a picture of a whiskey bottle. Leaves or feathers tied in her hair. Then her friend came up. Linda. She had dark eye makeup and purple feathers in a necklace, and a fringe poncho knitted out of yarn that she kept flouncing up with her arms, twirling like a dancer. Making sure he saw her, showing herself. I kept looking back at my watch. I would just have to take off back to the school.

What are you getting into now, I was thinking, as I ran back.

42

People Are Worried

"People are worried. I'm worried."

Muriel had me pressed against my locker next morning. Her look said No Excuses.

"What?"

"People are worried. I'm wondering. Who are you turning into?"

"What are you talking about? I'm the same person I always was!"

What was this? Had her trip to Washington made her so distant that we didn't know each other any more?

'But you aren't. People are talking. You're always with that guy now. You weren't at lunch. And I wanted to tell you all about Washington."

"That guy?"

"Brandon."

"Yeah, Muriel. Brandon. He has a name. Not just 'that guy.' He is a human being."

"So you admit it, you know what I'm talking about. And I didn't say he wasn't human. I'm just saying . . . it seems like all of a sudden you're spending a lot of time with him."

"Well so what? We might be friends. Has anyone thought about that? We're on the team together. You spend a lot of time with all those music people. Oliver? And all of them. Are people worried about that?"

"You know what I'm saying. My symphony friends aren't like Brandon. We've known each other for a long time now. We've been in symphony for several years. And some of us knew each other before that. You've really just met him, Chris. It's just, I'm worried. You aren't like him. You didn't used to be. And . . . I don't want you to . . ."

"To what?"

"Well, I didn't know how to tell you, but people have been talking. Saying they saw you. With him. Going into the woods during lunch. Chris, someone could turn you in. What's going on? Is it true? I'm not even sure I should believe it. And you just got over being in a fight. I didn't think you were one of those kind of people."

"I'm not!"

I just looked away. I'm not. I don't skip school and take drugs and stand around smoking or any of that. Those "kind of people" sit out in the woods all day, rain or shine, in a little hut made of sticks with a broken ping pong table for a roof and a torn up old tarp for a carpet, in a ditch with trash and think they're cool. We run past their hideout every day and see the cigarette butts and drink bottles and food wrappers. And where they use the woods for a toilet. The school had to know about it. Why didn't the school people go out there and bust it all up?

"And, Chris, this guy Brandon, don't you know what he's up to? It's girls in the woods, nude photos, that kind of thing. Is that who you are?"

"Where did you hear something like that?"

"Everybody's saying that. A lot of people. I don't know. Something's not exactly right about him. Just wait. Can't you see it in him?"

"I never saw anything like that, Muriel. Do you think I was doing that? How long have we known each other? Since seventh grade. Me and Brandon were just looking at the running trail. Brandon's one of the fastest runners we have. He's been giving me tips on speed. Because I'm Distance. Just like always. I'm the same person you always knew. Distance. I'm durable. When it comes to speed, I'm terrible. He was just pointing out some things about running with speed. Which I know nothing about. If running were about endurance only, I would be going to the Olympics. We were looking at the trail. It just helps to be out there."

Wow. That sounded so convincing. I wasn't even sure how I'd just said all that. I didn't want to say anything about Brandon talking to those girls. I still didn't know what was going on. I didn't even ask him. I just decided I didn't want to know. And I started to tell Muriel about it. I wanted to. But I didn't know how to say it without making Brandon look like what she already thought he was. And I didn't think that was all there was to Brandon. Even if I couldn't convince Muriel.

But it did make sense. Photos, girls in the woods. And if that was what Brandon was doing, why did he take me along like that? The way he had kept on at me about going out there, if all he wanted was to deal with these girls. I had thought he was trying to cheer me up somehow, like he said, let me see that life was more than one messed up project. I had believed him. And we didn't get caught. So that was good. But someone must have seen us. But unless they came to get me, I wasn't going to worry about it. I had too much to worry about with my messed up project.

And when it comes to running, and whether or not I care enough to be worth it to my team, I ought to make a t-shirt that says "I endure," because that's exactly it. I endure all the way. I don't give up. Muriel used to always ask, how do you run like that? She hates running. In gym class she always does bad. It's all in your head, I'd tell her. In your heart. Inside you. It's a whole landscape inside you. A whole country. It's a place you can go to. It doesn't have to do with what's right there in your eyesight. It's inside you.

How can you explain something like that?

You can get better at it, I told her. Isn't that like music? If you start to falter, you talk to yourself. A voice comes to you. It says, Can you run another 5 minutes? Are you going to tell me that you can't even go 5 more minutes? You've already gone this long and you can't go 5 more minutes? And you keep going. And that voice comes back. It doesn't leave you. Because you know that once you've stopped, 5 minutes is nothing at all. It passes like one breath. But when you're running, time slows down.

"Chris? Where are you? Where did you just go?"

"So how do you play music like you do anyway? How do you practice so much, and how do you get that kind of sound out of that old wooden box?"

"Don't change the subject! You always do that. You zone out like you're a thousand miles away, like you couldn't possibly hear anything, and then when you get back, you're asking me about music."

"Yeah, so? How do you play music like you do, anyway?"

"How do I play it?"

"You play it great. If you didn't know that already. You amaze me, actually."

"OK. Don't try flattering me . . . "

"What!"

"Yeah. I'm still worried. About you."

43

Caracol and Cenote

Worry and fear rushed over me the way a line of fire eats up paper. My face glowed hot and sweat broke out on my scalp. It was pure panic, white-hot fever, the beginning of a sickness. I was glad no one saw me at that moment. I could just sink into myself, head in my hands, my body sinking into the wet ground to become a bed of moss somewhere in the dark woods.

Someone had seen us go into the woods. They might turn us in, like Muriel said. I didn't even to ask who. I just pushed it away from me. And all I really wanted was to tell her how bad my pictures had turned out, but I didn't, because all she would say is "What now?"

There wasn't enough time. We had a math test, my worst subject. We had a huge chunk of Gilgamesh reading for Mr. Collins.

Maybe I was making too much of it. This was a stupid project anyway. It didn't really mean anything. It would be forgotten right away.

But I couldn't convince myself of that.

I kept flipping through books. Maybe there was another idea?

Next day at lunch I went to the art room instead of the cafeteria. Mr. Blake met me at the door.

"Is Brandon in here?" I asked, trying to swallow down a bite of apple. "He was going to show me what he's working on."

"Yeah, OK, but absolutely no food in the dark room. Too many chemicals. Something toxic might jump down your mouth while your back's turned. Sit down and eat and I'll show you in when you're done."

I sat down in the deserted classroom to eat my homemade sandwich. The tabletop looked medieval, dark wood and scratch marks, ink spills and names and doodles.

Mr. Blake had posters on his walls, famous artwork. I knew some of them from French, some Matisse pictures, the jazz stars, a window on the Riviera, a lady playing piano while two boys in striped jackets played checkers.

Student drawings filled a huge cork board.

Then I saw something familiar tacked to the storage room door. I got up to have a look. I couldn't believe he had this.

"Mr. Blake, where'd you get this? It's what we've been studying. I'm doing my project on it, well, kind of. At least I was."

"Amazing, aren't they?" Mr. Blake looked back at me, smiling, speaking loudly over the gushing tap of water gonging into a metal sink where he was washing his hands. He was soaped up to the elbow. He had a short haircut like a teenager, but his hair was touched with silver.

"I got that poster a long time ago, after I had been to the ruins at Chichen Itza. You can see how beat up it is."

"You've actually been there? Did you see the Caracol?"

"Yeah, definitely. You know about that? Wouldn't go all that way and miss that. We went up in it." His eyes widened and brightened and he cut off the water and shook his hands into the sink. He turned toward me toweling his arms and hands.

"Kind of a pilgrimage, you know. We were young and foolish then," he added with a grin.

I saw a younger Mr. Blake, a backpacking hippie maybe, with other teachers like Mr. Collins, hitchhiking all the way to the Yucatan. They reached the edge of jungle in crazy house-painted buses, sleeping in tents and hammocks and living off grubs and leaves and fruit, swimming with electric eels, and then the jungle opened out onto the green plazas of archaeological Chichen Itza, where the saw-tooth pyramids zigzagged out of the treetops. They stepped out onto the hushed lawn looking upward.

"Fabulous," he continued, turning toward something he was working on.

"What was it like, going into it? I mean, like, how big is it? What are the stairs like?"

He laughed. "Oh, it's not very big. It's not like a coliseum or anything. It spirals up on the inside, it's round on the outside. Dark little round hallways.

Sits on a raised plaza. Not tiny, but not a huge building. Little windows on the upper floor. They point the way to important points, astronomical landmarks that the Maya found meaningful. Lined up for viewing the planet Venus and probably the moon. I've forgotten the details. They connect the structure to its environment in a conceptual sense, much the same way it connects visually to the surrounding structures through formal qualities. They respond to the outer world, in this case the Solar System, by allowing that to determine their placement and their purpose. Or some would prefer to think of it is as The Heavens."

"You mean the windows?"

"Well, and the builders."

"So, you think they really planned it all exactly like that?"

"Oh, no question. A building like that is not an experiment to see what shows up in an open window. It's an expression of a long search of the heavens, well, not a search really, more a long span, years, of observation, following the movements of Venus and the moon and other heavenly bodies. They involved the planet Venus in their religion pretty heavily, but to tell you the truth, I haven't kept up with the new ideas people are putting out on it these days. They designed that little building after a seashell, you know. At least that's the theory. Pretty amazing. We do know that conch shells were part of their iconography for Venus in some of the carvings, and there are records of Maya and other South American and Mesoamerican peoples still today blowing conch shells as horns. There are some pyramids that you can stand on and feel vibrations in your feet if someone blows a conch nearby. So the structures apparently incorporate an audible dimension as well as visual. Ingenious. And actually I have recently read an idea that in one pyramid you can clap your hands, and the echo makes the sound of the call of the quetzal bird, another important image for them. Talk about a way to build a holy space. I mean, wow, the building itself responds in a holy voice when the person takes action. I love it. I believe that building was Maya too, but actually, I've forgotten now. Old age, I'm afraid. You ought to get down there someday if you're interested. Planning a career in archaeology?"

"I haven't really thought about it before."

"Well, it's not for the ordinary tourist, maybe, someone looking for luxury. But it's a sight to behold. You want to get there at dawn, or late in the evening, away from the busy day in the heavier tourist seasons."

"Wow. I would like to see it. And what's at the top, does it open up to the sky?"

"No, the roof just slopes up over you. Kind of cramped, actually."

"Oh, yeah."

"It's like those corbel vaults, like in the rooms at the tops of the pyramids. You know about them? That's what's in the passageways of the observatory."

We had learned about corbel vaults and arches. It was where you stair-stepped two sets of blocks toward each other, over you, until they met and supported each other. The space under that became your room or passage-way or whatever you were building.

"And from the main ruins it's a short walk on the Sacbe, the Sacred Causeway, out to the Cenote. Beautiful place. Turquoise blue like a swim-ming pool, about 50 meters down in a cavern, shining with sunlight. Fin-ished eating? Brandon's in there." He pointed to a black plastic cylinder built into the wall. It looked like a dark, round phone booth.

"We are extraordinarily fortunate as a public school to have this," Mr. Blake said. "It was the gift of a benefactor. Very expensive."

It was like outer space transport. You had to stand alone inside the cylinder, arms to your sides. I pulled the handle like he'd shown me, heard a whirring sound, a whisking sound, and I really wasn't sure if it was me mov-ing or the wall. Maybe the floor. Everything was black, pitch dark, and then the wall opened behind me. I felt cool air and smelled the chemicals before I saw anything. I stepped out into dim red light. The Dark Room. Brandon was in his black fleece jacket, leaning over a table full of trays.

"Chris," he whispered. His eyes were intent on the work he was doing, moving a photograph with tongs in a tray of clear liquid.

Even in the low light the photographs were shining. I stood by him looking down at a raccoon. The animal filled the whole page. Its fur was bristling, silver and black. Just to see it there, framed on a page, made it something I had never seen before. Both of us had been there on the road when Brandon took the photo, but he had seen something that I had not seen.

He lifted the wet photograph with the tongs and slipped it into an upright clear container. Water was washing over the photographs floating there.

"They need water," he said. They were dead animals but the way he took the photographs, the way the dark places and the white places worked, they were alive.

The clear container was gurgling softly as it washed them, and I saw the animals' eyes shining out from the water.

At practice, I just ran. I tried to enter the distance. In a daze. I didn't even know where we were. Think of all the kids you've ever known, I told myself, who joked so much about not doing their homework, sounding so cool, waving their F papers like trophies out on the sidewalk in front of the buses. Like failing was good for them. Now I was looking at that kind of attitude for myself, and I didn't want it. It wasn't me. Maybe something was wrong with me? I didn't want a bad grade.

At home Dad was making the carpet look good, like a professional had done it. It felt springy to my sock feet. The new smell filled the house. I helped after supper. We had to pull as tightly as possible and try to hold it down for the staples to bite. Then I went to my room to do my homework. I had been joking when I told Muriel this would be the downfall of my life. Or whatever it was I had said. The hurricane. Now it really was. I was going to be embarrassed. That was it. Embarrassment. All those kids at the lunch table. The music people always had themselves together. All they had to do was keep practicing. The plan was always laid out for them. Put the music in front of you and go to it. Delve in, dive in, be submersed. Live in the world of music, and you get to live with Bach and Beethoven and all those people. And the church people, they always knew everything. They never experience any kind of doubt. They were comfortable.

What in the world had I been thinking when I took those pictures? Time was speeding up, like water swirling down the bathtub drain. Faster and faster the closer it got to being gone. The drain was a gorging mouth and I was the drowning man locked in the swirl.

At the end of our running that day I was at the back, letting them get farther and farther ahead. I took a quick turn into the trees before anybody knew it. Somehow that might help me. The few towering poplar trees. The little chapels between them. The high places where late sunlight came through the trunks and shadow covered you at the ground.

When Gilgamesh and Enkidu entered the Pine Forest to chop down trees, the guardian Huwawa tried to fend them off. He roared, and his voice roared like the sound of a waterfall. He had the frightening face of a lion. But Gilgamesh and Enkidu were stronger. The sun god Shamash helped them. Shamash sent thirteen winds to blow against Huwawa, and Huwawa was beat. So he tried to bargain with them. Make a deal. I'll give you some trees if you'll leave the forest. And Gilgamesh was willing to. But Enkidu said no. He thought it was a trick. And in the end, Gilgamesh and Enkidu took Huwawa's life and then they took all the trees they wanted. They tied the trees together to make a raft and floated away down the river, and from the wood of those trees they made a huge unbelievable door for some palace or temple.

Maybe the Caracol? Was there any project I could do about it? It was in my mind now, the spiral that led up to the heavens. I wanted to build one.

And maybe—the Jaguar? You said I could call you Inha. And that shimmering thing, Hummingbird the butterfly?

Either come and help me, or send a puma here to kill me in the woods, and let me be finished. Let me lie still on the surface of the Earth, like an uncomplicated deer who knew his time. The way of all life. Until I disappear.

Out there on our running trail in the woods behind the school.

44

Seraph

I went back to the library Wednesday during lunch. I had to. Another book was waiting there. I had seen it before, but it was old and plain, and I had not bothered to look at it. But now I was grasping for help.

This old book had pictures, all in black and white, little ink drawings. No photos. Nothing to catch your eye. It was from sometime like 1905. It hadn't been checked out for over thirty years. How old was this school, anyway? I found it again, right where I'd seen it before. It was in no danger of being checked out. Nobody would come looking for it. But all this time, I had been making the mistake of judging a book by its plain, faded cover. I slid into a seat at a corner table near the windows. No one else was even in the library. The librarians were behind their glass, in their sanctuary eating yogurt or something. And just a few yards away from all this quiet, all this solitude, through the wall and across the atrium students were in the cafeteria talking and jabbering and cutting up.

"Right, Chris," I smiled to myself, "you really are dumb."

This book had something I had found nowhere else: cut-away views of the Caracol. It showed the inside hallways. The drawings were little, old-fashioned, black ink drawings. Not photographs. Some person way back then had sat down and patiently drawn this, line by line, dipping a pen into a bottle of ink. What had Muriel said? In the quiet of the room, sitting at a corner table, my eyes traced over the lines of these ink drawings. I felt myself grow calm. I was paying attention to these old pictures. And there standing by me as I looked was the patient man who had drawn these same lines long ago. His hand was on my shoulder. And here I was sitting still beside him, on blocks of ancient stone, in the Yucatan, at Chichen Itza, at the Caracol. I heard the scratch of the pen, heard the metal nib tap the glass of the ink bottle. He was making his quiet observations.

Thank you, I whispered.

One side-view showed four hallways, ceilinged over with corbel arches, and I thought these hallways must wind around, that's the famous spiral. But then an overhead cut-away view showed that they were two circular hallways, one outer and one inner, concentric circles connecting to each other by four doorways. Which wasn't a spiral, wasn't like a seashell, not exactly. Was the Caracol not really like a sea shell, after all, after what I had heard and read?

But it was.

In the middle of these circles was a stocky core, a central pillar. It was within that core that you curled around through a true spiraling passage, up to a higher level where windows opened out. So that was the seashell, the 'caracol.' It really was an ancient, secret spiral, deep within this stout core. From the drawings it looked like a passage cut into solid stone, and still there, even though a lot of the building was in ruins. To get into that spiral you had to get up about 10 feet, as high as a basketball goal, to an opening about the size of an ordinary house window, it looked like. I could hit a basketball goal with the tip of my fingers, but I could not grab the rim with my hand. What's the point of having a door you can't get into?

At the upper level were windows, where the stars and planets and the moon appeared in their right seasons. Some of these windows were aligned with sunrise or moonrise on the Equinoxes or with the stations of the Planet Venus. At this desperate moment it was too tedious to read through all that. It wasn't the astronomy or any astrology that I cared about. I just wanted what my mind instantly gave me: the ancient stargazers up there, ingenious in their observations and their calculations, having built this place to line up with the motions of the heavens, this sea spiral, their faces appearing in the frames of the windows at the proper times for observing. Finally, at the right moment, the moon would be rising, robust, smooth, and beaming over the tree tops. Moonlight would fall in through the window, curve round the seashell walls. Maybe they had polished the inner stone, made it like a real shell, and then the moon shining on that smooth surface would fill that place all the way down through the core with glowing white moonlight.

I spoke harshly to myself. Put my hands to my head. Maybe I could have built an observatory. I could have built a short, spiraling stairway. Not out of stone, but we had a bunch of old lumber in our shed. And we had enough space in our back yard.

Mr. Blake had said something about the Sacbe, the sacred walkway. I saw it on the book's map of the ruins at Chichen Itza. It led to the Sacred Cenote, one of the underground pools that formed over ages, where rainwater washed away the limestone. The city was named for this cenote: The Mouth of the Well of the Itza. The Sacbe was not a road to be taken lightly. The Cenote was a perilous place. People made sacrifices there.

The old book had a good picture of Chaac. His eyes were spinning round. Hypnotized by a hurricane. Or was he using his eyes to spin a hurricane? His nostrils flared, his breath steaming out.

Then, in another section of the book, the word 'blood-letting' caught my eye. The picture showed a stone tablet, a "stele." The carving on the tablet was hard to figure. At first it looked like swirling lines and decorations. I looked long to find a human face, and even then in all the catching eyes of other beings and the swirling lines I had to keep finding my way back to that human face. The human's eyes were closed, the head upturned. The caption said they used bloodlettings as a way to get a vision. Above this person hovered another person emerging from the mouth of a dragon, or was it a bird, or a decorated snake, I couldn't tell, but it was about to pierce the head of the human with a spear. I had already heard something like this: the burning seraphim from church. And Mr. Collins had talked about seraphim too when he was telling us how cherubim weren't little babies flying around. The seraphim were winged fiery beings within the elements of air and fire. Burning. It was a seraph of six wings who reached down and touched a live burning coal from the temple altar and put it to the prophet Isaiah's mouth.

Here am I, Isaiah had said, a man of unclean lips, and my people are unclean people. The burning coal took away his uncleanness, according to the seraph.

The Maya king went up to the top of a pyramid, to the little hut-shaped room on top, for the bloodletting. He would have to pierce himself with a stingray spine or with a sharp needle of obsidian right in his most delicate parts. Or use a shark tooth. He would drip his own blood onto a piece of paper, and they would burn the paper, maybe a priest would, and the smoke from that burning would go up among spirits, among the ancestors. To bring a message from the spirit world.

Maybe they were not so different from Isaiah. Maybe the Maya person was saying, "I need help from another dimension. I need help from beyond myself."

The bell rang. I hurried to the desk to check out the book. The librarian looked up, shocked to see someone in the library, the same librarian I had annoyed during break.

Bloodletting. It was so extreme and desperate. It seemed dirty somehow, the more I considered it. Too desperate. Like you couldn't get comfortable back at home anymore after you've done something like that. You would have scars. Like people taking drugs or something. It seemed illicit. This is not something to do in real life. It was too much. You could infect yourself and die. I put away that idea. Just like nobody should take a live hot coal after reading the Bible and touch it to their mouth. Only holy beings are permitted to handle things like that.

But when an idea came, would it pierce my head like a spear?

Maybe this afternoon, in my running, I could run myself into the extreme, run so hard I would come into a vision of some kind. Run myself so hard I would start ideas flowing from deep within me. Or from outside me? Maybe that was the point of bloodletting. Opening yourself up. It didn't have to be literal. Was I that desperate? Could I push myself to it, or did I have to wait for it to come to me? How could you know what you might end up with?

45

Cherub

Chilly Wednesday night I slumped in the circle of light from my desk lamp. I had to seal myself in and get this work done. The weather people were calling for wintry mix, at the weekend, maybe sleet, maybe snow, maybe freezing rain. It was too much to hope the wintry mix would come in time to rescue me from the project deadline, that it would bless us with a day out of school. The deadline would come to blast me, and the wintry mix would build a tomb of ice around my corpse.

Where I should have found math notes in my notebook I saw pumas and jaguars staring out of dark places. I saw half-men half-jaguars running and leaping. I saw hurricanes and the sun, planets and solar system turning their turns. So I held the paper of math problems up to the warm light bulb. Let it ignite and burn away into smoke and ash.

I took up one of the books from the library and just sat there, letting my tired eyes dwell on the pictures.

These Jaguar Men. Were they shamans, enchanters, story-tellers, priests? Were they half man, half jaguar, like, did wearing the pelt make you take on part of each? Sometimes the jaguar suit covered the whole body, like pajamas. Another picture showed the pelt of a jaguar draped over the man's back. The jaguar head was his headdress, open-mouthed, studded with teeth. The jaguar face creased and growled, the eyes a dark void, a dream life.

But it's hard to know exactly what ancient people thought about it. Experts make educated guesses. When I looked up Ezekiel like Mr. Collins had said, I found cherubim in the temple of Jerusalem that were half man, half lion. They stood among palm trees. The notes said they stood guard in holy places. The jaguar, and sometimes the puma, guarded the entrance to the Underworld. They were able to go from this world into the Underworld. They fought the water dragons, the crocodiles. They were able to go above the earth, and under the earth, and into the deep places inside the earth. The jaguar was as the sun, a nocturnal sun, as it moved through the night under the earth. And so for the man who wore a jaguar skin?

There are openings to the Underworld: the caverns in a mountainside, and the cenotes. Openings bright with water, openings black with darkness. Passages that take you to places you would not want to go, cold places or burning hot places. Tight spaces where you can barely move, where you start to think you will never get back to the surface and the light and blue sky and nice clean air.

In the Maya stories, it was related to the planting of corn. How a seed goes into the earth, the mystery in the dark, where the seed dies but a plant grows up into the light. And how new seeds grow from that plant, and people eat corn and live, and people are made of corn.

But to get hold of a jaguar skin? It was power. You would have to kill a jaguar. But how? Burn it with torches, or pierce it with a spear? It was hard to understand. Was it really acceptable to kill a jaguar, something so important?

Look at a jaguar. The face, the strength, the jaws, the muscles. You would die. Your skull would be crushed. The ground would be marked by a trail where the jaguar dragged you. The spots on the fur, mesmerizing, not spots at all, except for on his legs and head. They were open circles, clouds, oblong shapes. They were wandering thoughts, the way you let a brush with ink make its own marks.

And that's when I saw it.

The jaguar's circles and spots were like the Maya writing. They were rounded shapes, little pictures grouped in round-cornered squares, shapes and pictures side by side. It couldn't be a coincidence? Could they have designed their way of writing from looking at a jaguar's marks?

Words written on the pelt of a fiery cat. He enters the passages inside the Earth, alive even underground. He goes into a person's thoughts and comes out with writing on him. The sun goes down and the sun comes up. Plants grow out alive of the earth. And it is Night, and it is Day. The earth turning, the sun blazing. The sapphire sky, the deep indigo of night. The daylight sky a solid blue stone star-struck to blinding splendor.

Muriel was always telling me "Day" is just us being up close to a star. "Night" is just a shadow, because the earth is poised in the heavens. The night sky seems like a flat screen, the original movie screen, her teacher said, and the constellations seem like lines and shapes, but really it's all wide open space. And I was beginning to understand. Night is us having the whole earth between us and the sun. Because Earth is an object. It makes a deep shadow. And then, in the shadow, we see the sky full of stars. They're always there, and we are floating in this Universe. Circling. Orbiting. Rotating.

The sun comes up and the sun goes down and then the sun makes its passage through the water under the earth. That kind of night is a passage. The jaguar a guardian, running, burning, who goes into the underworld, burning but in secret, even in that darkest place.

As When Someone Blows Breath.

Inha the Jaguar stood stark against the shadows of the woodland. His golden coat was marked with the marks like the sheen on blue ink.

Looking. Waiting.

He did not roar like a waterfall, like Huwawa.

"Be quiet, my son. You called upon me. Come with me."

His eyes are amber jewels filled with light.

"You see the markings on me, the markings I carry, stars and the indigo sky.

He did not have the look of ferocity on his face, the look to make me fall in terror. His silence was as the living silence of trees. But when I looked it was as if I saw a face in each side of the turn, the face of a man and the face of a cat, jaguar, and trees on either side.

Night was falling, shadows in the edges. I saw light flare as his body took breath.

And I waited. He was quiet. Looking at me. This was not the waiting of the hunter before it takes its prey. And as I waited his quietness came over me. I felt myself being at peace.

Run with me, he said. And again I thought: we would fly into the night sky. That would be how it happened, flight through the spiral, into the galaxy. The nocturnal sun, taking its place among the stars.

No. This is not the journey of the Solar System. The sun does not go around the earth. Don't be afraid to know that this journey is not like that.

The shadows darkened. All I could see of him was the gleam of his breathing as he waited.

"Be quiet, my son," he said. "In all your talking you are taking my eyes from me. There is a way of shining white. There are mirror waters and black stone glass." He stood looking, waiting.

I saw a way into the forest. And the peace he felt, I felt. I would go with him. Fog and mist, pale ancient green of the woodland, came all around us.

We went beneath trees, a woodland way in darkness, and then darkness opened. The indigo of night sky came clear above us, the pattern and fabric of stars filling the limits of sky. And before us stood drawn out in silver lines the looming dark bulk and roundness of the Caracol.

Up the stairs he leapt. I followed. He turned to the right and we walked without sound the length of the platform at the edge. We turned at the corner and walked the length of that side of the platform. We turned at the corner and walked the length of the back of the platform and he led.

Are you trying to measure every footstep? But I didn't say anything. And then we approached the structure of the Caracol.

In the lower passages we went around each circling hallway inside, and through each door. And then we came to the upper doorway that went up into the Caracol. That doorway stood open above me, entirely beyond my reach. But he leapt, able, and stood upon that upper threshold, and it was only then that I understood, as if he had said it out loud: this place is set apart on purpose. The height of the threshold makes it so. It is the way into the spiral, and it is holy. And he put his paw to my forehead as if to mark me and to make me able, and I leapt. And we went over the threshold. We walked in silence the smooth stone inside the shell. We went all the way around, and at every window we stopped. Like he wanted to account for every window. And from each window we looked upward and outward across the land and toward the indigo sky. I saw the patterns of stars. I saw how in the distance stars seemed to sit blazing above the horizon. And I saw that the distances between windows corresponded to far distances in the sky, as if lines marked by his sight went out into the distances. He saw where the heavenly spaces corresponded to places that lay beyond me in the earthly plains of starlight. I followed his sight but I did not see as much as he saw. I saw no person anywhere, like everyone was gone, asleep maybe, but the land was there, land of gardens and homelands and woodlands. In his sight and in his measurement all that place and all its distances were accounted for. They were kept, at least, and secure, even if it seemed no one was there to know it.

I came to cleared land. I saw gardens. I saw plants growing food. I brushed my way through cornstalks. Tomato plants grew glistening along the path, cold and gelatinous, waxy green with a bitter smell of wet earth.

But I had fallen behind. The sky was golden all the way round, sunset, with branches of pine at the edges. Brandon and Corin were already there, talking. I had to catch up. A flash of silver: Brandon taking pictures. I raced ahead. The pine tops danced golden in and out of the rays of sunset. Rustling birds clattered upward through treetops and broke out singing, twittering.

But I lost my footing. Branches and twigs snapped as I fell, hitting my face and neck and head. A head-clogging scent rushed over me. My breath thickened with fumes. Cold mint burned the back of my throat. My eyes squinted with it. Everything was dewy, and I was coughing, with the damp leaves in a thicket arched up around me like an animal's den. Sickness? A reaction happens here, an inflammation in the body. You're starting to burn and you're wet inside with blood and water. The burning comes green as chlorophyll, dark green as smoke from heavy tobacco, like fever, like hacking up stuff.

A man stood there, hand against bare chest. Was it he who worked this garden? Blood ran down from behind his hand. But I saw no wound. His eyes were like a cat's, impossible to understand. The sky lowered, clouds and humidity, weird and gold-green, like looking through pharmacy bottles. His chest was bleeding as he tilled the soil. He held up his hand to me, open, and showed the glistening bright blood. The blood mark on his chest was black and shining wet and in its wetness was a reflection.

"No," I was saying through the thick congestion.

He gripped his sodden hand onto my shoulder. I felt the wet and I felt the grip conform to the shape of my muscle, my bone. I was coughing and wheeling and staggering, hacking out yellow fumes and trying to run, fighting my lack of breath, my closed nostrils. But I heard a sound, a glittering wrangle of rattles, shrill piping, rumble of drumbeats. It was the sound of distant human song.

Why was my desk lamp on? Why was I at my desk? Stiffness and pain cracked in my neck. The clock by my bed said 3:32. My radio was on.

3:32.

AM?

I tried to understand.

3:32?

My arm was stuck to the pages of my book. Slobbering on my school book? I raised my arm, trying to get myself loose, and watched the page rip before my eyes. Watched it hang from my arm. I had never damaged a school book before. I just stared at it, still in a daze of waking.

The left side of my head was wet with sweat, or spit, slobber, mucus. A thrill ran through me, pounding my heart. I tore the page off my arm, cut off the light and threw myself down on the bed. I would have to be up in just a few hours. Suddenly I felt wide awake.

3:32 in the morning? I couldn't trust my own eyes. It felt like morning, and it felt like I still hadn't gone to bed, and it felt like I had gone in through a door and come out again to some different place. Like the middle of the night was the middle of somebody else's room, the middle of another country.

I had seen Inha. I had gone with him.

On the bed I lay a while, chest reeling, heartbeats, the ocean in my ear drum pulsing inside me. Was it even normal? After several minutes, or maybe an hour, or maybe half an hour, after my eyes got used to the dark, I realized that squares of brilliant white were laid out over me, at odds with the plaid of my blanket. I saw my own body, my arms and my chest and legs, all washed in ghastly white. I looked up behind my head. I hadn't even pulled down the window shade. A chunk of moon was cresting through torn and broken clouds, solid white, a perfect shining stone. And the Morning Star was already there beside it, harping silver strings on the hour of awakening.

46

O Shining One

Mr. Collins' classroom see-sawed and swung as the fluorescent lights flickered across the ceiling. I caught him just as he was unlocking the door. One of the lights didn't work right, a little lightning bolt zapping in a glass tube. Mr. Collins set his old leather book satchel by his desk and turned toward me.

"It won't take the whole period," I urged.

"You're talking about an entirely new idea, at this last minute? And it's something to be done in class?"

"It would be a presentation. Kind of like a drama, maybe, a one-person . . ."

"Well . . . we're already behind where I wanted us to be this quarter. Let me think about it."

"OK. Thank you."

I was turning to go when he said, "But are you sure you'll be able to pull it off, a whole new idea? That would be one of my main concerns. How would you be able to do that? I'd hate to see you hurt your standing just for the sake of a sudden brainstorm."

He was staring at me with genuine concern. I didn't want to have to tell him my other idea was a disaster. Should I tell him my new idea was something I saw in a dream? Maybe that's the same as a brainstorm?

"It just came to me in the night. And . . . my standing is about to get hurt anyway because the project I started didn't work out, except for one part of it, the main part, and that's covered up right now by brand new carpet at my house and I can't get it out."

Mr. Collins started to say something and then didn't. He looked puzzled and a little startled.

"I have photographs, but I can't use them. They didn't come out right. I've written the paper for that project and I can still hand it in, but I want to do something I feel better about."

"OK, Chris, I'll tell you what. Go ahead with your new idea, but turn in all the other stuff as well. Give me a write up of the new idea. Explain your intentions and the point of your thoughts. As long as you do your best, I'll back you up if the project committee has any problems with it. I know I can trust your work. So I'm counting on you. You see that clock up there," he tilted his head toward it, "and you've heard me say it enough: Every minute is precious to me."

"Thanks, Mr. Collins. I won't let you down. I really appreciate it."

All the hours of that day wore through me, every numeral on every clock as the hands ground their way around the circle. At lunch I went to the art room instead of the cafeteria because I knew Brandon was there, hunched over in the darkroom, quivering the trays of liquids, lifting the photographs gently with tongs, exactly like before. Like he'd never left there all week. Only thing different was more work was finished. He was absorbed and carried away, and I was getting power from the work going on. And I wanted another look at Mr. Blake's poster from Chichen Itza. Because if you get still and look at a picture quietly enough, you can go into that place.

Finally back at home I could get started. I had a fairly new black magic marker. I put it in my book bag first so I wouldn't be able to forget it. That was the easiest part. Now for the more difficult. By far.

I knew what Mom would say, but the time for drastic action was upon me. I would have to sacrifice a good bed sheet and suffer the consequences later. After supper I got out scissors. The bed sheet would have to do, and it would do OK. It was the only piece of cloth available to me at that late hour. Working in the orange circle of my room's light, I cleared an area on the floor and spread out the sheet. I hadn't thought about how thin a sheet is till I looked at it. It was flannel, but nothing like what the real fur of a jaguar would be. In the dream it had been deep, plush, shining. Like rich velvet, I thought, but then, I couldn't say whether I had really felt rich velvet.

But that was a dream, anyway. I had never touched a jaguar. But the memory of Inha was gigantic in front of my eyes, like if I'd seen it on a movie screen.

I couldn't sew. And I couldn't ask Mom, not at this last minute and definitely not since it was a good bed sheet. So no need to think of making this thicker by adding layers. Plus, that would mean using more and more stuff, more and more time. I should have started sooner. Too late now to worry about that. And with that thought I felt a sudden rush of freedom, like I was flying. No more time to haggle over choices, no more time to worry. Nothing to lose. Live or die, right now. The scissors made a sharp, precise sound as they cut. As beautiful and frightening as open heart surgery. Like you could hear every single fiber being sliced right through. No room for mistakes. No going back now.

Cloth this thin would fly up as I walked, or ran. It would flop over. I really needed something heavier.

Or I could attach this to a shirt. That would solve these problems. And it would have to be attached somewhere anyway. By doing that now I could just wear it under a coat or sweater and be ready to go.

But that meant sewing. But how hard could it be? It didn't have to be actual "sewing." It just needed to be thread and needle zig-zagging. It wouldn't have to look nice. Still, wouldn't there be an easier way than having to mess with thread and needles and all that? And I would have to find all that stuff without bothering Mom. Or I could walk in holding this cut up bed sheet. What would she say then?

Tape might work. It might be ugly. More likely it would come undone, like what if it rained? Glue? Would it have enough time to dry during the night?

I had a stapler.

Would this idea work at all?

I had a good T-shirt about the right color. Close enough. It didn't have to be perfect. And it didn't have to be a costume that hid me completely. In fact, that was what was good about it.

I heard the satisfying sound of a good staple connection.

It was a mixture of two things into one, instead of just one being covered up, so yes, it would be exactly right if my arms and face were showing through. Just like in the picture. Maybe it wasn't supposed to be a secret that those were really human beings under those masks and costumes.

I pulled off my shirt and pulled on the new combination, carefully over my head and gently.

No way. It was like wearing a branch of holly leaves. The staples had to go.

Maybe this was a strange idea. But Mr. Collins did say he liked my work. And some guy did write a bunch of symphonies to the planets.

I had some string in my room, not too thick. If I could get a large enough needle, I could attach the shirt without a whole lot of trouble. I ran downstairs to look around Mom's sewing machine.

Usually she kept stuff out on the sewing table or in the top drawer. She was in another room just then. I found a needle that looked about right, close enough. This wouldn't be too difficult.

I vaulted back upstairs. This was going to work just fine.

I flicked the light switch out of habit as I came back into my room, even though the light was already on. The power of electricity! Once I got this sewing done, and got the cut-out jaguar attached to my gold t-shirt, I would finish the paper. The golden flannel jaguar skin lay across my bed. Just waiting to come to life. The only thing missing were the spots and the circles and the cloudy rosettes that would make it into a jaguar.

O Shining One, O Shining One!

47

Sewing

S ewing. If the guys on the team find out about this . . . But here I am.
Making a costume. Anybody would think it was for Halloween.

I am sewing and I don't really know how to. All I know is that the thread goes through the eye of the needle; the needle goes through the crisscrossed threads of the cloth; the pieces of cloth join together. It is back and forth, back and forth, in and around, thread joining threads, threads that are already joined back and forth back and forth.

This is going to take forever. It's going to take all night long. I have never stayed up all night for any school work. This might be the night.

I am crazy for doing this. I raided the pantry for snacks about an hour ago. I hope Mom and Dad didn't wake up and think a burglar was here.

The best part about this costume will be the head. I'm making it exactly like the one in the pictures, where the guy's face looks out of the jaguar's mouth. Using the pillow case. The jaguar's head goes over the top of the man's head. So that might be the hardest part to make but that's how I'm going to make it.

48

Morning of Project

In the early still-darkness the harping of the multitudes collected against my window. All those wheels turning, engines whirring on the Interstate. A pulse point of car lights miles away bobbed and winked in the tree branches, like the cars weren't moving at all, like when you put your fingers to the blood moving in your own neck. You feel the heartbeat but not each moving blood cell.

Once I got to school everything went in a blur. When the time came, I was already in the room, already in my seat. The voices out in the hall were at a rough roar. Over Mr. Collins' desk the fluorescent lightning zapped and danced, storm in the distance.

I had the gold T-shirt on under my sweater. And the jaguar pelt was sewn on, attached at the shoulders and all along the sides in my own hatchet-blade stitches. Stitches angular, like my shoulders, blades and bones, catching it on. I had become a craftsman overnight.

Our English room was stark, the walls of cement blocks glossed to a high hard dental-white in the thin fluorescence. At the back bookshelves leaned with lines and stacks, textbooks and novels. Now I was seeing the room as it really was, as it would be all summer long with no one here: a chamber of barren loneliness. Up front were Mr. Collins' pictures and The English Speaking Countries of the World. Even those things, Shakespeare and van Gogh with his ear bandage, drained themselves of their colors in the pallor. The whole room was appalled at me, that I was going to steal some English time today. The only thing alive and moving was the clock, and it had no soul, but only mindless continuation.

I thought "Can't you people go ahead and sit down and get ready? Don't you realize you should be in place when it's time for class to begin? Don't you realize we have something important today?" And instantly I felt repulsed by my own self. I had already turned into a heartless teacher. I was abandoning my own people.

The bell sounded. Smiles and laughing dropped away and people spread out and filed down the rows to their places. Mr. Collins was up front.

"Good morning class. As you all know, Interdisciplinary Projects are due today. I'm sure you've all worked very hard, and we'll be proud of all of you. One of the students assigned to my group is in this class. His project is going to involve your participation. I've given him some of our class time this morning, so give him your attention and your full participation.

The way he gestured toward me then, suddenly, and without any warning, was like a boatman offering a hand into an unsteady, shaky boat.

"Chris?"

I had nothing to do but stand up out of my seat and start moving forward down the row.

Time moves in ways you can't understand. Even if it is connected to something as solid as Planet Earth. Maybe it has to do with the speed of your heart, in moments when everything feels crazy. Everything is thrown to the air and you don't know where it will land.

I stepped into Mr. Collins' boat. I was stepping onto the sea.

Wow. I must be truly insane. I would have said I had thought about all this, but I hadn't thought for one second about having to put this to the class in spoken words. I had only imagined it happening, like watching myself from above. Now I was facing the class. I was in charge. I had to say something.

My eye caught sight of the mythology book on Mr. Collins' desk. The jaguar man, and Heracles in the Nemean Lion pelt, and the others. Muriel's words came to me: Just like a textbook. Maybe I could depend on that?

The room swallowed, with me in its throat. A sudden nervous heart race forced my breath. Suddenly this jaguar pelt seemed too strange. Why in the world would you bother with that, they would say? Why would you think that is a serious project for school? Coal Train in the back corner yelled out 'Whoo Chris.' People started clapping.

"Mr. Coltrane, enough," said Mr. Collins.

At the lectern I began pulling my sweater over my head. I had to do it carefully not to rip the jaguar pelt bed sheet loose from the t-shirt. It felt like half an hour of careful wriggling. My t-shirt started lifting up, making chill air run on bare skin. Currents of static zipped through my hair and left me feeling draped in spider webs, hair glued to my scalp or spreading around my head in rays. I scrambled my hair with my hands and shook my head.

"He's wearing a cape! Chris, are you about to fly?"

"Don't disturb him! He's turning into a moth!"

Everyone laughed. But this was supposed to be serious. And I didn't want to stand here explaining. I wanted it to happen. Pressure bore forward against me. Sweat started to break out on my scalp.

This was the edge. No going back. I knew Coal Train would lead all the guys in a good laugh, for the rest of the year probably, but I had to keep going.

And just like a textbook didn't seem right. Not for this.

I took the jaguar pillow case mask and slipped it on, and settled the unfolded pelt around me. Now a jaguar stood before them. I felt the room change to a different kind of quiet. Somehow words came to me, but exactly what I said is hidden away in those moments as the clock ground up time around that hour of English.

The Jaguar is here. He stands before you. To the ancient people, or to anybody who lives where he is, he is a lord of the forest, a lord of night. He's the top predator, and he can go on land or go in water. He can touch the sky from tree tops. He can cross boundaries, and go into the Underworld or into the world above in the sky.

People want food. They want life. They are growing crops of corn. They are growing whatever grain is their most important food, their staple food, the food they depend on. They have been given grain so they can eat in peace. Their crops need rain. Without water their gardens would be dry. Their plants would die. These people are growing corn. They call to the Jaguar.

Jaguar, they say, you have helped us. We are able to call to you. We have language. We have words, and you understand our words. Raise your voice. Call down thunder. You are the one who can go for us. Call to the god Chaac to wield his axe, to open the way for rains. We have no way to get rain for ourselves. Send the Child Rain to come and dance in our fields.

People, says the Jaguar, you are the people who have been given the earth. Remember that. You have been trusted. All who live on Planet Earth wait to know how you will tend to us, the animals and plants. You have been given the care of gardens and the care of forests. You have been given the care of remembering. You have been given this child, Tender Corn, that you not devour each other. It will be reborn for you. It will be for your food now. You will tend gardens, and you will tend memory. I will show you a way to remember. Follow my way. Follow the markings on me. They will give you a way of writing.

Make marks of your own now. You know the black spots that mark me. Because of those marks, people will fear me. People fall back at the sight of me, the way people fall back when they see a marked serpent. They know the black markings on my golden fur.

The people know that night is coming. The sun is going down. Darkness comes. No one can see. Only one can see for them. The people call to him.

Jaguar, we cannot see. Who will bring the sun? Who knows the path of the starry sky? Help us again. Hold up your light, O Shining One. Our fire is warm, but we do not have enough fire to light the world. We do not have enough fire to make day.

Jaguar, you are among those who go. You have given us help. You do things we cannot do. You make the shadow on mountain rocks and you go into darkness, into the mouth beneath the mountains. We have seen the word of your silent feet. You sink into water unafraid. You rule over the water dragons, the caiman and alligator.

People, I will show you a way to remember. I will teach you. Make marks of your own now. Write upon my fur. These are the stars, these are the planets. These are the bodies of the heavens that I will carry, lights in the firmament, words written on me by the powers of heaven. Now you, write your words on me. Take my marks and make your own words. I will carry your words as I go. I will keep the light as I go. I will call the Child Rain to dance in your fields. I will go into dark places. I will give you a way to remember. And light of day will return to you.

"This is your project?"

"Is this about food?"

"Did you make all this up? It sounds like you're reading a children's book."

"Did you say you're supposed to be dressed up like a jaguar? But don't jaguars have spots?"

"Is this some kind of one man drama? Who's supposed to be talking, anyway? Is the jaguar saying all this, or different characters?"

"Chris?"

I pulled the mask off and looked at the class. "Come on people, don't interrupt! The Jaguar was standing in front of you. Couldn't you feel it?"

"Well, Chris. A little explanation might help?"

That was Mr. Collins. OK, a little explanation.

"Yes, jaguars have spots. Of course they do. Even the jaguars that people call black panthers have spots. And jaguars have more than one kind of spot."

Now it was just like a textbook. Jaguars, leopards, cheetahs and the spots. Cherubim and sphinx guarding a holy place, and a jaguar in the sun's Underworld passage. But this wasn't supposed to be like a textbook. The Jaguar was standing in front of you!

"Yeah," Bradley broke in as I spoke, "but if all that was true, this nocturnal sun stuff, the jaguar would just burn up."

Jeannie replied, "That doesn't matter, Bradley. How could it?"

"If all that was true," Bradley kept on, "they'd keep finding charcoaled jaguars every morning. Is that what these people ate? But I'm just saying, they couldn't know what we know about the sun or they wouldn't be able to say things like that. And they wouldn't have needed to or wanted to. They can't have known anything about the sun, like how hot it is."

I saw Mr. Collins' eyes darting between the class to me. Did he want a big discussion? No sign of what he thought. Sometimes he liked to let us hack our way through. Or maybe part of my grade would be how I responded, how I handled being in charge? I had asked for this, to be in front of the class. Later on I wondered if he was testing me for whether or not I could be a teacher.

"It's not about that," countered Chantal. "Ugh! There's nothing wrong with having a story like that. It helps them understand things. They needed sunlight. They knew that. They knew about their crops. So they connected those things, the jaguar, the sun, the power. It has nothing to do with whether or not they knew the temperature of the sun."

"But that's what I'm talking about," Bradley continued. "Obviously these people didn't know anything about the sun. Not like we do. If they did, they would know that anything would die if it came anywhere near the sun."

"But they know a lot about the sun. They knew what they needed to know. And it's not like they can't think of symbolic things. Right? They didn't have to think a jaguar really was the sun to make a symbolic connection."

Several people were talking at the same time.

"Are you talking about a flying jaguar going around the earth with the sun all night long? Because . . . everyone knows the sun doesn't go around the earth."

"That's why they should have known better. That's why this is a crazy idea to begin with!"

"This is wrong," Martin was saying, his eyes tight against me. "You're actually praying to a demonic god and making us listen to it." At the exact same time Will was asking, "How long would that take, anyway?"

"Would what take?" I said.

"Going around the earth like that. Like, what is the circumference of the Earth? We can calculate the amount of time needed."

"Well," said James, who never said anything, "I think it's more like the jaguar fighting his way through the Zodiac, going against Scorpio and Cancer, and the constellation Draco, and Taurus and Leo, all the way through to the break of day."

Now Mr. Collins spoke. "This is a great area of discussion for us. In fact, I'm making some notes from your comments. We can return to some of these thoughts, because we are going to be talking about the role of mythology in human life. For now, Chris, go ahead with what you have planned. We don't have a lot of time left."

It was in the dream: Inha running down a path in the forest, me running after him. Running with him. I saw the regular jaguar markings on him, but in the dream letters and words were written on him.

"So that's where you come in. There's a black magic marker on my desk. I'm wearing a jaguar skin but the spots are only penciled in, blank. You will fill them with writing. I want you to write something."

"Write what? I don't know anything to write. Is this for a grade? You didn't tell us we would have to do this."

I hadn't expected griping. Everybody was supposed to jump up, ready to write.

"Quiet," Mr. Collins demanded. "We only have a few minutes. Do you know a line of poetry, a song lyric? What would you say about your life, or about the world as you know it? What can you put into words on the spur of the moment? What is of true importance to you? Write only your name if you must, but everyone must write something. Let's go."

I saw Eddie taking the marker from my desk.

"Here it is. I'm not going first." He threw it away from himself, toward Chantal, like it was a defiling object. She looked startled but caught it with a quick movement.

"What?" she asked. "I can catch. Don't look so surprised."

She stood and came to the front. I hadn't thought of this: I would have to turn, not see what was going on. Everyone got quiet, like they were waiting for the words to come singing out as she wrote. Her palm pressed and pushed against my shoulder, turning me as she wrote. A tiny wavering line began, weird coolness from the magic marker, loops and marks. I couldn't make out the letters. And then the fumes, like liquid plastic sliming into my throat, tingling my nostrils. I hadn't thought about fumes. I heard a click and then soft whirring, Mr. Collins' desk fan. Would he say it was not OK to keep going?

"Who's next," she said in a hushed voice.

Someone else started. I could feel the class watching. They wrote on my back and shoulders, and my eyes followed the shapes of the letters at my face, words on Mr. Collins' board. He marched them in all capitals forward across the board at a timed pace.

Every minute is precious.

And like a whisper, I heard each person, close, breathing, concentrating. They weighed their hands on my shoulder as they wrote. I heard the tiny grinding of the clock and I saw gear upon gear above me clicking in the depths, in the secret interior where things run unseen, the clocks, the calendars, and the center of the earth turning, groaning, gathering, gaining, spending, another minute, another hour, a day and a night, we sleeping and waking.

I didn't begin to sweat again. I was at peace. And they kept coming.

Like a whisper, they said it,

Jaguar

They all came forward,

They marked the stars and the constellations

They wrote their words

Their writing

Jaguar, Jaguar,

They turned me around, and around

"Is that everyone?"

Spun me around,

Put the jaguar mask back on me: they understood it without explaining,

And they opened the door and sent me out and closed it behind me and I turned and fell headlong in the hallway over legs outstretched, running shoes, and Brandon sitting there on the floor. He looked stunned, drew away, and then recognized me.

"What took you so long?" he whined. "I just about got nailed for being out here."

"What are you doing? Why didn't just you come in? Just come in the room."

"What's that?" He nodded toward my chest.

Black, a circle of black spreading outward from the pocket in my t-shirt.

I snatched out the capless marker.

"Here, write something on my back, like they did. That's what this is. I've got to get out of here as quick as I can."

"Write what?"

"Anything. Anything. Just do it!"

Was I shouting?

"Who's going to read this? What is this, this cape? This is your project?"

"Nothing, nobody, come on. The jaguar has to go before they come out. It's the Lord of Night, Nocturnal Sun. Write something. The jaguar is going to run, the sun passing into the Underworld. Fire under the Earth. Down to the track and then take this off and come back for the rest of school and the rest of life."

He began to write. The bell would be ringing any minute.

"Come on."

"OK, that's it. You're going to take this down to the track and burn it? Right?"

"Chris?"

"What?"

"I said, that's it. I've done it."

And the jaguar was running.

Daylight at the end, double door sky gleaming on the floor, and my feet lit within it. The doors wheeled back, wheezing at the hinges. The jaguar was running, and I was the jaguar, and the jaguar was before me and the jaguar was in me. He saw a path.

A white way shining.

Arc of sunlight drove him into the green shadow-forest. Plants hid him, the fanning palmetto under shafts of light. Massive ribbed vaults of the holy ceiba trees soared upward, branches trumpeting silver flowers.

Drumming and music came through the trees. A community shimmered in and out of sight just through to a clearing, dreams of music rattling and rasping, shakers and singers and dancers.

Night was falling, a blue water silk draping over day. The ancient people were sending away the sun.

The jaguar traced the edges in shadows. The people did not see him, but they knew he was there. They knew his time for moving. His footsteps came near them. His gleaming coat brushed among known trees and landmarks. And the voices chanted, song on the evening air:

Ember flaring

As When Someone Blows Breath

Go, rejoice, run your course

Make your way

Remember us this night at the Face of the Waters

We will remember you

The rattling and drumming grew strong, pushing his legs, catching his heart in quickening rhythm. Like the movement of pistons, strength of youth, steps rising and steps falling to carry him over ground.

The sun fell and it was a sign: what if forever? And darkness came. Would there be nothing to light our way? No, let us cling together and be a people and while we wait let us remember a way to tremble light out of sticks and sulphur and flints.

At their fire people gather, faces made by fire from darkness, nodding, smiling, looking deep and far away into the orange light of the hot coals and glowing embers.

People offer their songs and stories. They offer the shadows of dance, flickering candlelight, curling smoke of incense, fragrant cloud of burning tree resin billowing up from embers within. People kneel in a cloak of shadow and raising a bright face of worship in profile with the sound of bells and chimes. They spread a table laden with gifts and offerings of thanksgiving.

And a voice from within the smoke came to me, the voice from within the embers,

Inha, as the smoke rose among holy ceiba trees:

To the place where soil is scarce, ground is thin, and water below.

Where sky rests upon the face of waters

Do you know how fire burns in water?

"This is the way," the jaguar said.

It is darkness, and the jaguar goes among shadows.

He scruffed over thin ground, thin soil, earth drumming with footsteps. The trees opened, sky darkened, indigo. Gold and vermilion stars lay fallen to the ground, the riches of the earth, to gravel, up an incline, to the gate. The heart of the jaguar joined the drumming and the rattling, breathing the music into and out of his body, on streams that surround the world. He had the sun inside himself, the power to transport daylight, sunlight that flexed in rays and fiery spikes, corona at horizon. He had not left me. He was with me.

And the sun dropped over the horizon.

The limestone walls sang as I passed. The circular face of the waters crashed open. Green light from the world of plants, the world of life, tried to reach me. But I shot through the surface, into the depths. Away from sky and away from light. Blue-green waters swirled around me, deeper and darker as I sank. Lower and lower, farther and farther. The body of water held me, surrounded me, and I was plunging deep, deep.

"Inha," I tried to say.

But I hit. A muffled thump, tangled feet, falling forward. My hands met it, in front of me, and it was solid, but it gave way. I was desperate, in darkness, for air, for air, at the bottom of water, gasping but not getting air, and I could see the surface a mirror of light. I couldn't get there. Pure darkness before me, and I couldn't speak. I had no breath.

49

Crash

No breath.

Guttural emptiness sucked like a drain, suffering, a gorging horror and it was me. Or it was under me. It was fighting me. I squirmed and pushed. I saw teeth, the red inside of a mouth, hot air and bad breath, cigarette, ash and spit-spray, gurgling blood bubbles and the voice under me yelled, cursing, pushing. My head, my arms came back stinging me, lashed. Hands gripped my shoulders and threw me hard away. A voice yelled in my ear, but it was gargled and muffled like when you have a cold.

"What the hell? What are you . . . ?"

But I had no breath.

He kicked clear of me as I rolled, trying to get up. He was up spit-ting, coughing, hands to his face, blood as red as paint seething through his hands. His sleeve then the front of his shirt wiped at his face. Blood ran over his mouth, his teeth, dripping from his chin, tongue licking out, tasting to believe it. Then he was slantwise, coughing and tripping out of the gate and down the row of pine trees toward the road. And there was the black sports car. Gleaming like it had a way of pulling down light and holding it in the shadows, making itself shine.

Deep breaths. Bits of gravel pocked and clung to the underside of my forearms. Head starting to feel pain. I brushed myself off.

Little blood lines erupted on my arms.

Bright shining blood was guttered all down my shirt. My own nose? No. No blood wiped off my nose.

The monotone electric voice went straight up into the sky. The bell. My legs were shaking. I heard the black car roaring in fury, tires screaming and gripping, and it flew away. And then the wheeze of the hall doors. In seconds the grounds overflowed with motion, chatter, a ziggurat of human sound.

Anger surged through me. Who was that? Hiding out back here? And now the wet glop of his nose blood slapped against my skin. I walked a few steps along the pine row holding my shirt out, trying to shake blood off.

I had to get back across the yard. I had to get to Mr. Collins' room. Get my stuff. My arms were scratched up. I had to get to the bathroom and wash up. My shirt was bright with someone else's blood. Cold and wet. Flopping against me with every step. Which bathroom? The closest was in the atrium by the cafeteria, right in the crowd of people changing classes.

I had no other shirt with me. All I had was my sweater back in the room.

Idiot! You can't go into a high school looking like this. Half-hiding in the bristling pine branches I started to pull off the blood marked jaguar shirt. I would just run into the building without a shirt. According to my project idea, I was going to run out of the school and down to the track. I had a little pocket knife so that when I got to the track I could cut away the jaguar part and just wear the shirt. The jaguar would have run on, and I would return to school as a regular person. But the knife wasn't in my pocket. Had I put it in my book bag? But what would be worse, running shirtless back to the building, or all this blood? No one can go around school without a shirt on. So I made a dash for the building. I could grab my sweater and my book bag and rush to the bathroom in the atrium and maybe not be late. Not too late. Once I got into the crowd, maybe it would be too crowded for people to notice what was on my shirt.

But within seconds all I heard was "Oh my God" and "Is that blood" and "What's up with these sophomores" and "That's the same doofus kid who wouldn't fight back in the cafeteria." People drew back at the hall doors, either side of me and made a little passage. "The one who was fighting in the cafeteria," someone repeated.

I just had to keep going.

Mr. Collins, when I got to his room, was writing on his board.

"Chris, that was . . . interesting." His hesitancy stopped me. "Did that go as you had planned? We'll talk about it later."

Before I could think what to say, he took a second look at me.

"But what's happened? Is that blood? Your arm's bleeding."

I saw the trickles on my arm and a few dots behind me to the door. And blood was splattered on my pants leg.

"Is your forehead bruised? That's a pretty good knock. Chris, if I didn't know you better I would say you'd been in a fight. Or a murder. Is that your blood?" I reached up to feel my forehead. It was numb and tight but not hurting that much.

"Here." He had some tissues on the shelf. Students for the next class would be coming in at any moment.

"I kind of got tripped up. I was running and kind of slid on some gravel. I'm not really hurt. I don't think. I ran into somebody, this guy was out there, I don't know, I think he got a bloody nose . . ."

"Here, use some of this." Mr. Collins rummaged around in his cabinet and brought out a bottle half full of rubbing alcohol. "Have you got something else to wear? You must have planned on changing after this project."

No, I must not have. He wiped my arms with stinging alcohol, wiped cold alcohol on my knotted forehead. I just wanted to get out of there before the room started filling up with the next class.

"Yeah, I've got this." I held up the sweater. "Thanks, Mr. Collins."

Do you mind, I was about to say, if I just get out of here?

"Did that go as you wanted, Chris?"

That sounded ominous.

"I didn't think about it starting a debate," he continued. "But then," and he glanced around like he wanted to see who was listening, "your class has been argumentative all year. Lots of energy. Maybe you've touched on something this morning that we can build on."

Yeah, well, I wasn't sure about that.

"Well, I didn't plan any of that part," I said. "Thanks for letting me do this at the last minute. And thanks for the alcohol. I guess I better get on to my next class."

Mr. Collins wrote me a note so I could be late. I went straight to the bathroom, but people saw me on the way. Who wouldn't stare at someone wearing a jaguar pelt and with fresh blood on their clothes? I locked myself into a stall and ripped off wads of toilet paper to dry up the blood from my shirt as best I could. Outside and inside. I took off the shirt, and then found the little Swiss Army knife in my book bag. I cut right through all those stitches I had labored over the night before. And they were good stitches, strong. In my fumbling around trying not to let the legs or the tail of the jaguar pelt dip into the toilet the knife dropped to the floor and skipped out from under the stall. I had to kneel down and reach out to get it. The toilet water looked gross spiraling with blood from wet toilet paper and I thought about leaving it to shock the next person, but I didn't. The wet blood on my shirt felt less gloppy when I put it back on, but still cold, but I couldn't wear only the wooly sweater and suffer the itchiness like some hair-shirted monk for the rest of the day. And the blood on my jeans was already stiffening. It wasn't red looking. I got as much of it wiped off as possible. So I had to live with the grossness and lament the fact that I had not planned well enough to bring another shirt. But anyway, who would have been able to expect anything like this? I stuffed the jaguar pelt into my book bag, flushed the blood stained toilet paper, and bustled out of the cramped stall. My eye caught the eye of someone else just leaving the bathroom. I hadn't even heard anyone else in there. It was Archer, one of Martin's lunchroom disciples. I didn't really know him.

At the sink I washed my hands and arms, felt all around the bump on my head, threw water over my face and hair, tried to arrange myself, and then made my way to class. Imagine everybody sitting around me, in all my classes, and at lunch. They could see the dark stains on my jeans, but they had no idea I was wearing the blood of some dude who had been hiding out behind the stadium gate and concession stand. If raw blood stank, I couldn't smell it, but then I thought again of what Brandon had said, and I wondered. Maybe I was giving off offensive odors everywhere I went. Everything I had done in class, the jaguar standing there, seemed like a few days ago. I was a bit dazed and not sure what exactly had just happened.

Brandon wasn't at lunch, and Muriel wasn't either, and later that afternoon strange messages had spread around school. Somebody had "filled the library with dead animals" was the way I heard it in fifth period. That weird hurricane guy was "running around with blood all over himself" after he "got slammed by some guy in front of the stadium." Some girls I passed in B Hall mentioned the dead animals. Their bodies contorted involuntarily. "It's so disgusting." "It's like, really morbid." Guys at the end of C Hall were laughing about a smashed raccoon. "It's the one I nailed last weekend," one of them said.

So Mr. Blake must have put Brandon's pictures in the library. How all these students had seen it I didn't know. I had never heard anyone talking about any of the displays in the library before. But by the time I got there, I couldn't find the pictures anywhere. In another part of the school? I couldn't find them.

During the afternoon I realized I didn't know where my jaguar mask was. I didn't remember having it with me when I was in the bathroom cleaning up.

Finally, in the locker room, I would get to hear from Brandon how it all went. I knew Mr. Blake thought highly of Brandon's photographs. Brandon would get a good grade, but even more, the honor of being an artist. A real artist. How had all this come together for him? It was because he was willing to take a stand. He was making an important statement. He got people talking. He was in touch with the power of art. How does someone know how to do that?

"Hey jaguar man, you're marked for life now. Look at those spots!"

Coal Train was pointing at me from across the locker room.

I twisted my head back to look over my shoulder. I hadn't even thought about the magic marker printing through to my skin, even though I'd stood there feeling the weird coolness as each person was writing. But there it was on me: prints of what had been written on the jaguar pelt. A lot of it, anyway. Jaguar's marks on my own back. We usually ran without shirts for practice, and even in chilly weather like this, to be tough. But I pulled on one of the school practice shirts as quick as I could. Why, I was thinking later. It would have been fun to be out there marked like that. A couple of the senior guys had real tattoos. I knew Mom and Dad would never say yes to that. But I didn't know what people had written. And I had this voice saying, "Keep it to yourself." It just seemed like the thing to do.

Brandon was usually in the locker room before me. But not today.

Coach came in a few minutes later than usual too.

He looked straight at me with the most serious eyes I had ever seen on him and then he addressed the whole room.

"Brandon will not be running with us today or ever again. I just found out he's been suspended, and, based on his record at his previous school and on the events of this morning, he probably won't be back at this school again."

What?

I stared at Coach, expecting more. How could this be right? Was he even supposed to be telling us something like this about another student?

"Coach? . . ." I started.

And then he was staring straight at me again.

"And you, Fuller, get your regular clothes back on ASAP and get to the principal's office. You can explain yourself to him."

Explain myself?

"What? Coach?"

"You heard me. Everybody else, to the track, pronto! I'm in no mood for any more stupidity today!" And he turned and went into his office and shut the door. The room was dead silent. Was this about Brandon? Or, dread filling me at the thought, had they found out about me and Brandon going into the woods? Muriel said I'd been seen. So they would be wanting to interrogate me, now that they had caught Brandon. Had he been in the woods today? It was the only thing I could think of. No way he would have given them my name?

Mr. Givens was in just as bad a mood as Coach. All this tension on a Friday afternoon. Wouldn't he rather just get home for the weekend?

"You, young man, did you or did you not bring a knife on this school campus today?"

But I just stood there dumb for a couple of seconds. How would he know that? They can't have cameras in the bathrooms. He seemed so furious, and it was so unnecessary.

"A knife. You heard me. I want a straight answer, and I have the right to search your book bag. You were witnessed using a knife this morning and even now you stand here in clothes stained with blood. I have heard about the blood all over you—nearly the entire school appears to have seen you—and it has taken me a while to get it all together, the student with blood everywhere, the strange costume, and now I have had a witness reporting you with a knife."

All I could think to say was "who?"

"Don't ask me who. That is not the question. Yes or no, son?"

Son? That felt weird. He barely knew me.

"Mr. Givens, I can explain everything. It wasn't anything. It was just something for my project this morning. The blood was just a weird accident. It had nothing to do with the knife. There was this guy . . ."

"So there is a knife? You freely admit it? Hand it over. Surely you knew better."

"Yes, there is a knife. But really, it was nothing."

He was holding out his hand. Like I was some baby in elementary school. "This means suspension."

"Wait, can you just hold on a second, I can explain all of this."

"No, I cannot 'just hold on a second,' young man. You do not comprehend the situation you are in. We have regulations that must be followed and you have been seen with a knife in the school building and now you have shown me the knife and I have no choice. And I have just recently seen you here in this office on charges of fighting in the cafeteria during lunch hour –had you forgotten about that—which you did not deny-- and here you stand talking to me in clothes stained with human blood. There is paperwork to be done, so sit down and let's get this done. Dealing with these projects all day and now all this, you boys, I've had enough of this. We're not even halfway through the year. And we will have to contact your parents. Really, Chris, I am completely astonished at you."

I was completely astonished too. I couldn't keep from stammering around.

"But the blood's not mine. It's from some weird guy hiding out in the stadium. I don't even know him. And the knife is just a little pocketknife I needed for my project. I didn't even have it with me when I ran into this guy. It was in my book bag in Mr. Collins' room. I had to cut some strings. You can ask Mr. Collins. He knows all about it. He gave me permission. He can back me up on any of it."

He called on the intercom for Mr. Collins to come up to the office and then got out the papers to start the paperwork. How could this be such a big deal? A little Swiss army knife. And Mr. Collins came in. He looked ready to be on his way, Friday afternoon, jacket over his arm and leather book satchel in his hand.

"What's all this," he asked, looking from the principal to me and back again.

He backed me up about the blood. He must not have thought about such a large amount of blood on my clothes. I told them the whole thing, about the guy I ran into. That I had no idea who it was. I did not tell them I was pretty sure I had seen his car before, that day he chased me and Brandon in my car. Because I didn't want to tell them we had been at school that day during our break. It couldn't matter to them if we had been there, because we didn't do anything wrong. But I thought telling them would just add to the confusion. And the more I thought about it, the more sure I was that this was the same guy I had seen talking to Brandon when Brandon first came to this school. But I didn't want to bring Brandon into this. Anyway, I could ask him who the guy was when I finally got to see him. If he was suspended, he must be back at his house by now. They would have called his parents to come get him. But this is all insane, I kept thinking. But it wasn't going to turn out in my favor. The conversation between the principal and Mr. Collins heated up.

"Really, I'm telling you, Chris' project was not something you turn in but more like a performance. He needed to leave my classroom as part of the project, he was wearing a costume, and I had no problem with that, because Chris has proven to be a trustworthy student, and then when he returned, he had scratched his arms. There was blood, and he had bumped his head. He told me he had fallen on gravel and I have no reason to doubt him. I gave him some alcohol to clean the scratches, and sent him to the bathroom to straighten himself up, and I wrote him a note to be late to his next class. I did not know anything about this run-in or crash with this other person, but I didn't have time to ask Chris too many questions at that moment. It would have been better if you had mentioned it," he said, looking at me. "Or maybe you did mention it? But OK, we know about it now. We can take action. We've had hints of possible drug dealing going on around the stadium buildings. This may be connected to that." They both looked at me, like maybe the idea was just now taking shape that I had something to do with drug dealings. My throat got instantly dry, because I would not be able to deny going into the woods during school. Not without lying. Even if it didn't have anything to do with drug dealing. I did not want to have to lie to Mr. Collins.

So anyway, did I dare ask, was I still really in trouble? Mr. Collins asked for me.

"So I can't see much more to keep us here? I don't think Chris has done anything intentionally wrong. It is a strange turn of events, no doubt, but nothing malicious, and why, for heaven's sake, Chris, are you still in those foul clothes soaked in blood? Have you really worn that all day long?"

I was about to reply, Yes, I didn't have anything else to wear, when the principal spoke.

"Robert, there remains the issue of the knife. My hands are tied. No student is permitted to bring a knife on campus, let alone to use it on campus, in a school building. This boy has been seen and reported, he has admitted having the knife and has turned it in. I must suspend him. I'm going to telephone his parents now."

The world became crazy. Of course Mr. Collins had known nothing about the knife. It was so much a matter of nothing he would have had no reason to know about it. I felt my throat tighten and thought, I'm not about to cry? But no, not tears but a red flush of hot anger broke out over me. Mr. Collins held his hand up in front of me as if to stop a force, and shook his head. The look on his face said "Don't make it worse." But he took me by the shoulder and turned me away as the principal made the phone call. It will be OK, he told me. I will help you not get too far behind.

I wanted to explain it all again. But that wouldn't change anything. I had broken a serious rule without even knowing it. Well, without even thinking about it. I guess I had heard these rules at some time or other, but when you have no intention of doing harm, how can it matter if by accident you broke a rule? Mr. Givens calmly chunked my knife into a drawer in his desk. I would never see it again. Mom and Dad would be demanding an explanation. From me.

I was suspended.

50

Footsteps

Wouldn't a pair of scissors have worked just as well? Mom said after she calmed down.

Mom and Dad almost insisted on coming to the school but in the end they didn't. It was just one of those things, Dad told me later when I got home. Things like this happen. We learn from them and we grow because of them. But it was a serious situation. I would have this on my record. He had stern words for me. I must begin to think more realistically, think for myself, think about what I was doing. Make myself more aware of not letting my ideas run away with my good sense. Stuff like that. We would get through this. Maybe I needed some quiet time to contemplate all of this, Dad said.

And why didn't you just tell me your photos didn't turn out? he asked.

So when I asked permission to stop off at Brandon's house on the way home, so that I could ask him what had happened to him, and really to ask him about this guy with the black sports car, I had no expectation that they would let me. But they did.

In my headlights the sky descended, micro jewel mist, dissolving solid objects right in front of me. My sweater got beaded with particles of cloud. I watched my wipers cutting through it, watched it swirl in the air. Everything swirled around me: the project, the jaguar, all those words I had spoken; the crash, the blood, the knock on the head; and now I was suspended. An outcast. Piney Groves Estates. The gold letters on the fancy brickwork struck dull, fog over shine. Flames licked in the antique lamps. I wanted to find out about this freak in the stadium. And Mr. Collins talking about drug dealing, looking straight at me. And Brandon suspended, Coach saying he would never run with us again.

No one came to the door. But it looked like a faint light was on. The twin TVs that never stopped? I knocked again, and then pounded on the door with my fist.

"Brandon. I just want to know what happened. What's going on? And you won't believe what happened to me."

No answer. I went around to the side, Brandon's window. Dark. Blinds closed tight. I was getting wet. The mist gathered on you, invisible in the air. My feet were getting wet. Getting cold. I tapped on the window, but nothing. People had to think I was trying to break in.

I looked toward the white plastic fence, the Rocks, and to where the secret path went to Corin's. That was the place to go next.

A couple of his windows were lit, beacons in the dimness, and his outdoor lamp was on by the driveway. The clinging mist was making all lights glow, magnifying the orange and gold.

"Corin?"

I banged on his front door, waited, and then walked around back.

"Hey, Corin, are you here?"

Sheets of misty droplets swirled through the arc of lamplight.

Maybe he had seen Brandon.

"Corin?" My voice sounded raw in the cedar groves. The spongy ground under the shaggy trees was still dry. The huddle of birds burst away in one wing from their feeders when they heard me. Corin was coming up from the shed. Out in this refilling the bird feeders. Carrying one of those old fashioned oil lanterns you light with a match, the light bobbing back and forth with his steps. Like the old man of the woods, lamping around under the groves.

"What is it, lad?"

"Is Brandon here?"

"No, haven't seen him. But what is it? You've had a knock on the head. Not fighting each other, tell me?"

"No! Not at all. It's too crazy to explain right now. I just want to speak to him if I can. I've got to get on home in a minute."

"Well, I wonder . . . If you've already been to his house, I have a thought where to look. Come on."

Cars on Gilead Road sprayed past in gauzy headlights. We finally caught a gap and Corin was at the yellow lines and then on across to the tall grass. Faster than I expected, straight for the Interstate. In my dizzy head

I felt a rush of exhilaration, like an unstoppable song suddenly coming to me, at the scene in front of me: Corin with his antique lantern, legs and feet in grassy lamplight, upper body a shadow of falling evening, Gilead Road a rushing water-sheet of tire splash and traffic, mist ranging all around us like the air itself had a grain, a sea-body that went all the way overhead, the whole sky wide foggy storm glass and water. And breaking into view, the whispering arc of light on the evening Interstate. I was small.

"Where do you think he is?"

But he hadn't heard me. He was barely willing to wait at the on-ramp. He crossed at the slightest break, a car's horn strafing rudely at us, our offensiveness at being in its way, and I burst past while it bleated down the ramp toward the flow of red taillights.

Corin went toward the underside of the bridge. I had never been there before.

Between us a few yards of grass sloped downhill to a place where you could get under the bridge on a little footpath. All along where Corin walked the silver gleam was so bright I could see his footsteps marking a trail in the grass. And then the air, the mist, seemed almost blue. It was the particular moment when every tiny crystal of mist was a lens to magnify the glowing twilight. Suddenly everything was hovering with it.

I caught him at the point where we both looked together round the bend toward the underside of the bridge.

My breath stopped. A pair of running shoes, just the fronts tips visible, side by side on the line between blue twilight and the solid black shadow under the bridge.

"Brandon!"

No answer, no movement.

Corin started down, but then pulled back. "Go down there, lad, I'll hold ya."

I edged down, Corin holding my arm, straining to see without slipping in red mud. Then I was out of his grip, hands on the bridge beam in front of me.

"Brandon? Nope," I called back up. "Just a pair of old shoes." But they were like his. I ducked into the shadows under the bridge. Let my eyes adjust. It was a concrete place, smelling damp and stale and filthy. The smell, the evidence, of human waste. Not much different from the smell of a dead animal. I saw food wrappers, trash, old clothes up in the low tight angle where the bridge joined the land. The road above quivered and rumbled. I thought I saw a section of it moving, shaking loose.

"Brandon?"

The smell was sticking in my throat and making me turn away.

"No," I said coming out, "nobody. What do you think? On the other side?" I tried to see into the dim angle across the Interstate.

"I don't know. Let's go. You go on home now and get your supper. They'll be waiting for you and there's no need to keep them worrying on a wet night like this."

But I wanted to keep looking. The only place left I could think of was the Out Back. The Rocks. But in this weather?

I was hungry. And if I was going out to the Rocks, I wanted to get some boots. And a flashlight.

"I used to be able to walk to town unbothered," Corin was saying to the cars as they whipped past. "Used to be able to stand out here in the middle of the road if I wanted to, and come to no harm."

"Why did you think Brandon . . ." I started to ask, but Corin said 'Come on!' and headed out into the road at the first break.

The cars rushing by had gravity of their own. It pulled me and the air with it.

"Here lad, you head on home. Don't trouble yourself, he'll turn up."

"OK. I know he will. I just want to know what's going on."

I left him going into his front door. He said leave the car there, in his driveway. I could move it later when the traffic died down. Our kitchen windows were glowing, impossible to miss in the silver blue air-water. The old post oaks armed up dark and mossy around the house, heavy trunks, heavy branches. I would not like to face having no place to come in to, to try and live under a bridge, on a falling night like this.

51

Incense

Of course the phone call from school was only the first round of explanation. Mom and Dad wanted to hear it all again. The bang on the head was unavoidably visible, so the explaining had to begin right in the doorway.

And why was I so wet, and why so late?

Then I dashed upstairs and flung off the wet sweater, the blood stiffened shirt and the blood splattered jeans. I got into clean clothes, good and warm. I slid into my chair at the supper table. They had eaten ahead of me, which is exactly what I had hoped they would do. They were sensible parents.

Until they saw for themselves the scratches on my hands. And the gravel lashes on my arms. Just when I thought we had this all settled.

"Is this more fighting, Chris?"

No. Not more fighting. How could I explain all this? The whole thing was so crazy. I was running along in the jaguar costume, and bam, I just run into this weird guy who wasn't even supposed to be there.

But how in the world could you be running and not see a person there? If someone attacked you on the school grounds we should be on the phone to Mr. Givens this minute.

No. I've already told Mr. Givens. It wasn't an attack. It was a collision. I don't know how I didn't see him. He must have come from behind the concession stand. He came out of nowhere! Right at the exact moment when I got there.

But how could you be so unaware? Weren't you looking?

But trying to explain that would be impossible. Because for those few minutes, I was the jaguar. My eyes were open but I wasn't seeing what was in front of me. Maybe it was a weird kind of blindness. I saw the ceiba trees and the path of the forest, the dark and brilliant flames, the edge of the gardens. I saw the pathway where the jaguar ran. I really saw that.

After a few minutes they quieted down. Finally they saw I wasn't hurt bad. Just a bruise on my forehead. Put some alcohol on all those scrapes, Mom said.

But they weren't 100% satisfied. Why hadn't I told someone right away what had happened? Why hadn't I asked to come home to get different clothes? Why hadn't my teacher gone out there right away to go after this guy? Why was I out of the classroom anyway?

None of this would have happened if you had been in your classroom, Mom said.

Then it was back to Brandon.

Was I absolutely sure my suspension and his were not related? It's just too much of a coincidence. You're telling us everything? You know you can talk to us. If you two have gotten into something, whatever it is, you know you can tell us. You can trust us to do the right thing.

Yes, I said. I know. I don't know what happened with Brandon, but I got suspended because of the stupid knife!

I ate my spaghetti and bread and salad during all this, while Mom and Dad washed and dried dishes. The news people on TV were going on about their political world.

I was halfway to the Out Back with a flashlight when Dad yelled for me from the back steps.

"Corin's on the phone. He's found Brandon." As I jogged past him he added, "I've already told him its OK with me. Let's get to the bottom of this." I took the phone. He was looking at me like I was still holding out on explaining everything.

"Hey Corin, what's happened?"

"It's Brandon. I've found him. Curled up on the ground down at the back of my place, if you can believe it, in all the leaves at the compost pile. Wet, soaked through with rain, dirty. Down in that far corner near the pylon. He's had a rough time, torn up about something. Would you come over and talk to him? He was talking crazy. Says they threw him out and he can't go home and he doesn't want to if he could, if you can believe it. I finally got him up to the house. Don't even know for sure if he recognized me at first. I told him to just stay here, but we need to call his mom and dad. They're bound to be worried bad about him."

"We'll call Brandon's parents. I've met them, met his mom. Or step mom. But I don't really know them. I guess they would remember me. I could just go up there and tell them where he is. Is that OK?"

"No," Dad said, shaking his head. "You're not going anywhere other than Corin's and not there either if it wasn't Corin. Brandon's father can get himself over there and get his own son."

Dad had to call Information to get their number.

"Wow," he said when he hung up. "That's an angry man. Corin was right. They did throw him out. He says they don't want him back. Sounds like he's in a lot of trouble. Now listen, son. Did you know anything about this? I mean, was there anything going on that you knew about? Are you absolutely sure this has nothing to do with all this that happened to you? This is just too crazy to be a coincidence. Is there anything at all you should tell me about this? Shouldn't I call Mr. Givens and talk to him right now?"

"No, Dad, nothing. Truly, nothing. Brandon seemed like he was getting along fine. I mean, I don't have classes with him, but he never said anything about having problems. Mostly all he ever talks about is surfing and basketball and running shoes."

"Mr. Calaveras said it's the last straw. They've had all they can take from him. Could you hear him? Apparently Brandon was in some kind of trouble before? That's why they moved here, trying to get a fresh start? You've never heard anything about any of that?"

"No. He never talks about where he's from. Except to mention mountain lions. I've never heard him say anything about it."

"Go on over there and see what he's got to say. We'll be here if you need us. If we don't hear from you we'll assume you're staying over there. And you are not to leave Corin's at all, under no circumstances, unless to come back here. No where."

I crammed some stuff into my book bag and headed over. It was colder now. The cypress fronds were silver, gleaming, dripping with the mist rain. The beam of the flashlight went all the way up against the sky, where like my breath everything was white.

I knocked on the back door, thinking I would walk in and see Brandon and Corin sitting there eating cake and drinking green tea.

Corin came to the door. He looked tired.

"He's sleeping now, finally." That sounded like the way people talk about somebody in the hospital.

"Upstairs. I'll show ya. Thanks for coming. It'll be good for you to be here."

"OK."

"I wanted you to be able to talk to him. Something's troubling him bad. Maybe you could stay over here tonight? There's plenty of room."

"Yeah, that's fine."

Corin turned and began to climb the stairs.

In Corin's house wood and stone were everywhere. The fireplace and chimney were old field stone, rusty earth-colored and stoney white. The floors and walls were wide boards, well worn and shining clean. Always a smell of pine. The ceiling beams showed through overhead. It was a strong house. The moldings over doorways were cut with a design of leaves, and over each window the same way. The floor creaked when you stepped, telling you the whole house was built together, old wooden boards making these rooms, and I got the idea I was walking around in an antique chest of fine carved wood.

At the top of the stairs we were in a hallway. I saw several doors. Corin turned to the right, where a door was partly open. Light made a pathway into the dark of the room. Our shadows gathered as we stood at the door.

Wild angels of firelight flew up the walls from the fireplace.

"I wanted you to be here when he wakes up. There's another bed here, plenty of room."

It was too early to go to sleep. But I was already feeling the weight of everything coming down over me.

"So what happened?"

"After you went home, I came in to get something to eat, and then I said, I'll just have a look round the back. I went in the greenhouse, the shed, and then on down past the blueberry bushes, to the compost. I've had deer bed down there before. I've startled them sometimes. I've stood there for long minutes sometimes watching little fawns sleep, peaceful little babes in a beautiful world. And I've had to run out wild dogs from there before, with a rake, one time, dogs that had been running around and had killed some people's calves. But that was a long time ago, and tonight's the first time I've found a fellow human being lying right out in the wet leaf pile like he didn't care, like he was right out of his mind. Right up against the wooden fence."

I heard rain hitting the roof now, up here in the top of the house, a blanket of sound over us in the wood paneled hallway.

"A right shock it was. Brandon, I said, What is it son, but he didn't say nothing. I put my hand on his shoulder and he raised up a little, eyes of blood, they were so red, and I knew he wasn't right. I've seen a share of drunk lads in my day."

"Drunk?"

"No, I don't think so now. Well, I don't know. I might say drunk. Wore out, maybe. Terribly distraught. Almost like he just wanted to fall there and not get up."

"How did you get him up here?"

"I didn't at first. Just sat by him, talking to him. After a while he started pulling himself up. Lean on me, lad, I said. I can walk, he said. He came with me. Both of us soaked with wet. Found him some dry clothes. He wouldn't tell me what's wrong."

"Something at school," I said. "But also something at home, something about where he lived before. His dad's real angry. They said they don't want him to come back home, that's what his dad…"

"Shh, not so loud. Don't let him hear words like that."

"But that's what his dad said. I don't know what it's all about."

"He'll tell us. I think he will. He's been a good lad since I met him. Least, I thought he was. Go on in, and keep an eye on him. Let's get some rest. I'll be downstairs if you need me."

I was tired. Maybe it was the knock on the head. Mom had made me take something. It had been a long day.

The room was big, old, part of the attic I thought. Wooden floor reflected the firelight. I could hear Brandon breathing. Even by that glowering fireplace I could see that he looked scratched up and dirty, little pieces of leaves stuck to his hair. And on the floor.

I lay there awhile, listening to the rain. Or sleet? A tinsel sound pecked and sparked at the window. Was it cold enough? I saw nothing but ink darkness outside. Tiny crystalline ticks struck the window glass. Maybe it was just hard rain?

No, that had to be sleet. Could it be that cold already?

I couldn't remember what I had brought with me, what books. It wouldn't be easy to read in this fireplace light anyway. Even if colonial people did it. But I did have my flashlight. I had clean clothes for tomorrow. Maybe it was already tomorrow. But it couldn't be that late. I reached into my book bag, and then I remembered.

The jaguar skin. The pelt, the precious fur of the cat marked with celestial bodies. Put on my coat, Inha had said. Be my son.

I hadn't read anything anybody had written.

Maybe I shouldn't? I hadn't told them I was going to. But I didn't say I wouldn't, either.

But nobody had said not to read what they wrote. I held the pelt up before the fire. Flames leaping at the hearth showed through, fiery, vermilion, and the spots darker. Half by the blocky light and shadow of my flashlight, half by fire light, I beheld it. Fantastic. The color was exactly right. A fiery, beaming cat. I admired my drawing, the toes and claws. It had gotten a little roughed up in the fall, dirt, splatters of blood on one edge. But that only suited it the more and now it had been through all that, blood and gravel, and it was still here. Now it was a relic. The class had done the writing just like I wanted, in the shapes I had penciled in. They had done it. So my project, that part of it, had gone right after all. It was not a failure. The jaguar's spots were there, in rosettes, spots and circles, shapes within shapes and clusters of spots. Made with words. Some people had colored in outlines of the spots. Just like the real thing.

Some of the writing was addressed to me.

"Chris, just wanted you to know, you're crazy. But that's good. I like that about you." –Darius Coltrane.

"Chris, you're one of a kind."

"Yes I can! Visualize Success." That had to be Chantal. She always said that.

But I felt a little let down. What had I expected? Profound statements, love songs to the universe, something like that. These were more like things you write in a yearbook.

Even Mr. Collins had written something. I could easily tell his writing: "My mistress' eyes are nothing like the sun. W.S." What!

Some people had wrote their names. Someone wrote "peace" in small letters with a little hand making a peace sign with a heart drawn around the hand. Handwriting that I didn't recognize said, "I think my parents hate me, and I understand why."

Someone, maybe Gilford, had written most mystically of all, "The wheel turns up and up."

And then I saw Brandon's handwriting. As sharp as his accent, block letters, all angles, all capitals.

"I swore to kill someone, in front of his own children. And the only thing that stopped me is I couldn't do it before they grabbed me. And I'm sorry for it but I can't take it back."

What? There he lay across the room, breathing loud and slow, fast asleep.

Was it a joke? I couldn't remember him ever making any jokes, not really. But this wasn't funny as a joke, anyway, unless I really didn't get it. Swearing to kill someone?

I clicked the flashlight off and lay back, watched the firelight dance and flicker.

He was strange. Would he write that just as a crazy thing?

But those words. Killing someone. Swearing to. I read it again. Did it matter if you swore something? Seeing the letters written out made me hear his voice saying the words. They were too serious. Should I just act like I had never read it? But why would you put something like that in writing, ever, and let it run out the door, if you wanted it to stay secret? Trying to get rid of it? It felt like he was speaking directly to me. Maybe he really did do it, but can't bring himself to say it?

The fire was blazing right there. I could toss the pelt right in, watch the orange embers eat into it, race across it to white ash. The magic marker writing would go up with smoke outside to the mist and rain.

Maybe I should just hold on. Don't say anything, but wait. See if he says anything, like "Did you read what I wrote . . ."

But why was I so hungry? My stomach was rumbling. I could smell something cooking, something familiar that I hadn't smelled for a long time.

I threw the jaguar skin on the bed, stepped softly out the door. Faint knocking and pinging came from below, a metallic sound. The fragrance was soaring up the stairway, invisible smoke of heavenly incense.

I smiled at how crazy Corin was. When I got down to the kitchen there he was standing at the stove humming. As if he expected me.

"Corin, I'm starving. I didn't know I was so hungry until I smelled that popcorn."

"Well," he said, "I just thought, I'm hungry, so, I said, I'll make us some popcorn. Have a seat, lad."

He was popping the corn in an old pot on the stove top, the old-fashioned way.

The popcorn finished with a roll of thunder. It filled a big bowl. He brought the bowl in both hands over to the table and set it in the circle of light that fell from the fixture over the center of the wooden table. Steam and the fragrance swirled up into the light. I was so hungry. Corin brought a salt shaker over, a little glass one with a chrome lid like the one Brandon had broken in the locker room. The sprinkling salt showered over the popcorn and sounded like the noise I was hearing on the windows.

There we sat crunching our way through handfuls. We were like men who have been away shipwrecked, or in deserts, starving. Corin made the popcorn perfect, exactly the right amount of salt.

"Corin," I said at the end of a big swallow, "has Brandon ever told you anything about his old school? Like, anything that went on? Where he was from?"

I gulped down more popcorn and didn't wait for his reply.

"Because there's something Brandon wrote that I think you should hear about. To see what you think about it. If it's important. Or maybe he was just kidding."

Corin looked at me, waiting to hear more.

"Something about him almost killing someone. He tried to kill someone. Do you think that could be true? Would something like that bother someone enough to affect their life?"

"Hold up, Chris lad, I think you better go back to the beginning. Where did he write that? What was the situation?"

The jaguar, the water under the Earth, the man in a jaguar skin, all of that . . . I started to explain, but Corin looked at me like it was interesting but too confusing.

"Could you eat more? Let's make another round." He got up and moved toward the stove. I heard the popcorn pouring into the metal pot. It would be easier just to show him the jaguar skin. I stood up, turned to run upstairs, and the jaguar appeared before us in the doorway, spread out, fiery, golden, spotted.

"Yeah," it said, "make a lot more. I'm famished."

"Brandon!"

I pinned him against the door jamb. He looked like he'd been through a tornado, face scratched, eyes red, hair twisted and sleep-shaped. He cowered back from me.

"OK, I'll tell you," he said. He thought I was about to punch him.

"Hey, I'm not mad at you. I went by your house. Coach told us . . . I just want to know what's going on." Before he could say anything else I put him in a headlock.

"Chris, easy. It will all be told. Sit down both of you and eat."

The popcorn was suddenly louder, thumping, rolling. The fragrance was wondrous, sweet, flavorful. White steam rose up around Corin's face as he poured the popcorn into the bowl.

"Corin, I have to say, this is the best popcorn I've ever had. It's just, it's unbelievably good."

"Angel brought this popcorn. Flew in with it in a little bag and dropped it on the outdoor table one afternoon as I sat there." And he went on fixing Brandon a glass of water as if that was a 100% normal thing to say.

"Take these. The power of the willow tree."

We both looked to see white aspirin in the palm of his hand.

Brandon took them and drank the whole glass of water. Corin filled it again.

We sat there crunching. Brandon devoured like we had. It was so good. Corin laughed and said there was plenty more. I just smiled and leaned back in my chair. The tinsel sound was still at the window.

"That sounds like sleet to me. What was the weather supposed to be?"

The window was solid black, ice cold.

From the back door our flashlight woke isolated areas of the yard, bushes, the bird feeders, the outdoor chairs. They told the secret, that layers of freezing rain, cold glass, were falling and shaping solid over everything. Everything watered away and faded under layers of glittering ice, like shining the flashlight into a pool.

I beamed the flashlight toward the sky. The falling ice was arcing down like millions of tiny meteors from outer space.

Corin pushed the door shut. The cold air whooshed out from behind it in a tightness that sealed us in. The latch snapped firm and fast. As we sat back down, Brandon pulled the jaguar skin off his back and folded it so that part of the writing was face up.

His part.

He put it in the middle of the table, in the center of light, and after a few silent seconds, looked up at me from across the table.

"You're right Chris. I wrote this. And it's the truth about me."

52

Ice

I felt like I could see light waves coming down over the table.

"But I swear to you, it wasn't like what you're going to hear when you get back to school. It was all a big mix-up, an idiotic thing, a mistake."

"What was?"

"What I did was wrong. I'm not denying any of it. But I'm not a danger to anyone. I just want to say that at the start."

"I never thought you were a danger to anybody. A little annoying sometimes maybe. Did they say you were a danger? But you'd be in jail, or something like that, if you were, wouldn't you?"

"The principal today said there was reasonable cause to believe that I was dangerous to his person, or something like that. That's what you're going to hear when you get back to school. Everybody there is going to know about it. They came and got me in the middle of class. I did threaten to kill a teacher at my old school, and I'm not denying that. You might as well get all my stuff out of my locker, cause they're never going to let me near the school after this."

"That guy in that black car has something to do with all of this. He was at school today."

"What?" He looked truly shocked. "You don't even know him."

"I knew him alright. I recognized him. I've seen him before."

"That day when I was hiding from his car? You couldn't have had a good look at him."

"No. Way before that. Back when you first came here. You showed up in my English class. That was the day we found the crow and brought him back here. The next day you didn't show up in class, but then I thought I saw you outside at lunch and that guy was there too. I saw him walk away and you went into the woods at the edge of the practice field. I was about to go over there after you but then it was time for class."

Brandon looked down at the table.

"Later that day you said you hadn't been at school except for about an hour. But I knew it was you. I mean, it didn't matter, I just wondered, cause it looked like you, and I thought it was you."

He looked up. "It was me. I lied to you. I was afraid. And I'm really sorry now. If I had known you better then, I wouldn't have lied. I would have known that it would be OK to tell you the truth. I should have, especially after you took me home that first day and after we found the crow and all that."

He breathed out a huge sigh that sounded like weary relief. But he looked sick.

"I was scared of anybody finding out."

He was looking at his hands, fingers spread out, palms open.

"It's OK Brandon. You didn't know me from anybody. But all this time, since the day we found the crow, I've been thinking we were friends."

"I'm going to need some friends after what happened today."

"What did happen today?" I said loudly. "I don't even care what happened at the other school."

Corin was watching us back and forth, his eyes bright and dark.

"I went to the library first thing, early, to meet Mr. Blake. We finished putting my pictures up. They looked good. I felt like we had everything ready.

"I went on to class, like normal. Mr. Carr was going on and on and somebody knocked on the door. It was Mr. Blake and he said could he see me, so I went out in the hall with him. I thought something was wrong with the way we hung the pictures or there was something we could adjust to make it better, something like that.

"He said the committee was having problems. What problems, I said. With the photographs, he said. With their content. He just wanted me to know ahead of time before I heard it from anybody else.

"I didn't care. I mean, I expected people not to like it. That was part of the point of doing it. Well, he said, I want you to know I support you and your work 100%. He said it was some of the strongest student work he's seen since he started teaching high school. Mr. Blake is awesome. He said he would let his opinion be known to whoever, it didn't matter."

"Well, you remember that preacher that comes on TV that my step mom watches? Man, God must be against me for everything I've ever done, cause that dude is on my grading committee, and he's evil. When I got to the library, he was standing there like a giant waiting for me. He's huge. And I just stood there thinking he's about to clamp a rat trap around my neck."

"Wait, you mean the same guy that's on TV? He lives around here?"

"Yeah, no lie, the exact same guy. It was a shock to see him standing there in person. He's huge. And his voice is extremely loud. When I walked in with Mr. Blake, he was standing there in the middle of the library breaking everybody's eardrums, pointing to my pictures and telling the whole place how my pictures showed the degradation of youth or something like that. He's just so loud, it's unnatural. It's uncomfortable. It's painful. I don't see how anybody could live in the same house. He's a bellowing giant and everybody was kind of falling backwards in all the noise. And he wouldn't stop. He talked louder than the school bell, and that's when I knew I was in trouble, cause they said you don't need to worry about that bell, just stay where you are.

"He was going like a freight train: These are the kind of pictures that show the erosion of our culture, that I was just giving back the stuff I had learned in evolution class about animal rights and it was the displacement of man and making animals into persons and then animals would be divine, it was the front edge of a wedge to take over the schools and our minds and next thing you know we'll have the church of the holy animal and all this other idiotic stuff I can't even remember. My head was spinning. I was like some little guy in cartoons with stars spinning around his head. I just stood there with my heart pounding inside my ear drums, trying to think what to say."

"But he can't give you your grade. He's not a teacher."

"Yeah, but he wouldn't stop. His voice just filled up everything anybody tried to say. Only Mr. Blake was on my side.

"Anyway, they made me go to a separate room in the back of the library, and when I got inside they made me sit down in front of them. They were sitting in chairs kind of in a half circle. He was all red in the face, boiling over. He said let's get them down right now. Mr. Blake said wait, we owe him a chance to explain. The preacher kept getting so mad, he lifted his chair off the floor and hopped over towards me. Bang bang bang. I just sat there watching him getting closer and closer. I was like, what are you doing. He said this was an example of the stuff that was taking our country down, that I was fascinated by death and morbidity. Why don't you take pictures of something worthwhile. Why don't you take pictures of people's dogs, if you want pictures of animals, something nice like that, something that shows home and society and the way people have put order into the world. I was just thinking who put this freak on a committee? Who thinks that somebody like this ought to be working with kids? One of the teachers said . . ."

"Wait, who was it?"

"I don't know, some lady. She had silver eye makeup like fish skin and you had to notice it because she talked with her eyes closed. She said my project would be found unacceptable. Even before I had a chance to present anything.

"Mr. Blake was great. He kept saying this is exactly the kind of work we're looking for in art, that my pictures were doing exactly what art does. The preacher said just exactly what do you think that mess of filth is doing. Mr. Blake said if you can't see that for yourself you ought to leave education to the educated. Something like that. It got intense. He was saying art is a gift to help us see ourselves, and if you don't like what you see you don't blame the mirror. Stuff like that. I wish I had a recording of it. Mr. Blake is normally so calm and with all this tranquility but he was coming right back at that giant guy."

He took a drink from a cup of tea Corin had set in front of him, holding it with fingertips of both hands like it was some kind of forest broth of herbal roots and leaves Corin had concocted.

"So what happened? They really found it unacceptable?"

"I don't know. When we came out of the room the pictures were already gone. The display cases were empty. If it weren't for Mr. Blake I guess I'd be asking you to sneak up there with me to go look for them in the dumpsters. Mr. Blake managed to tell me that he would get hold of them and keep them safe."

"But I can't see how that could get you suspended. Or almost expelled. Or whatever Coach said, that you might not be back at school?"

"Well, that's because I was sitting there listening to this fish-eyed lady talking about my pictures with her eyes closed and I just was thinking about my pictures. I was thinking about those animals we found and these people didn't want to be bothered to notice anything outside their front windshields except the parking space they're pulling into and the big fat cheeseburger they're chewing on and I just got more and more angry until I just got up and told them that this was the work I had done and that I wouldn't be changing any of it. They could look at it or not look at it, take it or leave it."

He laughed his breath laugh and shook his head.

"Well, that was it. All downhill from there. It isn't for us to take or leave anything young man, she said. It's for you to do your work like you ought to in the first place and take the consequences when you don't. And leave the judging to us. That started her on the whole list of what grade was I in, who was my homeroom teacher, who did I have for homeroom last year, what kind of grades did I usually make, what did I normally do last year. What is my life like at home. I knew it was all over when she said she was going to the office to look into my record.

"They told me to go. I wasn't even sure what period it was. I guess that was when they called my old school and found out I'd been expelled from there. About half an hour later they came and got me and told me I was suspended and that I might get expelled. So now I'm suspended from school under the discretion of the principal and I don't even know where my pictures are. My dad came and got me. He took me home without saying a word until we got there and then he said get out and don't come back here again, what did I think I was, the god of the world. Or something like that."

The ice was still ticking at the windows. The refrigerator had started a whirring sound. Chroma had joined us at some time and Corin got up to give her a snack.

"That's why we moved here, because I was in trouble. This was supposed to be a new start. That's why he's so angry."

"So you never even had a chance to talk about your pictures? That's not right. You should have had the chance to explain them. You know what Mr. Blake said, anybody who can put together work like that has a lot going for him. I heard him say that in the art room, and that's worth a whole lot more than a grade on one little school project."

"Yeah." Brandon was staring at the table in front of him.

Corin stood up and yawned like a big white cat.

"OK. Let's get some rest, lads. There's firewood here on the back porch. Both of you get a couple arms full and take it upstairs. Stoke up the fire. I reckon the whole town is sealed over with ice. We can talk more in the morning. We can go outside and see what's going on. Things will look better in the light of day. So go on up and take your rest. I'll be down here if you need me. And tomorrow we can get in touch with your parents. That is most important."

The fire in the upstairs room had dwindled down to a couple handfuls of bright embers, nodding little eyes about to go to sleep. We stoked it up and stacked more wood to the side.

"But you came by my class during my project." I said, "When was that, with all the other stuff that was going on?"

"I don't even remember. It's like it didn't even happen. But it must have happened. My writing's on that leopard skin you made."

Leopard.

I got into the deep covers of the bed by the window. All those tattoos on my back. I was wiped out and weary and the blaze of fire was singing me to sleep.

I let my eyes dance around with the flames and the wings going up the ceiling. It was nice having a fire in your room. Brandon's voice came out of the dark and it sounded a little shaky.

"So you're not afraid to sleep in the same room as a sworn killer?"

Brandon creeping around the room with a murder weapon, blood all over him? I tried to think of something funny to say. I couldn't see it. It just about made me laugh, but I didn't think he was joking. I did want to hear about it, all that stuff from his old school. But Brandon, a killer? I'm the one who spent the day walking around in someone else's blood.

"Well," I said after a few seconds, "we are still going to Hatteras, aren't we? I'll just have to go ahead and risk it."

53

Otherworld

I saw brilliant turquoise, I saw blue-green, I saw rays of sunlight follow me into the water's depths.

I had run with Inha. I had taken his coat upon me.

"This is no way to go," I yelled.

The golden light of his coat was gone. Sunlight from the surface reaches a limit.

Water does not allow fire.

Everything is dark.

This is no way to go.

"Be quiet, my son.

Follow me now. I will lead you through."

It is cold burning. Like inflammation, like lightning in rain clouds, like fever in the body.

"This is the Mirror," he said.

We journeyed. The watery cavern was an opening, and it was a passage of both water and of rock and of not knowing where I was. The water swelled like a tempest and spit us, to a slippery crawl, to a climb of rock and no hold for human hand. We rolled, we were flat, we folded, along smooth ancient rocks. We faced cliff-rock and face-rock, rock greater than all of my experience, rock that forbid me any knowledge of its fullness. We scraped in tight places and brushed sheer formations. We struggled and I would not have been able without him.

He was an emerging form in the darkness, the way the moon strikes ripples on a lake, silver in the flex more than in the body, shimmering on the contour, his form bending the palest light to shape a silver crescent. His fur was rich like the deep indigo sky in high moonlight. The ever-changing luster was the only light, the whispering embers of fire hidden inside him.

This was the keeping of the light, the keeping of fire. A tarnish, a crust on the ember that keeps the fiery colors hidden. This was the fire that burns in water, the fire that burns in secret hidden under the mountain.

All talk was kept within us now. All talk and all hearing was within.

Where are we? I was calling out. Are we not to see the glory of the sun?

I heard his voice though he did not turn when he spoke, did not face me, and we did not speak aloud.

Where are we? he said. Behold yourself, if you can. We are where elements roam, where elemental abundance runs to abandon, to crest and wave and flood, teeming, held back at borders that life might come to order and not be overwhelmed beyond measure. It might be called the Abandonment, but it is not abandoned. We pass through the Waters.

I tried to behold myself. I held my hands out in front of me. I put my hands to my face. I could feel myself existing but I could see nothing of myself. On him were the markings, I saw them, keeping hidden light as we ran and all around us came torrents of water, and my feet swept away from me. We were again in a Sea, for all I knew it was the Atlantic or some ancient body greater than the word Atlantic, the sea that bounded Pangea, when all the continents were locked like puzzle-pieces in one, when seeds of future generations of plants, and cells of future animals, were being scattered and settling, spreading out into the broader world we know today.

I tell you, he was saying to me, stay close by my side or you are utterly and completely lost. It is by these markings and these eyes that you are kept. By no passage at all may a human being come through except by word of one of my kind. It is my trust, this journey. Do not stray from me in the least or you are utterly undone. For all about you are what have been called the Deeps and the Emptiness and the Utter Waste.

Even as he spoke these words, I felt as though, I knew, I would never breath again. As though a stealthy hand came fingering its way over my mouth. As though hands held my ears. And I could not take my eyes from him, for as he spoke, the spots and circles and rosettes of his pelt flickered, livened, glowing silvery blue as they were, becoming as the stars seen from the darkest mountain, billowy stars, and they were becoming as living eyes, how many I could never count. And each eye was living and moving and watching all about, and it was as if we were running or swimming, I do not know. And around each of them appeared the letters of words circling each eye, words beyond any knowledge I had to read them. Power was coming from each eye, as if in rays, each one spreading a cone of watching power into the darkness, moving and watching.

"Take cover at my side," I heard his voice saying in front of me.

And the whole night sky covered me in a moment, a sparkling canopy, and I knew I was in safety. My breathing returned. In the dark of the wings was the vigil of a holy night surrounding me. Currents of light traced over me, around me, coursed through air and molecule, energies that pulse the world's atmosphere. Mosaics of purple and indigo, sparks twinkling like jewels in cavern walls under torchlight. I felt the great power of strength carrying me forward. It was as though I were under wings but those wings were flying. I felt the great pull of them. I was carried. I don't know how we flew and I don't know how I was carried. We were moving in a great rush of power. Hail storms clattered around us and bright bolts of lightning flashed, bright charges of friction throwing from us, but we soared in warmth and safety.

We came to the end of dark churning waters. We came to the beginning of open land. It was like a wilderness. A desert. A resting place. Sandy, grainy, gravelly under foot. It was a narrow way in rocky land but the ground felt solid under my feet. My ankles did not turn. My steps did not falter. No stone was in the way to make us stumble. He was leading a good way.

The land lay at rest under the night sky, terrain made silver by moonlight on the blades and the spikes and leaves of desert plants. A pathway was there trailing up to the mountains where moonlight lay white at the crest. And other people were there too. Pilgrims. We were joined. We became as a band together. I did not know each one. I did not need to. We were there together.

Put away the things of your former selves. Shed your clothes. Take new, take these things, they told me. Make new clothes for yourself. They showed me how. I did not know. They were simple things, simple clothing of plain cotton. They showed me. We sewed with fine wool thread. Pictures of Guardians we sewed onto our clothing. They showed me what to do. What Guardians called to us: Seeds, pumpkin seeds, corn and bean seeds. The gifts of food. Each little seed a shape, a capsule of protected life. I made these with colored wool threads onto the plain cotton of my clothing. Ochre yellow and earth greens, moss and dark storm grays, bright blues, iron reds. Other Guardians called out to us. We hold the Lamp for you. Saints, angels. The Lion, the Ox, the Eagle. I made them onto my shirt and my trousers of plain cotton. What other Guardians called out to us: Leaves of plants. Holly.

Evergreen. The enduring green of cedar and pine. Good herbs like mint and rosemary. The tower of oak, the promise of acorn. The star of sweet gum. And the fruits of plants. Apple and almond. And holy minerals: salt, in cubic crystals of silver and white.

We are the people on the journey, they told me. Are you not too young, some asked. Welcome, some said. You will journey with us. But are you not too young? We do not eat except what little we must. We do not sleep, except what little we must. We do not leave the circle of the fire by night, we do not relieve the body, except what we must. Are you not too young?

"You are as a fool," the Jaguar said to me. "You are as a baby now. Do not leave me or be unguided or you will come to destruction."

"He is as a baby," he said. "Is he too young? Where are his long years and his toil? But he is with me and I will be his guardian."

You are come to make this journey, they said to me. The people of the journey gathered around me. You are ready. You are here. We will show you how to make clothes for yourself. They handed me the simple cotton shirt, the simple cotton trousers. They showed me how to make the designs using colored fine wool threads.

The Jaguar Inha, silent as a rising moon, lay at the edge, burning like the darkened embers of a sleeping fire. He was noble in profile, undisturbed, able to present such a face that nothing would take his eye from the place where he was looking. He lay with forearm forward, half-sphinx.

And Hummingbird, the butterfly, was there. She can change shapes. She has the power of transformation, and she stood there speaking to me on the trail at the near slope of the silver mountains.

"You have come safely in," she said. "In peace, in silence, be still."

And Brandon was standing by her side.

54

White

Deep in the night I heard shrieking in the ice.
And again.

It couldn't be a gunshot? Firecrackers? But now? Here? In the middle of the night?

And then a rustling, a rushing, like water falling or like sharp wind, and then a mumble, a thud, a thump.

The fire had withered away, ash and embers. Our stash of firewood lay by the hearth.

Another popping shot, another whooshing water-rush, another dull thump. The crackings and thumpings were coming every half minute or so. I leaned up and wedged my face to the dark glass, the chill of glassy sea water. Outside all lights were long ago engulfed and extinguished. But then I knew without seeing. Trees were breaking under layers of ice.

Another crack. Live branches were tearing away and crashing to the ground.

The house had fallen to a silence deeper than regular nighttime, and that meant no power. The lines would have been pulled down somewhere by ice or by falling branches.

I looked again at the firewood waiting at the hearth. Quick. Dancing, tiptoe, a crazy Puck tossing firewood, I built up a pyramid into the last embers. The shiny pine floor was mirror cold, and I was leaping and sinking and wrapping back into the warm cavern of bed.

Fire was quick. The pleasant crackling took right to the dry wood, popping and sparking. And then I heard another, different sound. The only description possible was "chordant thunder." Even if I had never heard those words together. Thunder ringing in chords, like bells, the very chimes they ring in the heavens. Did it thunder during ice storms? The sky, solid with clouds and ice, bore down close upon us. Sounds were trapped with us here below, rebounding off the clouds and hitting my eardrums. Again. Chimes, from the sky. I looked for car lights or something on the road. Maybe it was the police, an emergency signal? It was like ships sounding for the depths, muffled by distance. Chordant. Chiming. We were sunk to the bottom of a sea, cloud and ice, our trees crashing down upon us. But no noise came from the road, no sound of traffic, no gush of tires in slush and rain. No hushed tire whispering on snow. No passing headlights. This was ice and darkness and falling tree branches. I entombed myself deeper into the covers.

When I woke I saw bright whiteness shining upward from outside. It filled the windows. Brandon was still out, breathing like a steamer.

My nose and face were arctic, like I'd been camping outside. Maybe the power would come back. Within seconds. I counted five, ten. But the whole house was quiet, shivering, and there was a secret creaking and the sound of little snaps and that, I thought, was the ice stealing in through the copper electric lines, racing back through the dead electric conduits, where nothing held it back, frost gushing from the outlets, splintering the sockets, snapping our wires and window glass, blowing out light bulbs. The floor along the walls was piling up with freezing white pestilential anthills, the mineral growths of deep caverns going up to the ceiling. I buried my head down deeper into the blankets.

When I woke again I felt the blankets being pressed down in small forceful pokes at my thighs and stomach and chest and neck and then I opened my eyes to a sniffing nose and whiskers tickling my face and a snuffling loud breath.

"Chroma, where did you come from? Are you frozen?" I ventured my hand out into the cold air. Her loud breathing rumbling and she walked around purring all across me.

Even without power we had breakfast because Corin had a big fire going. We toasted bread and cooked sweet potatoes, and we still had hot water because Corin's hot water heater had a pilot light under it. We went crouching down the stone steps for him, under the house, where it smelled like cold clay, to make sure it was OK.

Outside, clouds still banked over us. White sky, white ground. Not snow, but sleet had driven down like a salt crust, and on every surface, sheaths of ice thick and knobby as glass bottles. The sun was nowhere to be seen.

So much freezing rain had fallen so fast. It was devastation. Corin was stunned, walking around gently laying his hand on tree branches, on tree trunks, saying nothing. Did he have the power to restore them like that, just laying his hands on them? But I knew that wouldn't happen. It would have to be the roar of a chainsaw and the brutality of broken tree trunks. We were out with shovels to see if we could get Corin's steps and walk cleared so he would be able to get in and out of the house safely.

We had to step over and around broken tree branches, through them and under them. The bigger branches would be for firewood. The ice held globs of cedar green like twisted hands, crystal deformities, and those branches lay there strangely bright, like the cold had burned them to a vivid green. Open flesh was torn raw on the live wood. Blank white sky filled gaps of missing branches, in places that had been covered for so many years. Corin was truly shocked. I felt we should do something to help him, but what? In movies, people offer brandy or strong tea at moments like this.

"Wow, I'm breathing this," I said. Taking deep breaths. It was wondrous, the cedar smell in the air from all the broken places and bruised green. It was like oranges, tangerines, like Christmas trees and pine and cinnamon fresh and sharp. It cleared my head, my throat. It was clean.

Brandon spat loudly toward the side of the walk, and then again. "He's the biggest liar on the face of the earth. He told me to call him Star Man, when I first met him."

"That's dumb."

Brandon kicked his feet on the icy walk.

"I've thought about this so much. It never goes away. I wake up scared in the middle of the night. I see his face up against mine. I smell the cigarette smoke. I can't get away from him. I'm back in the middle of it even though I remember I'm moving on. In the dark, I just lay there knowing it's all real, even if we don't live back there anymore. It just recycles through my mind, some idiotic kid who did something really stupid, who messed up everything, and that stupid kid is me and I can't get away."

I just stood there kicking at the ice with him.

"Brandon, I don't know anything about all of that. If you wanted to make a clean start, you already have. You're here now. Haven't you already been punished for whatever happened at the other school?"

"Yeah. Massively. And it didn't go away."

He belted an ice-chunk against the papery bark of one of the blasted cedars.

"And you didn't actually do it. It was just words, wasn't it, swearing? You didn't kill anybody."

"But I spoke those words. They happened, like, when they went out into the world, that made them real. They're on me now."

I belted an ice-chunk against the bark of a tree.

"I guess you already figured out it's about drugs," he said. "I'm one of the kids who fell for that."

"Well, I hadn't really thought about it." But as I said that I remembered the principal and Mr. Collins talking about drug dealings around the stadium.

"'Can't you see when you look at me I was born under the sign of the devil?' That's what he used to tell us. 'Don't touch me, I'm a magic person. One touch and you're burning.' He was always saying stuff like that. 'Don't even come near. I've fallen from the sky. You aren't ready for what I can bring on you. Spiritual creatures like me need their space. I came into this world to do evil.' He would make you sit in the back seat and look down when you were around him. He would never shake hands with anybody. 'Why would you ever want to shake my hand? You touch me under peril. I bear a magic that can turn against you.' Psycho stuff like that. Then you would look over and the stuff would be laying there on the seat beside you. He told me he drank blood before and he would drink it again if I messed with him and then I would find out what the devil looks like. But that's so stupid, and I let that scare me. But after all that's happened I'm not sure if he really said that or if I dreamed it. Cause I started having nightmares real bad back then. Really bad. But back then, when he said things like that, I got caught up. I got mesmerized. I saw how dark it was but I wanted to hear it anyway. It was like a place I could go into. Way better than school. It was real to me and nothing else mattered. And my parents were driving me crazy all the time. The idea of being kind of magical, of being so powerful that people should stay back. That kept me fascinated. Stupid, I know. You can go ahead and say it. I know you're thinking it."

I just smiled. The little breath-laugh. Well, I was thinking, how could you want to be around a person like that?

But I thought I knew what he was talking about. Stuff like that might be more interesting than what we were doing in math. It would all depend on the situation you were in.

"What happened was at a football game, a Friday night. My school had a stadium like the one here, with concrete bleachers going up a slope.

"I don't remember a lot. I don't even know exactly what I took. All he had to say was 'ride the lightning outta here.' That was enough to catch a stupid kid like me. I thought I was doing something so great. We were out in the parking lot. It was perfect. Friday night, Autumn weather. Football weather. People were laughing, other kids. People were just having a good time. Kids were throwing a football. Meeting their girlfriends or the girls they liked. That's what it was all supposed to be about. Having a good time. 'Have a good time,' he would say, 'Come on, have a good time.' That was his little saying. It was after the time changes back, getting dark early. The game had already started. I wish I had been in the stadium watching it. I got so fascinated by the sky. I probably looked exactly like what I was, a doped up kid standing there looking at the sky. It was dark blue with lights in it, like airplanes coming in close and I was just standing there watching them. That was the first thing that came back into my memory after it all happened, these big bowls of light pouring down to earth and then I was just blurring across everything. Suddenly my legs had unbelievable power. I was running over the ground and everything was rushing past. I was so powerful. Big bowls of light were being poured down to us, it was angels, and I could go to them. I held out my arms. The bowls of light were pouring out staircases for me and I was going up there. I was so stupid. It was like water running. Like if you go white water rafting. I was suddenly inside the stadium and noise was everywhere, chuckling and laughing, voices all around, happy, louder than normal, and I was rushing on it. I thought I was surfing I guess. The best way to say it is the rush of it. Everything rushed, it all just rushed against me and I rushed into it and I was in the middle of it. I rode it. It was holding me up and I was going to reach the light coming out of the bowls.

"Later on, people told me I was running up and down the stadium hill, from where the gate was to where the bleachers started going down. A bunch of people, lots of the crowd, stopped watching the game so they could watch me. People were gathering around. They told me people were amazed at how fast I was going. Some people said they tried to talk to me and my eyes were glowing bright red and I couldn't keep still. I just kept going everywhere. But I didn't know I was doing that. I ran down the hill near the end zone. And then they said I turned and ran for the bleachers. I was leaping the seats, over people, around people. People were having to scramble out of the way until I finally came up against this teacher.

"I remember the lights, and I was going to the angels, and everything else looked red. And there were voices coming to me. That's when I said I was going to kill him. He was a teacher. I came up against him and he was in my way. He was keeping me from the bowls of light. Before he had a chance to do anything, I was shouting down on him. 'I'm going to kill you, I swear I will kill you.' I just kept on and on shouting it.

"Those words came out of me. I don't know how. Every person in the whole stadium saw me and heard me. I've started remembering parts of it. Little parts. When I wake up at night. Or I'll just be sitting in class or anywhere and a scene will come into my head and I'll be remembering it.

"It's the guy's face I finally remembered. The teacher. He's just looking at me so afraid and shocked and drawing back. It was like I saw into his mind and I could tell that he felt like he was the only person in the whole world at that moment. He felt like no one was with him. And he was thinking I really was going to kill him, and he couldn't stop me, and his kids were there beside him. And they would see me killing him."

"So what did stop you?"

"Other people. They grabbed me. They threw me down. I got scraped up against the bleachers. But I mean, and I'm not saying this for an excuse, who knows what I was really going to do? Maybe I was just going to laugh. Maybe I really was going to do something. They told me later I was fighting back. They had to hold me down against the concrete. The only reason I didn't get put in jail is because the teacher didn't press charges. He could have. My mom keeps thinking he will, like one day he'll change his mind. She keeps saying I've put myself under his power now and stuff like that, and its a debt we'll never get out of, like he could decide to sue us at any time, and that's all she talks about when I go up there. I didn't know him or have him for any classes. I don't know why I would say that to someone. I tried to talk to him later, I mean, I did talk to him, just to tell him I didn't mean it. He said don't worry about it, it's just one of those things. I wanted to say I wish I could take it all back but I didn't say that, because it seemed like he would be thinking, 'yeah, sure.' He said he didn't take it personally, he has worked in schools enough to know that kids are growing and changing and going through difficulties. But what he said didn't matter, as far as me getting expelled from school.

"My dad wanted to kill me. I think he tried to get me put in jail. He said jail would be better for me. He and my mom hadn't been getting along anyway, so all they did then was yell and argue and mom would run off crying while dad yelled after her. It would get dark with them yelling and nobody even turned on any lights in the house and I never knew if I could come out of my room or not without getting yelled at. My dad made me go to a shelter for a couple of weeks."

"A shelter? What do you mean? To live there?"

"Yeah, just for a while. About ten days. A homeless youth shelter. I had to go to a drug group with a couple of other guys about getting off drugs.

And at first I was like, I'm not on drugs, I only did it a few times. But then it was cool after that cause this one kid started telling all this stuff and I could see how messed up he was. He was so much worse. So after that I just kind of quit worrying about it and just listened. That was at a place for homeless people where you could get lunch but you couldn't stay the night, and they didn't have supper. It was on the other side of the downtown from the place where we slept."

"You really did that? Weren't your parents worried something would happen to you? You could have gotten killed or something."

"I could have, I guess. But really, it was a relief not to be around my parents arguing all the time. I guess it was kind of like I was camping out. I just kind of stuck with these guys who seemed pretty stable. Not everybody out there is safe to be around but these guys were OK, really. They came to eat supper every night and didn't cause trouble and just kept to themselves. They didn't want trouble. They just talked about stuff during the day. We walked all over downtown and looked at stuff I've never seen, like the way the roads look from under the bridge when nobody thinks anybody's looking. You can walk all around the big buildings. You just kind of disappear and watch everything. But you're right, I wouldn't want to be out there by myself and I was just lucky when I got in with those guys. They're not bad guys, the ones I was with. Some of them do drink a lot and that's what's got them where they are today, I guess. I just kind of laughed and tried to fit in and not stand out cause I guess I was scared, I admit it. But they were funny. One guy would talk about stuff from the Bible all the time, and then he would just start singing so loud, about fifty times a day. All those guys were older than me except this one kid named TJ. They had this thing where this lady was doing an art project where homeless people could draw and paint on an old wall outside, where an old house used to be. TJ showed up out there for about three days. But then he said he was moving on. He said 'got to find a place to lay my head.' And I was like, hey, come with us, but he didn't. You could just see in his eyes, how far away he was. And there are some scary people out there too."

"And then, one time at the lunch place these people brought all this food, and they had vegetarian chili, with cornbread and salad and chocolate cake and I was so blown away I just walked back to my table in a total trance of elation like I was holding the Holy Grail of food. I just sat there looking at it before I ate it, without even picking up my fork or anything, just because I was so glad to see it. I just watched the steam coming off it. I can still see it and I can still smell it and I can still taste it. And this lady, one of the people who fixed it, came up and sat across from me and I was like Oh no, here comes all the church talk, because they were from a church. So I just kept my eyes on the food and the steam.

"And that lady didn't say anything. I kept waiting. I could feel she was looking at me. And then, I had my hands on the table near my bowl, I felt her hands come and lay on top of mine, like she just took my hands in hers. And I didn't even look at her but I could feel how her hands were smooth and warm, and I guess this sounds dumb but there was this smell of rose lotion exactly like my grandmother used to have. All she said was one thing, and it floated around with me from then on. 'He made darkness his secret place.' That was it. No sermon. And like, I knew she meant God because she was from a church. He made darkness his secret place. I was like, Wow. His secret place.

"And I always wonder who she was. And if I ever see her again, I will get down on my knees and thank her for bringing us that food."

"Wasn't it hard to talk to those other guys though, I mean, cause you knew you were going back home. Didn't you? Where they were there for the rest of their life. I mean, that is their life."

"Yeah, exactly. I just didn't say much. You're exactly right. All of them are there for real and I was just kind of visiting. I knew I would be going back home. But I was there for a real reason, and I had been expelled from school. But that's not really right about all of them. Some of them do move on. Some of them do make it out of there. But some of them are crazy for real, I mean like really messed up. Frighteningly, believe me. Psychologically. Like that guy who would break out singing. I don't see how he would be able to make it. But he's one of the nicest, I mean, you would know instantly if you met him, he wouldn't hurt you at all. I ate with him and walked all over the place and spent whole days with him.

"Anyway, all during that time, my parents were splitting up. My dad was looking for a new job and a new place to live, all because of me. He was ashamed of me. That started the whole process of us moving here. A new start in a new place. I never wanted to be here."

I watched my breath blow out all around my head in curls of white vapor, like they were curls of white paper, and they were filling with black letters trying to take up all the things Brandon had just said.

55

Plan

Then on the way back in Brandon stopped. Turned back and looked at me. Behind him the crow family flapped down into the trees, shining black against the dull white ice.

"Wait. Did you say you had seen him?"

I'd been waiting for this.

"Yep."

"How? When?"

"That's how I got this knot on my head. I didn't just see him, I busted his face."

"What? What are you talking about?"

I drew it all out for him, the coughing, bubbling, blood-spitting face I saw when I opened my eyes. The black shining sports car screaming in fury.

"Chris, man, you're turning out so different than I ever took you for. Are you joking? This guy carries weapons. You're just a kid, a little boy compared to him. This isn't playground wrestling."

What?

"Well you can tell him that, Brandon. Tell him I'm just a little kid. He's the one who went running away with blood pouring out of his face. His nose must have been broken wide open. It's not like I planned any of that, anyway. It was a crazy accident."

"Chris. Man. Dude. No offense, but you're crazy. He'll be back. Mark my word. He will be back. He won't care if it was an accident. He'll be back. And he will mess you up. He's going to be looking for both of us now. He's seen us together in your car. He's going to be outside your house one night when you get home from school. That's what he does. And he says all this stuff, to mess with you. And he means it."

"Like what?"

"Like he'll put all your teeth in your pocket. That's what he used to say to me, what he would do if I told."

"What does he do, walk around with pliers in his pocket? Don't worry so much. Man."

"No, Chris. This is something to worry about. This is for real. You have no idea. I'm serious. You need to be serious about this. He will mess you up. Dude. Chris. Believe me..."

And he put his hands on his head and started muttering about 'Why have I gotten you into this.'

"You didn't get me into anything. I'm the one who ran into him. It just happened . . ."

"But he was there because of me."

". . . And I'm not afraid, Brandon." I wasn't. I had told Mr. Collins and the principal about him, and the principal would be digging into Brandon's past anyway. So it would all come out. The school would get the police to arrest this guy and that would be it.

But, of course, the school never did anything about the skippers. And they had to know they were out there sitting in their dilapidated hideout.

What I was afraid of was that Mom might ban me from ever going anywhere again. And I was supposed to be going to Muriel's concert, and me and her were supposed to go out to eat after it was over.

"Hey. OK. So the police will be wanting to catch this guy, right? And the school doesn't want him lurking around. What if there is a way to catch him? He's going to be looking for us. What if we could get him caught? Set a cunning trap.

"You mean with us as the bait?"

"Yeah. Something like that."

He breathed out a big long breath. "Yeah, but you don't know when he's going to turn up. Or where. He could show up at your house. It could be at any time. He's going to be looking for blood."

Like a vampire.

"Does he know where I live? How would he? Does he know where you live?"

"I don't know. I don't think he does. I've been watching for him. I probably would have seen him in the neighborhood by now. That's what he does, just sits in his car on a street where he knows you'll see him, and he knows that you know he's watching. And that puts you up against the wall. So yeah, anyway, that makes sense. He's showing up at school because he doesn't know where I live."

"So to find you, and to find me, he's still going to have keep lurking around school. And that is where we set our trap. We have to make contact with him somehow. But we're in control, because we know he'll be there. We should make the first move. Not let him catch us by surprise. We'll make a plan and entice him into it. You have to make some kind of arrangement with him, a meeting, and that's where the police will get him."

Brandon's face went dark again, clouded over like when I first met him. Like he saw nothing but impossibility, far distances that were too far away. Which way, which way, which is the right direction.

"Unless he remembers your car, Chris. That's all he needs. All he has to do is follow us home one day."

"Why is this guy even here, anyway? Are you saying he followed you all the way from Colorado?"

Brandon threw back his head and yelled. Like a painful gulping howl. From the upper tree shadows the crow voices called an alarm.

"I'm so sick of him. None of this happened in Colorado. If I had stayed out there I would never have met him." He looked straight at me. "That was another lie, too, I guess I have to call it. In a way. I did live in Colorado, and everything I told you about the mountain lions is true. We saw one in our own yard, one time, but then we moved to North Carolina. We were living near Winston-Salem when all this happened. That's where I met him. And he wants to keep me quiet. And he wants to get me back onto his lightning. He can't stand to lose somebody. It's about control. That's something I learned from the counseling. And he doesn't want me to expose him for what he is. And I . . ."

"That's why we have to get him caught. We have to."

"I don't know. I don't know!"

56

Sliding

The ice built up heaviest on pine trees, it seemed like, and pulled some of them all the way over. Deep places of red clay lay open where the trees' roots had been pulled up. In one of those places we found a mystery: glistening black coals of charred wood, deep down three or four feet in the ground, set in red clay like dark jewels. We knelt around it, looking, wondering. Corin thought it was the remains of a fire from long ages ago, and then later a pine tree sprouted there and grew. Would it take centuries for the coals of a fire to end up so far down in the ground? Does the ground build up on itself? Had an ancient settlement been here? Was this the night campfire of one who stopped here on a lonely journey?

"People were in this place long before ever we came here," Corin said. He looked a little troubled and then a look of peace came over him.

"Yes. This is the way of things. Like waves passing over. Time passes over us. We get buried and new people, new generations, carry on. Carry on above, under the sky. I have been here and now . . .

"You fellows, I might as well say this to you now. I hadn't wanted to tell you yet but I know I must. The time for my leaving is not too long from now. It'll be next year in the early Summer."

"You're about to die?" I couldn't help myself.

"No, least I don't think so. I'll be moving. Moving in with my son and his family, in Raleigh. They've got it all figured out. They've got plenty of room for me. And this place will have to be sold. Not until the early Summer.

Don't be thinking I've asked you to do all these things, all this work, for no reason, it hasn't been like that, it was a gift to me to have you here . . ."

"Corin, what? But how can you just go? What about the house, what about the garden and all the plants and your trees and everything? How can you just let it go?"

Brandon looked at me like, Don't ask, Can't you see it will just hurt him? But I kept on.

"Well, it's hard Chris. It's not easy to let it go, but nobody can hold on to anything when their time comes. I don't want to go, but it's one of those things. The world keeps turning and days add up into years and, well, a person grows old. My son cannot move here. His work is elsewhere. He cannot keep this old house and all this yard, and that's how it will be. I will have a place there with him, and he has a garden too. He's all into growing native plants, so I'll learn about that. And you know, my Dear One told me I would know when it's time to go. And I do know. I feel it. I feel it within me. I know it's time."

Corin. It felt like a new devastation. I stood there not knowing what to say.

"This old place," he kept on, looking around. "I had dreamt of a place like this. My Dear One dreamed of it. We made it, and it grew, and somehow it became so much what we had dreamed of that I don't know now if it was made after my dreams or my dreams were made from it. And if I dreamed it before it came to be, I know it will go with me like a dream after I'm gone from it. And who knows? We may find a buyer who loves trees and who would keep it like this."

But it will all get torn down. I almost said it out loud. It will end up bulldozed. But I didn't say it. He was smiling a little and looking fine. Looking like he always did, calm and OK, him and Brandon, like somehow they knew something I might not know.

Me and Brandon walked right up the middle of Gilead Road. No cars came at all. On the bridge we stood and watched a line of power company trucks creeping up the Interstate. The shopping centers were closed. All along Gilead everything was shut, and up at the old Square. You could walk everywhere. Kids were out sliding and playing. We heard them shouting. We went down there, behind the old elementary school. It wasn't real sledding, it wasn't as good as snow, but down by the ball field it was good, the way it slopes down. We slid on lunchroom trays somebody found at the back door of the cafeteria. It was ice and sleet, layer upon layer, with rough edges when you slammed up against a jagged place. No banks of soft powder to crash into.

But by afternoon the ice was already melting. It snapped with the sound of glass and shattered on the ground. Sheets of it peeled and slid off branches. Long sheaths fell from the power lines. The shells and skins of an old world slough off and shed, and make room for the emergence. A new world, or the same old world as before? It was always like that, melting away so fast.

The knot on my head felt better. I knew it would be getting bluer, greener, weirder. I saw people staring and couldn't help feeling I had a trophy. They thought I had banged myself up sliding on the jagged ice. We just wanted to go down to the shops, even with it all closed, go up to the Square and see who else was out walking. People were walking around. It was so different from when the town was full of rushing cars. Like this you can see people. People could stare at my banged up, crazy head. People could look at me and wonder and think, I bet that's a kid who just got in a bunch of trouble at school. That's how he got that knot on his head. I hope he learned something from it. And look at the pair of them.

Both of us suspended now. This was new territory for me. I didn't know how to feel about it. And people already knew about it. Some kids were asking about it. Knew I'd been called to the office late in the day. Been fighting again, they thought. Everywhere we went, I kept thinking, everybody knows. Everybody's looking. We got suspended. We might be criminal kids. We might get into anything.

Not really. But I tried to enjoy acting like it. Tried not to feel worried that I was becoming a lost person, a failure.

We stayed out sliding for hours. Got ice-wet from falling. I would have stayed out all night probably, if that had been possible without getting into worse trouble. But it came time to go back home. Brandon went back to Corin's but somehow it got worked out with his Dad and he ended up going back home too.

The power came back on late in the night, while we were asleep, without us knowing till we woke on Sunday. Church was called off. Corin's yard was truly a battle scene. Our yard was. Every yard was. We started some of the work of clearing, even on Sunday, to get our and Corin's driveways and walkways open. Lots of work would be waiting for us, cutting branches into firewood, clearing away broken limbs. It was our earliest ice storm that anyone could remember, and some trees still had leaves, like some oaks, so those trees got ripped up because the ice had clung more fiercely to them.

Later, riding in the car, we could see that just like at Corin's, the cedar trees along country roads and pastures had split open. The splitting revealed their inner purple wood. Purple like beef, like deep muscle, ripped open.

But it was that smell that I could never forget, fresh and powerful in the air, like oranges and cinnamon and Christmas.

57

Going to the Planets

"You'll be there, for real? Tuesday night?"

"Yeah, for real. I said I would."

"Just asking. Just making sure. It's going to be so good. You're going to love it!"

"I know. You've told me."

"I know. But it is, for real. You're going to finally hear what we've been talking about all this time. It's like, I've had all this other reality all this time that you've never even seen or heard of. You've just heard us talking about it. You've never even heard the music."

"I know. I've never even heard the music. I'm completely in your hands here. But I have seen the planets, at least a couple of them. Venus for one. And Mars. And something else that I think was Saturn or maybe it was Jupiter, I don't know for sure. And some of the Earth."

"You do know what they are?"

"Yeah, I know. They're symphonies. Obviously. That's why you're playing them in Youth . . . Symphony."

"You're crazy. They aren't symphonies."

"Yes they are. That's what symphonies are, little pieces of music for orchestras like yours to play."

"They're not little! You really don't know."

"Don't tell me this is going to be some four or five hour thing, Muriel, I'll be dead before it's over and you'll come out looking for me and I'll be slumped over petrified in my chair. You'll have to call the authorities to have my body removed."

"You're crazy. You won't die from this. You'll come alive. And they're not symphonies, they're tone poems. But I'm not even talking about that."

"You never said anything about poetry!"

"You like poetry! But I'm not talking about them anyway, I was talking about the planets. In the sky."

"In the universe you mean. In the Solar System."

"OK, in the Solar System. But that's still the sky."

"No it isn't, the sky stops where the blue stops. After that it's Universe. Somewhere in between it's Atmosphere."

"So where does the blue stop?"

"When the sun goes down."

"You're crazy. You're still a Flat Earth Person."

"No, I've improved. I'm leaving that flat world behind. I'm sailing off from it in a spaceship. A little spacecraft."

"Well, what I was talking about is the planets. The ones out there."

"And I'm out there with you. All that space everywhere, all those little planets, us circling around in our little spacecraft. Maybe they serve supper on board. What will we have? What were you going to say about them?"

"I don't remember now."

"Say something anyway."

"Like what?"

"I don't know. Maybe something about the little twinkling stars."

"The stars are not little Christmas light bulbs, you know."

"How do you know?"

"They aren't! They're giant burning fires. Don't go too close to them while you're in your spacecraft, they'll toast you before you even get close enough to know it. They're bigger than the Sun. Most of them are. Are you looking out of your window? See how bright that is?"

I shuffled with the blinds.

"In the west. That's Venus. But the light isn't coming out of it, it's coming from the sun to us, reflecting off Venus. If we were standing up there on the surface of Venus right now it would be daytime. You might want sunglasses."

"You would want more than sunglasses if you were standing on Venus."

"Because it isn't a star, it's a planet."

"I know. You've told me."

"So if people were standing on Venus, at some time they would probably be able to see Earth the way we're seeing them. Like if you were standing in their dark part when we're having our Earth day time, we would be shining like that to them."

"Yeah, I know."

"See? Like right now it's just now getting dark for us. We're just turning away from the sun and they're getting hit with the sun and we're seeing them. So if somebody was standing on the edge of their day the way we're here on the edge of our day, they would be looking at us maybe, at the day part of earth, which is just a few states over from here really, just over there somewhere."

"I know, it's awesome."

"So you'll be there. I'll see you after. You're still coming with us to get something to eat?"

"Yeah, I'll be there. I'll see you after. I'm still coming with you. I won't fall asleep. I'll be listening. And I'll be watching. Where will you be, anyway?"

"On the stage? I think?"

"Oh. Really! No, I mean, where on the stage?"

"With the violins? Do you think maybe?"

"How do I know where the violins will be?"

"Oh my goodness, you really do need help!"

"I've told you. I've been knocked on the head, remember? I'm not my right self."

Isn't that the truth. I had a lot to tell her. She must not have heard anything at all about it. So yeah, I had a lot to tell her.

But somehow I felt OK.

I had the jaguar pelt in my room, and I thought it would go good on the wall beside the maps. But it seemed better to keep it folded, closed up and secret, just for now anyway.

And I kept having this thought, an idea, and I got to work. I got out paper, pencils. The drawing came out dark on dark.

A jaguar.

The Jaguar. Inha, when I had not seen him.

Dark on dark. Just a thin line of light, like a crescent moon. The contour, the wordless look of a jaguar.

Brandon was right. I could be making designs. I could be making pictures.

58

Monday, Return to School

Monday morning it was like the solid white sky of the storm had cracked and fallen. Shards of it lay in all the shadowy places. Everything above was bright blue, bright sun.

And I was up already and outside, even though I didn't have to be. I didn't feel heroic anymore. I felt the weight of my classes going on without me.

Just be glad to have a break, a voice in my head was telling me. But that was crazy. It wasn't a break. It was damage. It was me getting destroyed. My schoolwork, my future. My reputation. I was getting behind. What would people think of me now? I couldn't not care. I even walked out to the road, like standing out there would somehow connect me to everything I was missing. In my mind I arrived at school and pulled into my usual place in the parking lot, over at the far edge. But the white pines stood silent now, wounded and sap-ripped and arm-broken from the ice. It was my papers blowing away across the parking lot, and I couldn't catch them.

Crow noises sounded right beside me, right in my ear. I could have punched him one time for that. How he got down there so quietly, I don't know, coming up from Corin's shadowy ramparts. Or was I just so lost in my mind that I couldn't hear anything? He had that maniac glint in his eye. But after all this I knew him better now. He wasn't hiding stuff. And he had a plan. It was insane.

"Yeah," he said. "We're going to take them some lunch. They sit out there even in weather like this, cold and wet, and they don't get much of anything to eat if they don't bring it with them. They'll be sitting out in this icy wetness. And they've been good to me, and that's what I'm going to do for them. I'm getting them lunch, and I need help. And it will be awesome to be at the school like that, after all this. You don't deserve to be suspended. Why shouldn't we go back up there?"

Because we could get into a thousand times more trouble. That's one good reason.

"How," I asked him. "You're crazy. There's no way I'm driving back to school today."

"No, we're not driving up to the school. You know I'm not that dumb. Just trust me."

Sometimes you do things that are unexplainable, even to yourself, even when you are the person deciding to do it. It would not make any sense for me to go down to the school. Was it the woods? The idea that we would be going secretly into the woods, the woods we knew from running, that we would be hidden from the whole school right when school was going on? Was I a defiant person? What was Brandon really after?

"Is this so you can contact Star Man? If it is, we need to get our plan together first, don't we?"

"Just let me think about all that. I don't know yet. I don't know!"

The road that goes by the school woods is our coming home route every evening. That was Brandon's plan. It's no trouble to park in the grass alongside that road, he was telling me, and to climb up the bank and go into the woods. We can easily do all that so quickly. We can do it while no cars are coming. No one will see us.

Like this was something he did two or three times a week.

Once we get in the woods, he said, we already know our way. And we just go up to the hideout. They'll be up there, sitting in the cold. Hungry. And we are going to take them some lunch. Come on, man, you like the woods anyway.

"Yeah, but the warm school building is right there. The cafeteria is right there. Why are you feeling sorry for them? They could be inside. They don't have to be out there." They're a bunch of low life trouble makers, I wanted to say. They're throwing away their free education. They're throwing away opportunities. They don't need somebody to take them lunch.

"OK. You're right. They don't have to be sitting out there in the cold. But they are. They have stuff to deal with sometimes. They have trouble. Do I need to say that you might not know all the things they're dealing with? Some of them get abused at home, in ways you don't want to know about.

And they've helped me. And I am taking them some lunch. So are you with me or not? Come on, man. You like the woods. You've come this far . . ."

"I do like the woods. And you don't have any way of getting down there without me. Do you?" Putting it like that, we both had to laugh. It was true. And I had come a far way now. I had a record. I had brought a violent weapon onto campus. Into the building. And I had been in a fight. But getting caught in the woods while I was already suspended would seriously mess me up. It would be impossible to explain this. I would never be able to say it was something that happened to me. It was a choice I was making. It would make everybody wonder what was going on with me. And Mom and Dad would truly kill me. But it was like feeling you were going to war or something, a bond of togetherness. We were both in trouble and neither of us had done anything truly bad. Any truly bad thing Brandon had done he had already paid for. He had already been punished for it. And this was taking lunch to someone hungry.

Parking on the side of the road did scare me. We would be leaving the car for as long as it took us to get through the woods and then for however long we stayed with them at the hideout. We would be going all the way across the woods, all the way through, from the road to the playing field near the new elementary school. And with Brandon, you never knew. And these girls, people I didn't know at all, not anymore. Not since elementary school. They had gone so wild so long ago that I had lost all contact with them.

And if they saw me out there they would know that I was like them. I wouldn't be different anymore. I would be like them. And I didn't like that.

Brandon refused to get regular fast food. Something easy like burgers and fries. But that would cost a lot anyway. So we went to a grocery store to get bread and cheese and stuff like that to make vegetarian sandwiches. How he had money for all that I do not know. I guess from the hay or from Corin. I didn't ask. I was half afraid he would confess to robbery. So we had to go shopping, then go home and make these sandwiches. And eat a couple. Bread, cheese, lettuce. Stuff like that. He bought the kind of bread you have to slice yourself with a knife like a sword. And then we would head for school, on our going home route but in the opposite direction.

And the people in the grocery store looked at us weird. I could feel it. While we were getting the lettuce and other greens, a grocery guy was doing stuff in there and he looked at us like, Why are you in here? Why are young dudes buying lettuce? What kind of mischief is possible with lettuce? And the checkout lady, while she was taking his money, was looking like Why aren't you at school? Why are you buying this? Delinquents like us are supposed to try to buy beer and cigarettes. No, we were buying bread and lettuce and cheese. We are not normal people.

I thought we would park right by the woods, climb up the bank from the road, like he had been talking about, and then make our way on the familiar running trails. But now just like when we were hunting the dead animals on the roadways, Brandon was back to his maddening way of yelling out right when he wanted me to pull over.

"Stop!"

"Here? Wouldn't it be better to go down and turn around, and then we could pull off on the same side as the woods. There's plenty of room there. And quit yelling like that. Haven't I told you?"

"No. Right here. This is the way."

"Right here" was on the other side of the road from the woods we needed to go through. He wanted to go straight down the bank, the opposite way. And then into a little creek that ran under the road and along the back of our running woods. It did go up to the hideout, but why not just use the trails?

"You want to walk in the creek?"

"Not in it. Along it. This is the way," and he was already down the bank. Down into icy shadows, in ankle-grabbing vines, foot-twisting steepness, face-slapping tree twigs. And at the bottom, a quick leap over a depth of murky creek water.

"Now," he said, pointing with his head as he clung to low slung branches, "through there."

"There" was the gaping mouth of the pipe where the creek ran under the road. It was tall enough. You could to see through to the bright opening at the other end. And you could see cold creek water running through, glinting silver. We could straddle the run of water but I knew I'd be going home with wet shoes.

But I felt wild. I felt abandoned by the school, by all my hard work at school. The breezy weather, the woods, the leftover ice, the cavern doorway opening in the creek pipe, worked an effect on me. Wet shoes, wet hair, I didn't care. We set off clambering toward the pipe. We were on our way into the woods, into the school grounds from outside. We weren't supposed to be there. We had sandwiches. We were unexpected. If the school wouldn't have us, we would have the school. We would encounter these wild people, and now I was one of them. A new feeling surged in me.

It was Brandon leading and me following into the shadow of the pipe. But right away he stopped short, thrashing his hands around his face and head. Head and face wrapped in spiderweb like a death gauze. Going insane. Wait, I told him. A few seconds later I was back with a deer antler of a stick.

I went in front with the stick to clear the way. Like a man with a torch. The sound of the road above us came earthy and thick because we now were in the ground, muffled in the pipe. We were stagger-walking where water ran between our feet, the serpent stream silver in the mouth of the pipe. We had to bend and lean. I tore away heavy webs like ripping cloth and at the far mouth of another world we leapt. Our feet landed among ice-beaten ferns, thudding into crusty sand bed. We were in the creek-side now under high mossy walls of earth, a place washed deep by the eons of rain water. Dinosaur bones might lie in the open here, or the traces of the ancient people and their arrow points. Old fallen trees lay criss-crossing the banks over us. The evergreen Christmas ferns draped the mosses. We did not run down here during our running. High oaks and round-trunked tulip trees pillared up. We were quiet. We were half subterranean and half open to the sky. We found enough ground to walk on. Small caves opened on the bank sides, kneeling-chambers of blue clay if anyone cared to kneel and pray there, where the rain waters dripped down from the playing fields.

We came to a place where the creek went under a trio of living trees. A wonder-place where we walked through the ground under living trees. The roots stretched a network, a roof-thatch, over the creek. We crouched and scuttled silent, bent forward and it was there we had no choice but to step into water. The clay walls hung with roots and webs, with dark holes to vanish your hand. Daylight ran in at the edges on a few currents of creek water but the roots above us darkened the water around our feet. A deeper pool waited as we emerged from this and we had to leap up, and then, right at a bend where ferns draped thick, someone jumped and we were both startled. And we had scared him. And I saw it was Stenson, someone I had known in elementary school, but had long ago quit seeing or knowing. Not because I decided not to know him, but just because we had gone in different directions. Everybody knew that he had never been quite right. For all I had kept up with him, he might as well have been dead. Or maybe I would have known more about him if he had been dead, because dead students are usually talked about and heard about. He used to go to rehab or therapy or whatever they called it, in elementary school. What was he doing out here? With him, you never knew. But we had known each other way back. He spoke to Brandon first but he was looking straight at me.

"Speed, you can pass on by. You belong. But this one? Chris? Smart as a whip? You don't come out here. What are you doing? You out here to turn us in?"

Speed?

Smart as a whip? I was getting the whip now, being suspended. I had never been punished like this at school, for anything. Everybody knew it.

That fact was stuck to me, even if I tried to act like I was liberated to roam among school skippers and delinquents. I didn't know what to say.

"You out here to turn us in?"

"No, of course not."

"Because you don't belong out here. Speed can come out here but not you. You don't come out here."

Brandon spoke up. "It's OK. He's coming along, isn't he? Learning the dark side now. Don't worry. We aren't here to turn anybody in. How would we? And look at him. Look at that knot on his head. Look out he doesn't throw a punch at you, Stens. Watch out now."

No. Don't say that. I'm not here to punch anybody.

And I'm not about to join in with these people either. Stenson is right. I am different.

He was looking at me like I needed to say something. I started to say "We run out here everyday," but that wouldn't mean anything. Kids like Stenson weren't out here then.

"I'm just going up here," I said. Then Stenson sat back down, and we went on, and he just stayed there, like it was 100% normal for someone to be sitting in that damp sandy place, cold, feet nearly in running water, right in the middle of a school day. Then from behind us we heard, "Is that food? Can I have something, just some fries or something? Hey, you can't pass unless you hand over some of that food." Suddenly he was back in front of us, and I lost track of whether he was joking or what. He looked crazy, holding up his hand, like "You shall not pass." And Brandon laughed and handed him something out of the bag. "OK, Stens, no problem. Don't worry, man. We're not here to bust through your ground without paying our due. But you know how I am, what I eat. So you have to deal with cheese and lettuce and tomato. No burgers. I'm not putting animals to death so I can eat."

We left as Stenson was unwrapping one of the sandwiches.

"That's what I brought this stuff for, anyway," Brandon said as we moved on. "You have to be careful with that one," he said. "You never know with him."

"Yeah, I know."

The creek banks were lower now and we walked on moss carpets out in the open. But when the sides got higher and the creek bed deeper, we went back that way, hidden again. We passed through the curviest parts of the creek here, side-winding around small islands of the bank. Then we came to the muddy wash-out trodden with runners' prints. It was the low spot where our running trail crossed, where we runners would make our leaps across from bank to bank. This time we clambered up from below. The hideout was within sight if you knew how to see it. Up in the drier woods a few thirty, forty yards, banked by red clay on both sides. Scrub pines and brambles blocked the view from the long playing fields. I saw the broken branches, the old two by fours. Any junk they could get hold of out here. The worn out ping pong table for a roof, and a little black hearth for fires on cold days, if they felt like risking the smoke. I tried to hold back. Not go. I was out of place and I felt it like a crawl on my skin.

The skippers were there, inside. They were gathered round, tending the smallest fire in the world, just a few twigs burning. The cigarettes they were smoking made more smoke. All of them were smoking, orange eyes burning in the shadows. Brandon walked up like he knew them all. Right at home.

"Speed, son, what you doing here. We thought you got kicked out of school. Get in here. You want more pictures? How's everything going?" That was a guy called Bird. Girls and boys were there, about seven people or so. I couldn't see all the way into the dark at the back of the hideout. I knew Linda. She noticed me this time right away.

"You brought him out here? Chris?" She looked around, looking to the others. "You shouldn't be out here with the losers. You gotta to make it big in this world. Somebody's gotta take care of things while we get high." She laughed with mouth open, lounging back, like Delilah or Cleopatra.

I wasn't one of these cool people who knew how to be so sophisticated sitting in a scrap heap. How could you be so calm about skipping school, breaking rules in the woods? How would you ever get used to that? Here they were, like people at a river picnic.

"I'm just out here," I stammered. Feeling like an idiot. Out here they don't hide what they're doing. I wasn't supposed to be seeing this. And now I had seen it. And I had already said the words: No, I wasn't here to turn you in.

And now I had been seen.

"Well don't just stand there, waiting for someone to see you," Bird said. "Get in, get in. We got room. We can make accommodations!" They shuffled around to make room for me.

The seating was boards on bare earth. The cigarette smoke was heavy around me. I was in it now. The hideout. Wreathed in the blue-grey smoke that came ghosting double barreled out of their nostrils. I was sitting beside these people, and they were tearing up Brandon's sandwiches and passing them around, and they included us too even when Brandon said they for them, not for us. We all took some and we all ate. So I was thinking, is this something I'll be doing from now on? I've eaten here with them. Are these people going to know me now when I pass by them outside of C Hall? My head was swirling. The smoke, I thought. And the idea that I was out here. I had broken something. Something big. They had seen me. I was wrapped up in this, and when one of them offered me a turn with some kind of cigarette, I felt my hand reaching up to take it, like, it would be OK. But then at the last second I just said, "That's OK dude" without even knowing why. Just impulse. I'm not one of them, I was saying to myself. But Brandon took a turn with a cigarette, and I thought, wow, this is the real Brandon now. I know him now.

"I just wanted to bring you guys something to eat. A little food to say I appreciate you letting me take some pictures. If they let me come back to school, it will be my next project. And even if I don't get back in school, Mr. Blake's already told me he can help me get some pictures put in a gallery. A real gallery. And you can go see it. And all your identities are hidden. I've only shown pictures to Mr. Blake that don't show your face. Nobody will recognize you."

"I wanna be recognized," one of the boys said.

"Shut up, dope head," another told him. "Speed, we got to ask you. People are saying you killed somebody. That's why you got suspended. And this kid, I don't even know you, but all that blood you had on you. Everybody saw that. I don't know who you were fighting, but that was some kind of fighting you done."

"No, really, it was just an accident."

"OK," he laughed. "I see how it is. You don't want to talk about it. That's OK. But out here, we got nothing to hide. And I see that knock you wearing on your head."

"No, really. It was just an accident."

I had just repeated myself, automatically.

But I felt a gush a pride. My face got red. Half of me wanted to say I had killed someone. But someone from further in was talking.

"Speed, you do all this with your camera? When you were taking those pictures. You got this all together. I don't see how you did it. You got all this going for you. I wish I could do that stuff, man."

"It's not that big of a deal. You just have to do something. You just have to care about something and then do something about it."

"Seems like I can't. I can't stop getting in-school suspension and my mom driving me crazy. I can't sit in class all day. I just can't sit there. I just need something like this, being outside. Just being free. Taking pictures or something. Or making something. But I don't see how you put all that together. You just came out here taking pictures, but then it all came together, like, an idea. That's what they ought to be teaching us. But I'm glad you got this. That's cool. But I'm just out here, living in the woods, smoking my smokes."

You're being stupid, I wanted to shout. You don't live out here. And smoking is bad for you. You could be in class learning right now.

But I was in awe of how Brandon was talking to them. He had a real connection. It had to be said: He was one of them. I would never have given them a thought. Other than to turn away from them. Linda had said, You shouldn't be out here. And Stieg had said, You don't belong out here. And they were right. I did not belong out here. And now I would have to figure out how to get the smell of cigarette smoke off me.

But not belonging out here didn't mean I couldn't know these people. The next time I saw some of them at the end of C Hall, I would speak to them. I would talk to them.

Brandon gave away all the sandwiches we had made. We said our goodbyes. We said, Let's sprint back. We tore off through our regular trails, instead of going back through the spider webs and the bewildering depths of clay caves and tree roots. We didn't need to pass by Stenson again. We sped along our trails and made the whole circle, we were flying, right up to the school fields, daring Mr. Givens to see us, Brandon crow-calling as we went, and back around till we burst out into bright sunlight at the roadside. We leapt the bank, leapt icy shadows, and ran down to my car. Uncaught, unscathed. We had visited the school skippers, we had entered the school woods, we had run our trail despite the school having suspended us. We rode home yelling out of the windows.

59

Paper Lantern

After supper Mom said OK to me going up to Brandon's. But don't stay too long. I needed rest, she said, after all this that had gone on, and how did my head feel, and did I have my homework done, and all that stuff.

I was fine.

Walking up the road in the dark of evening is no big deal. I would rather walk, with the Autumn weather, with the indigo sky. The only part of the roadside that is hard to walk on is a little bit past Corin's driveway where it drops down a little toward the ditch. The rest of the way has wide places where you can get off the road if cars come. But by that time of evening the wheels are at rest, in the regular world. The thing of being outside after dark is fine. Nothing scary. It's so dark, Mom said. But I was adapted to the indigo, the stars, and the way the trees and the horizon look darker than the sky. It's lighter out there than it looks from inside house windows. You notice these things if you go out there. Outdoor lamplight is like blue green lanterns lit among tree branches. Some street lights are mint green, some orange, some yellow. All of that under the grainy night sky, the indigo blue. I could see all around and be unseen. Almost unseen. A moving shape in the night, a little crescent of human shape. Light goes a long way, even small lights.

Then on the way up, the giant preacher appeared, floating over me, thundering down upon me with that mighty voice. Lightning flashed from his teeth as he growled at me.

"Out in the dark! You don't even know you're in the dark. And Brandon is in the dark. This is exactly what happens! You dwell in spiritual darkness and you are deep in it. Error takes hold in the lives of the people of earth and gives root to all forms of evil. Rot and wickedness multiply on the earth. Loss of reverence! Adoration of death! Mourning the loss of animals when you yourselves are lost! What are you doing? Where are you going?"

Leftover ice crunched under my shoes. One car came sailing round the curve, glazing me and the ground and the ice with bands of gold. And then darkness inked back over me. They thought I was some freak, some wanderer lost. Suspended. I would go and live among pine trees and lie still on pine needle beds. I started counting my footsteps for some reason.

Corin's windows of fireplace orange glowed among his trees. Every step moved them among the dark trunks. He was inside probably eating popcorn and listening to his radio. Up ahead, through the branches, the ancient flame-flickering lamps at Piney Grove Estates were licking up the dark.

And I had the rarest gift, one I never expected, just then. In the dark, the pine forest was still safe. If I didn't look for it, I felt it. I saw it. It was real. It was inside me. It was there. It was a secret. It had been photographed or written into my mind. Kept safe. It would come back to me. It was still there. All I had to do was be still. Like, somehow, I had won the gift without even knowing it was happening. Like Hummingbird said it would: it came to me.

Maybe it had to with walking, the way your mind gets at ease. Or maybe it was because of love?

Brandon's step mom let me in. I couldn't keep my face from burning red. Here I was, some kid who walked up here in the dark. To her, no different from any other delinquent that Brandon was always mixed up with.

I opened his door and stepped into a cave of almost total darkness. Car light ran a watery flow of shadow strips across the wall. The only other light was a strange halo floating around the room: Brandon shining a flashlight on the walls and ceiling.

The blurry light wavered, struggled, glinted off Brandon's animal photographs. He had tiled the walls with them, maybe a hundred, pinned up over the bed all the way to the ceiling. On the wall around the closet, and the wall around the door. The glossy smashed fur and limbs and eyes of dead animals, the grit of road pavement, dark and grainy like charcoal drawings. The photographic black flared and disappeared in the glare of the beam and then flashed silver in the angle as the beam passed. Because of something in the process, something in the chemicals.

Brandon had told me about photography. The film in the camera is treated with a chemical to let it receive light. Inside the camera it's dark.

When you take the picture, you are opening the shutter, which is like a door to a tiny room. Light rushes in and strikes the film for a fraction of a second. The image comes in on the light and gets caught by the chemical on the film. Then later, when you print the picture, you are doing the same thing again but onto a piece of specially treated paper instead of film. And you do that inside the dark room, which is like a camera that you go into. And all the stuff that could go wrong, like how my photos turned out too dark, was because of all the things I just said. You might not have the shutter opening at the right speed, and it stays open too long, or you might have it opening so wide that too much light gets in, and in photography too much light, or light for too long, is exactly like too much light going into your eye. Instant blindness. Instead of making you see more, too much light makes a solid black photo.

He was just staring and moving the light without speaking.

"Brandon," I muttered.

He was just laying there.

I already knew it was because of something Corin had said that afternoon. A slick looking car had come up his driveway, he told us, and when he went out to see who it was, to speak to them, they backed right out into the road and sped away. Corin thought it was strange.

A car what color? Brandon had asked.

Black, Corin had said.

"So they let you come back home then?" I stammered.

Of course they had. I already knew that. He seemed so deep in silence that I was just looking for something to say.

"So how did you get to come home, anyway, I mean, what made your dad let you come back?"

"I don't know. He just let me. Corin talked to him a long time. I didn't hear what they said."

I watched the light going up the walls, across the ceiling. A flashlight has those grey shapes in the light, like the grey parts on the moon. He stopped the light on one of the pictures, a squirrel maybe, flattened there with the white line of the road going right under it. I hadn't seen it before.

"On the day when people are in Heaven all the animals are going to have a word to say. They're going to stand up all together and say, 'We lived on earth. We had dignity that you in all your human greatness never came close to. Never understood. We lived, we slept and walked and found our food and died on all the hard surfaces of your man made world, all the concrete and the asphalt and all the car metal you could come up with and we never lost our dignity. We were noble.' That's what the animals are going to say in Heaven."

This was a strange thought and I didn't know what to say, and we just sat there for a few minutes watching the wavering light float over the grainy pictures on the walls. Then Brandon leaned up and seemed to wake up.

"Yeah, we're dead, man."

"What? Because we got suspended? Or do you mean Star Man, and it's only a matter of time until he catches us? Because I don't think he will, I mean, I've told the principal, and Mr. Collins, and they'll have the police . . ."

"I don't mean that. I mean, we're dead. You and me. We died. Today was the first evidence of it. Of our deaths. We're walking in the world of the dead now. Here." He sat up and then got off the bed. "Take your shirt off."

"What?"

"I'll show you. I saw it today when we were washing clothes." We had thrown our clothes into the wash to get the smoke out.

"See?" he said. He turned my back to the mirror and shined the flashlight on me.

I did see. All the jaguar spots of magic marker writing had gone weird and blurry, spreading out blue, green, just like the green blue bruise that shone on the front of my head. It was the jaguar's spots. It was like my whole back was bruised green with decay. It had to run its course over me like the poison oak death blisters had. Like the marks of a skin disease on me.

"Like green mold and death rot," Brandon said. "So you see, we are dead already."

Then he went to his desk, clicked the lamp on, opened the drawer and took out a cigar. Starting cutting the end. When he went to strike the first match, I said, "What?"

"Here," he said, already with the window open. Puffing the cigar into a billow of smoke. "Take some of this."

The look on my face must have said everything, because the next thing he said was, "OK. This is absolutely the only time I will ever ask you to smoke anything. It's nothing but real tobacco. Just take one drag on it. Just one. Because we are dead, and the smoke is the way to show it. It's a way to say 'we're here now.' Land of the Dead."

He puffed out a big billow. It smelled good. Different from cigarettes.

"Just once. A death. Symbolic, if I have to spell it out. I'm not asking you to become an addict."

When I was coughing, he was laughing, and that was it. I had done it.

"Dead," he said. "That means we're free."

"Free?"

"Not being held down. Like when we were running our trails today without the school knowing. It's the way we'll be able to defeat Star Man. It's the way we're going to win. By being dead."

I was squinting at him. I'd never heard of any symbol like that, smoking. But I had another question eating at me.

"So what was all that about today, anyway? The girls, the woods, pictures? What's up with all that? I don't really know what you're into with them, and it's not my business really, but you've got to know by now what kind of girls they are. I'm not really into all that kind of wild living. If you are, that's cool I guess, I mean, I think you shouldn't be, but when it comes down to it, it's your choice. Just don't get the idea that I'm planning to get into that."

"What are you talking about? Stop being so crazy." Then the smirking laugh.

"I've never told you. I'm doing another project, another group of pictures. Not for school. Although Mr. Blake has been helping me. He's got me hooked up with a gallery that does art shows for young people, teens, kids. He helped me get into a show there. So I've been working on pictures for that."

"Pictures of girls?"

I was still thinking about what Muriel said, that everybody was saying Brandon was taking pictures of naked girls in the woods.

"Yeah, girls," he said, with his eye wide. "Wanna see?"

He took out a plain folder from the bottom desk drawer, a pocket folder like you use for school papers. He turned on the lamp by the bed.

"Sure you're ready for this? You just said you didn't want to be involved in my wild living." He stood there holding the unopened folder, eyeing me, eyebrows raised. "Come on. One look can't hurt you too bad."

He opened the folder and brought out the photos. Spread them out on the bed.

And then he laughed. "Not what you were expecting?"

I couldn't hide my surprise.

"Do you think something like naked pictures would be in a youth art show? It's pictures about kids who skip school. It's about what they're going through. I'm just trying to find a way to show what it's like to be a kid that doesn't make the honor roll or a sports team or the popularity contest. To be a kid who gets lost in this world. And these two agreed to let me use some pictures of them. And a couple of the guys too. A few of them wrote down some of their own situations, their statement of why they ended up like this. Why they don't go to class. Those will be included with the photos in the show. But no faces. No identities. No way to trace who they are."

No faces. Just a few kids in the woods, standing around, sitting. But there was the t-shirt I had seen, the Wild West with a whiskey bottle and a pistol on it. There was the feather jewelry I saw the day I had gone out there. Had he been taking pictures that same day? I recognized the places. Up there where the trail came out at those people's little farm, where the pear tree was. In one picture the skippers were sprawled in the grass like people at the beach.

"That was Halloween," he said. "Remember? The school had an outdoor 'party' during lunch, and everybody could go down to the stadium and get a grilled hamburger?"

"So how did you do this? How did you just go out into the woods and take these pictures? It had to have been during school. You had to have been out there skipping too, to be out there doing this."

"Yeah, well, I had a way, let's just say. I had permission to be outside doing an art project, and this is what happened for that."

The smirking laugh again. The cool demeanor. The way he was when he first got here. He packed the photos back into the folder and clicked the lamps off.

And then, "Well, to be honest, Mr. Blake is the one who made it happen. He gave me permission to go outside and he knew I was going to go out there but he didn't stop me. So . . . now I've told you that and it's just between us. He told me not to tell anyone, because it would get him in trouble, but now I've told you. But you aren't going to turn him in, I expect."

"No, I'm not going to turn him in. I'm not going to turn anybody in."

The Brandenburg cassette was in his player on the desk and I clicked it on. The hunting horns bellowed out and we didn't say anything.

So Mr. Blake had been letting him go outside. The pictures would be in a real gallery in a town just a few miles away. It seemed just like this music. It was serious music in a real orchestra, played by my friends from the lunch room. I was surrounded by real artists doing real artwork.

I, on the other hand, had some ideas for drawing on a t-shirt with a magic marker.

"That's awesome, man. A real art show. But I do keep thinking, it's still bugging me, the school has to know those kids are out there. They've got to know where that stupid little hideout is. I never understand why they don't go get them. Because those kids are just wasting their life. They're throwing away their opportunity. They're all just dead people out there before they even get started in life. And smoking is bad for you."

"Before they even get started? Some kids have a harder life than anything you know about, Chris. From day one of their life. You really don't know. And the school people don't go down there looking for them because they know they'll find them, and then they'll have to do something about them. And it's too much trouble. They can just count them absent. Don't have to worry about them."

The music carried on, a force of its own, not troubled by what we were saying.

I just sat there. I know some kids have a harder life. I do know that. But I didn't argue. I knew he was right.

"So today. You really just wanted to take them something to eat."

"Yeah. That's it. What else. Dude, really, if you're thinking I'm after more trouble, you need to know, I'm finished with the way I used to be. Don't be thinking I want to get back into any of that."

"But just going out there is doing something wrong, isn't it? How can you say you're not after more trouble?"

"OK, yeah, it is wrong because it's against the rules. But what I'm saying is, I didn't go out there looking for a good time, or something like that. Like Star Man used to say."

"I thought maybe you wanted to go out there today so you could spy on him. Star Man or Sun Dog or whatever idiotic name he goes by."

"Yeah, well, I was keeping an eye out for him. I was thinking he wouldn't come around today, after you ran into him on Friday. Because he'll be thinking you will have told the school about him, and they'd be out looking for him. I wouldn't have gone if I thought he'd be around."

The Brandenburg soared around us.

"So anyway," he continued, "if you want to say these kids are dead, what will get them back alive again?"

Then I heard a voice that made me go listen through the door without opening it. Brandon's stepmom was talking like syrup, like melting marshmallows and, could it be, that giant TV preacher's booming voice?

'Come in, my goodness, what a special surprise, how are you, my goodness gracious.'

Yes, it was the television preacher's booming voice, right there in the living room. Brandon's door vibrated against it.

"Brandon," we heard, "come on out hon. The pastor wants to place prayer cover over you. Pastor, I was so sorry to hear about your accident. That was so awful, I just can't imagine, how are you? Why don't you just sit right down and rest? What can I get you, a little something to drink? How about a piece of pie?"

Then a buzz of muted mumbled words. Then, nearer,

" . . . didn't realize at first he was yours, you all being new to the church and all . . . never see him around church . . . thought I'd come around . . . yes . . . been hunting and had a little accident . . . yes, ma'am, it was, that's right .

. . a trophy prize buck, kind of thing you go out there for, just staring me in the face and . . . yeah, and I'm telling you the next thing I know I'm laying there on this here moss bed holding my hand to my chest saying 'Lord Jesus, not now, I got too much to do, this flock of yours ain't ready . . . the people ain't ready . . . we are living in the end times and we are not ready . . . and this boy, I've been worried about him . . . yes . . . we need to put a hedge . . . desperately . . . you see, he's living out some of the signs . . . I've got to speak with him . . . "

"Pastor, my goodness! Brandon, come out here, the pastor needs to speak to you."

I jumped back when she knocked. I thought Brandon would automatically get up and go out there. But he was already halfway out the window. The smell of chilly damp swirled across the room.

"You can go in there if you want to," he said. "I'm not." The flashlight beam rolled wildly around the room for a few seconds as he moved through and out.

"Hey," I said, head outside, "I'm coming with you, but you're already in a lot of trouble. You sure you want to leave like this? Maybe that's not cool."

"I don't care. I've had enough."

We crept away around back where ice still crunched, this opposite world where shadows fall out white. The neighborhood streetlights draped down big tents of fluorescent white. I glanced back at the SUV pulled up in their driveway. It was a vehicle made to measure for such a mammoth person, such a bone rattling voice. Brandon was headed for the back way, down through rough grass and weeds to the Rocks and over to Corin's. At the end of the cul-de-sac middle school kids were skateboarding on a home-made ramp. White plumes laughed out from their mouths as they skated and joked. I didn't want them to see us going the secret way.

But you don't own the Out Back, anyway, I told myself. You don't own the Rocks. Any kid who wants to has already been down there.

"What's up Sean, Kev, Brady, Dantay," Brandon called to them.

"Brandon," they said. One of them ran up and shook hands with Brandon, skateboard under his arm, running and talking at the same time.

"Dude, you won't believe Sean just now, he was so awesome like in midair, it was so cool, he was just like you and he came down and you should have seen it! You got to come skating with us again! Where you been?"

So we did. We stayed out for a while under the pale green street bulbs, the tents of fluorescent light, skateboarding. "Vagabond/Savage/Animal" was Brandon's word for my skating. He had the skills. I just went at it. Mostly falling, when I got away from the most basic things. But they were teachers. They like showing you how, because they like skating.

And that was the beginning of our plan. We didn't know it then, but that was the beginning.

Because I went into an animal fit, like the way a cat suddenly runs wild for no visible reason. Maybe it was the photographs, the impact of the Wild Hunt suddenly catching me up. Suddenly skating, crouching, I was finding a way to stay up, rolling on the ground when I fell. I did ridiculous things, made-up possum jumps and animal dances, raccoon moves just to aggravate laughter, because I didn't know what I was doing. And it gave me power to do something.

And Brandon was back at it, sidling up to me, saying it again. Making me smile and shake my head.

"Yeah. You're proving it now. These vagabond animals nobody cares about. Nobody ever says a possum is cute, and you said yourself, it's the most killed animal in the world. It's like I've been telling you. We're dead now. So that could be bad, or we could use it for good. Good stuff from the grave, a true shock to everybody."

The younger guys were cool. They were funny. It was weird to have other kids nearby to home. Maybe I could live with this neighborhood after all. Then they had to say goodbye, called to go in.

And we disappeared. We folded into the shadows of a house. We ducked round the end of the Gaunt Jaw. Down into the high grass, into the brambling weeds, into the dumped loads of chunk gravel. We had to walk foot-holding, side-clambering, until we got where we could jump to the Rocks. Then we were far enough away to turn the flashlight on. I got mad all over again at how the developers didn't care. The land was nothing to them. Dumping ground. They left ditches and junk places, rank grass and strewn rock. It was easy to turn your foot, twist an ankle. On the Rocks we stood a moment and then like cats we were down. We knew the way to scramble, the places a person can grapple down those round boulder faces. Seen from Piney Groves we were two shadows, or one, or three, impossible to be sure, a beaming flashlight, bobbing, white halo on the ground in a blurry circle.

It wasn't far to Corin's. I couldn't believe other people didn't know this way. They had to. It was too easy. His place had been scraped open, exposed to the world outside. Brandon had tried to avoid making an obvious trail.

Our light flashed ripples at the bottom on unfrozen ditch water, and we leapt. The other side was muddy but I went for a patch of grass. For a second I wondered about the scene at Brandon's. Had they opened his door by now to find the room dark, the music playing, and us gone?

From the Rocks we had seen the light on in the greenhouse. Corin's whole place looked little, misaligned, out of place. Old fashioned and angular. Like it could never last long in this new way of the world. The bulldozers would be waiting to get their teeth in. The little round-ribbed greenhouse was glowing like a lantern, like an origami spaceship thin as paper.

60

Message

Our shadows zigzagged down through wavy grass and weeds and among them I saw shadows of the animals from Brandon's walls, animals dark and shining, gleaming like ancient coal and dark stone fossils, photographs like charcoal drawings. They ran with us.

My shadow jumped with a raccoon jump over a broken tree branch, and moved with a possum move through the weeds.

It's like Inha was standing there with the Wild Hunt's animals running all around him.

Up from the weedy thickets then we came, into the back of Corin's yard, through the wooden slat fence, past the compost pile of old leaves, past broken tree limbs.

At the glowing greenhouse we made the crow sounds.

No answer. He wasn't there.

Into the knot of pathways, the shrubbery, the azalea camellia rhododendron, and the Himalayan cedar like a pavilion over all this. No one. We kept going.

Then we heard voices. Corin and someone, around the corner of the house. In the driveway. We went closer. Nobody had ever been there except us.

And Brandon stopped, threw back his hand.

Don't step into the light.

Star Man. Standing right there, shadow hands of cypress draping his face. Asking Corin, we heard him, Where are the boys? They live here, right?

Fire flared in me. How could this freak come here and bother Corin?

"We could bust him right here," I whispered, pushing forward. I was still crazy from the animal jumps and the possum skating, all that stuff.

"No." Brandon pushed me back. "Don't be crazy. He'll cut us up or shoot us all right here. Or he'll come back later and kill Corin."

But Corin was no fool. Nothing came away from him.

They aren't here right now, he was saying. I don't know where they might have gone. They come and go as they choose these days. Boys like them? I've no way to keep hold of them.

I'm someone they know, Star Man was saying. They'll want to get in touch with me.

Listen to him trying to sound local, trying to sound like he's from North Carolina. Fake accents stand out.

I'll be wanting to see them, he was saying, shrugging. Tell them, will ya, tell 'em all I'm wanting is a ballgame. Just a little roundball. Any idea where they could be? When they'll be around? Give them that message, won't you. A little roundball.

No idea, Corin said. They come and go as they choose, he said again. He let Star Man keep on thinking we might live here.

I'll be back, he said. Deep City, Up North coming back into his voice now. I'll be seeing ya. Bet on it. He winked and pointed his finger, a little gesture to show how cool he was. A shadow moved up the drive and the car's engine roared up. The speakers thumped a rattling racket into Corin's own driveway, like Star Man was reaching his hand to shake this elderly man, to shake his house, to shake everything nice about a person's home. His headlights turned away and I wanted to grab stones to dash him.

Crow sounds again and we stepped out.

"I knew you were somewhere hereabouts," Corin said. "Heard you down there. I don't know who that fellow is, but I know enough to know there's something not good with him."

"He didn't try to hurt you, did he? I can't believe he came here. We should've done something. We should've grabbed him."

Corin shook his head. Just like Brandon.

"He was unpleasant enough. But I saw bruises on his face, Chris." Corin was looking at me. "Like the knock on your own head. You're connected to him, I believe."

My mind started spinning. Connected to him?

I looked at Brandon. We had to get our plan. We had to call the police. We didn't need this guy coming around here.

"Now both of you," Corin said, "come here." He stepped into the light inside the house.

"With all this damage from the ice, I'll have plenty of work for you if you want it, and I'm more grateful to you for all you've done than ever I can say." He had an envelope for each of us. He grasped our hands. "Now go on straight back home, both of you. I'll be fine. And you be careful. Don't be looking to get into something."

"He wants a ball game?" Brandon said, turning toward me as our shadows went before us from the outside lamp. I heard the smirking breath-laugh, saw the upward nod. In the shadowy lamplight a broken-tooth smile came over his skull bone buzz-headed face.

"I'm pretty sure he is actually better than us. He can shoot better and he is probably tall enough to dunk. So he's going to beat us on the court, and I think that's how we're going to defeat him."

61

Gift

Flickering thoughts grow into full realities and I was there, unseen. Like remembering a dream. You don't make it happen. It comes to you. Like Corin said, a dream that goes on with you, because you dreamed it. It came to you and it's real and somehow it keeps on being with you, in you, even when you don't know it's with you.

It was the most unexpected gift. I had crossed the boundary. I stood in shadow under the towering heights. They were ancient pine trees. I was walking the path again, standing among the pillars, standing on the shady needle pathway. I gazed and gazed at the towering forest. I held my hand to the bark of a tree, the way I always had done. Like I could bring comfort or help or at least share the tragedy. The trees welcomed me. I loved them. I heard the wind moving, soft among the branches. I heard the wind arriving from a distance. I heard the wind moving among the branches.

62

Chris + Muriel

I looked back at jaguars I had drawn in my math notebooks.

I got out a white t-shirt. One of my newer, better ones. More destruction of property.

I made the design on paper first, because on paper you can erase. You can get the design like you want it. Then I cut out the paper. I made a kind of stencil.

A jaguar standing, looking. The eyes are able to see into the distance. The tail curved, the ears alert. But the marker was getting old, almost out of ink. But then I thought, it looks good that way. I kept coloring with that marker. It wasn't solid black. It gave the jaguar its silver sheen. I got another marker to finish it, to darken up the places that needed to be a deeper dark.

It was a dark jaguar. The melanistic. It had the dark jaguar marks, the water silk, the silver sheen of darkness.

But it still wasn't exactly right. What if I dyed the shirt dark blue? Like blue jeans, denim, indigo blue. The jaguar would almost disappear.

Brandon said No, leave it. It's perfect. But I thought dying it would work. I went to the grocery store, found some dye, read the instructions. The blue was dark but light enough to be different from the black. And it was good.

The jaguar was there.

I could wear this and take the jaguar with me. Nobody would know who he was.

Brandon said, You have to make more of these. People would want this. What have I been telling you? People would buy this. I would buy this.

He got out the neon orange long sleeve t-shirt.

That's when I started thinking. That's when my ideas started swirling. Like the way a hurricane begins. Warm air, cold air. One thought turning another. Following one idea brings you to another. My hurricane designs, thunderstorm designs, Solar System designs.

Muriel said, Hmm, a panther. She was trying to figure it out. She saw a pattern in me.

Still drawing these cats, she said. Since 8th grade? Still drawing these wild animals. And such a quiet boy. Deep waters run deep, she said.

When I showed her the shirt, I was afraid. I thought she was going to be angry about me getting suspended. I thought she was going to turn and say, Don't bother talking to me anymore. Don't even come near me. Because she has everything figured out. She has music. I thought she was going to say I was turning into a trashy person or something like that. Somebody she didn't want to be around.

But she didn't say any of that. She just wanted to know what happened. How could any of that happen, she said. Didn't the principal understand that I didn't mean any harm. She wanted to understand it, and she was just as angry as I had been about the stupid knife. Because it really was stupid. She ran her fingertips over the knot on my forehead. I told her all about what happened. But she did say, How could you not have known you shouldn't bring a knife to school? And I kept saying, I just didn't think about it that way. I didn't mean any harm. Well, she said, someone could have stolen it from you and done harm, and you would be connected to that because it was your knife.

I hadn't thought about it like that. I had to agree she was right.

I would do it different now if I could, I told her.

And she kept saying, Who turned you in? Who knew you had a knife anyway?

But I didn't say anything about that. I didn't care anymore. I didn't want to bother with it. I was just glad I would be able to go back to school. Get back to normal. I was "permitted back on school property to resume appropriate activities and regular school functioning" or something like that, was the way the official word from the school said it. Brandon would still be out a couple more days. His situation was more serious than a knife. Even though he really had already been punished for everything that went on at his old school. He hadn't brought anything more dangerous than photographs to school. But he would come back too. Things were different now. I didn't care anymore about the church people. I mean, I cared about them as human beings, but I wasn't troubled by what they said anymore. Me and Brandon were cool, and the music people, and it was awesome.

I went to Muriel's concert. And with the music, the Planets, the feeling of soaring into Outer Space, and Muriel shimmering in that black dress, all the starry Universe in one person, I couldn't take my eyes off her.

Brandon came to the concert too. After it was over, a bunch of them and some of their parents were going to La Verona Pizza, a place I had never been. It had red velvet designed wall paper, and they said come on, you're going aren't you? And you, Brandon. So I was thinking, before I knew where we were going, here's Brandon going to make another speech in front of everyone about being a vegetarian. So I tried to head that off by making a speech for him, making a joke about he can't go if it involves eating meat, and I won't be able to go either because he won't have a way home. But then one of the symphony girls standing nearby heard all that, a girl who goes to a different school from us, and she said, Yes! At last I'm not the only vegetarian. So it just fell into place, like it was the course of nature. She's the harp player of the youth symphony, Anise, from across the county, and automatically she and Brandon had everything to talk about for about 3 or 4 hours it seemed like. And Muriel got worried because she thought one of her friends was about to get mixed up with a trouble making boy, some kind of disagreeable guy, because Brandon does look like that, and I was trying to tell her it was OK. She just hadn't really met him yet. It's OK, I whispered to her. I'll explain everything. Don't worry about him. He's not going to cause trouble. He is unusual, that's true, but he's OK.

"And you," she said, while we were sitting at the corner table. The others from our table had gone to play songs on the juke box before the food got there.

"You wore that homemade panther t-shirt, that you made with magic markers, to a classical music concert."

"I'm a trouble maker," I said. "So many bad influences come over me. Can't help myself sometimes."

"Don't joke like that. Bad things are real, and lots of people are messed up because of . . . "

"I know. I'm just kidding. I know lots of kids make bad choices."

"And besides," I continued, "this is a jaguar shirt. You take Spanish. Isn't that a Spanish word?"

Jaguar.

Sounds like a whisper.

I whispered. She whispered. And I knew that was the moment.

63

About Your Project

"Well," Mr. Collins said, "Let's talk about this project. It was interesting, no question, but I'm not sure it qualifies as strictly academic. It was more like a kind of performance art."

I knew he would say something like that. Where was my analysis, where were my critical thinking skills? All those things he had come to expect of me?

Me dressing up in a costume wasn't enough. Somehow the meaning of it all needed to be brought out more. Was it important if the costume didn't cover me all the way up? Did it matter if people saw a human being underneath?

I don't know, Mr. Collins. I don't know. I haven't got all those thoughts worked out.

But the Jaguar had been there with us, in our classroom. The people saw him, and the jaguar spoke, and the people came up. They wrote on the pelt and the jaguar ran. That was what I wanted. That was what I had seen happening. Whatever it meant. Wasn't it the same as what Muriel said, how music lives in our hearts?

64

Ball Game

I already know how we're going to defeat him, Brandon said. He went dribbling toward the basket with a spin move. His dunk attempt cuffed the net right up under the rim.

"That's the worst dunk attempt ever seen," I told him.

"And you're about to show me how?"

Neither of us is tall enough but we are getting better, getting our hands to the rim.

Out here in Piney Groves, next to the little kids' playground, they have a full size rubberized blue paved basketball court. And the goals have heavy steel frames and poles. At least the Piney Groves people got that right.

I heard the skate kids laughing not far away, heard the run of their boards on their homemade plywood ramps. Streetlights are already coming on. Some trees are already bare for winter, silver under late day sky. Up here on the Gaunt Jaw we have a view of the pylons and the way to the Rocks and the dark line of pines beyond the Out Back.

We look like we're just messing around, trying to dunk, trying to grab the rim, taking long shots, making lay-ups. Just one-on-one silly scuffling basketball. We even try skateboarding layups. It's skateboard basketball, a game we might invent.

And a few streets up, at a place where the street curved round, lay the black sports car. Easy to see. Like a venomous mouth waiting to spring. The way they make cars, I was just starting to notice, the way they design them: It looks like it's already flying.

It's like the bouncing of the ball stirs him up from some dank place below ground, Brandon said. He just shows up.

This was the beginning of our plan. It's like we had gained power.

I can already tell you what he's going to say, Brandon said. And I already know what we're going to do. It's how we're going to defeat him.

He dribbled the ball hard on the pavement. Turned his head like he was listening for the way the thump drove down into rock hard earth. *Thump, thump, thump.* Looking at me. The upward nod. Like that was a way to say something.

"Let him hear it," Brandon said. "It'll draw him in. He wants us to see him. But don't look at him. Just keep a side view. Just make a little noise with the ball. Just be your normal crazy self."

"You're the one who went around with dead crow feathers on your head."

He wants a ballgame? We'll give him a ballgame. We'll give him a reply to the message he left with Corin. Round ball. Like he has his own little language for basketball. Like he's so good. In his mind he's the god of basketball.

I grew up on the streets, he'll tell you. I know street ball, he'll say.

He doesn't. It's the one thing in his life where he's normal: he can't stop believing he's so good at basketball. No more of his magic talk: "Don't touch me, I'm too powerful for you to withstand;" all that psycho "I'll drink your blood" talk. Basketball is the thing that'll get him out of his car. Get him on his feet. He'll strut out here like he owns the court. Like he's really good. Cause he grew up on the streets, he'll tell you. Somewhere up north.

Let him talk. We had talked to Corin, gave him the word. When Star Man comes back, when he's wanting to know where we are, tell him this: Where would any kids like them be? I can't keep them away from the ball courts up there. They're not even doing their school work anymore. Might not even be going to school at all. For them it's all about the ball court.

Thump, thump, thump. Listen to the ball on the face of the earth, Brandon said. And you standing there dead already. Skin turning green and blue. Dead already.

I stood there feeling the pine trees around me, me among the ghosts, me on my trails, even as I stood on that stage of land overlooking the humming power lines and the way that went all the way to California. I stood there hearing the wind in the pines, the voice of the land of North Carolina before the virgin pines got torn down. *Thump, thump, thump.* I stood there knowing that now I could see two places at one time. I can be in two places at one time. The pine forest is inside me. When I lay down to rest, I will go back and walk among my trees. I dove, I stole the ball from Brandon and made for the rim. A spinning thundering dunk move. Almost.

65

Costume

People all over the world wear animal costumes. Why don't we have anything like that?

In China, Korea, Vietnam, at New Year, it's a dragon and a lion, or a tiger.

In Peru, in the Andes, men dress as bears and climb a mountain to get sacred ice.

In West Africa, people wear masks of birds, or masks with horns like wild cattle.

In North America, the ancient people wear masks of raven, wolf, orca, bear.

People see the human being under the costume. The fact that people are there is not kept secret. Nobody thinks the dragon dancers aren't there. It could be any one of us inside that costume.

Why don't we have anything like that?

Put your hand on the shoulder of a wild jaguar.

Brandon had moments of doubts before we got our plan together. He almost gave up. I had to keep talking to him. What is it? I said. Don't you want to put an end to this? You want to keep on trying to avoid him all the time? That's being dead. You'll never be free. We know he's at school now. We've got to do something.

You're coming through this, I said. You have real friends now. You're the one who has courage, facing him like this.

It took a while but at last he spoke.

You don't understand, he said. His voice was shaking. I could see without him saying it: a deep fear was in him. Like he was afraid to even say words. He wasn't a coward. He was afraid because of all the stuff from the past. Yes, he said, I want to stop him. I don't want to keep thinking he might be around. But you don't understand.

Tell me, I said. You're just telling your friend something real.

When you're around him, Brandon said, he has power. You feel it. You feel yourself going back to him, back like it was, even though you don't want it. The memory comes over you. You can just go back down into it, like you don't have to think about anything then. And even if it wasn't good, you remember it being good. What you remember is so strong. It was like everything was taken care of, and you don't have to do anything. You just hide in it. The only thing I can think of to explain it is if you've ever been at the beach when it's summer and the ocean is warm and then it starts raining and you don't even feel the rain. Everything is warm water. At the beach it's fun, but with this, you're in warm water that's drowning you and you don't really know it. Or maybe you just don't care.

You're right, I said. I don't understand. I haven't done all of those things like you have. I've always thought I was different from people who do stuff like that. But I might have done it, if my life had been different. I don't know. But I know we've got to do this. I'm with you. You won't be alone. You're not going back to the old way. But what you said, Down in it. If being around him, or even thinking about it, takes you back down into it, this time you're not going down into it alone. Think of all those animals. I keep thinking about them after I saw them all together on your wall. They were real animals, and now they're gone but they aren't gone either. Because you made all those photographs, and even if those photographs are just thin paper, they exist now because somebody made them. I mean, photos are fragile but people are going to protect them because of what they are and what they mean. Mr. Blake would protect them, or anybody else like him. So anyway, it's like the animals are still here, and you're surrounded by them, a whole bunch of animals in the dark with you. That's what I keep thinking.

Muriel was afraid. She kept on at me to tell her what was going on. She could see the seriousness on us. We were different. And she made me angry, a little bit, because she kept saying Brandon was involved in all this bad stuff, and who could trust somebody like that?

Muriel, no, I said. Stop worrying about Brandon. He really is OK. You'll see.

Then, down at the Rocks, me and Brandon discovered something. All of a sudden both of us were yelling, swearing, slapping. Scrambling out of there. It was yellow jackets. One of us, or both of us, had disturbed a nest. They're wasps that live in the ground. Down there under the Rocks, in that sheltered place, they had survived the ice storm. All of a sudden, both of us were getting stung like fire. We ran out and fell down on the ground in the weedy grass. And that made it OK, somehow. Laying there, flat contact with the earth, laughing at our idiot selves, how much it stung. After we calmed down, Brandon looked at me and held out his hand and said, OK, Chris, I'll do it. I'll face it.

He was able to give the police good information about Star Man. He probably knew where he lived. He wouldn't tell me, but I didn't care, even when Muriel said doesn't that make you feel like a baby?

The police would be waiting. And they wanted to be assured that we wouldn't try anything foolish. Because there could be consequences. We knew that, didn't we? Consequences of the law and consequences of danger resulting from any foolish action we might take. Consequences of bodily harm or endangerment.

"Yes," we said. "We know that."

At home I had work to do. It had to be good. I didn't need a gold colored bed sheet. And I had been in trouble for destroying that. It was reckless of me to have done that. I was caught up in the moment and didn't think about what I was doing. So now I had to get something dark blue. Indigo.

"You know we could get killed. This could all go wrong," Brandon said.

"We won't. He won't have any idea what's hit him. The police will be there."

"You don't have any idea. He would kill someone as easy as you would drink a glass of water. He has a gun."

"We'll be OK. We have a plan. Stealth and cunning, like a jaguar. Like the puma. From on high, I leap down!"

Brandon was shaking his head at me.

"Where's that blue paint you had on you that night on my roof? Let me borrow some of that for a little while."

"You're crazy."

"No. I've seen his blood," I said, as I held up indigo blue cloth I got from the cloth store clearance rack. What made me say that, I have no idea.

I was acting like the fact that I had seen his blood would give me power over him. Like I didn't think I was full of blood too, and skin is not a very sturdy container when everything that can come against it is said and done. But I had seen his blood, after all, and it was just like mine or anybody else's.

In some parts of the American West, the ancient people wear masks and costumes and they turn into the animals even for a little while. Why don't we have things like that?

"Unfurl an arm of power against him," I told Brandon, flexing my arm. "Where's that blue paint?"

He was shaking his head.

"Absolute maniac," he said.

66

A Pair of Freaks

Finally the time came. Everything has to be ready. Dark of night falls ever earlier now, and for this to work we need it to still be light.

We'd got hold of some old jack o'lanterns. We had to hope they didn't rot too fast, and we had to hide them from the middle school kids because they only wanted to smash them.

I went up on foot. Walker and runner. My feet are Sure and Able, I said to all who dwell in the high places of late afternoon sapphire sky. Brandon would be meeting Star Man at the Piney Groves common area. And him and Brandon had made a devil's bargain or whatever people call it. Like staking your soul. Our souls, on a ball game. We were in this together, but it was Brandon who was going to face him during this.

So if Brandon lost, he was back in it again and he had to bring new blood, this wretched kid who wanted to ride the lightning. That was me. Could anybody really fall for that?

Brandon had set it all up so nice. Sold him the weak line so easy. So helpless. He did it so good I almost believed he meant it. I almost believed Muriel was right, he was giving me up to Star Man too. That he would tell Star Man where I lived. But it was because he had said all those words before, when it was for real. Now it was for a different kind of real.

And that idiot swallowed every bit of it. He can't imagine that anybody has any life outside of the foul world he lives in. He thinks he can do anything. Like he can always get away with it no matter how bad it is. He can squeeze down flat in the seat of his car and get through any little crevice.

He would probably be proud of that.

"Any little crevice," I can hear him saying.

Any little crevice. Jabbing his finger at me.

Brandon got him a message. Meet me behind the dumpsters at Town Hall. Right there by the back of Town Hall, in the shadow of bushes and Leyland cypress, arborvitae. It was a place Brandon knew Star Man used. Because nobody would suspect a deal was going down right there under the eaves of town government. It was a different kind of deal this time. They were making arrangements for the ball game.

We had other arrangements with Corin. When Star Man comes back, this is what you tell him, we told Corin. Tell him, Yes, we'll have a ball game. Tell him he can meet the boys at the ball court at Piney Groves Estates. Just up the road. That's where they are.

"I've known you since before you were born." Star Man's voice had sneered in the shadows behind town hall. "I'm in your blood."

"OK," Brandon had said, so plaintively. "OK. You're right. But it's got to be tomorrow night. It has to be like that. I can't help it."

"Why get up with me if you aren't for real? You know not to mess with me," Star Man was saying. "It's bad for you."

I only heard him. He has a way of never being fully seen, always finds the shadow to drape his face with. I was crouched down in the narrow space behind the dumpsters. Across Brandon's face I saw the forest shadows of arborvitae, reaching out to give him life. I had to hold my breath, it stank so bad there, and I had to end up throwing those shoes away because I didn't realize I had been standing in some kind of piss-slop-grunge crap without knowing it at the time. My shoes stank so bad, and Mom said "absolutely not young man" when I went to put them in the washer. But just in case something should happen, something go wrong in baiting this villain, I was there and I was going to spring out and land a punch right on him and bust that dude's face again if I had to. I already had his blood on me one time. So it was like my hand would automatically know how to find its place, and reopen that vein and throw him down again.

Brandon said I was a complete idiot to speak like that, because I didn't have any beginning of an idea what he would do to me and that he would have a gun and a knife, anyway.

Brandon was at the edge of the common area now, by the children's little playground, waiting at a bench. All perfectly normal. Nothing would be more unremarkable than a playground ball game between friends. All of this would happen with houses near. Anybody might be around. These things happen among ordinary living people. Other kids might be playing out there at the other basket, but if they were, Brandon would just say, We can't join in right now. We've got to play this. A little bet we have between us. So they would be there on the ordinary ball court. And right by the court we had lined up the old worn out jack o'lanterns. Old pumpkins past their prime, most already patched with the green dusky mold.

But the Rocks was the place. I was already out there.

Because we know a secret about this place. Something happens when you live somewhere, when you aren't stuck in a car all day, when you get out into the natural world. You find out things about that place. You begin to read the land and the inhabitants of it. We've already found it, and we've already been struck by it, and we hit the ground because of it. We got knocked off our feet. We're going to raise up a cloak of stars out of the ground to wrap this Star Man in, a piece of clothing he will never forget. A garment of power to suit this hawker of lies. This agent of the big liar.

And I knew a secret about Brandon. He knew it too, even if he didn't know it to say it. From my place now at the Rocks I could see something that Star Man never would see, at least not the way he was then. Brandon wasn't alone up there. Standing with him were the animals he had called together, the animals of the Wild Hunt. I could see them, even if nobody else happened to see them that afternoon. Brandon had called them all together, taken them under his wing, you might say, and there they were, around him, near him, alongside him. Brandon was not alone. They were going to help him. Maybe they seem like just shadows, but the thing that made Brandon call them together in the first place was stronger even than sunlight.

It's like a heavenly visitor would appear. The unexpected. The elemental surprise.

Star Man would be astonished and unable. He would be out of his car. That was vital to it all. He thrived in his car, as if he had given away his own body and no longer used it. He slouched and hid in the seat, running the windows up and down, thumping the speakers like he controlled thunder with buttons. He could no longer function on his own two feet. He had to have that key, that ignition, that explosion behind wheels in metal casing.

Me and Brandon, however, are not like that. We know the roads by our feet. Speed and Distance.

Speed and Distance.

Suddenly it was all beginning.

The dark car, gleaming as it rolled, making its arrival under the Piney Groves sky. The constant thumping of his speakers, easily crossing the distance to the Rocks, dissonant with the playground and the running kids at the swings.

I saw him get out, sling shut the door. The long feathered hair. The strutting walk. He had brought his own basketball, just like Brandon said he would. He would only play if they used his ball. This special big city basketball, this I know how to play better than anybody down here in this hick state basketball.

Brandon and Star Man talk for a moment, and then their shadows stretch out in front of them as they wind into sudden play. Basketball moves, one on one. Sun shadows, late afternoon November, dancing with them. I'm watching from the Rocks. Basketball, one on one, North Carolina autumn afternoon. Dark outline of high pines across the Outback. Nothing more normal. But this time, Brandon was not going to win.

It was two out of three, like people always do. Nobody plays just one little game. Two out of three. I heard them saying it. Brandon wasn't going to make it out of this alive. But we already knew that.

So when Brandon had the ball, driving toward the basketball, right when he most needed to score, he dribbled it off his own leg. But really he was kicking it, knocking it well out of play and out of bounds, acting like he fell. Even throwing in a little possum dance on the way down, like I had done. All the way the ball rolled, out into the waste land, jumped the chunk gravel. Right where I would be able to get it and hide it at the Rocks.

Brandon goes into a fit of craziness now. The possum dunks, the raccoon skating we had practiced. Using his own basketball. But that ball isn't good enough for Star Man, and it's driving him crazy.

Stop trying to avoid your destiny, I hear him saying. Suddenly he cares about rules. You can't have an extended time out, he whines. You're losing and you won't change that by acting like an idiot. Time's up. You're losing. This cheap junk ball of yours, look at it anyway, scraped up and worn out. Inside showing. Just like those rotten pumpkins there. That's your head, numbskull. Those dead pumpkins. Jack, I'm gonna start calling you. Jack O Lantern. You, Jacko.

All the way at the Rocks: You, You, You. Deep city accent.

Let's use the pumpkins, Brandon says. Come on. A dunk contest! There's enough here.

Smash.

The first one didn't even make it to the basket. It slipped from his hand, crushed into mush against the pole of the backboard. But it's really just possum dancing, raccoon basketball.

The second one couldn't even stand the weight of a human hand, but gave through, slid down the arm, a slimy slime wash up the sleeve. The court under that basket was a pumpkin slick now.

You brought me out here for this? Real anger was growing in Star Man now. I heard the tone, the same tenor of voice, the big city tremor I'd heard that day when it was me in the gravel, jaguar, blood pouring out.

I'm for real here, I'm serious, and you brought me out here for this? My ball is down there somewhere stuck in that hole and you wanna play like this?

That's my moment. That's when I come into action: Push Star Man's ball out within view, like it's been there all along, rolled down there all along and he just missed it when he was looking that way.

And I had already given the signal for Corin. It was really starting now. Looking this way from his fence, toward the rocks, snowy hair set among his shadowy trees. When you see me hold up my hand, I had told him.

Down they come, Brandon and Star Man, side climbing the chunk gravel.

"You dragging me out here? That's a real basketball you've let run down into this junk hole. Real leather. High class. Top grade natural leather." What a big city cry baby. "You making me step into this nasty place? Letting my ball get lost in this mud pit? You know I don't go for junk. You know I'm not cheap. You're going to be paying out big for this. You know I don't play with no skull bone like that piece of junk you got . . . "

But I was dressed with garments of power. Think of all the people around the world who know when to wear animal costumes. The forest trees drape us with their good shadows, and animals don't mind joining the good spirits of the holy world to do good. Animals don't mind lending their forms for something good.

Out in my place, out at the Rocks, it was indigo blue. Deepest night sky when you're out under stars, when all the world's asleep around you and the Universe wheels its secret above you. And I was painted with blue-green death rot.

Brandon and Star Man closing in. The high class basketball lay waiting in the entrance to the Rocks. This was our plan and it was working.

The Night Sun, burning and cold, with fever and inflammation, burning like the tiny phosphorescent bodies sparkling in the salt sea:

Inha leaps out.

I am from Shadow and from Light.

From on high, from down below, I leap. You will look and you will not see.

I said the words. I wore the pelt. I became all the jaguars I had drawn, all that I had seen. I roared, I was invincible, I was invisible.

I covered myself with lightning, letters of the holy alphabet.

From the secret place, when we stirred the ground, a host of stars would rise up. The most unexpected thing, burning stars from below the ground. Sparks of fire from under the earth and a jaguar from on high.

67

Darkness Made Plain

Through waters, and through black stone glass . . .
"Tongue in your blood!"

The open teeth and twisted, angry lips of Star Man rose toward me. I followed the wide white turn of his eyes as I fell. Voices shouted. A sound rushed like wind. My legs and ankles, my arms, were burning. I heard cursing, saw arms swatting.

A booming came down like thunder, the might of the heavens. Bright light was gold, yellow, white. I was not able to endure the power of it. I crumpled, face at my feet. For days, it must have been, my eyes were stark with the lasting power of it. I was shaken. If my eyes were open or closed it was the same between darkness and light. The last I saw of Inha was golden light pouring from him, through him, all the spots and dashes and rosettes of his coat streaming rays of light, and he was gone. The sun in all the majesty of dawning was there before me. It was a threshold of power and I had to fall away for shadow and for shelter.

We men exult.

The forest, at last, dimly lit. We have come here over a walk of several days. Each night we made our camp along the way. And we took care. We did not neglect what is right. We bowed unto our gods. We made known our reverence. We opened the ground, we poured out a blessing, water and wine. Each night we took our rest and in the turning of the nights our sleeping eyes saw dreams. We took omens, and at dawn we rose to keep our way.

We are men. And we are mighty. We want the trees that are here in this land. We have come here to cut them. We have nothing like this, and we want to build. We want to make beautiful things. We will build. We have beautiful things to express. We will express magnificence.

You will not go into that deep land, they said to us. You will not stand long in that place. You will come to the shadow of the woods and you will fall. Gods only enter there. You will not stand before the one who lives there. You will turn. You will fall and you will run back. You will hear his voice but you will not see him. He will appear and you will not stand. You will fall.

Do not go, my dear friend said to me. Listen to me, friend. Let me speak a word unto you. I have known the pathways of these mountains. I have lived in these fields. Have I not lived nights sleeping and days hunting in these lands? I have heard the shrieking. I have heard the clamor. His voice is fear, his voice is waters rising, his voice is mankind drowning. You will hear it and you will never clear your mind again. You will hear it and you will falter and you will fall. Do not go.

Do not be a coward, I said to my friend. Dear friend, do not tremble so. I will go, and you, come with me. You who know this land, who know this mountain, you will come with me. I will trust you and as companions we will go. We will walk the days together. We will lose count of our steps over hills and rocks. We will share food together each night and when we rise at dawn we will speak our dreams and we will take our omens and we will make our way together. If fear come in the night we will each shake the other from it at sunrise.

We are able. We have covered ourselves with strength. We have courage enough.

Who is this guardian of the forest, whose voice has made you tremble?

A shape, they whisper. "Something moves in the shadows!" they shout. "Turn back! Turn back!"

Who is this guardian of the forest? A terrible sound, they tell us. A roaring voice who shouts, who paralyzes, like a flood of overpowering walls of water.

We might have had to turn back. We might have wondered if we could fight it and we might have lost faith. But tonight it is not so. Tonight we men exult. Tonight we have stood firm.

A spear thrust into the jaguar's side, up under the rib cage but with care not to ruin the pelt. We want that. The animal screeches an unearthly screech. A gasping sound begins, rough with growling. The animal fell back, like lying down to sleep, and then it rose up, dizzy, staggered, still coming forward. It had leapt at my brother, deadly claws in the air. But my brother stood and did not flinch, he became a man, and the spear shot in. My uncle forced it, jabbed it, his whole body the force of hand and arm behind it.

The jaguar had not been afraid of us, even such a number of us who had gone out for it. From the shadows it sprang, roaring. Roaring like waterfalls, like hurricane wind. We knew we might lose anything or everything. The cost could have been someone's eye, someone's face, someone's life. The claws are ruthless and like the sharpness of the sharpest cutting edge. Hands seized him, hands appearing from the darkness. Blades savagely lashed from the darkness, glinting like teeth, and blood sprayed from the throat. Hands disappeared into the flesh. Even in the dimness, even with its own darkness, the obsidian blade gleamed hard, blue black like the raven's wing. The hole they cut and the jagged line soon glistened wet in the fur, bright as red fruit, the bloody line, the fur dripping. Man's hand disappeared into the neck, vanished into the throat of the jaguar, the jaguar's eyes staring. Its jaws of yellow blades hung poised, tongue lapping and jiggling alive with the motion of the cutting, as if the beast might yet wake and take my friend by hand, arm, and body into the horrible gash and away, into night where he is lord and has his kingdom.

But it was we who had seized him, we who dragged him forward into the light of our hands, into the circle of our torches, out of his place of secret. It was we who looked upon him. It was our hands that entered his body and spilled out his blood. My friend's hand kept the savage passage round the circle of the neck, bobbed into the black, and emerged glowing, glowering, red and purple to the forearms. The fierce head fell free. Ours.

They took it, cradled it close. They eyed it, faced it, held it up. No one mocked it. It was a trophy and a divine at the same time.
They came to candlelight
They set it up high upon a place, and
The blood still dripping
The eyes still staring
But dead
The golden sunlight gone out
The fierce glint become the dull glare of glass lit from outside
They ignited charcoal and lit censers,
Rounded their lips and blew breath, glow the coals, glow the coals
A memorial for all time: humankind had won this fight.
The smoke of incense, a choking fragrant cloud of tree resin, billowed from embers deep within the censers.
They lit pipes and on the rake of breath
The bowls flared,

Smoke in rich layering scents,
Scent of sweet earth and rain,
Scent of fresh cut wood,

Of rain upon dry land, and they blew the smoke from their rounded lips, polished the jaguar's face with cloudiness, the fur gleaming like old rich garments worn down.

And they breathed out curling smoke
And from their guttering throats came a graveling speech,
And they blew their breath upon it.
They curled smoke up to it.

But something stirred me. Something stood before me as I lay there, near my face, with small dark muzzle and silken whiskers. And it spoke.

"Are you here, Young One? I was here in the early dawning time of all, when the thundering dragons walked upon Earth, before men set their footsteps and made their roads upon the world. Take heart. Many devastations have fallen on the world since those moments when I witnessed Earth's first dawning. I have had to keep in shadow many times. I have seen my home destroyed. I have seen the trees I loved pulled down and cut away. I have had to flee the roaring saws. I have had to keep out of sight, quiet and running. I have been unable many times to fight back and to keep out the ones who come to destroy. Keep within yourself my same endurance. Take heart and show your teeth sometimes when you must. You are one who loves, and you have been carried in the wilderness. And remember how when you heard devourers come, it was your own heart's beating that you heard. The jaguar has sent me to speak to you, and now I have. He has kept the sunlight, and I am he who in my ancient age opens the sky for dawning as I go my simple way. And when you chance again to see me, remember my words."

Who was this? It was not Hummingbird, and it was not Inha, whom I had seen go into the realm of shining light. And I saw trailing away from where I lay the behind-side, the long tail, of a grey-white opossum on its way.

But I woke.

The hospital room was dim with window blinds. The TV was on some ridiculous show I would never watch. My head was banging like a gong. I was starving. My eyes hurt. Mom, Dad, Corin, and Brandon were there. Others had come and gone. People from church had been there. Muriel had been by earlier, they told me.

Now I knew what happened when you get shot. I had been transported in an ambulance. I had been on the television news laid out on a stretcher, a local kid shot in bizarre circumstances in a successful drug arrest. Star Man had put me down, put me in the hospital. I had to have surgery, and now I was alive and awake, and he was in jail.

All the marks from the magic marker, my tattoos of writing from the project, were completely gone, to the wonder and astonishment of my mother and everyone else, once she pointed it out. I was not surprised, though. It came back to me, the way dreams sometimes do, at the odd moment when you remember them suddenly. You can relive them for a little while, if you're quiet and don't get in their way. I had seen the writing glowing blue-green on my own body, cold traceries of flames as blue as terrifying snakes of lightning. I had seen myself as if from above.

The words of one of the angry policeman at the scene suddenly came back to me too. "You two are the damnedest pair of freaks I've ever seen. What is this? Yellow jackets? And you? Halloween was weeks ago." I lay there laughing while everyone else in the room smiled down at me like I was probably crazy and mostly pathetic.

68

Zero Twins

"Looks like the zero twins are back," I heard as I curved into a seat beside Brandon in the cafeteria. The music people had seen to it that we still had a place.

Zero?

People stared at me, my first day back. And it was the same as always. I would never be without the hurricane reputation, and now I had been on the local TV news, involved in a drug arrest. Involved, me and Brandon, both of us, on the news. People stared at us. We had done something strange, we were mixed up in it, but it was something heroic too, and foolhardy and probably foolish.

But things were different now too. When math let out and I went out the double doors of C Hall, I walked by guys I knew to be some of the hide-out people. Guys I had sat with in the smoke. The outside steps of C Hall was their hang out place if they were on campus. They nodded to me, spoke to me. Here he is, they said. Here's this one. All that blood. He doesn't say much. I stopped and talked to them. They knew all about what Brandon and I had done. Knew some of it. How did it all happen, they asked. They were glad Star Man was caught. And that surprised me. I had assumed they were into his kind of thing. Part of his drug deals. But they weren't. They didn't like him.

Martin came through the doors just as I was turning to go down the steps and on to H Hall.

"This some more of 'your people', is it, Chris?" I saw his eyes darting arrows of ridicule to his friends, seeing that they heard the remark. Looking at me like "I don't know what you are anymore."

Some of my people? "Yes," I said. "I believe so."

"So, just so I understand, you think that just because these apes have similarities to us, that means we should think we are related to them? Like, say, for example, because orangutans have hands almost like ours?"

These apes? He thought he could provoke me. Like when I had provoked him, asking him to hold up his hand to mine. That had left me feeling like a hole was in my stomach, even though he was the one who hit me. Because I had been trying to aggravate him. I didn't want to have that feeling again.

"Yes, Martin. I do think that. Apes have hands like ours, and they're almost like us, but not exactly. That's the main point. The 'almost.' We're close to them, but we're not apes. We're human. We are the only ones who can be human. If being human means anything? Just because we have physical connections to them does not make us less human."

"Chris, you're so strange now. I barely recognize you."

"I'm not really strange. I've been thinking about all of this for a while. Thinking about it but not saying anything. Now I'm not afraid to say what I'm thinking about."

The lunch ladies had made the Green Jello again, complete with little fossils embedded in. But this time it wasn't the pale death-grapes. It was shards of yellow cheese, exquisitely preserved in glowing green amber.

The music people welcomed us back to lunch with crazy handshakes they had made up. Always talking more music. We sat there eating lunch and I felt an idea dawning in my mind.

"Brandon, when is this art show of your other photographs? Have I missed it?" I knew I hadn't, but I wanted this to be said out loud.

"You haven't missed it. It starts at the end of the week. They're having an opening reception."

"What's that?"

"Kind of like a little party with food and stuff for the beginning of an art show. That's what they tell me. This is my first ever art show."

"And are the kids in the pictures coming to that?"

"Said they would. Who knows."

"So, Muriel, how would your symphony people like to show some support for the visual arts? Gather up a crowd of music people to come out and support a fellow artist?" I said, pointing with my thumb at Brandon beside me.

After we ate, as we were standing in the line at the dish window, Martin turned out to be right in front of us. And I said in perfect green-jello coolness, "Zero is weird, isn't it? If you add to it, it's like it was never there, but anything times zero, it's still zero. That's weird."

Martin turned his head back about halfway, and then stepped up to empty his tray. I was just thinking out loud.

"In fact, everything times zero is still zero. One or one million or one billion. Zero is untouchable. I mean, is it at the top or is it at the bottom? How can you know?"

Brandon just looked at me, dark eyes, eyebrows raised.

Martin turned back and faced Brandon like he was looking at a poisonous snake. He jostled Brandon's tray just enough to make everything rattle, but not spill off. "You watch your step, Zero, or I'll find a way to get you sent back forever to wherever you came from." Fire rushed across my face, a mix of indignation, embarrassment and anger. I'd never thrown the first punch in a fight before, but there might be a first time. I stared at Martin. I'm the one talking, not Brandon, I was about to say.

And I'm the one trying to provoke, again. I had let myself go. Maybe I would never learn. I glanced at Brandon, and thought, Martin, you don't have any idea what kind of things this kid has faced. He could probably punch you down to the floor right now. But he didn't. Brandon was just as cool as that green jello.

And something came to me later. The words Inha had said to me. Taking away his eyes and leaving ourselves blind. I had run with him, and I had seen him, but I still didn't know if I understood him or the shimmering blue-green, Hummingbird, all the way.

69

Sabbath Labor

We have the weirdest church. And I wanted Brandon to see that not all churches are like the one that is always on TV at his house. Not all preachers are like that one. And he would get to hear Corin read the readings.

They make the whole room dark. The sanctuary. And silent. They start the services this way every year during Advent. Lights turned off. No one says anything. No music, not to start with.

You just sit there at the start of the service and absorb the dark and the quiet. It is getting toward the darkest time of year. While you are waiting in the quietness, you notice little things you don't usually see. Like the way the only light is the pale window light on a gray day of early December. Unseen rays of light graze across the high beams of the ceiling. Glossy things start to show up, like the hand-worn places on the wood of the pew in front of you, and the altar rails. Soft light. The lines of the wooden panels of the choir. The glistening of weave in the banners and the altar cloths. And the gleam of brass, the candlestands and the cross they carry in. Only those things catch light, like the hair of the people in front of you or the eyes of the person beside you.

You realize that you don't usually sit still like that. You don't often let things come to your eyes. Usually you're pushing yourself around, doing stuff. Going places. But now, no one talks. It is quiet. They do it this way every year during Advent. And then, from out of the dark in the back, comes the voice of the priest calling out, just a simple human voice:

"Come to the banks of the River Jordan, and hear again,
'The voice of one shouting: In the wilderness . . .'"

After lunch we were meeting the girls, Anise and Muriel. Going to a Sunday afternoon movie. They wanted us to be there exactly on time. We both nodded obediently and then smiled to each other at exactly the same moment. No way, we were thinking. Now was our moment to be late and show them what it felt like. There was strength in numbers, we said.

Not much strength in just two, it turns out. Not against the wrath of girls forced to wait. They were not happy. They decided not to come out for it seemed like an hour, just sitting in the car being dumb, no matter what we said. We tried silliness, macho humor, foreign accents, really dumb sexy dancing, fake anger, real anger. We missed the start of the movie and probably everything else. It just goes to show, don't mess with women. They're incomprehensible.

"OK, Muriel. We've missed the beginning of the movie now. And I'm not paying to go into a movie half way through. I'm not made of money, you know."

"Well. I never thought I would be seen out with a cheap-skate boy."

I knew she was just playing but I did wonder, what in the world would it be like to be providing for a wife and a family someday? Would I have to be made of money then? It seemed frightening, but at the same time I couldn't help thinking, "I'm up to that, Muriel, just wait and see."

"OK," Muriel said. "I know somewhere else we can go. Even better."

"Do you, now. What's that."

"Just you wait and see. Wearing that jaguar t-shirt. Don't tell me you wore that to church too. Follow my directions. Jaguar T! That's who you are. Come on! No argument. You're the ones who made us miss the movie. So now you're under my control."

"OK, Muriel but this better not just be some..."

"Some what? Just you wait and see. Don't trust me?"

Well. It turned out Muriel really did know something better. Better than sitting inside on a beautiful day like this. Like she really did know how to see into some place inside me, and know how to find what was secret in there. What I was keeping sacred, and what I was scared of losing. Where I was keeping memory and hope locked inside. And how had she known about this place all this time, and I had lived here all my life and I had never seen it and never been here?

I followed her directions like I was blindfolded, and she led us to a public park that I had never been to. That I had never even heard of. Right here up the road just a few miles from our town. And there just past the grassy area of swing sets and climbing gyms for little kids, past the tennis courts and some basketball goals, was a nature trail. Right through a forest of mighty tulip poplars big as barrels, and the ground festooned with Christmas ferns. Native holly trees darkened the way with deep shadows. Park benches marked the way here and there. It was a public park, and a few other people were going here and there. But I was in the woods again. Big woods. Deep woods far from any cars.

"Don't stop there," she said, when I stood gazing up at the towering poplar trees. "Come on. We aren't all the way there yet."

We kept on down the trail, and then up a little rise, around a bend, and toward the light of bright day coming in beams among the shadowy trees. And there in front of us was open land, land that looked like nobody had cared about it for a long time, and a group of kids, teenagers like us, and other people, bent over like farm workers.

"Come on," she laughed. And we took our place too among them. The leader smiled and said Welcome, and he handed me a handful, a bundle, of tree seedlings, and a little digging trowel. All around me, people were planting trees in the cool sweet earth. I heard Brandon say "Sweet." I looked at Muriel and she looked at me and we smiled to each other. How had she known about this? She really is a wonder to behold.

Author's Note

The mythology book Chris' English class reads is fictional, but the stories he reads there are real stories from ancient mythology. Hunahpu and Xbalanque are in the *Popol Vuh*, which I read in Dennis Tedlock's translation. Stories of Gilgamesh and Enkidu are from ancient Mesopotamia. I read them in Stephanie Dalley's translation. I found both these translations wonderful and engaging in a way that shows their stories aren't locked in the past but are as real as the world around me today.

It was in art history lectures that I first heard the idea of a "jaguar god of the underworld" and a "night sun" or "nocturnal sun" jaguar who conducts the sun through the underworld. I was fascinated but details were scarce. I began to imagine a jaguar figure, even a sacrifice victim, who would conduct someone safely through a perilous passage. In the depths of Davidson College's library I found some information, such as in Mary Miller and Karl Taube's *An Illustrated Dictionary of The Gods and Symbols of Ancient Mexico and the Maya*, and Daniel Finamore and Stephen Houston's *Fiery Pool*. I found an old translation of the *Popol Vuh* there but then one afternoon in Chapel Hill I found Dennis Tedlock's translation. It is so readable and alive that I came to love and marvel at this wondrous book and the ancient minds who conceived it.

Other elements of mythology I depended on are in the Bible's books of Genesis, Psalms, Isaiah, Ezekiel, and the Acts of the Apostles. Observations about the creation stories in Genesis may be well known; good resources that I depended on are the Harper Collins Study Bible, Robert Alter's translation and commentary and Nahum Sarna's *Understanding Genesis*. Quotations from the Bible in my book are from the Authorized Version, also known as the King James Version. The psalm Chris half hears through sleep at church is Psalm 18; and Psalm 36 that comes to the forefront of his thoughts as he was on his way to do violence.

The old book of ink drawings Chris finds in the library is inspired by a book I came upon unexpectedly, *The Caracol at Chichen Itza,* by Karl Ruppert. For an image of a Maya altar where people are praying to Chaak for rain, and for information about the layout of buildings at Chichen Itza and their relationship to cenotes I found invaluable Alma Guillermoprieto's article in *National Geographic,* "Secrets of the Maya Otherworld." For the image of pilgrims making new clothes and conducting themselves with spare means as part of a wilderness journey I was inspired by Barbara G. Myerhoff's beautiful book *Peyote Hunt.* The things Brandon tells Chris about pumas in Colorado are inspired by David Baron's gripping accounts in *The Beast in the Garden.*

See the bibliography for these books and sources.

Bibliography

Alter, Robert. *Genesis: Translation and Commentary*. New York: W.W. Norton & Company, 1996.

Baron, David. *The Beast in the Garden*. New York: W.W. Norton & Company, 2004.

Finamore, Daniel and Stephen D. Houston et al. *Fiery Pool: The Maya and the Mythic Sea*. Salem, MA: Peabody Essex Museum in association with Yale University Press, 2010.

Guillermoprieto, Alma. "Secrets of the Maya Otherworld." *National Geographic* 224 no. 2 (August 2013) 99–121.

Hendel, Ronald. "Genesis." In the *Harper Collins Study Bible: New Revised Standard Version, with the Apocryphal Deuterocanonical Books, Revised Edition*, edited by Wayne A. Meeks et al., 3–10. New York: HarperCollins, 2006.

Miller, Mary Ellen. *The Art of Mesoamerica: From Olmec to Aztec*. London: Thames and Hudson, 1996.

———— and Karl Taube. *An Illustrated Dictionary of The Gods and Symbols of Ancient Mexico and the Maya*. London: Thames and Hudson, 1997.

Myerhoff, Barbara G. *Peyote Hunt: The Sacred Journey of the Huichol Indians*. Ithaca: Cornell University Press, 1974.

Myths from Mesopotamia: Creation, The Flood, Gilgamesh, and Others. Translated by Stephanie Dalley. New York: Oxford University Press, 1989.

Popol Vuh: The Mayan Book of the Dawn of Life. Translated by Dennis Tedlock. New York: Simon and Schuster, 1996.

Ruppert, Karl. *The Caracol at Chichen Itza*. Washington, DC: Carnegie Institution of Washington, 1935.

Sarna, Nahum. *Understanding Genesis: The World of the Bible in the Light of History*. New York: Schoken Books Inc, 1966.

* 9 7 8 1 6 6 6 7 4 8 3 6 9 *